BRIEF CHRONICLE
OF
ANOTHER
STUPID HEARTBREAK

Also by Adi Alsaid
available from Inkyard Press

Let's Get Lost
Never Always Sometimes
North of Happy

Books edited by Adi Alsaid
available from Inkyard Press

Come On In

ADI ALSAID

BRIEF CHRONICLE OF ANOTHER STUPID HEARTBREAK

Recycling programs for this product may not exist in your area.

ISBN-13: 978-1-335-14569-7

Brief Chronicle of Another Stupid Heartbreak

This edition published by arrangement with Harlequin Books S.A.

For questions and comments about the quality of this book, please contact us at CustomerService@Harlequin.com.

Inkyard Press
22 Adelaide St. West, 40th Floor
Toronto, Ontario M5H 4E3, Canada
www.InkyardPress.com

Printed in U.S.A.

1
TANGLED UP

I would have called bullshit on the whole thing from the beginning if I didn't see both Iris and Cal get the same look in their eyes. Constantly. When Iris hums to herself as they walk hand in hand, when Cal insists on doing the dishes at her parents' house, when she underlines whole paragraphs in novels then simply has to voice her appreciation for what she's just read, and how he'll stop whatever he's doing to listen, even if he clearly has no idea what she's talking about.

One eighteen-year-old gets that look, you start feeling sorry for them. Two of them give that look to each other and no matter what kind of cynic you are, you start thinking only teenagers really understand love. How insane it's supposed to be.

Leo was running late again.

My stupid, beautiful ex-boyfriend—who'd spent the entirety of our relationship arriving on time—had not even texted to give me a heads-up. I was waiting for him at Madison Square Park, and even out of the sun it was uncomfortably hot and made worse by the smell of garbage. Every person that entered my periphery was potentially Leo, so my heart quickened with excitement and then fell into disappointment as soon as I realized it wasn't him. He wasn't hurrying to come. He was happy he'd left me. He wasn't going to give me a chance to talk him back into our love.

I heard the snap of a soda can opening and turned to see my new bench mate.

Skinny white boy, thick-framed hipster glasses, cute enough to make me forget about Leo and the long stretch of summer ahead without him. He took a sip from his Coke and then looked at me. Right away, I knew he wouldn't be just one more face in the nameless masses you see every day in a big city. He had a face that I knew would stay with me, that would pop into my mind months later and for no apparent reason other than the persistent question of what might have been. He smiled at me, and I forgot about what time it was and the fact that Leo was probably blowing me off for the second time this week.

Okay, maybe I didn't entirely forget. It was in the back of my mind, like it had been for the three weeks since summer had started and Leo had thrown away what we had. You can't have love in your life for nearly a year, tangled up in a single person, then transition into its absence without feeling the loss. An attractive face helps, but cures nothing.

A French couple stopped in front of our bench, looking over a map of Manhattan. They were speaking loudly and gesturing wildly, their words a blur of vowels and those throat-tickling soft French *r*'s. I looked to my right again and my eyes met his. He raised his eyebrows and smiled at me, gesturing at the couple, whose argument was getting more heated. I tried to smile back, but couldn't guarantee that what I did qualified. It was an awkward facial muscle contortion at best.

"Do you understand what they're saying?" he asked, in a stage whisper.

"What?" I said, because conversations with strangers are hard.

He gestured at the French couple. "Do you understand any of that?"

"No, sorry."

"I wonder what they're arguing about." He looked at them wistfully, and I wished I could get a glimpse inside his head.

"I imagine they're lost," I said, eyes more on him than on the couple.

"Where do you think they're going? All the tourist spots are on that map. The city's a grid, and it's pretty easy to get around."

"Maybe they're arguing about which way the map should be held. I hear in France they hold their maps diagonally." The boy laughed; a laugh like rising bread, warm and doughy.

"I don't know what that means. Sorry," I said, assuming he'd laughed out of politeness. "Maybe they're looking for something super specific that's not on the map."

"Don't apologize. That was funny," he said calmly, leaning forward with his forearms resting on his knees, looking at me intently. He took another baby sip from his Coke. "I'm irrationally intrigued by them. What could they possibly be looking for?"

"I don't know. Treasure? The spot where John Lennon once picked his nose in a photograph? Tourists are weird."

The boy laughed, then leaned back into the bench. He turned and took in the sights of the park, which gave me a little time to admire his face for a bit. *Take that, Leo*, I thought. *I'm staring at a cute boy and I don't feel guilty about it.*

I scanned the morning crowd at the park, still hoping to catch sight of Leo despite my previous thought. The sun shone through the leaves, casting dancing shadows at Bench Boy's feet. As usual, I kept my ear out for some eavesdropping opportunities, which I'd been trying to use as writing inspiration. Nothing else had worked since Leo left me. I could only hear the French couple trying to make sense of their map.

"There is a legitimate chance that they're using this lost tourist act as a cover so that they can talk about us," Bench Boy said.

"Define *legitimate*."

"You don't think that it's possible?" We turned to look at each other at the same moment. How is it that mere eye contact with an attractive stranger can do all sorts of things to your insides?

I looked ahead so as to not give myself away. "I mean it's possible, but what would they be saying about us?"

Immediately, the boy put on a thick, completely unconvincing French accent. "Oh my God, Celine! Ze people here are unbelievably attractive! Just look at zat boy on ze bench. Mon dieu, he's so attractive I want to stab my eyeballs out and serve zem at a restaurant like escargot!"

I raised my eyebrows at him, unable to contain a chuckle and only slightly worried that I was sitting next to one of those creepy people that can hide their grossness just long enough to get close to you. "I didn't know it was possible to offend French people so quickly, but I think you just did."

He leaned toward me, not smiling, though his eyes betrayed a twinkle of amusement. "No, you have to be her. What's she saying?"

I'm not sure what it was that kept me on that bench. Maybe it was a hope that Leo would still show, or maybe it was nice to have this moment without him. I looked away from the boy and studied the woman in the couple. She was holding the map with one hand, her perfectly manicured fingernails painted royal blue. Her blond hair spilled over her shoulders as she scrunched her mouth to one side of her face and continued studying the map.

"I swear to God, François," I said, in my own terrible French accent, causing the boy to smile adorably. "You make zat threat everywhere we go. One of zees days I'm going to really pluck out your eyeballs myself and feed zem to ze locals."

"Zey should be so lucky," the boy replied with a laugh.

We watched the couple for a second, and in the silence Leo slipped into my thoughts again. I started thinking about how it had felt to see him for the first time every day. The instant swell of joy that his mere presence provided. How I couldn't resist smiling. I thought about how that was just the beginning of the delights Leo brought to my days: his thoughtfulness, his sense of humor, the way his lips on the back of my neck made it seem as if I had a pleasure button which only he knew about and was willing to press repeatedly. I hadn't had that in three weeks, nor, it seemed, would I have it again.

"Should we go up to them and pretend to be French too?" Bench Boy asked, leaning in slightly.

"Absolutely. Just give me a second to transform into an entirely different person with acting skills and the confidence to make a fool out of myself in front of others."

"Is there a way for me to compliment you on the confidence you had to already pretend to be French with me, without implying that you made a fool out of yourself?"

"Well, not when you put it that way, man."

The boy laughed and raised the Coke can to his lips, but before he could take a sip he chuckled again and put the can down.

"I hope I haven't discouraged you from any future fake accent work in public. It would be a great loss to the world if you never said 'feed zem to ze locals' again."

"Hell no. That's my catchphrase, and I'm not going to let a stranger ruin it for me."

"Oh good," the boy said. "Just wondering here, in what other situations does your catchphrase come in handy?"

"If you criticize my catchphrase one more time," I said, going back into the terrible French accent and raising my voice, "I will feed you to ze locals!"

The boy laughed again, a deep-bellied, full-bodied laugh that made me want to actually adopt a catchphrase and see how often I could slip it into conversations throughout my day.

He looked like he was about to say something, but then the French couple had another burst of arguing, both of them pointing furiously at the map.

Bench Boy stood up and walked over to them. There he goes, I thought, never to be seen again. He offered a quiet French "pardon" followed by "Can I help you?" while pointing at the map. He stood with them for a couple of minutes, using mostly hand gestures and mumbling as the couple continued to argue in rapid French. They departed with softly muttered thank-yous and smiles, then, amazingly, fatefully, he sat back down next to me.

"That was nice of you," I said.

"God, that was surprisingly easy," he said, beaming. "Invigorating." He brought the can of soda up to his lips but stopped, as if a thought had occurred to him that shouldn't be interrupted by mere thirst. "I think I'm going to start doing that more often."

"Help tourists find treasure? Practice that terrible French accent?"

He chuckled, which was nice of him, because that was another stupid joke. "No. Just...helping people. That felt good." I had no idea what to say to that, so I kept quiet and felt the acute strangeness of myself for a little bit. "I get that urge to help more often than I act on it. I feel like everyone does. But I've just decided, right now, sitting here on this bench with you, I'm going to act on it more often. Help people."

"Um, okay," I said, kind of desperate to turn to my phone and write down what he was saying word for word into my notes app.

"Sorry if that's weird. I'm in a weird mood. It's been a weird hour."

"I dunno, we just pretended to be a French couple serving your eyeballs as if they were snails," I said. "Nothing weird about that."

He smiled and took a sip of his Coke. "Imagine you've spent the last two years on an undefeated two-person paintball team. The excitement of win after win, of kicking so much ass that it basically feels like you've been beating life itself. Every day you experience that thrill. Until now. I think we're going to lose."

I bit my lip, stealing another glance at his face.

"Weird."

"Très weird," he replied with another wry smile. I thought maybe we'd go back into our repartee, which had eased some of the sorrow I'd felt sitting on my own, but he looked away, lost in his thoughts.

I looked at the time on my phone. Leo was never going to come. I wouldn't get that shot of joy from seeing him. I was keenly aware of the boy sitting there next to me, but I was also aware of the chatter of the park, the constant din of traffic, a basketball bouncing nearby. On the grass to my left, a squirrel was hanging around the base of a tree. I was most aware, however, of the pain that still sat squarely in my gut. Of how I wanted to leave it behind and at the same time drown in it. Of how I hated Leo and missed him dearly in tiny moments of the day, and how the two feelings did not exist separately, but were intertwined, tangled up like sweat-soaked bedsheets.

The boy leaned back and groaned, turning his head up to the beautifully blue, stupidly hot sky, keeping his eyes closed to it, as if refusing to take note of the weather. "It's such a bizarre thing we do," he said, not looking at me.

"What is? Help French tourists?"

"Love," he said, just like that, as if strangers went around talking about these things all the time.

A few moments passed by. The boy opened his eyes, took another sip of his Coke before getting up to chuck it in a nearby trash bin. The clunk the can made as it went in told me it was almost full, as if he hadn't been able to stomach any of the soda. He came back, wiped his glasses on the hem of his shirt, squinting at me because the sun was in his face. Then he said sorry, and thanks, and left me on the bench. Alone.

Later, I met my friend Pete at our favorite bookstore, The Strand, before our shift at a nearby chain movie theater. "You should probably stop trying to meet up with him," Pete said, thumbing through a graphic novel. Pete doesn't say much, but when he does you can pretty much always count on honesty, rarely on tact. I guess I appreciate honesty more than tact, because almost as soon as Pete and I met at the theater two summers ago, I latched on to him and haven't let go since.

"I wish he came while that boy and I were talking," I said. "I wanted to make him jealous. It's crazy, I know. But the heart and its wants and all that." I picked up a hardcover, read the first line, put it back down. "I can't believe he didn't show."

"Suspend your disbelief, Lu. That's the fourth time by my count."

I sighed. Pete was probably sick of hearing about Leo. That made sense to me. I was sick of thinking about him. I picked up a couple of new arrivals, flipped through them absently, nothing catching my eye. I ran my fingers over the covers, looking around at the other shoppers.

"Pete?"

"Yeah?"

"Why do you think Leo left me?"

Pete stopped reading for a second. He brushed his black hair out of his eyes, closing the pages of the book around his finger to keep his place. He looked at me with those intense green eyes of his. I feel like Pete could force people to do his bidding with a single look. "We know why he left you," he said in his faint Irish brogue. "He didn't love you as much as you loved him." He turned his attention back to the graphic novel. "I'm gonna finish reading. I'll see you at work."

I sighed and made my way downstairs. Starla, our favorite bookseller, was at the help desk and waved hello. She's tattooed and in her thirties, and never treated us in that eye-rolling "damn teenagers" way that so many adults adopt as their general attitude toward people our age. I waved back, wanting to go talk to her, in no real rush to get to work. But she was busy with a customer, so I just ambled around the bottom floor trying to eavesdrop on people.

Work-space drama; the half conversations of people on cell phones; high school gossip. It'd turned into a compulsion after everything had happened with me and Leo and all my own words dried up.

I used to write my column once a week, and I posted almost daily on my personal blog, wrote in a journal, jotted down novel ideas, the occasional poem, and—more than I cared to admit—little entries into my phone's note function in which I either came up with how to cure all the world's ills or jotted down ideas for animated TV shows.

Since the breakup, I hadn't been able to write anything

which my editor, Hafsah, wasn't loving, to say the least. I'd been a columnist for *Misnomer*, one of the most highly trafficked online teen magazines, for a year now. The day Hafsah called me to say I'd been hired as the love and dating columnist was probably the happiest day of my life. I'd always suffered from this idea that I wasn't a writer unless I had readers. And suddenly the world called and said, "Okay, we're on board. You are, in fact, this thing you've always felt yourself to be."

Now, instead of writing, I eavesdropped. I hadn't sent Hafsah anything since the breakup, which was three weeks ago, and even through her emails I could feel her intense eyes narrowing with impatience, her neatly manicured nails tap-tap-tapping on her desk.

I don't know why I turned to eavesdropping. Sometimes I felt like I was chronicling life, or the city, the connections between people. Sometimes I felt like I was addicted to stories, and I was giving normal people a chance to get theirs out there, even if it was just a fraction of them, even if it was just a snippet in a notebook that would never make it into the world at large.

That was probably bullshit. All that was happening was that I had writer's block and I was stealing other people's words. Or I was just nosy.

I scanned the crowd for potential subjects. A middle-aged dude bugging the employee at customer service for books with yellow covers. Two women scanning the self-help aisle talking about auras. A bunch of people on their own, eyes on the shelves, giving nothing away.

Then, I spotted her. Full-bodied Latina, pretty, two perfect mascara streaks running down her cheeks to her pinup-model-red lips. She was on the phone, near Thrillers, W–Z. If it weren't for the tears, she might have looked older, but the kind of sadness on her face resonated with me. Teenage heartbreak. Scurrying to the aisle behind hers, I picked out a random novel, trying to keep my eyes on her through the space I'd made on the shelf, straining to hear her over the hum of the store.

"I don't know what I'm going to do, okay?" she said, wiping the back of her hand across her cheek. I reached into my bag, grabbed the notebook I always kept on me for just this occasion, scrawled her question onto the page, thinking about how it would go on my blog later, the story I could shape from it. The girl clutched at the fabric of her dress as if it were responsible for her tears. "No. No. I don't know how to tell him, that's what I'm saying." She brought a finger up to her mouth, nibbled at the nail, chipped with long-faded red polish. "Yeah, I know I have to."

I held my breath, wanting her to say more, needing it.

"I have to go. Yeah. He's here." She gave a sniffle, another back-of-the-hand swipe across her cheeks, a smudge of mascara by her temple. "Okay, bye."

Then I watched her hang up the phone and slip it into the pocket of her dress. She sighed, made a few more attempts to clean up her appearance, her eyes locked ahead. I didn't want to look away from her, wanted to soak her in, write all of her, because she looked the way I felt. Then I watched her walk down the aisle and across the store toward the entrance to meet the boy I'd talked to on the bench.

2

THINGS HAVE CHANGED

Bench Boy and Crying Girl left the store together, and I rushed after them, almost knocking down a display of new arrivals on my way out the door. The sidewalk was crowded and a fire truck was wailing loudly on its way down Broadway; for a moment, I looked left and right, worried they had disappeared into the ether.

But life is not a spy movie: they were only a few feet away, heading in the opposite direction of the movie theater where my shift was starting in ten minutes. I probably shouldn't have cared enough to follow them, should have shrugged and sighed a brief lament to myself that I'd miss out on hearing their conversation, then gone on to work. Instead, I immediately followed behind.

The thing with eavesdropping is that it's rarely interesting, and if this was the only thing I could write about now, I sure as hell wanted to follow the one good lead I'd come across.

I texted Pete, asking him to cover for me if I was late for my shift, then I opened my notebook and got a little closer to the couple, ears cocked, ready to eavesdrop to my little heart's content. I was only a few steps behind, confident that New York's crowded sidewalks would shroud me in anonymity. Even if they turned around, I'd be just another one of the millions of people who stormed up and down the streets every day.

They crossed Thirteenth Street, expertly maneuvering around an onslaught of oncoming fellow pedestrians. A woman in a green T-shirt wearing big headphones passed by, and a few steps behind me I could hear a girl on her cell phone, saying "literally" way too often. There was a constant whir of tires on pavement, of footsteps on the sidewalk, the chatter of millions.

Bench Boy and Crying Girl weren't talking to each other. His hands were shoved in his pockets, she was picking at the hem of her dress. They walked slowly, and I waited in anticipation for their conversation to begin. I thought about what the boy had told me on the bench, about being on an undefeated two-person paintball team. It had sounded a little nonsensical and perplexing at the time, but now, with their body language and the space in between them, I thought I understood a little more.

"Look, Cal," the girl finally said, just loud enough for me to make it out over the honking taxis making their way down Broadway. But she seemed to run out of steam. Her hands dropped to her sides, clutched at her hemline again.

"What, Iris?"

"I don't know," Iris said.

"I think you do," Cal responded, his voice like cracked glass.

She wiped at her eyes again, took a deep breath. I readied my pen. "I've been thinking and… I don't think I can do long distance. Four years only touching in the summers? Four years of wondering where I am if I don't text you back right away? Four years of our lives growing in different directions?"

The words nearly froze me. Leo had said almost the exact same thing to me. After months of lobbing L-bombs at each other, months of ever-increasing intimacy, sometimes in waves and leaps (like the first entire day we'd spent in each other's company, all twenty-four hours, on the subway and eating pizza and watching a movie, sleeping, talking), and sometimes in inches (one handhold at a time, one little confession at a time)—after months of enjoying each other's company, making plans to continue doing just that, Leo looked into my eyes and told me he didn't think our love could survive four years apart.

My hands shook as I tried to write the scene down in my notebook while keeping pace with them.

"Love," Cal said. The word left him like a whimper. "We have love. What else matters?"

The girl was crying again. I caught the shimmer of light reflecting off her wet cheeks. A honk from a cab driver drowned out something she said, and I got a little closer, almost at their heels. They were moving forward at such a glacial pace that I had to actively think about walking so that I wouldn't run into them. "We're eighteen. Of course we're going to think it can last forever. But it's not that easy."

"That's not true, Iris. I've never once said it will be."

"That's how you talk about us though. Like we're the greatest romance of our time or something. Like we can overcome all these things that everyone else fails at, like we're somehow different." We reached Union Square, and they waited at the stoplight to cross the street. Traffic was sparse and they easily could have crossed, but they weren't paying enough attention to notice.

"You used to talk like that too," Cal said.

I was almost torn apart by that line. I could hear all the heartbreak that I felt for Leo in Cal's voice. But Iris shrugged it off easily. "Yes, but things have changed, Cal. You have to adapt to the world, to life."

"So now I'm being punished for being a romantic?"

Iris groaned, raising her hands in frustration. Someone pushed past me and then in between them, calling us idiots under his breath as he crossed the street. Cal and Iris didn't notice that either.

I was probably late for work by now, but I couldn't pull myself away. I kept listening, kept writing it all down.

"I'm not punishing you. I'm just saying that there's a difference between our relationship in theory and what happens when we're faced with reality. You want to stay in the city. I want to go to California. I *am* going to California."

"So we'll do long distance," Cal exclaimed. "I thought that was the plan."

I'd said the same thing to Leo three weeks ago, only more tearfully. I could imagine exactly how the rest of the breakup would go, based on my own experience. The shock of the words spoken. The immediate quiet afterward. The person who'd been dumped scampering away.

Usually, in these eavesdropped conversations, I was rooting for drama, for the stuff that makes good stories. But I felt myself dreading what would come next, how they would follow the same steps Leo and I took.

"No," Iris said simply. The light turned green, a throng of people surrounded us, little bumps and shoves to the three of us, everyone as unaware of the fight as Cal and Iris were of them.

The scene unfolded exactly how I didn't want it to. Cal pulling out his phone, in my opinion to keep himself from crying. Then silence, which was probably only meant for the two of them but somehow pulled me into it, so that the sounds of the city fell away as if they'd been physically removed from the world. Iris glanced at Cal, fraught with worry, as if she knew she'd broken him.

Then Cal shoved his hands in his pockets and turned around brusquely. As he stormed off, his shoulder bumped mine, and he mumbled a "sorry" as he sped past me, no recognition in his eyes.

Iris turned around too, watching him go. She didn't immediately call out for him, just watched, tears welling in her eyes. I realized the light was still green and I was the only one standing next to them, which was a total amateur spy move. As much as I wanted to stick around, whatever part of my brain that experienced social awkwardness was buzzing like crazy, so I crossed over toward Union Square. I wrote down everything that happened, the look on Cal's face when he was fleeing the scene, Iris's silence. For the first time in weeks I felt moved to write my own words. But I didn't have a grasp on them, so the only thing I could write down was this gut-wrenching déjà vu moment of the event that had caused my writer's block to begin with.

I wondered how many teens go through the same thing every summer, how many times that conversation is repeated with every end of another school year. I wondered how many survive, not just as a couple in the long term, but the conversation itself. How many people can maneuver through its hidden land mines and invisible walls and crawl out the other end intact?

When I reached the park, I turned back around so I could make my way to work. At the street corner where we'd stood, something caught my eye. On the ground near where Cal had been standing. It was a wallet, cheap and plastic, the design looked like one of those airplane safety cards they put on the back of the seat. I leaned down to pick it up, a little amazed that it hadn't been spotted by anyone else yet, though I guess it did look a little bit like spilled trash.

Even before I opened it, I knew it was his.

"Pete?"

"Yes?"

"Do you think they broke up?"

"Jesus, Lu. Is this going to be the driving question of your life from now on?"

"Would you rather I go back to 'why did Leo leave me?'"

We were sitting at the box office, each logged in to adjacent computers. It was our favorite spot to work because it faced the street and provided the best opportunities for people watching. But at that moment I couldn't care less. I was fumbling with Cal's wallet, studying its contents. One school ID (some prep school in Brooklyn), one well-worn Metro card, a receipt for dinner at an Indian restaurant dated almost two years earlier. A sticky note curling at the edges, neat block letters on it: "I like you. Quite a bit."

And, most important, a half-filled-out raffle ticket from a YMCA. On it, in smooshed, scrawled handwriting, was Iris's full name, address, phone number, and email.

"Debatable," Pete said with a sigh. "What game are we going to play today? How about What Would You Do with That Weirdo? Count the Moles? I Would Bone That Person?"

"You never want to bone anyone," I said, turning the raffle ticket over in my hands. Pete leaned back in his chair, eyes focused on the people passing by the theater. It was the usual array of Lower East Siders that might be wandering around on a weekday morning: some young professionals heading out for an early lunch, the NYU students that stuck around for the summer, the smattering of unclassifiables that are at every New York City street corner, their entire lives a mystery. I kept looking for Cal and Iris to walk past the window, somehow longing to rewatch their breakup happen in real time, even if it felt like watching my own breakup.

"We could play I Would Cuddle That Person," Pete offered. "Dibs on Alice."

"You can't call dibs on Alice. We share Alice." Alice was this adorable old lady who came in without fail once a week to watch a movie. She got a box of Milk Duds, and snuck in a flask of what we were pretty sure was straight-up whiskey. "But I'm not ready to change the subject yet. I want to talk about the couple. I want to know if they're still together."

Pete gave me a little side-eye. "Clearly they broke up."

"You don't know that," I said, though I have no idea what made me so defiant. They had almost certainly broken up.

He turned his attention to a couple of guys in their twenties who'd approached his window. I looked down at my phone. Every day, dozens of times, I'd check that screen, hoping to see Leo's name in it, hoping he was going to offer some sort of apology, or beg for a reconciliation, or even just check in and say hi. Just like that, no capitalization or punctuation or anything. The minimal amount of care one can show electronically, that's all I wanted. Just:

Leo
hi

He hadn't even apologized for missing our meeting that morning. Next to my phone was my notebook, open to the day's writing, Iris and Cal's fight. Without their names in there and a few other details, it could have been about me and Leo, the only thing I would have written about us since breaking up.

I pictured how my night would go after work: my little brother, Jase, playing video games on the couch, his shouts ringing out through our little apartment. Mom would be cooking some sort of Italian food. I'd sit with my laptop on my knees, typing up what I'd eavesdropped, failing to come up with anything of my own. I'd watch for Leo's name to pop up on my notifications. I'd stumble about on the internet, reaching for something that would make me feel okay.

I read the last few lines I'd written in the notebook. Iris's "no." Cal's departure.

Pete slid the customers their change, then looked over at me. I could see something in his eyes. Pity or concern or frustration, who the hell knows? "What's on your mind, Lu?"

I put Cal's things back in his wallet. "I need to know..." I trailed off.

A guy appeared at my window. In his forties, velvet tracksuit, mustard stain on the shirt beneath. He was looking over my head at where the showtimes were displayed. I smiled like I was supposed to, then gestured to Pete to add the guy to our running tally of tracksuits we'd seen since we started working (543 so far). He bought one ticket for the matinee of *Shit Blowing Up* or something like that.

Pete was still studying me, those clever eyes of his boring into me and reading all my thoughts. "I should probably return the wallet," I said, pointing lamely at it. "Her address is in here. I could take it to her."

Pete's kind of like my wise, old uncle. He asks poignant questions, and delivers poignant answers. He's like Bilbo Baggins. Wait, is Bilbo Baggins the wise, old uncle? Like, he has a beard which he strokes before saying wise, old things? I haven't read those books, but I picture him as having a great beard.

Sadly, Pete has zero facial hair. He's also freakishly adverse to hand gestures, so even if he had a long white beard, he probably wouldn't be the type to stroke it.

I waited for him to unload his speech, all insight and logic and moustache stroking. Honesty and tactlessness.

"Yeah," he said, after a long pause. "That'd be nice of you."

On Becoming Uncrushed
BY LU CHARLES, SEPTEMBER 5

For the first time in my life, I have wriggled out from beneath the weight of a crush unscathed. More than that: I have escaped triumphant. I'm sure someone smarter than me has already waxed poetic on our dubious word choice for the act of becoming romantically interested in someone, so I'll skip the diatribe.

The important part is this: I'm out. Relationships, dating, kissing, those are real things that exist in our world. I can confirm. That door has been pushed open, and I've been allowed inside. I know I've been writing about all the aforementioned things with an air of authority for a few months now, but you guys haven't been coming to me for advice, right? God, I hope you haven't been coming to me for advice. I've mostly relied on the testimony and wisdom of others. No longer.

"How?" is the big question, of course. Aside from "Why are we here?" and "Why is the Midwest always covered in mayo?" Truth be told, I'm not quite sure how it happened. My memories of the transformation are shrouded in mystery, still. I'd run you through the course of events but I just tried that and immediately deleted them because they were trite and uninteresting.

All my previous crushes have ended in disappointment. Not

quite rejection, because I never pushed myself to try and get to the next step. Disappointment in myself, mostly. Occasionally in the other person, who proved themselves not to be worthy of my interest. Often, these crushes ended in disappointment in the way love refused to enter my life (regardless of what I did to make it feel welcome). I've had the thought that maybe love is not for me, not at this stage of my life anyway. Maybe I was just meant to chronicle what others experienced, examine life as others lived it. Not the ideal fate, but there have been worse.

It's weird to be on this side of things now. Through a three-week span of escalations, I now find myself seeing someone regularly. Kissing someone regularly. We text each other throughout the night without the eternal question of whether or not something will happen hanging over the conversation.

I don't mean to gloat, readers. I mean to marvel. I have been granted a thing I've wished for. Not the only thing I've wished for, and not the only thing worth wishing for. But a thing that brings me joy. A thing for the first time. That's something.

Who knows for how long I'll be granted this joy, for how long I've left unrequited crushes behind. I'm stepping into new territory, territory I'm not entirely sure I'm good at yet.

I wasn't quite good at crushes either, I think. I enjoyed the way they cast their spells on me and then moved on, like passing thunderstorms, or gross smells wafting by. But if the point of a crush is to lead to a relationship (or a kiss or sex or whatever), then I failed them the way they failed me.

Until now. So for those of you who have been allowed through the door and into this room: let me know what I can do to be better at this new, scary, wonderful thing. And for those still unsure that real people actually kiss and stuff, I will do my best to describe my experiences. We're on this journey together.

3
WHERE WE'D GONE WRONG

By the time I got home that night, there was an email from Hafsah waiting in my inbox.

My mom was on the phone speaking in Tagalog, probably with my grandma, who we call Lola. Jase was on the couch, playing video games like I knew he would be, barking insults into his headset. It sounded like explosions were going off in every corner of the apartment. I figured I'd go into my room and blast some music and try to force some writing.

But as soon as I tried to cross the living room, my mom yelled for me to eat some leftovers. I could still smell the basil in the air. Mom only ever cooks Italian food. Every night. We're not Italian, we're Filipino. But I guess the heart wants what it wants, even if it's spaghetti Bolognese five nights a week.

I sat down next to Jase on the couch with a plate of reheated pasta, watching him murder perfectly nice-seeming animated dudes with guns. My notebook was by my side, but I knew any attempts to pick it up would bring a tirade from my mother about how she wouldn't let her child starve under her watch, so I put the pen down and finished my food.

"How was your day, Jase?"

"Awesome," he answered, before calling his friend a "cheese dick," which I seriously hope is not a real thing.

"You just did this all day, didn't you?"

"I love summer." He smashed on his controller then shouted some more incomprehensible curse words, prompting my mom to yell at him about watching his language.

"Aren't you old enough to start working?" I asked between forkfuls of pasta. "You should really start getting a résumé together. You're almost fourteen. I think child labor laws are about to get reformed. It can only help the economy. Plus you're the only male in the house. Isn't the patriarchy teaching you to be ashamed of not being a breadwinner like Mom and I are?"

Jase gave me a puzzled look, then turned back to murdering people virtually. "My sister is so weird," he mumbled into the mic.

I slurped up some more spaghetti and continued to take in the cacophony of my apartment. Mom was complaining again about Dad traveling so much and not hosting us every other weekend like he was supposed to, the pub down the street was having a busy night, the voices carrying through our window and somehow making themselves heard over video game explosions. For some reason it made me feel lonely, hearing people out there, carefree, laughing together.

As soon as I was done eating I went to my room and lay on my bed with my laptop and my notebook nearby, my crappy little fan blowing and ruffling the sheets of paper. I could see the first line from Hafsah's email in the preview: Look, Lu, I'm sorry but if we don't have...

I clicked over to Facebook. Cal's wallet was next to me, and on a whim I typed his name into the search bar. There were about a dozen results, most of them locked accounts with profile pics that looked nothing like him or were too vague to make out.

The sticky note and the receipt that were in the wallet were laid out next to my notebook, as if they were evidence of something I understood. I read the address on the raffle ticket, and though I felt like a creep doing it, I typed it into Google.

Iris lived on the Upper West Side, near Morningside Heights. A nice building with a golden awning, balconies rich with plants and wicker patio furniture. I'd already made up my mind about going the next day, since I didn't have to be at work until the afternoon shift. I had no specific plan, per se, but I figured worst-case scenario I could give the wallet to the doorman.

I clicked over to Tumblr, scrolled through mindlessly for a while, doing my best to avoid Hafsah's email.

When I'd had my fill of that, I started transcribing Cal and Iris's breakup. Not breakup; fight. After rereading it a few times, I had to agree with Pete that it seemed pretty obvious they had split. But something in me fought against that conclusion.

Finally, I could no longer ignore the nagging presence of Hafsah's email.

Look, Lu, I'm sorry but if we don't have something from you soon, we'll have to terminate your contract. I hate to get all ultimatum on you, but the longer you go without a column, the more your readers forget about you and the less it matters when another column comes out. It's been a few weeks already, and I'm worried that if you don't send something in soon, we'll lose all the momentum we've built up for you. People forget easily these days. I'm guessing things were a little crazy with the end of school, and I don't want you to lose your scholarship, so I'll give you until the end of the month. Any longer than that and I'll have pressure to fill your space with another regular contributor.

Hope all is well,

Hafsah

I looked back to my notebook, flipped through the pages of hastily scrawled handwriting trying to capture others' words. My job at the magazine was tied to a scholarship for young women working in journalism, and without it, I wouldn't be able to afford going to NYU in the fall. So, poor timing there, writer's block.

I reread Cal and Iris's fight, wishing I had the same play-by-play from when Leo and I had broken up, though I wasn't sure what good that would do. Maybe I could use their story to figure out where exactly Leo and I had gone wrong. Maybe reading about their heartbreak could mend my heartbreak. Maybe there was a cure for my writer's block in them, somehow. After all, when I was walking behind them, I'd felt the urge to write for the first time in weeks.

I relived their breakup, and mine. I opened up a Word document on my computer, my fingers resting idly on the keyboard for a few minutes before I added my column's usual header. I gave it a title: On Heartbreak.

Then I shut my computer and went to sleep.

The next morning, Mom was at work, Jase was back in front of his screen, and I was on my way out the door to return Cal's wallet to Iris.

There are very few reasons why I would subject myself to the New York City subway on a summer day. The suffocating heat turning each platform into a sauna, everyone's sweat glands working overdrive. It brought out the worst in men, leering at any girl in a sundress or shorts, as if we didn't equally deserve to contribute to the sauna by freely sweating into the atmosphere without being stared at for it.

That day, though, the stops zoomed past without me noticing. A wallet should not have been reason enough, but I was inexplicably driven to return it.

I got off the train and walked the six blocks to Iris's building in a daze. Part of me knew that whatever I was doing was not entirely reasonable, I should have been working on a column, I should have just called the number on the raffle ticket and have them come pick it up. But most of me didn't really care. I felt like I was on a mission, even if I didn't yet know what that mission was.

Before I knew it, I was in front of the address written on the ticket. I looked up as best I could at the tenth floor, almost hoping to see Iris in the window, but there was nothing to be seen except the city reflected in the glass.

I texted Pete.

Lu
I'm outside Crying Girl's building.

Pete
Returning the wallet?

Lu
In theory.

Pete
Um…what could possibly be theoretical about it?

I didn't respond. I wasn't even sure what I had meant by that.

I wasn't sure what my plan here was either. The easy answer was to just go buzz her apartment and return the wallet. But that's not what I did. I took a lap around the block, holding the wallet in my hands, going through its contents, imagining Iris in her room feeling post-breakup blues. I pictured Cal on the bench where we met, thinking up paintball metaphors that only slightly made sense and wanting to help strange French couples. I pictured myself sitting right there with him, waiting on Leo, both of us feeling the same thing in different ways.

When I finally hit the buzzer, I was met with silence. I sighed with relief, then noticed that there was someone behind me. A girl with a skateboard tucked under her arm was crossing from the elevator to the entrance. She had comically large and bright pads on her knees and elbows, and a matching neon green helmet, her long curly hair unfurling in uncontainable waves from beneath. A green backpack hung over her shoulder.

"Hi," she said, her voice as bright as her skating accoutrements. "Are you new here?"

"Um," I said, because conversations with people were hard. Even if they were young, adorable people who knew how to be friendly. "I'm, uh...looking for a friend. Iris?"

"Iris Castillo? She's awesome. She babysits me sometimes. Lets me eat whatever I want and then we sing Broadway hits." She shifted her skateboard and looked over her shoulder. "Don't tell my mom I said that."

I chuckled. "Yeah, I won't. I just came by to give Iris this wallet. I don't think she's home though." I looked over at the intercom to show I'd tried.

"I can get it to her if you want. I live down the hall from her."

"Um," I said, this time because I didn't want to part with the wallet. It felt too soon, like the coincidence of Iris and

Cal and me and Leo and the wallet falling into my hands was too meaningful to easily let go of, especially without seeing one of them again.

"My name is Grace, if you wanna text her and check that I live here or something," she said with a smile. I was a little intimidated by the fact that she was better at conversations than me. Grace smiled again, then dropped her skateboard and started rummaging through her backpack.

At the same time, I held out the wallet for her. But she was busy jingling things around, and before she noticed me offering it, I pulled back my hand. I tried to access that part of me that I use when I'm interviewing people.

I'm not sure what happens during those situations. The strange shell I present to the world falls away in favor of my true self, which is a lot like my everyday self, but more comfortable with who I am. Like when I interviewed with Hafsah for the *Misnomer* job, or that time I approached half the sophomore class at my school to ask them about masturbation habits. For a column, not just my own curiosities, of course. People I couldn't ask to borrow pens from, I was suddenly inquiring about their most intimate, private moments.

In those scenarios, I kind of felt the way I did with Leo. Things were easy. Like those mornings when we would meet up before school. He'd greet me with a coffee, slip his fingers between mine, kiss me on the cheek. We'd walk to school together, and for blocks, for months, I didn't have to actively think of what to say. I didn't have to juggle the thoughts at the surface of my brain and those lurking beneath. I could make my dumb jokes without hesitation, without that damn thought that came before I otherwise opened my mouth, the thought that said don't do it, the thought that said you are not valuable to others. I was fully present, fully myself, and Leo loved me for it.

"You know what, I think I can maybe meet up with her later," I said, stepping away from the door.

"Cool," Grace responded, still searching. "See ya!"

"Bye," I said, and turned away, my cheeks starting to flush. I turned down the street and back toward the subway, the wallet still in my hand.

4

THE ATTEMPT TO UNDERSTAND

I shoveled another scoop of overbuttered popcorn into a bucket, unsuccessfully offered the customer the chance to upgrade to a mega-large, and took their money. I was stuck at concessions, which was a strict no-phone zone. That meant I was cut off from the wider world, stuck in this sixteen-theater microcosm of the city, with no idea what was happening outside my scope of vision. It was crazy to me that humans used to live like that, completely separate from the rest of the planet, knowing only what was in front of them. Not that my phone could really tell me much about the things I kept churning over in my mind: Iris and Cal, whether or not they'd broken up, why the hell I hadn't returned the wallet, Leo's back while he slept.

In front of me, lines formed for the latest summer blockbuster. Brad the manager was tearing tickets up front, two kids were killing time by playing one of the three barely functioning arcade games in the lobby. Popcorn spills and lost napkins were starting to pile up, the way they always did when it started getting busy.

"Hey, Lu."

Pulled away from my thoughts, I looked up at my next customer and was greeted by Leo's stupid, beautiful face. Dark eyes highlighted by lashes that looked Photoshopped, unblemished brown skin that was a shade darker than mine and so soft I always wanted to just press myself against his cheek. Behind him, his friends Miguel and Karl were trying to hide their snickering, giving each other looks and then smacking each other on the shoulder.

"I didn't know you'd be working today," Leo said, running a hand through his hair, which he was wearing down, instead of in the samurai-esque topknot he usually sported. "Sorry I bailed yesterday. I thought it'd be a little weird."

You know how sometimes your thoughts fill up so quickly that your mind might as well be blank for all the noise it's causing? I stared at the boy I had loved and wondered if he was suffering at all. I didn't say anything. This boy used to do everything for me, once upon a time. He'd offer to write essays for me so that I could get an extra hour of sleep, watch movies I knew he had no interest in seeing, just for me. He even walked forty blocks once to see me because his Metro-Card was empty.

It must have been October, judging from the length I remembered his hair being, and the layers of clothes he'd been wearing. He'd arrived at my door ruddy-cheeked and slightly sweaty, a cup of tea in hand. "Don't you have a huge math test tomorrow?"

"It's a regular-sized test," he'd said, his smile lighting up the hallway.

"I meant the degree of difficulty."

"It was harder not to come here."

"Eww but also aww." I'd let him in, accepting the kind of deep kiss that now made me angry to remember.

"Also, I studied while walking. Did you know they made calculus podcasts?"

"You did not listen to a calculus podcast," I'd said. "You were probably rehearsing for the play."

"I don't *just* sing, Lu, Jesus. I have other interests." We'd made it to my room by then, flopped onto the bed to lay next to each other, my head finding its resting spot on his chest. I'd craned my neck to look at him, judging his last statement. "Fine, I was singing. But, still, I contain multitudes."

I snapped out of the memory to realize I'd been staring at Leo.

"I guess this isn't much better," Leo said with a grimace, which made Miguel and Karl burst out laughing.

I looked past Leo and his jackass friends to my still-long line. I wished Pete were around to rescue me from this, but his shift had finished an hour ago and he was waiting for me at The Strand. I could feel myself start to blush. Rage-blushing, I think it was.

"Um," Leo said, starting to shift uncomfortably. This was the first time we'd seen each other since he broke up with me. This wasn't exactly how I was picturing it, with my co-workers around and the next person in line looking exasperated at any motion that wasn't strictly in my job description.

"We're gonna do the friends combo." He pushed a couple of twenties across the counter. I stared at the money, wishing it was something else. Maybe one of the bills had a love letter written on the back, or an apology. He was a theater geek after all; this could all be some elaborate, dramatic ploy. More chuckles from the jackasses. Leo bit his bottom lip, then looked back at his friends and told them to shut up. He turned toward me but didn't meet my eyes at all, his cheeks reddening. Shame-blushing, I guessed.

I started filling tubs of popcorn, my hands shaking enough that half the kernels spilled onto the floor. The other day at Madison Square Park, I'd had this whole speech prepared for him. I was going to try to convince him that we shouldn't break up, not for something as easily overcome as distance. I'd gone over the words in my head about a thousand times during all those hours when I couldn't sleep because of him, tinkered with their arrangement, wanting every damn sentence to punch him right in the heart so that I could then nurse him back to health. Now though, none of those words came to mind.

I slammed two tubs of popcorn on the counter and tried to ask him what he wanted to drink. But my voice was about to do that whole squeak-when-you're-about-to-cry thing, so I just picked up a couple of large cups and raised my eyebrows at him.

How I wanted those cups to be bottomless. How I wish I could just fill them up with his choice of orange soda for an hour straight until my shift was over, watch the bubbles fizz incessantly so I wouldn't have to face him in this state.

"So…" he said, with a long pause, as if he was trying to decide whether or not he should follow it up with anything or if he just let the words speak for themselves. Relationships don't end in periods, they end in ellipses, stretching the end out as if they don't know it's arrived. "What'd you want to talk to me about the other day?"

I slid the sodas over to him and punched in the order into my register. I thought about Cal's words to me on the bench. *What a weird thing we do*, he'd said. *Love.*

I grabbed Leo's change but just held it in my hand for a moment, looking up at him. "What do you think, Leo?" I managed to say. Instead of meeting my eyes, he looked down at the floor and shrugged. We'd been in love so recently, and now here I was trying to decide whether I should place the bills and coins on the counter to show him how hurt I was or if I should reach out and drop it into his hand for the pleasure of brushing his fingertips with mine.

The last time we'd held hands and meant it we were out on his fire escape, watching the neighbors. It hadn't been the dead of summer yet, the night warm but comfortable. Leo had just come up with a new song to add to the ongoing R & B album of our relationship. This one was titled "Fire Escape Boners" which I promise was a much sweeter song than what it sounds like. He had such a lovely singing voice, and he could come up with song lyrics that fit my sense of humor and made me swoon at the same time.

Nine months we'd dated. If I got to live until I was eighty, our relationship would only take up 0.9% of my lifetime. I tried to tell myself that 0.9% of my lifetime couldn't possibly have this much of an effect on me. It was meaningless. That's how long I spent in karate classes when I was eight, and I sure as hell didn't know any karate now, nor miss its presence in my life. I watched him open his mouth stupidly with no response. He brushed his hair back again.

"My movie's starting," he said, calling his friends over to help him with the snacks. They muttered hellos as if we hadn't noticed each other yet, then scurried away. "Sorry," Leo said.

Again, instead of saying all those words I'd prepared just for Leo the other day, I thought of Cal's, *We have love. Isn't that enough?*

He finally met my gaze and I looked into his eyes, eyes that I'd looked into most days for the last nine months, eyes that, on more than one occasion, had been the first thing I'd seen in the morning. I wished our time together had endowed me with the ability to know what he was thinking, to identify exactly the amount of love he had for me. But I had no clue, and didn't want to guess.

Then Leo turned and left, a trail of spilled popcorn in his wake.

As soon as I got off work, I grabbed my bag from the employee room and bolted down the street toward The Strand. I found Pete hanging out at the customer service desk with Starla, the two of them leaning over a crossword puzzle. The store was quiet, only a handful of people wandering about half an hour before closing. Indie rock was playing quietly on overhead speakers, and the soft, warm lighting made it feel like we were in a movie.

Starla spotted me first, and she smiled as I approached. "What's up, babycakes?" She did that whole antiquated-term-of-affection thing that usually only sweet, elderly ladies can pull off unironically.

"Oh you know, just my angst," I sighed and plopped my forehead onto the desk.

"Uh-oh," Pete said. "Shift not go so well? Are you disillusioned by the masses swallowing up Hollywood franchises again?"

I kept my head down on the wooden surface, turning so that I could see them, my cheek smooshed and making my words come out garbled. "I mean, yeah, that doesn't help. But..." A groan escaped me. "Leo showed up."

"Is that the ex?" Starla asked in an unsubtle aside to Pete.

"The very one. Let me guess, he didn't try to serenade you back into his arms?"

"Not quite." I stood up, feeling like no amount of sighing could ever help the queasiness in my stomach. "More like he showed up to swallow Hollywood franchises."

"That's a weird way to put it," Pete said. Then he snapped his fingers and grabbed the pen from Starla to write into the crossword. "*Swallow!* Seventeen-down." They high-fived, Starla's many bracelets jingling with the impact. "So, did you confront him?" Pete went on. "Unload the speech that's been building up inside of you lo these many days?"

"Again, no. More like stared into his stupidly pretty eyes and silently begged him to still love me."

"Yeesh," Starla said, eyebrows angled in concern. "Running into exes is never fun. It's just so easy to tell that at least one party involved is holding back some pain, some longing. It lingers there like a fart, making normal conversation impossible."

"Especially when you're the one who farted," Pete chipped in.

"Thanks, Pete, that's helpful."

"Sorry." He chewed on the back of the pen, looked up from the crossword. "Of all the movie theaters in all the world, why'd the dick have to walk into yours?"

"'I didn't know you'd be working today,'" I said, dropping my voice and making it sound as dumb as possible in imitation of Leo. It's not what he sounded like at all. Again, the jerk's voice was beautiful. But I was angry that he hadn't let me convince him to still be an us, hadn't bothered to show up to our meeting but had waltzed into my theater as if he didn't know I'd be there, angry that he wasn't still singing R & B songs with me. I groaned and looked around the shop, trying to find comfort in one of my favorite places, the quiet beauty of colorful, nearly endless stacks of books. All of them chock-full of love and heartache, couples killing themselves because they couldn't be together, couples traveling into hell to find each other, couples climbing over and fighting through and barreling past obstacles to be together. How had that not prepared me for a precollege breakup?

"You alright, girly?" Starla asked me.

"What percentage of these books do you think are about love, in some way?" I asked, ignoring her question and turning my back toward them so I could look out at the whole store. "Or at least have a romantic element in them?"

"Shiiiiiit," Starla said, stretching out the vowel. "If you leave out nonfiction and all the reference books, I'd guess 90 percent."

"That's so crazy," I said. "Why? Why this one thing? Life's much more than just love."

An old, balding white guy picked up a thick paperback from the classics table, turning it over to read the back cover. A black woman and her two tween daughters roamed the children's section, one girl holding her mom's hand, the other rushing ahead and gathering a pile of books.

I turned back to Starla and Pete, who had stopped doing their crossword puzzle and were looking out at the store too. "Because," Starla said, "love's the pinnacle of the human experience, yet it's still a mystery to us. The joys and the pains alike, not to mention the awkward mumblings of seeing an ex for the first time since your breakup. It's the best thing that happens to us—"

"Love's the worst thing that happened to me," I interrupted.

"—but we don't really know why," Starla continued, acknowledging me with a chuckle and a couple of reassuring shoulder pats. "All that art, it's just...the attempt to understand it."

"You should know more than anyone," Pete added, the words half-mumbled because of the pen in his mouth. Starla reached over and grabbed the pen from him.

"Gross, dude, that's my pen."

"Me? Why would I understand it?"

"Don't you write about it professionally? Love, specifically."

"Well, yeah. But I've never claimed to be a love expert. I'm

wading through the murky shitswamp that is love, and bringing my readers along for the ride."

"Wow, was that your pitch?"

"My love-hate relationship with love is part of my relatable charm. I'm not doling out advice, I'm chronicling what
it's like to be a teen maneuvering through this…" I waved my
hand and gestured at all these stupid books about love, then
at myself for added emphasis.

They went back to their crossword puzzle and I looked
out at the store a little longer, thinking about what Starla had
said. I spotted the aisle where I first eavesdropped on Iris,
wondered how she would deal with her first run-in with Cal
after their breakup.

"You're going to be okay," Starla reassured me, offering a
light forearm touch, her bracelets cold on my wrist.

"Yeah," I said. "That's what the books and movies keep
telling me."

I took my time walking home, not really in a hurry to deal
with my mom, or with another failed attempt at sleep. I tried
eavesdropping a few times on people around me, even pausing near a few bars with patios and pretending to text so that
I could listen in, but I couldn't seem to focus.

I climbed up the five short steps of my stoop, unlocked
the front door that led into the mail vestibule, then the inside
door that led to the stairway. We'd been living in this apartment since my parents got divorced and my dad moved to
New Jersey, but for some reason I'd never really noticed how
many stains were on the gray carpet, how the paint along the
walls was peeling so much that it looked like it was trying to
escape the building. Every apartment I passed by was replete
with noise, TVs blasting, music thumping, feet stomping. It
was like I was suddenly attuned to something about the city
that I'd never really focused on before.

When I unlocked my apartment door, Mom immediately pushed her chair away from the kitchen table. "Oh thank God," she said. "I was so tired." She walked over to the kitchen, setting a mostly empty red-wine glass by the sink. "Hope your day was good. Eggplant parm in the fridge, you can heat it in the microwave for a minute and a half. Good night." She planted a kiss on my forehead, which made me just want to fall into her arms.

I wrapped her into a hug, and she let out a soft "oh" in surprise, then held me tighter, probably thinking all sorts of mom thoughts. I wondered for a moment if I should tell her about Leo. I wanted to, felt the urge rising in my chest, though it was too easily suppressed. After Leo and I broke up, my mom had asked me if I was okay, and I managed to shrug and say a weak, "Yeah." After a few repetitions of this, she didn't bring it up again.

I don't know when Mom and I settled into the kind of relationship where love was not discussed, but it had happened too long ago for me to do anything about it now. I remember when my parents got divorced, I was old enough to see some sort of heartbreak in her, to sense her sorrow past my own. But I was thirteen and didn't know how to ask her about it, and the topic hadn't been broached since.

"G'night," I said, letting go of her and turning away, hoping she wouldn't call attention to my hug. "Please make pancit one day. Or lumpia. Literally anything not covered in tomato sauce."

"Very funny," she called down the hall. "Don't be loud, you'll wake your brother."

A record-breaking day for sighs, no doubt. I made myself a plate, threw it into the microwave, checked my email. Hafsah's warning still sat there. I read it again, wondered what I would do if I lost the job, lost my scholarship. I grabbed the book I was reading and set it on the kitchen table along with a glass of water, but struggled to read even a page.

Too many thoughts raged through my head, all of them uncomfortable to linger on. Bad furniture, that's what my thoughts were.

I ate as much of my dinner as I could stomach, then went into my room and fell on top of the sheets, wanting to cry but not exactly knowing what had changed from yesterday to today. I'd known Leo was unlikely to change his mind even with a speech, and all I'd done that day was muttered a sentence and handed him his change. *What a weird thing we do to ourselves*, I thought.

Then I sat up with a start. Inspiration poked at me for the first time in months, jabbing its persistent finger into the small of my back. I reached for my phone on the nightstand and clicked to reply to Hafsah's email.

Sorry, H. Been struggling with some heartbreak-induced writer's block. Fitting, right? But I have an idea. Are you free for coffee tomorrow?

5

PANIC VINAIGRETTE

Explaining dreams to someone when you don't really remember the details is one of the worst things a person can do, so I'll spare you. What you should know though, is that when I woke up I was happy. Overwhelmingly happy for just an instant, until I realized that I was happy because I'd dreamed about Leo. We'd been sitting on that bench in Union Square Park where I met Cal, but instead of Leo bailing on me, he'd shown up and taken my hand without a word. I was back within that comfort, within the joy of sitting next to someone you love and just feeling your hand in theirs. He started singing one of our R & B songs for me, then leaned in and kissed me.

I lay in bed, the feeling of being loved lingering even though it had come from a fictionalized version of a person who no longer loved me. I checked my phone and saw that Hafsah had emailed, saying we could meet at noon in Midtown. The desire to fall back asleep and into the dream made my bed a little more comfortable than it usually was, and the relief from Hafsah's email made me want to sink as deep into my mattress as possible. I snoozed my first alarm, not ready to start the day or to think about what it meant to be so happy after a dream like that. It's bizarre how dreams can just bleed into the day after they're done, like they're something tangible, like they're clothes you wear until you go to bed again. I was just about to doze back off when my backup alarm rang out. I groaned into my pillow and pulled myself out of bed. Cal's wallet was still on my nightstand, and I picked it up and rummaged through it for the millionth time before deciding it was best kept out of sight and chucking it into my drawer.

In the living room, Jase was back on the couch with his video games. Mom was at work. I got myself a bowl of cereal and watched Jase kill a few more people, trying to clear my head of the dream. "Don't you have any social interactions planned today?"

"What are you talking about? I'm playing with literally all my friends right now."

"What if you read a book today? Just, like, a page."

"This game actually has a really good storyline." Jase paused his game for a second to take a bite of leftover eggplant parmesan. There were four pieces piled onto the plate, and that's not even counting however many he had devoured before I'd woken up. He used to be such a sweet, small kid. So small. I could pick him up and even physically intimidate him when I needed to. But now he was eating as much in one meal as I was in a week, and his limbs looked like a magician pulling a colored handkerchief out of his sleeve. They just kept going and going.

"What about some community service hours? Volunteer work? Meditation? Any plans to do those today?"

"Prolly not."

"Your generation will be the end of us all," I said, getting up to go shower.

I still had plenty of time, so I decided to save myself the subway fare from Chinatown and walk to Midtown. I wanted to
corral my thoughts, so that I could make a good pitch to Hafsah. But my thoughts were un-corral-able, and altogether too
painfully focused on Leo. I ended up just eavesdropping the
whole way there. Nothing meaningful really. I wasn't within
earshot of anyone long enough to get a full conversation. Just
lines, words I plucked out of the air.

The restaurant I was meeting Hafsah at was obviously a
business-lunch meet up. It was empty at 11:45 when I got in,
and at exactly noon the line snaked out the door, all thirty-,
forty-, and fiftysomethings in business attire. There was a
staggering number of blazers.

I felt weird as hell sitting there, obviously out of place.
Well, not that exactly. But like everyone else thought I was
out of place. I'd been meeting with Hafsah at places like this
for over a year now.

I'd checked into the front desk of the building she worked
in and saw the looks the security guards gave me, their eyebrows raised, the contemptuous stares of middle-aged white
dudes wondering what I was doing in the elevator with them.
In their eyes, I was lost. I'd wandered in accidentally.

But here of all places, I was not lost.

I'd found *Misnomer*'s call for writers online in a Tumblr post,
shared hundreds of times before I'd even laid eyes on it. I was
probably supposed to be doing homework at the time, but of
course had gotten sucked into the black hole of the internet.

The post said the site was looking for "fresh teen voices"
in a handful of categories, which immediately filled me with
hope that they were looking for exactly me, while also making me question whether my voice was fresh or even typically
teenage or what category I was suited for. I'd seen "love" on
the list, but had assumed I could do humor or current events

or lifestyle, whatever that one meant. They'd asked for a cover letter and a portfolio of writing samples, so I'd spent the next few hours shirking my academic responsibilities in order to go through everything I'd ever written. After overcoming nausea from reading the garbage I'd written over the years, I managed to find a handful of blog entries, essays, and stories that I felt strongly enough about to submit.

A week later I had an email from Hafsah, the managing editor, telling me that since I lived in New York, I should come in for an interview, ready to discuss ideas. I filled three pages in my notebook with pitches on what I could write for her.

That first time in the *Misnomer* offices, I'd felt out of place, sure. Up until I sat down in front of Hafsah's desk. There were many ways I could describe Hafsah, but above all else, she's a badass. At twenty-nine she was the managing editor for a magazine, had a publishing deal for two books of essays, had her work featured in the *New York Times*, the *Atlantic*, and the *Wall Street Journal*, as well as having been interviewed a handful of times on TV for her insight into a number of social issues. I'd researched all of this before coming in for my interview, and I was in the presence of the woman whom I aspired to be someday.

"What do you want to write about, Lu?" she'd asked, right off the bat.

I thought for a second. "Is it a bad interview answer to say 'anything'?"

"Not necessarily." She'd turned to some papers in front of her, presumably my printed writing samples, but they could have easily been, like, hidden Harry Potter manuscripts or classified Pentagon papers or something. She's was *that* cool. "How often do you write?"

"Most days."

"Do you schedule time to do it, or wait for inspiration?"

"At least a half hour before bed. And usually during math classes, as a stimulant. Except on days when I need a break."

She'd smiled. "How do you feel about love?"

"Um."

"I'm sure you saw that one of the positions we're looking to fill is a regular romance and relationship columnist. Not a Dear Abby thing, per se, more like a Carrie Bradshaw thing."

I tilted my head. "The quarterback?"

"As in *Sex and the City*?"

I snapped my fingers. "Right. I knew that." I noticed that the usual discomfort that came after I said something stupid didn't rage in my thoughts. My comment dissipated in my memory. It was a wonderful thing, being unbothered.

Hafsah flipped through the pages in front of her, leaning her chin in her cupped hand for a moment before looking back up at me.

"How would you feel about writing about love?"

"I mean, writing is writing. I'm not too…experienced, or whatever. But I'd be happy to do it."

"Well, (a), that doesn't matter. I just love your voice, and some of these blog posts are exactly what we're looking for. Those two weeks when you had a crush on the kid in chess club led to some compelling, funny reading. And, (b), being in a relationship isn't the sole experience of teen love. God knows it wasn't for me. We're not looking for a relationship advice person, that's too passé. We want someone to muse about love and dating, the absence and longing of both."

"That," I said, "I can write about."

Hafsah smiled again, and I almost felt like my life as a writer-with-an-audience was already beginning. "You've got these insights that I think could resonate with readers. Even now I'm looking forward to reading more from you."

It didn't sound like I was interviewing for a job anymore,

which almost prompted me to run a victory lap in her office. I didn't, which is probably why I got the job.

I knew what I had to offer the world, and it was my writing. And ever since I'd started at *Misnomer*, regardless of how I moved within the world, I'd felt more a part of it than ever before. So they could raise their eyebrows all they wanted.

At the fancy restaurant I didn't/did belong in, I sipped on seltzer water until Hafsah arrived, smiling at the hostess and pointing me out as she strode past the line of people waiting for a table.

"Have you been here long?" Hafsah asked as she sat down. She pushed her menu aside and looked around for a waiter, one arm raised slightly, two fingers stretched just enough to catch someone's attention, but not enough that someone might think her desperate for it.

"No, I just got here."

We chatted small stuff for a while, mostly her asking me how it felt to be done with school. To be honest it still just felt like any other summer. A stupidly heartbroken one, but whatever. I wasn't thinking about starting college in the fall yet.

When our food arrived, Hafsah went into business mode. "Alright, what's your pitch?" She unraveled her silverware from its little cloth napkin sleeping bag and started poking away at her pasta. I had a great-looking ahi tuna salad with soy vinaigrette in front of me, but now that it was time for me to tell her my idea, I couldn't bring myself to casually eat while unloading the speech I had been going over in my mind all morning.

It took some stammering and a few expectant looks from Hafsah before I could actually start speaking intelligently. "So, the other day, I eavesdropped on this couple," I said, fidgeting with my fork, my glass of water, my phone, the tablecloth, my tuna, anything within reach. "They were talking about how the girl was leaving to go to college, and the guy was staying here, and the conversation turned to…"

Hafsah waited for me to finish.

"A breakup, I guess. You know, classic summer before college stuff."

"Just like you, huh?"

"Slaying me with the casualness there, H."

"Sorry," she said, offering a forced grimace before turning to her pasta again, probably not wanting to let the afternoon flitter away unproductively. "So, you're thinking a piece about precollege breakups?"

I toyed with my fork for a little while, rubbing some wasabi across the side of a piece of seared tuna. "A series. I was thinking I could profile specific couples. Starting with those two."

"How would you find them again? Didn't you just overhear them?"

"I, uh, have the boy's wallet. It's a weird, long story where I promise I am in no way implicated for any legal wrongdoing. But I have a way to get in touch with them. I could interview them, fresh from their recent heartbreak. And then I could do a whole series of other couples going through the same thing. I could write about it from so many different angles, right? It'd be interesting. Couples who are staying together long-distance, couples who decided to change plans to be together, couples who…didn't."

Hafsah chewed thoughtfully on her pasta, eyeing me. I tried not to squirm. I wasn't uncomfortable in her presence. She was in no way a mean person. It was just intense to be under the scrutiny of someone you admired, someone you knew was damn good at life.

"Are you going to write yourself into the pieces?" she said, finally, wiping at the corner of her mouth with a napkin.

"Um, I hadn't really thought about that," I said, because

those words were easier to say than, *Sure, but thinking about my failed relationship is crippling me and I'd rather think about anything else.*

"It would help make it more relatable. Be transparent about what led you to this interest. The readers would love that." She shrugged, maybe because she saw the panic on my face. "Just a thought. But, yeah, I like it. We'll see how the first one turns out before committing to a series. Monday work for you?"

"Oh." I finally managed to take a bite of tuna, buying myself time while chewing. I looked around the restaurant at all the business people going about their days, having conversations about performance, sales, accounting, or... I guess I don't really know what those people talked about over business lunches. I couldn't fathom sitting down to actually write a reflection on Iris and Cal, and definitely not one on myself. But I couldn't risk getting my column dropped. Partly because it would completely unravel the external validation crucial to my (admittedly dwindling) mental health. Mostly, though, if I lost the scholarship that was tied to my job, I wouldn't be able to go to school at all.

"Lu?" Hafsah said. "Can I see a draft by Monday?"

"Yeah, sure." I took another bite of my salad, which was probably delicious but kind of tasted like a dusty slab of clay at that point. "Wait, what day is it today?"

"Thursday."

I heroically resisted throwing up. "Yeah, sure. Monday. Cool, cool. All weekend. And then some! Ha!"

Understandably, Hafsah looked at me as if I'd just turned into one of those homeless dudes who doesn't really carry a sign or has any sort of clear goal he's trying to accomplish, but rather spends his time yelling out random strings of nonsense words. Luckily, Hafsah knows that I'm much better at stringing words together on paper. "If the couple's slow to get back for an interview, let me know and we'll push it back, but I'd really prefer to see something by Monday."

"Monday," I said again, nodding my head vigorously to reassure my editor that I was totally normal and capable of writing and not a babbling maniac. "Cool."

"Great," Hafsah said. She set her fork and knife neatly across the plate, done with her food and ready to move on to whatever super important badass thing she was doing next. She got a waiter's attention again and set down her corporate card to pay for the bill. I told her I was fine on my own and so she took off, saying she was looking forward to reading what I came up with.

Now I was free to enjoy my panic salad and try to come up with a way to introduce myself to Cal and Iris without coming off as a stalker. Although I'd already kinda met Cal, and now I had his wallet, so I was definitely going to come across as at least a little stalkerish. Which meant they'd have to be really naive about the ways of the world to let me anywhere near them again. Which meant I wouldn't have anything to send Hafsah on Monday. Which meant bye-bye to college and my ability to ever write again.

6
OFF THE RECORD

I spent the rest of that day just kind of staring at the computer and making low guttural sounds. Then on Friday I decided I should probably at least try to find a way to talk to the lovebirds. Cal's name hadn't worked on Facebook, but I realized I had Iris's full name from the raffle ticket, and when I typed it in she came up right away. Her privacy settings weren't superintense either, so I opened up a private message.

Then I stared at it for a long time and made some more guttural sounds. When that didn't seem to cause words to appear on my screen, I texted Pete.

Lu
Help, I need to human.

Pete
Why? You have the day off. Be a slug.
Slugs have good lives.

Lu
Are slugs good at making introductions
with strangers on whom they've eavesdropped?

> **Pete**
> No conclusive evidence either way on that one.

I told him about my pitch to Hafsah, which I knew would really get him on board with the whole helping me thing. Pete's the biggest fan of my writing, and he takes every opportunity he can to encourage me to do more of it. Which was great at the moment because of the whole sucking-at-writing-since-Leo-dumped-me thing. Just say you found the wallet and want to return it, Pete wrote, oversimplifyingly.

Shut up, that's a word.

> **Lu**
> And how do I approach the whole we're-strangers-but-I-want-to-interview-you-and-your-very-recently-ex-boyfriend thing?

> **Pete**
> ...Journalistically?

> **Lu**
> Shut up, that's not a word.

> **Pete**
> You're a journalist, Lu. A writer mostly,
> but technically a journalist. Just tell them
> what the situation is. It's really not that weird.
> Worst thing they can say is no.

> **Lu**
> And then I get fired and lose my scholarship and don't go to college and die in vain, another wasted human life lost into the folds of history.

I slouched deeper into the couch and let loose a few more guttural sounds. Weird how an audible expression of discomfort helped ease the discomfort itself, even if just for a second. It probably increased Jase's discomfort, since he was sitting right next to me, and no amount of video games can distract from your older sister low-key imitating a walrus half the morning.

Finally, feeling on the verge of an existential crisis if I didn't even attempt to hang on to my columnist job, and only after many, many drafts, I sent Iris Castillo, aka Crying Girl, aka Bench Boy's version of Leo, a message: Hi! This is going to sound weird, but I found someone named Cal's wallet the other day. His name didn't lead to anything on Facebook, but there was a raffle ticket with your name in there, which is how I found you. Lemme know if I should get in touch with him or where we should meet to give you the wallet or whatever you want to do.

Hitting Send felt like the onset of a mild panic attack.

Thankfully I only have normal teen levels of angst-xiety, and my uncomfortable morning was made calm when Iris responded fifteen minutes later. OMG! That's so nice of you. Can you come to the address on the raffle ticket? I'll pass it along. I'm free any time before three.

I trekked back uptown to Iris's apartment building. This time, when I got out of the subway I looked around for some coffee to prepare for the conversation I was about to have. It's a weird compulsion, getting coffee in advance of a potentially nerve-racking situation. Maybe it was comforting to have something in my hands, or the constant motion of sipping was somehow soothing. Very often, it ended up being a terrible mistake that made me need to use the bathroom right in the middle of the nerve-racking situation, but I somehow still thought of it as a security blanket.

The night Leo and I broke up, I stormed out of his apartment and went straight to our favorite Vietnamese restaurant to get an iced coffee. We'd had pho there about once a week since we started dating, but even the suddenly painful experience of being in there—the bitter taste of what had once been a happy place now marred by the end of the relationship—wasn't a match for my craving of sweet, stomach-gurgling coffee. I'd sat on the curb, holding the coffee close to me in the early summer heat, wishing its comforts could extend deeper than my taste buds.

On the Upper West Side, I picked up a dollar cup of hot coffee from a bagel cart and walked to Iris's building, the whole time tinkering with how I would ask if I could write about her and Cal. I'd done it a bunch of times already for other articles I'd written, approached someone for permission, or for an interview. For some reason this one felt different. I couldn't put my finger on why, though if I had to guess I'd probably say that my finger would have landed somewhere in or around the awkwardness of eavesdropping on someone's breakup and then introducing yourself.

I checked the time to make sure I wasn't late or freakishly early, then texted her so she would come down. A moment later, as I stepped around the corner, someone coming the other way plowed into me, splashing scalding coffee all over the front of my shirt. I bellowed in pain and looked up to face my attacker, which is when I saw Grace chasing after her skateboard down the street.

"Owwww," I said.

"I'm sorry!" Grace cried. "You were just there suddenly."

I pinched the front of my shirt and pulled it away from my body, so that it wouldn't melt into my skin. "It's okay," I said, recovering from the shock. "I spill things too."

I looked around lamely for a napkin or something to sop up the mess and saw Iris emerging from her building a few doors down. She stood there for a bit before noticing us, and gave one of those looks you give people you're about to meet but have never seen before except for little profile pictures online. You tilt your head and squint your eyes and try to reconcile how they appear in person with the digital version of themselves you've seen before. Then she broke out into an earnest, charming smile and waved as she came toward us. I doubt I'd smiled at anyone since my breakup with Leo.

"Lu?" she asked, sticking her hands into the pockets of her dress. Noticing Grace, she frowned for a moment and said hi to her too, then started piecing together what had happened.

"Let's go upstairs," Iris said, looking at my shirt, which was basically just one big coffee stain. "We'll get napkins or something. Grace, are you okay?" Grace, probably happy to take this as absolution for causing the coffee spill, nodded, hopped on her skateboard, and rolled away, weaving around a couple slow-walking down the sidewalk.

Before I could protest, Iris turned back toward her apartment, gesturing for me to follow along. Her building had a nice elevator with a mirror wall and shiny chrome panels, which we stood in awkwardly for the ten-floor journey upstairs. We passed through an elegant, spacious hallway, the kind you see in hotels, but with fewer rooms. Iris opened the door inside and jetted away, saying she was going to get one of those magical detergent pens. I stood in the entrance to her place, wondering just what the hell I was doing. *Returning the wallet, confessing the eavesdropping, asking for permission to interview her, keeping your job,* the practical side of my brain said. *Figuring out how someone else wades through the insanities of heartbreak,* some other side of my brain retorted. To keep those two sides of my brain from arguing, a third chimed in and said, *Isn't that artisanal rug hanging on the wall over there pretty? It looks Oaxacan!*

Shut up, we don't know what Oaxacan rugs look like! The other two parts of my brain shouted in unison.

Iris came speed-walking back, the pen in her hand. "I'm

sorry this happened. The universe really chose to reward your good deed by being a prick, huh?"

"Totally," I said. I uncapped the pen and started dabbing uselessly at the damp coffee stain, which easily covered half of my shirt. There was a quiet moment, thick with the awkwardness of our unfamiliarity.

"Damn, that's not doing much, is it?" Iris said, pouting.

"It's okay. This happens to me about forty times a week."

"Oof."

"Yeah, I'm a lost cause. Like this shirt." I shrugged and capped the pen, giving it back to her.

"I'm sorry you have to walk around like that all day. Do you live nearby?"

"Not really, I live in Chinatown. But it's okay. I don't have any street cred or anything, so it's fine if people judge me on the R train."

Iris laughed, harder than she had to. She even did that thing only '50s starlets do where they cover their mouths with their hands, as if laughter could be contained, or even should be for the sake of propriety. On the way over to her place, I'd imagined her looking as heartbroken as I'd felt, but looking at her now, and over her shoulder at the living room behind her, I saw no evidence that she'd taken her breakup harshly. There were no blankets crumpled on the couch, Netflix wasn't paused on the TV. Iris even looked like she'd managed to shower at some point in the past few days, which was more than I could say for myself post-breakup.

"Well, I guess I should thank you for coming all this way. Especially since it came at such a high cost." She gestured to my shirt.

"It's really okay," I said, reaching into my bag to grab Cal's wallet. "I found out this shirt is from one of those evil places that uses sweatshops, so I've been meaning to, like, donate it and buy something more humane, or burn it in protest. I don't know which is the most ethical option. Anyway, spilling coffee on it was probably just my guilt lashing out."

Iris snapped her fingers. "Oh! I know what I'll do." She turned and walked away again, leaving me holding the wallet out to no one. I hoped there wasn't anyone else in the apartment that might appear and ask me who I was. "I've got a bunch of shirts here," Iris called out from what I assumed was her room. "You can borrow one."

"You don't have to do that! It's almost dry." I picked at the shirt, which was clinging to my ribs. "Kind of."

Iris came back, holding a baby blue V-neck. "Please, I insist. I've got like three of the same one. It's the least I can do for you coming out of your way to return my stupid boyfriend's wallet."

I froze, my jaw succumbing to gravity and clichés. *I'm sorry, did you just say 'ex-boyfriend'? Because if so you were super quiet on the ex part*, I thought, but didn't say, because I can still sometimes human. "Oh, he's your boyfriend?"

"Yeah. He sucks at hanging on to his belongings. I swear he can't go to a movie theater without leaving his cell phone under the seat with the day-old popcorn. The amount of times we've had to go back and…" She trailed off. "Sorry, I'm rambling. Anyway." She stepped forward and held her hand out, offering the T-shirt. "Thanks again. This really means so much."

Gingerly, I reached out and grabbed it, leaving Cal's wallet in her open palm instead. "Yeah, it's no problem," I said, almost a whisper.

There could have been a different outcome.

Iris said "boyfriend," not "ex-boyfriend," so there existed a world, a universe, some parallel dimension where two people like me and Leo could love each other the way we did and not be split up by the circumstances of our collegiate plans. I'd entered that universe somehow, and now I knew why I'd hung on to that wallet.

I'd unknowingly pitched Hafsah gold. It wasn't just a decent idea, an exploration of the murky ground of post-senior-year relationships, it was an actual blueprint. These two had lived through the same fight I'd had with Leo and survived. I wanted to know how. I wanted to share that how with others and help them avoid this stupid feeling I was in the midst of. Hell, maybe I could somehow be saved too.

"The bathroom is just here on the left." Iris stepped aside and pointed at a door. "I was gonna make a pot of coffee. You want some? Your shirt made me crave it." She smiled, humor in her eyes.

I nodded yes, then went into the bathroom to change. I was glad to get the wet shirt off me, and happy that Iris had offered coffee, not just for the comfort, but for the opportunity to linger there and work up the guts to bring up my ulterior motive.

When I walked out of the bathroom, I found Iris sitting on a stool at the kitchen counter looking at her phone. The smell of coffee was strong, the machine burbling loudly. Iris looked up at me and smiled again, flipping her phone facedown on the granite counter.

That was probably the moment that I'd been waiting for, to come clean about eavesdropping. I opened my mouth, then realized how hard it is to say the words, *hey, so, the other day I was spying on you.* Instead, I again opted for words that were easier to say, "So, you and Cal, huh? How long's that been going on for?"

She answered politely at first, but I kept prying, my journalistic instinct kicking in (and kicking aside my subnormal social skills). She was clearly in the mood to talk too, running me through a brief history of their relationship. They'd met online, on Tumblr. They'd started off liking/reblogging each other's posts, many of them little love notes to New York City. After enough of this casual e-flirting, Iris had sent him a private message. "I felt like we'd been looking at each other across a room all night, and I couldn't take the eye-dancing anymore without saying hi. So, I just sent a 'hi' with a little emoticon smiley face." They kept flirting online for a while after that, and a couple of months later they went on their first date. This was almost two years ago. Since then, it seemed like it was all roses and puppy love. No mention of fighting in the streets outside The Strand.

"What are you guys doing for college?" I asked, dipping my toes farther into ulterior-motive territory. Iris's expression didn't give anything away, but she didn't answer immediately either. "I'm just asking because… Okay, this is weird, but have you heard of *Misnomer*?"

She nodded. "Yeah, but I've never really gone on it."

"Well, I actually have this column on it that's all about love and relationships and stuff." I looked down at my lap, fiddling with my hands. "My newest piece is gonna be about couples who are facing the summer before college and the decision to go long-distance, or break up, or go to the same school or whatever. It's so funny that you're in that situation too!"

Iris raised her eyebrows, graciously passing over my stupid comment. "Wow, you have your own column?"

"It's not that big of a deal. I don't think a lot of people read it."

"Still. What's it like interviewing people about their love lives?"

"You can find out, if you let me interview you."

She laughed, then flipped her hair over and ran her hand through the curls, fluffing them out. There was something enchanting about the action, something that spoke of a comfort within her own body that I just didn't have. "Damn, girl, that was smooth," she said. She pushed away from the counter and took our empty mugs to the sink. "I don't know if I'm into that though. He and I had kind of a touchy talk about the topic the other day, and I'd rather not delve into it, especially in front of a stranger." The faucet turned on, and she rinsed the mugs and put them away in the dishwasher. "No offense."

She flashed a smile that I easily recognized as the desire to stop the conversation, but I wasn't quite ready to face the turmoil of my thoughts if I walked away from here without the article that would bust me out of my writer's block. "This is going to sound like I'm prying, but it's just an excuse to say a phrase I've been dying to say since I became a quote-unquote journalist. Off the record, what was the touchy talk about?" Another polite smile, eyes averted. She bided her time by turning on the dishwasher. "I'm only asking because, well…" I trailed off, surprised I was ready to broach the subject with anyone but Pete. "I got dumped recently. My boyfriend and I had planned to stay together after graduation, then he… I dunno. Changed his mind, I guess."

Iris looked at me for a moment, long enough for me to really think about what a weirdo I was. Here I was standing in this Upper West Side kitchen—with its granite countertops, decorative Mexican plates, and a freakin' dishwasher, the light coming in through the big windows that didn't just show the neighboring building but had an actual view—in front of a girl whose nonbreakup I'd witnessed and now wanted to take advantage of for my own personal reasons. And I was revealing my own broken heart to her. Within an hour of meeting her.

"I don't know," Iris said. "This seems…personal."

"Personal is what my column is all about."

"Yeah, but, I don't know you."

"Okay, what do you want to know?"

"Why us? For all you know we're boring as hell."

"Fair question," I said. I couldn't admit the fact that I'd eavesdropped on their conversation, heard lines coming out of her mouth that Leo had spat at me. "For one, I'll admit, it's convenience." I threw out my most casual shrug. "I'm standing in your kitchen and you just told me you're going through the exact thing I want to write about. I also like the coincidence of it all. I found your boyfriend's wallet on the ground and it just so happens you fit the profile for my column. That's kinda cool, right?" Iris considered this for a moment, then conceded my point with a nod. "Most of all, though, I'm just curious. My relationship failed where yours went right. I wanna know how you did it."

The dishwasher started to whir. Iris looked down at it as if she was thankful for its interruption. "I don't know what to say. We talked through it." She fluffed her hair out again and looked at me, maybe hoping I would change the subject. Unfortunately for her, my journalistic instinct was still on, and I knew that if I didn't say anything for a bit she'd feel the need to fill the silence. She turned her back to me and grabbed a dishrag that was folded by the sink, running it across the counter as if there was anything there to clean. "I don't talk easily about personal stuff. You can?"

Of course, I'd talked about the breakup with Pete already. And a little bit with my cousin Cindy when she texted a couple of nights after. But there's something about breakups and certain kinds of sadness that makes you want to return to the subject again and again, no matter how emotionally draining it can be. I guess that's what heartbreak does to you. It makes you long to feel drained.

"To a fault," I chuckled. "I work at a movie theater, and the other day during the thirty-second interaction I had with a customer buying a ticket, I managed to tell them not only that I'd recently been dumped, but that I was planning on a really great speech to win my ex back."

Iris cringed, which was the most appropriate reaction she could have had. "Did the speech work?"

"I've tried to deliver it three times now. He's bailed on me every time."

The dishwasher whirred again. Iris folded the dishrag back up. She looked me in the eyes like she was really trying to look inside. Probably assessing whether I was on some nerfarious mission to tickle them or rearrange their furniture or something, which is a good assessment to attempt on strangers inside your home. "I'll tell you what," Iris said, adding a warm smile. "You and I can chat some other time. You can return the shirt, and maybe by then I'll feel more like opening up. We'll talk about boys and breakups and all that." Then she led me toward the door, her hand touching my shoulder briefly to lead me out of the kitchen. "Off the record."

On Being Super Annoying and Happy

BY LU CHARLES, SEPTEMBER 27

Readers, I have to confess something. This weekend, I made out at Starbucks. Excessively, and unapologetically. I was responsible for propagating the image the world has of the uncontrollable, sex-crazed, inconsiderate teen. And it felt great.

We've all been on the witnessing side of this interaction, and it doesn't feel great. That gross, wet lip smacking, the cringe-inducing prolonged eye contact, the not-at-all-inconspicuous butt grabs. It's uncomfortable for everyone but the people involved in the make-out, oblivious to anything but their little world of two.

For those who haven't shamelessly made out in a public place, I'd like to present a case on its behalf.

Imagine, if you will, a seventeen-year-old girl who's been conditioned by art and media to crave companionship, and who's been coaxed by her hormones and/or society to crave touch. Imagine (or perhaps I should say, recall) the lonely days and nights without companionship or touch. She spends her time thinking about love and why so many are so obsessed with it, to the point where she actually gets paid to do the pondering (how meta).

Then comes a boy. Sweet brown skin, a commandingly sexy stage presence when he's in school plays, the ability to make every moment feel special. He laughs at the girl's jokes and reaches for her hand often, every now and then bringing their clasped hands to his mouth and kissing her fingers, telling her he's lucky he has her in his life. Kisses the way poetry describes kissing.

Now the girl and the boy are at a coffee shop, and they peck each other on the lips just to remind each other that this lovely thing exists in their lives. And it's not like the outside world just falls away. They don't forget about the people in the coffee shop trying to work on their computers or read their books or grumble to each other about their days. They just see each other more than anything else. The pecks escalate.

Should we fault the couple that is so enamored with each other? Why not dive into the joy? The world isn't exactly considerate of its behavior toward them, it does nothing to avoid annoying teens, and in fact annoys them quite often. So why not make out at the Starbucks? Why not take on the sneers and frowns the world so often casts in their direction anyway? They're momentarily protected by this force field of lips and tongues and flesh. What looks like PDA feels like refuge.

So, yes, for those who have been wondering in the comments, I am still in this wacky world of experiencing a relationship rather than philosophizing about them. It's going well, I think, even if I have become a little more annoying. I'm in a safe haven of smooching, and your dirty looks will not bring me down.

7

CARTOONISHLY THWARTED

"Pete, save me."

Someone else would have had the decency to at least offer a weary sigh before continuing on. Pete didn't so much as inhale semiheavily into the phone. "You don't need saving. You've still got a good idea for a column. It just won't be about those two."

"Will you let me mope for a second?"

"No. It even sounds like this Iris girl is interested in being your friend. You have nothing to mope about."

I groaned, really doubling down on my effort just to show Pete how normal people were supposed to act. "I'm going down into the subway. I'll meet you at The Strand in twenty minutes? Three hours? I don't know how long it takes to get back from the Upper West Side."

"Okay." Pete hung up, and I reentered the sweaty underworld of New York. Good, the underworld. A fitting place for me and my doomed writing career and love life. Of course Iris and Cal hadn't broken up. They were hip romantics with a true understanding of love. It was only me who sucked at these things, me who didn't deserve the entirely unlikely but still wholly possible scenario of love extending beyond high school and into college.

It was pretty empty at the station, just one white dude with a backpack and headphones on. Great idea, White Dude in His Twenties. I pulled my headphones out of my bag and put on a thought-suppressing podcast.

About thirty-five minutes later I was standing in front of Pete by the biographies.

"Dude, who reads biographies?"

"No book shaming," he murmured. "People are interesting. There's some comfort in knowing that lives continue on as stories."

I rolled my eyes and picked up an entirely too-heavy tome of President Martin Van Buren. Although I guess if a book were written about my life, I'd be okay with it leaning heavy. "Anyway. You rudely interrupted my attempt to bitch about my article going to hell."

"You have an article. Just find someone else."

"Like who? I don't know anyone else in this situation."

"Look within yourself."

"I don't know the answer. Just tell me."

"I was talking about you and Leo."

I narrowed my eyes at him. "I can't wait to read the part in your biography where you got murdered in The Strand by your best friend."

Pete thumbed through the book he was reading. I nudged him to lift the cover so I could see it, but also to make sure he wouldn't get too engrossed. He eyed me over the brim. "Have you met Diane and Rachel? They're Colleen's friends, dating and just graduated. I could put you in touch."

I reshelved the Van Buren biography and ran my fingers along the book spines in front of me. It's such a cliché thing to do, but I can never resist it. "But I want to write about Cal and Iris."

"They said no. You can either complain about not having a subject, or you can complain about having one. You can't do both."

"Watch me!" I yelled, maybe a little too loudly. A few customers gave me a mean look. They had a definitive tourist vibe to them and I felt like I was giving them the authentic New York experience of rudeness or whatever, so I didn't apologize.

"For the record," Pete said, putting his book down, "I think it'd be really good for you to interview Leo. That is, if I believed he'd take the time to show up for an interview. Which he wouldn't. Because he's a selfish prick."

"There is no record, so your comment has disappeared into the ether," I mumbled. We wandered around the aisles a while longer, the way we usually did, absentmindedly looking at covers and reading back cover copy, occasionally diving into the first few pages of a novel. The store wasn't too busy, so we hung out with Starla at the registers and played one of our people-watching games: How Hard Would It Be to Get That Person to Murder You? Starla was really good at that game, always able to come up with a scenario in which even the most mild-mannered customers might murder her. Maybe it was because an extra decade or so on the planet had the tendency to lessen your faith in people, or maybe because she'd read more spy novels than all suburban middle-aged dads combined.

I also tried eavesdropping on people every chance I got, but didn't get anything too interesting. That's usually the case with eavesdropping. You get the minutiae of everyday life without the context, the lulls without any highlights. I could have eavesdropped for years without coming across another couple like Cal and Iris.

In the lulls, my thoughts went to Leo. Pete had called him a selfish prick, but that was just Pete taking my side, being protective. Leo had never once been selfish in our relationship. It was a new side to him that the breakup had dug up, and even in my stewing, I felt that it wasn't the real Leo.

Pete had always liked Leo while we were dating. He'd even come with me to Leo's plays at school and joined me when the cast and crew went out for burgers, so that I wouldn't be the only quiet nontheater person. I think they'd gone to watch a movie once without me, maybe?

After about an hour or so at the bookstore, my mom called me and told me dinner was almost ready so I should get my ass over to help her grate three pounds of parmesan cheese or something like that. I wasn't really listening. Before I left, I looked at Pete. "Alright, fine."

"Fine, what?"

"Fine, give me the info for Colleen's friends."

"Wise decision," he said, unable to contain a smirk.

"Your mom's a wise decision," I said, gathering my bag and heading out the door. "I have to write a draft by Monday, so can you put them in touch with me tonight?"

He and Starla both chuckled. "See you tomorrow," Pete called out.

I spent the next day mired in abject boredom on my couch, still unable to write. The one exciting thing of note was that Pete got me in touch with his sister Colleen's friends, and they'd agreed to meet up with me after Pete's shift was over. I thought a lot about Iris and Cal, but I was itchy to get to writing, and Pete was right. It was better to move on and actually write something than get bogged down with one couple.

I was still going to get to dive into the topic, pry into someone's life, pick this thing apart and try to discover if it was knowable, if I could understand where Leo and I failed and how. Sure, I was still thinking about Leo nonstop, and I couldn't exactly shake off my interest in Cal and Iris, but at least there were other things going on in my mind. At least I'd be writing.

I'd already told my mom that I had a dinner meeting for the magazine, so at around seven I left home and walked to the theater to meet up with Pete since he'd met Diane and Rachel before and could make things marginally less awkward. We were going to Mamoun's, which had this incredible hot sauce I just had to slather on everything. Unfortunately, this turned me into a sweating, sniffling mess that would surely cancel out any of Pete's efforts to make me seem normal.

They were already waiting for us when we got there, having claimed a table on the tiny patio overlooking St. Marks. They were both black and wore glasses, though Rachel's were thick-framed and square while Diane's were the little circular John Lennon kind. I liked them right away, if only for their choice of table. It wasn't super muggy out, and when the weather is nice in New York, choosing to sit inside is a crime of unparalleled moral depravity. Kind of.

Pete made the introductions, and then he and Diane went to put our order in at the counter. Rachel and I stayed outside, where there was plenty of noise coming from the street— groups of college students deciding where they should eat, a promoter at the nearby comedy club chatting loudly with the bouncer, faint thumping music from one of the bars.

"Have you ever been here before?" Rachel asked.

"Yeah, all the time," I said. "I work nearby, so sometimes I come here for lunch. Also, I've been trying to sneak into the kitchen for about three years in order to steal their hot sauce recipe, but I always get cartoonishly thwarted."

"'Cartoonishly' the way Wile E. Coyote would get

thwarted, or like the villain in an episode of Scooby-Doo? There's an important distinction."

"Oh, definitely on the Wile E. Coyote side. Kind of Wile E. meets Tom from *Tom and Jerry*. There's always a stick of dynamite involved."

Rachel laughed, playing with her braided hair. "What would you do with the recipe if you got it? Make millions?"

I pretended to think about it for a while. "Make a swimming pool full of it. I'm not in it for the money, just the love of the sauce. I want to be surrounded by it at all times."

"Oof, I'm not about that. Hot sauce is meant for mouths, absolutely nowhere else."

"Good point," I said, relaxing. You find someone you can joke with right away, it's funny how quickly other anxieties just seem to disappear. Pete and Diane came out then, holding a stack of napkins and a bottle each of hot sauce and tahini.

We ate first, Pete doing most of the talking to catch up with Diane and Rachel. When we finished eating, the table was overrun with crumpled, sweat-and-hot-sauce-stained napkins. "Oh my God, it hurts so good," I said. I tilted my water glass to get an ice cube to ease the heat.

"You weren't kidding about your love for that sauce," Rachel said.

"It's not a healthy relationship, but I can't seem to leave it."

Diane pushed herself away from the table, hand on her stomach. "So, what'd you want to talk to us about? Pete said it's some kind of writing thing, but he didn't really give us details."

I crunched through the ice cube, swirling the bits around my mouth to calm my tingling taste buds. It would have been wise to go easy on the sauce, maybe, but when I'm at Mamoun's wisdom is not my forte. I filled Rachel and Diane in on the magazine and what kind of stuff I liked to write, and then I told them my idea for the new series. I didn't want to bring up Cal and Iris or my breakup, but Pete, as usual, had zero tact.

"Lu here is heartbroken and looking for answers," he said, giving me a condescending arm tap.

"That's not why I'm doing this."

He rolled his eyes. "Sure, the parallels are totally unrelated."

I threw a napkin at him, which he calmly caught and placed back on the table. "Well, what do you wanna know from us?" Diane asked. "Shoot."

I took in a deep breath and opened up my notebook. "How long have you guys been dating?"

Our interview went on for about an hour. Pete ended up leaving us alone, and we felt bad hogging a table at Mamoun's so we just started walking and ended up at Washington Square Park.

Diane and Rachel were really cool and obviously in love. They'd struggled with what to do in the fall when they went to separate schools upstate, whether or not it was silly to believe they could stay together beyond high school. All the same things Leo and I had talked about. But after weeks of it, they decided there were many reasons to stay together.

They ticked off all the boxes that I would have needed for a column. Profiling them would have been exactly what I needed, an exploration of how love can overcome obstacles. They were in no way less than Cal and Iris. They were inherently interesting, so in love that it made me scroll through pictures of myself with Leo on social media later that night, torturing myself just for the slight pleasure that reliving the love could provide.

But there was something that just wasn't clicking for me. No matter how many details I wrote down, the little lines of dialogue that were better than eavesdropping because they weren't stolen away but given with full permission, nothing sparked. When I said goodbye to Diane and Rachel and went back home, I looked at my notebook and felt completely underwhelmed. I even tried to push through and force myself to write an article. Two sentences is what I managed to type out, and one of those was: I don't know what to write someone help me.

I spent the whole night in front of my computer, my notebook splayed open in front of me, begging the words to come, begging my heart to open itself up and transcribe itself, to capture life in the beautiful way only words can. Saturday turned to Sunday. Nothing came.

8

AS BASIC AS EATING

Pete and I were stationed at the box office the next day and I was trying to write in my notebook in between customers. "This is great. I work so much better under pressure."

"Totally," Pete said, tapping at the keyboard. "The Diane and Rachel column coming along?"

"No, couldn't get a single word out. But I have a backup plan!"

"Oh yeah? Who's that?"

"This supersweet couple from Montauk. Joel and Clementine. They tried to erase each other from their memories but their love is too strong and they've just found themselves back in each other's arms."

"That's the plot for *Eternal Sunshine of the Spotless Mind*."

"Are you saying that I'm not allowed to interview fictional characters?" I scoffed. "Don't be such a patriarchal tool, trying to control my behavior. I thought you were better than that."

Pete leaned back in his slightly comfortable office chair, brushing the hair away from his eyes. The afternoon sun shone in the ticket booth, reflecting off a handful of shiny surfaces.

We each had a large soda next to us, beads of condensation dripping down the sides. I don't actually like soda, but it was free at work and the act of sipping on something sweet made work at least momentarily easier. "I'm waiting on you to tell me about a backup plan."

"My neighbors, Elizabeth and Mr. Darcy."

"Pride and Prejudice."

"Okay, fine, real couple now. They had a really amazing time in Paris together, but violent circumstances led them to split up despite their very strong feelings for each other. Years later, they ran into each other at Rick's Café in Morocco and he helped save her from—"

Pete interrupted with a sigh, shifting in his chair so that it squeaked as he moved. "Are you done?"

I slammed my forehead down on my depressingly empty notebook. "Not even close."

Behind us, the door to the rest of the theater opened. I couldn't quite muster the energy to lift my head up, so I was hoping it wasn't our manager Brad. "Lu, you can sit up straight, or I can put you on cleanup crew. Which do you want?"

"I want a muse, Brad."

Brad looked over at Pete. "What's she talking about?"

"Probably not worth explaining," Pete said, then turned his attention to some customers.

"Have you ever been in love, Brad?" I said at the same time, turning to look at him. He was holding one of his beloved clipboards, wearing a short-sleeve mustard-yellow button-down with a brown tie. Brad looked like he'd be really at home working at an office in Kansas, but he was alright. He wasn't a dick, and only occasionally made dad jokes that made me want to quit my job in a rage.

"Um."

"What about in high school? Did you date anyone in high school? What happened when you graduated and you had to decide what to do? Did you ever step onto that particular romantic minefield, and if so, how did you survive it?"

Brad stared blankly at me for a moment and then sat down at the computer on my left. He started scribbling down something on his clipboard. Sure that he was going to ignore my tirade, I opened up my notebook, waited for my musings on love to come pouring out of me the way they had been for the last year at *Misnomer.* "I married my high school girlfriend," Brad said.

Now I sat up straight. "You did? What happened when you went to college? Did you guys have, like, a tumultuous on-again, off-again thing throughout the four years, your love for each other tenuously surviving distance and the changes of early adulthood? Would you wake up in the middle of the night terrified that your love would pull so taut that it would snap, sending you each hurtling in opposite directions?"

A silence took hold of the box office. I'm not quite sure why. The poignancy of my soliloquy, probably. Pete was looking over at me, biting his lip thoughtfully. Brad had stopped scribbling. There was even a customer at my window, frozen by how deep I'd delved into the fragile condition of teenage love.

"I didn't go to college," Brad said, shattering the silence. He calmly resumed his vaguely managerial duties. "My wife takes night classes, and sometimes we fight about money and how many kids we want to have, but other than that our love has not been 'pulled so taut it could snap.'" He used air quotes for the last part, then pointed at my window. "You have a customer."

As the day progressed, Pete and I tried to think of anyone we knew from our respective schools who I could write about,

with healthy interludes of Pete suggesting I write about myself, and then me trying my hardest to shoot knives at him
with my eyeballs. We scoured our phone contacts and social
media friends, asked all of our coworkers. We got a lot of
looks, but no stories. I found myself going back to Iris's Facebook, doing a wee bit of stalking, maybe even hoping that
she'd suddenly change her mind and message me. I thought
about it some more and would love the attention, as well
as the chance to be portrayed in your wonderful prose
and unique insight!

It was almost six o'clock and I still had nothing. Hafsah
would no doubt check her email first thing in the morning,
and if she didn't see anything from me I'm sure she'd be un-
apologetic and ruthless and fire my ass before I'd even woken
up.

It's hard to describe what having prolonged writer's block
feels like. Like missing a part of yourself, I guess. But not really. It's like you've suddenly forgotten how to do something
as basic as eating. Long after mom had said good-night and
my apartment had fallen quiet, long after even the city itself
seemed to have gone silent, I sat in the dark, sweating despite
the open window, bathed in the glow of my computer screen,
time ticking away. I had nothing.

I rested my fingers on the keys, as if I could fool myself into repeating the motions I'd successfully performed in
the past. Then I clicked back to Tumblr, scrolled through
my feed. Usually that helped stimulate my brain; reading
through other people's posts, the pictures they chose to share,
those little glimpses of personality visible online. It was almost like eavesdropping. Part of me thought that maybe I
could find someone posting about their relationship in a way
that would spark my creative juices. For a while I searched

through hashtags that I thought could lead me to pertinent posts: #relationshiptroubles, #precollegiatebreakups #inarelationshipwhichrecentlysurvivedorwasdestroyedbytheprospectofeachpersongoingtocollegeinadifferentplaceandwethoughtwecoulddoitbutturnsoutwearentevengonnatry.

But I was kidding myself. It was almost midnight, and even if I found someone interesting, the chances of them accepting an interview and responding to my questions in time were not great, and that wasn't even accounting for the time it would take me to write a full column. Then I stumbled onto Leo's blog. I still hadn't found the courage to unfollow him, and I got stuck scrolling through his stupid thoughts and selfies. Sweat made my tank top cling to my lower back, and that simultaneously gross and annoying sensation was exactly what it felt like to read Leo's blog.

He hadn't posted much recently, just a few vague entries that I'd already pored over dozens of times, trying to suss out just how hurt he was post-breakup. Which meant that almost immediately I was seeing pictures of us still together. My face buried in the crook of his perfect neck, his eyes looking straight at the camera, a smile to them, like he knew the hair falling across his face was absurdly sexy. The caption read: The cover to our future R & B album.

Just to further torture myself, I found the post from late September where he'd reblogged my *Misnomer* column and written: Me. She's writing about making out with me. I'm dating a talented beast of a writer.

For some reason, I thought of a moment that occurred a few months ago. It was after winter break, and my latest column had just gone up. We were sitting in homeroom, which was the place where Leo, with one seemingly innocuous shoulder-tap, had initially confessed to reading my column. Our friendship had blossomed because we talked about my column, talked about love all the time, the subject's intimacy naturally bringing us closer together. After we started dating, I asked Leo if I could keep writing about us, and his eyes had lit up. "Lu, that's all I've ever wanted."

But on that particular day, Leo had come into homeroom, sat down next to me, offering a school-chaste kiss on the cheek like he usually did, and never brought up my column. After months of it never slipping his mind, months of compliments and intimate, funny conversations—nothing. I'd felt bad that day, a queasy feeling in my stomach like something had changed between us without my knowing why. Then he'd been sweet to me in one way or another after school, and I hadn't brought it up ever, letting go of this lovely little thing we used to do without questioning why.

When I'd made myself feel sufficiently awful, I finally closed out of Tumblr.

I was screwed. I had nothing. My eyelids were starting to sag with sleep. I bit down on my forearm and yelled into my own skin, trying to unleash all my frustrations while not waking up my mom. Then, accepting my fate, I opened up an email to Hafsah. While I was trying to decide on a strategy (Confident yet humble request for more time? Or pity-inducing groveling to not get fired?), my phone buzzed on the nightstand. I stood from my desk to go check on it, figuring it was Pete asking how the writing was going. Getting up felt good, bringing fresh air to the sweaty creases of skin.

It wasn't Pete though. It was Iris. She'd messaged me on Facebook asking if I wanted to meet up some time that week and return her shirt. She'd also sent me a friend request. Which, what else, led me down a rabbit hole of trying to find out everything about her and Cal.

I still couldn't see Cal's profile, but I could now see every time he'd posted on her wall, I could see their shared pictures, all the times they'd been tagged at the same location. It seemed like Cal had a job at a coffee shop near Washington Square Park, which Iris went to visit all the time, sneaking pictures of Cal in his apron and posting the photos to Facebook. Her captions, which was where so many relationships become unbearable to the outside world, managed to avoid being of the suck-it-I'm-in-love variety, which only made me want to keep diving into their relationship. For example: Cal adorably mock-scowling behind the counter, his glasses slightly crooked. Look at this ugly hipster in his little apron.

Spare the judgments, but I went deep into their online lives that night. I just couldn't stop. It was like looking at the alternate-reality version of me and Leo. Iris had way better style than me, and both Leo and I were Pinoy and had darker skin, but other than that, we were like the same people. Oh, and the in-a-relationship bit too. Also, Cal wore glasses.

Before I knew it, it was 3:00 a.m. and I hadn't even emailed Hafsah yet. The time that I could have used to at least force a crappy article about myself and Leo had withered away. I threw my phone across the room onto my bed, chastising it for making me fall into the wormhole that was Cal and Iris's relationship.

I got up to get a glass of cold water and clear my mind for a bit, but Iris and Cal followed me to the kitchen, whispering sweet nothings to each other. I stood by the sad excuse for an air conditioner and put my forehead against the living room window, looking out at the quiet, tiny portion of the city visible from my apartment. I love New York at night, the thought of so many people simultaneously asleep. One of the greatest cities on earth so calm that you can walk in the middle of the street and nothing will hit you but the glow of a streetlight. I pictured Iris and Cal walking down my street hand in hand, laughing into each other's necks. A memory of me and Leo doing just that popped up too. How he would kiss my forehead as we walked, reach for my hand, hold me close.

Back at my desk, one leg curled beneath me, my eyes continuously flitted toward the corner of my computer screen, mockingly displaying the time. I clicked over to my disgracefully empty Word document and typed in a title. On (Not) Breaking Up the Summer before College.

"This is fine," I said to myself. "I'll just write a general intro to the topic and ask people to write in with their stories. A profile can wait until later. I'll just type something up and I'll send it to Hafsah." I cracked my fingers, set them back in the subtle, familiar grooves they'd formed in my keyboard after all my writing. Because I know how to write. I totally do it all the time. "Hafsah will be cool with it. She won't tell me that this isn't the article I pitched her, or that I'm being lazy, or that I will never write for *Misnomer* again."

My fingers wouldn't strike the keys at all. I found myself looking back over my shoulder to my bed, craving to have my phone back in my hands, wanting to delve even deeper into Iris's and Cal's lives. "No," I said again, this time actually out loud, forcing myself to focus. It didn't have to be good, just a first draft, something that I could present to Hafsah.

The seconds ticked by loudly, as if there was a grandfather clock nearby. Which made no sense because there wasn't any sort of clock in my room or my apartment or probably even in my building. I feel like I would have known earlier if there was a grandfather clock in my building.

"Ahhhh," I whisper-yelled, smacking my hands up and down on my laptop because they refused to produce words. Another over-the-shoulder glance at my bed, the comforter wrinkled from my few hours splayed on it, diving into an internet hole. My phone had landed right in the middle of the bed, faceup, the screen reflecting the glow from my computer in a way that made it look like I had a notification. Maybe another one from Iris? Maybe she'd gotten up in the middle of the night, awakened by a premonition that I was suffering. Maybe she'd been stirred by a cosmic sense that she could commit a good deed, with minimal effort.

I shut my computer and slid into bed, grabbing my phone as I slipped between the sheets. They were still warm from my wasted hours curled up in bed, so I kicked them away, muttering a complaint about the lingering heat. Sleep was so desperate to take hold of me, I could feel it coaxing my muscles into inactivity, begging my brain to let it take over. I unlocked my phone anyway, stepping sure-footed back into the wormhole.

9

SOAK UP EVERY OUNCE

I woke up to the sound of my mom knocking on my door. "Lucinda! I'm not letting you leave for work before you have breakfast. Wake up."

I moaned in response, because it was the only verbalization my brain could handle at the moment. My hand automatically felt around for my phone, which I found tucked under my pillow, battery nearly drained. "Lu! Wake up or I'll call your boss and tell him the reason you're late is that you still get treated like a petulant child who won't eat her breakfast. Wouldn't that be embarrassing?"

"I'm not hungry," I said, clearly not loudly enough because she kept banging on the door. I unlocked my phone and suddenly all of last night came rushing back to me, as if I'd been drunk or something. The failure to email Hafsah, the borderline obsessive perusal of Iris's Facebook. Then I saw that I'd responded to Iris's message. I sent it out at 3:05 a.m., which would either make Iris think I was way cooler than I really am, or give her the exact right idea of what I was like. At least the message itself wasn't too ridiculous. Sure thang! I get off work at five every day this week. Does tomorrow (er, today, I guess? Monday) work for you?

Iris had responded about an hour ago, blissfully ignoring my use of "thang." Sure! But can't come too far downtown. Columbus Circle at 6 okay with you?

My lips spread into a smile, right as my mom pushed the door open. She was wearing her hair in a ponytail, and she had a T-shirt on that looked suspiciously like mine. We're basically the exact same size, and even though I wouldn't advertise it too often, she has a pretty spot-on sense of style. Our clothes ended up in each other's closets all the time. She crossed her arms and raised her eyebrows at me.

"Mom, I'm not going to starve to death if I skip one meal."

"CPS disagrees." She stood in the doorway, one hand on her hip in that way that meant she wasn't going to cave. Although she never really caves, so the hand-on–the-hip thing wasn't necessary at all to drive home the point.

"Look at you, you're wide-awake. Might as well eat something. Come on, I made waffles."

"I'll be right out."

"I don't believe you."

"Go bug Jase for a while."

"Don't be rude, I'm your mother and I get to bug any one of my children that I want. Plus, I don't need to bug Jase, he eats all the food out of the fridge and then some." She gave me a wide-eyed look, as if she'd really proved some point. "Get up, or I'm grabbing my phone and putting pictures of you like this up on Facebook. I know how to do that now."

"Mom…"

"And, Lu, you're really sweaty. That picture would get so many yeses."

"They're called 'likes,'" I said, throwing my legs over the edge of the bed and sitting up. Waking up was best done in stages. Mom hung around until I stood up. I went to the bathroom we all share and stared in the mirror for a while, not looking at my own reflection or anything, just staring at a spot and waiting for my brain to wake up.

After a few minutes, I went to the living room and sat on the couch eating waffles with Jase, who was shoving them into his mouth two at a time, swallowing like an alligator does, just one or two seconds of chewing before he tilted his head back and let them slide down his throat.

I watched him play video games, trying and failing to follow the action on the screen. I expected to get bored with watching, like I usually do after about six seconds, but instead I noticed how other voices were coming through the TV, other kids talking into headsets in faraway places like Seoul and Long Island. They were all yelling at each other, trading insults, occasionally cracking those dumb thirteen-year-old-boy jokes that no one else in the world thinks are funny. But Jase did, and his laughter made it possible for me to avoid checking my email for a bit. I didn't want to see Hafsah's name in my inbox.

"Dad called," Jase said, after a while. "He's back from London, so he wants us to come over this weekend."

"'Kay. We'll go Friday when I get off work." God, Friday. By then I might be on my way to losing my scholarship. How the hell would I explain that to my parents?

Maybe I could cash in on divorce fallout? I'd never really lashed out, since my parents splitting up had not been traumatic. Or maybe it had. I wasn't a psychiatrist, who was I to exculpate my broken home as a reason for my struggles with love, and therefore my writer's block, and ultimately my loss of scholarship. None of this was my fault.

"Mom," I said, looking back over the couch at her sitting at the kitchen table, reading a newspaper. "Not bringing this up for any reason in particular, but is there a statute of limitations on how long I can use a traumatic childhood event as an excuse for doing something...um...you wouldn't approve of?"

"Lu, what did you do?" she asked, not looking up from the newspaper.

"Nice try, but I'm not going to incriminate myself. I just want to establish a standard, in case in some hypothetical future I need to use it in my defense."

"Then the statute of limitations is thirty-six seconds." She flipped the page and eyed me for a moment. "What traumatic childhood event are you talking about?"

Now's your chance, I thought to myself. Claim the divorce was the root cause of everything. The fact that my parents had never established a familial culture of speaking about the hardships of love, and had not provided an example of love upon which I could model my relationships, leading to my loss of scholarship and collegiate career.

"Lu, that look you're getting is no good. It means you're scheming."

"I'm not scheming. I'm rationalizing future scheming."

Mom turned the page again with dramatic flair. "Eat your waffles, Lulu Bear."

I looked at the time, wondering if maybe I could still send Hafsah an article by the end of the day. But the hours ticked away without inspiration striking.

Twenty minutes before I clocked out, Pete asked me if I wanted to go watch a movie, since we hadn't taken advantage of our employee benefits in a while.

"Um," I said, because admitting that I had done exactly as he'd predicted and become obsessed with Iris and Cal was hard. "I actually have plans."

"Your body language tells me I'm not going to like it if you elaborate."

"I'm meeting up with Iris."

Pete tightened his lips and nodded slowly. Then he reached over and grabbed the closest thing to him, which was a stack of napkins someone had left at the counter by my register. He picked them up, examined them, looked around the empty lobby, then tossed them at my chest. "Why?"

"Dude, what the hell?" I leaned down to pick up the scattered napkins.

"You know why I did that."

"Your ability to pick up on social cues is really diminishing. Does 'what the hell' not enter into your lexicon?" He put his hands on the glass and lowered his head, shaking it from side to side. "Get your greasy fingers off the counter," I added. "I just cleaned that. You know how Brad gets about smudges."

Pete pinched the bridge of his nose, which is totally not a thing a normal teenager does, further proving my whole notion that Pete is some wise, old uncle type. Sans facial hair. "Look. I get what's going on. But I'm worried you don't."

"What is the big deal?" I slammed the napkins I'd picked up down in front of him. "I'm giving her back a shirt she lent me. And sure, I'm still hanging on to the hope that I can write about her and Bench Boy. I don't see what's wrong with that. My deadline was today and I couldn't write anything about Diane and Rachel. If Iris changes her mind, I might be able to ask Hafsah for an extension."

"You don't understand how your fixation on this couple is a misguided hope that your relationship with Leo can be salvaged. You don't get that you're just avoiding writing or even thinking about your own broken heart. Glad to be proven right." He stood up straight as Brad walked by, and pretended to wipe the counter he'd dirtied. Brad eyed us like he suspected we weren't fully doing our jobs, then continued to go check on... I don't actually know all of Brad's duties, to be honest. Pete smiled, which is his secret weapon. It's totally disarming. My mom once offered him food and he said no with a smile and she was totally cool with it. It was bizarre.

"I'm gonna go clock out," I said to Pete. "I'll see you tomorrow."

"I wish you a very fulfilling T-shirt returning interview," Pete said.

Since I had an hour to kill, I walked uptown to Columbus Circle. I texted Jase to make sure he was still alive in the nonvirtual world, then texted my mom that I'd be home late, which turned into a whole thing about how I had to learn to be more appreciative of my family and start making an effort to love her and never grow up, or something along those lines.

When I got to Columbus Circle, I looked around for a while, somewhat tired from the walk, but excited about the meeting. I was even hoping I was early so I could get some eavesdropping in before Iris showed up. It wasn't a part of the city I went to very often, but the crowd was pretty great. Tourists heading to Central Park, the upper edges of the Midtown office crowd, a group of dudes practicing their juggling routines right by a group of protesters and then the people protesting the protesters. It was prime eavesdropping territory.

But Iris was already there, sitting at the steps of the fountain. She was wearing another sundress, that same bright red pinup-girl lipstick she had on the first time I saw her at The Strand. I walked over to her, ready to cheerfully greet her when I realized she was crying. Bawling, almost. To the point where several people were doing double takes as they walked by. A black woman in a pantsuit stopped for a moment, maybe considering saying something.

It was really tempting to just turn around and escape the whole scene. I could remember the looks people gave me the night Leo dumped me, when I was sitting on the curb in front of that Vietnamese restaurant. The pity and confusion, the occasional smirk and amusement. Yes, sometimes people mired in sorrow and misery want to receive compassion and care. But sometimes public sorrow is still sorrow you don't want anyone intruding in on.

I thought about just going to the park for a while, people watching, finding shade beneath a tree and reading. I could text Pete to come join me. He was leaving for school in Rhode Island soon, and it'd be nice to squeeze as much enjoyment out of our remaining time together before that happened. Then I shifted and felt the crumple of napkins in my pocket. I'd meant to throw them out at work. The black woman in the pantsuit saw me pull the napkins out of my pocket and she gave me a little head nod, like she was telling me to do the right thing. The universe and its damn signals.

"Hey, you okay?" I asked, approaching with the napkins out. "Sorry, that was a stupid question."

Iris looked up at me, squinting in the sun, or maybe at my stupidity. Smeared mascara streaked down her cheeks. It seemed to take her a moment to place me. Then she cracked a smile through her tears and grabbed the napkins. "Sorry I'm..." She gestured at her face.

"Oh no, totally okay. Fine. People cry. I cry all the time." I sat next to her, wondering whether she wanted a hand on her shoulder or me to go away or, like, a cup of tea or something. We sat quietly for a while, Iris dabbing at her cheeks with my wadded-up movie napkins while I fiddled with her T-shirt in my bag.

"I'm sorry in advance if I talk about the weather," I said.

Iris chuckled. "What?"

"It's just that I'm one of those people that starts making comments about the weather when they feel a little awkward. Which I do right now. Not because of you crying, necessarily.

It's not you at all. It's more my inability to handle social situations far outside my normal comfort level. Which this kind of is. So if I start talking about how it's as sweaty as a lower back after walking around with a backpack on all day, that's why." I snapped my fingers a couple of times and bit my lip. "Damn it, I did it. I warned you."

Iris laughed. "Thanks."

"Thanks? For the rant?"

"For trying to make me feel better. I've been doing such a good job holding it in all day. Then I sat here and saw some stupid guy wearing a T-shirt with the California flag on it and I just…" She crumpled a tear-soaked napkin in her fist and scrunched her mouth to the side. "Lost it."

I looked across the street toward the park. Guys in pedicabs were offering rides to the severely disinterested sunset picnic crowd. A group of middle-schoolers stood in a circle, kicking a soccer ball back and forth at each other. On the other side of the circle, people streamed in and out of the office buildings, a whole swarm of them entering the Whole Foods. "Do you want to talk about it?" I fiddled with my bag's cloth strap, running my fingernail across the little bumps. "Off the record?"

Iris seemed to consider it for a while. The tears had stopped flowing, and she'd rubbed away all the makeup streaks. Fully composed, she scooted back so she could lean against the step behind us. "I'm okay. It's just that… Well, Cal and I are…" She took a deep breath. "We're gonna split up."

I put on what I believed was an appropriately sympathetic face, angling my eyebrows just right. The sun was reflecting off the Columbus Circle shopping mall, making us both squint. "Wait. Did you just say 'gonna'? As in, future tense?"

Iris sighed, and then she ran her hand through her hair and fluffed it out, flipping her curls over to her other shoulder. "It's weird and complicated. But yeah, future tense."

"I know I'm the one being the supportive listener here, and I'm totally open to letting you decide whatever you want to talk about and nothing more than that, but I'm gonna really need you to elaborate on that."

Cal had texted Iris the day after their breakup, saying he wanted to meet up and talk. Unlike some people, Iris had agreed *and* shown up, willing to hear out the person she still loved.

"Then he asked me what day it was, and what day I was planning on leaving for California. Both of which he knew the answer to, which tipped me off that he was thinking something weird. He gets these out-there ideas and you can just tell by looking at him that his mind is whirring."

"I love it and hate it when they do that. The whole world is a possibility when they get that look, the most romantic sentiment you can imagine is on the tip of their tongues, but also your worst nightmare."

"Exactly!" Iris said. She laughed and wiped at the corner of her eye. "I thought he was just going to rehash the argument we'd had during our breakup about long distance not being all that bad."

I nodded, and was about to say how I knew all about that argument, but managed to shut my idiot mouth up. "So, what did he say?"

"He said that we had eight weeks before I left, and why the hell would we waste those being heartbroken?" Iris crumpled the napkin I'd given her, then tossed it in her lap, shaking her head. "Then he went on this superlong speech about how I was right, how there was a point in time when we thought we were in the greatest romance of our lives, but we were teenagers fooling ourselves. That love is more complicated than how it feels at first." Iris stopped as some taxis got into a honking match with each other. Someone on the street yelled at them to shut up and drive. "Then that smart-ass shrugged his shoulders and said our love always had an expiration date, whether it was the end of high school, our death, or something in between. But he believed the time hadn't arrived yet."

Iris grabbed a new napkin from the stack in my hand, twisting it into a rope. That little piece of paper was so tightly wound I'm sure it could have supported something of real heft. Like two people drifting apart from each other. "So much for me not feeling comfortable opening up, right?"

I laughed. "So, did he have, like, a pitch, or what?"

"He said we should wait. That we could still break up, but on August 4 when I go to California. He said we should do exactly what every song and book and movie relentlessly tells us to—soak up every ounce of love that we still have between us. He said we shouldn't take what we have for granted, at least while we can."

"Damn. So you said yes." Iris was teasing me with this stuff. A column could have written itself in the time it took for her to tell me this story. Writing about love wasn't the only way my words come pouring out of me. But there are certain topics that I don't *choose* whether I'm going to write about them or not. This was one of them, and not writing about Iris and Cal was starting to hurt me, at least spiritually.

"Of course I said yes." Iris sighed. "I hadn't been happy about breaking up, it was just a mature move I was trying to make. My love for Cal hadn't gone anywhere, it was still sitting right there alongside the heartache." Another burst of car honks, which I guess were there with us the whole time and I just noticed them occasionally. The air had cooled ever so slightly, so that sitting outside with Iris felt surprisingly comfortable. "I hadn't even had time to really process the heartache, you know. And here he was spouting poetry at me and the promise that I could have more joy, which is what I really wanted. The worst part is that now I can really feel it coming. Now I know it's there waiting for me."

She looked at me briefly, as if I was the embodiment of that future heartache.

"Yeah," I said. "It does that."

10
BACK TO COLUMBUS CIRCLE

It was not yet twilight, but that Manhattan-specific presunset brought on by the shadows of buildings, that canopy of steel and glass. Iris adjusted herself, crossing her legs in front of her. I mimicked her position, my heart quietly pounding with excitement. Glancing inside my bag, I noticed my notebook resting on top of Iris's shirt. God, I wanted to pull it out and write down all that she was telling me. My thoughts were swirling with questions and ruminations, *words*, those magnificent bastards. They were on the verge of returning, I could feel it.

"Sorry about talking for so long," Iris said. "You didn't sign up to be my therapist. I shouldn't have unloaded on you like that."

"It's okay, I love hearing about other people's lives. Remember?"

Iris gave me a tight-lipped smile, then looked away.

Subtle, Lu.

We both looked around us at the New Yorkers continuing on with their lives. Suits, briefcases, retail polo shirts, bike messengers with their tattoo-and-gauged-earring uniforms, the worn clothes of homeless people, the glamour of the rich, the more appealing glamour of those who fashioned stylish outfits from less, women in hijabs, tourists in socks and sandals. People watching in New York always leads to clichéd reflections about the lives of strangers, and surprise, surprise, at this point I had a particularly hackneyed thought about their love lives, a superficial curiosity to know the state of their romantic relationships, a fleeting desire to know more about them.

I glanced at Iris, wondering what I would have said if Leo had come up with a proposal like Cal's. "I should probably give you your shirt back." I reached in and pulled it out, smoothing out the wrinkles.

"Thanks." She set it on her lap.

"You okay?"

"Yeah, thanks. Just imagining how many people's social media accounts I ended up on."

"Oh, you're definitely on mine."

Iris laughed. "Great, good to know. You probably don't have a lot of followers though, right?"

"Nah, just a couple hundred thousand. Most of them people you admire."

"Cool, cool." She chuckled. "So, this is a totally normal way to hang out with someone for the first time."

"Technically it's our second hangout, which I think is a perfectly acceptable time to break down in tears. Life is short, right? Kiss on the first date, weep on the second. That's a saying."

"Absolutely." Iris smiled at me, looked across the street at the park. "So, your turn to cry, then?"

"Sure, just show me a viral video of a human being decent to another human and I'll instantly turn into a slobbering mess of tears and feelings."

A few quiet moments passed, and I started to wonder if I could try for an interview again, though I didn't want to press it so soon. "So, Lu. Tell me about yourself. You return wallets. You write things. You cry at people being nice to each other online. What else?"

"I think that's the whole list. Oh, I also won a spelling bee in fifth grade, but didn't accept the prize for political reasons."

"Wow. What were those?"

"It was a Halloween-themed spelling bee and the prize was a bunch of peanut-butter cups."

"So?"

"So, screw peanut butter."

Iris did the thing that everyone does when I say something to the effect of "peanut butter is a scourge upon this earth." She dropped her jaw and widened her eyes as if I'd just attempted to kill her mother. I nodded confidently to show I wasn't going to retract my statement.

After a few moments Iris ruffled her hair. "I guess it's good that you revealed yourself to be a sociopath now instead of later." She chuckled. "What about that writing gig you have? How long have you been doing it?"

I told her that it'd been about a year, then explained that I hadn't really set out to write about relationships until Hafsah pointed out that her favorite part of my writing was my musings on teenage love.

My phone buzzed in my pocket, probably my mom wondering when I was coming home. Just for the comfort of it, I grabbed my notebook from out of my bag. I opened it up and flipped through the few pages I'd filled out since my breakup. Eavesdropped snippets of dialogue, an ill-fated attempt at a poem about heartbreak and Leo's eyes, some crappy doodles. "So, have you thought about me maybe interviewing you? With this new info I'm even more interested in writing about you."

Iris took a deep breath. "No, not really. I've been bummed out all day so hadn't thought about it much, sorry."

"No worries."

I thought about what I could say to convince her, but the only thing going through my mind was just a video loop of me reaching my hand out hungrily and saying, "Give it to me!" That probably wouldn't sway her. I stretched my legs out, my eyes following a gorgeous Latino man walking his dog and grooving out to some music on his headphones.

"I guess I don't really know why you're interested in us," Iris said. "I'm sure there's plenty of other people in our position. Couldn't you just write about yourself?"

I watched as a group of tourists scampered across the road, trying to avoid getting hit by angry cabbies yelling out their windows. She'd shifted positions again, now sitting at the edge of the step, her arms down at her sides, elbows locked.

"The thing is, I haven't really been able to write since my breakup. Nothing comes out. But..." I paused so I wouldn't accidentally mention my initial eavesdropping. "Since we met the other night, I've had the specific urge to write about you. I don't understand why or how, but I don't really understand much about inspiration anyway. I'm sorry if that sounds creepy."

"No, it's not creepy. It's just I don't think we're that interesting."

She bit her bottom lip, avoiding eye contact with me. In her body language, I could see my article fading away before my eyes. I could picture too all of the repercussions unfurling like flowers shedding themselves of their petals. The emails that would flow in, one after the other. Hafsah terminating my contract, the foundation informing me that I no longer qualified for my scholarship, NYU asking for the first payment of the semester.

"'We are brought up in ethic to believe that others, any others, all others are by definition more interesting than ourselves,'" I said, quoting Joan Didion. "I think that's how it goes anyway. Maybe you're underestimating yourself."

Iris flicked away something that had landed on her dress, then kept brushing the same spot over and over again. "I mean, that's a nice sentiment, but whether or not we're interesting isn't really my main objection."

"What is?"

"I just don't want to dwell. You saw me a second ago, weeping in public."

"Yeah, the video's getting a ton of views already," I said, trying to win her over with some levity.

"I've got the summer left with Cal, after which I'll be consumed by heartbreak for a bit. I don't want to sully these next few weeks by overthinking our relationship, our decision to break up." Her voice nearly broke on the last sentence, and I wondered if I was being a bit of an asshole. I could have told her about the scholarship at that point, tried to convince her a little longer. But then I saw the sadness threatening to break through again and I just couldn't do it.

I could see her wanting to flee from the conversation the same way I want to flee…well…most conversations. Maybe changing the topic was a selfless thing to do then, or maybe just the obvious right thing to do. "Alright," I said. "You guys definitely are interesting enough to write about. Especially now that you have this new arrangement. But I did once write a whole column about the love lives of potatoes, so maybe I'm not the best judge of what's interesting."

Iris visibly relaxed, a throaty laugh emanating from deep within her lungs. Relief. "Really? And they ran it?"

"Hell no. I compared those little bumpy wart things they have to STDs. My editor thought it was a joke."

A breeze blew past, the first satisfying one of the day. "God, that felt good," Iris said, just as I was thinking it. She closed her eyes to the cool air, and for a moment I could see what a great match she and Cal made. The way he acted with me on the bench, of course he'd end up with a girl that closed her eyes to the breeze. It was either obvious hipster inclinations, or me reading a bit too much into two people I didn't know at all. "You wanna take a walk somewhere?" Iris asked.

Out of habit, I reached into my pocket to check my phone. As I'd suspected, my mom had texted. But I could read the tone of her message, which was still merely inquisitive, and not yet laced with passive-aggressiveness, and she was still a few texts away from full-on aggression. There was also a message from Pete, telling me that he was going to be at the Barnes and Noble at Union Square if I wanted to hang out.

"Sure," I said, putting my phone away. "I've got some time before my mom freaks out about my absence." I stood up, brushing my butt off.

We headed into the park, where the early evening athletes were out in hordes. Joggers stretched against light posts, and cyclists weaved around pedestrians, calling out "on your left" as they passed by. One of those peanut carts was parked at the entrance, the honey-roasted smell wafting over to us. All around the park, people were having the kind of day that made me realize I didn't come to Central Park often enough. Picnics and Frisbees and canoodling on blankets, sneaking sips from wineglasses.

"This is nice," I said, because neither one of us had said anything in a while.

"Yeah. I'm gonna miss this place when I'm gone."

"What made you pick California for college?"

"Mostly the school. I'm going to Pepperdine, and just seeing the pictures of the campus I knew I had to go. It's right on the water, which just fills me with this overwhelming sense of inner peace. They also have a decent international business program, which is what I told my parents the choice was about. But it's been my dream for a couple of years. I can't believe I get to finally go soon."

"Do you not like living in New York?"

We turned off West Drive down one of the smaller jogging paths. Iris crossed her arms in front of her chest as she walked. "It's not that. I love the city. But I don't want to spend my whole life here. I want to try a change of pace for a while. Something calmer. I don't want to just live in one place and not know what other cities have to offer."

"I have no idea what people want with calm lives," I said, stepping out of the way of a couple jogging in matching spandex. "I love chilling every now and then, yeah. But a calm life freaks me out. Too much time alone with my thoughts is literally the most terrifying thing I can imagine. Like, if you were a filmmaker, and wanted to scare the hell out of me, make a ninety-minute movie where it's nothing but a blank screen."

"Really? I love sitting with just my thoughts for a while." We turned within view of The Pond, which was glinting in the sun. I reached into my bag and grabbed my scratched-up pair of five-dollar sunglasses. "It's a bit of a trip, sure," Iris went on, "but in kind of an incredible way. I can time travel into memories or fantasies, I can picture a million different parallel universes, keep myself entertained for hours with nothing but a bunch of tiny bursts of electricity happening in my brain."

"God, that sounds like the worst."

Iris laughed, a full throaty sound, immensely pleasing because it wasn't one of those polite chuckles which is the usual response people give to my jokes. "I mean, aside from the abject horror of consciousness, it's pretty amazing."

We wandered through the park as the sun slowly set, as if it had a choice on when to give way to night. Iris talked a little more about California, and how she was legitimately excited about studying international business and trying to learn Mandarin. I was curious about how Cal felt when she talked like this around him, since I remembered what it felt like when Leo got psyched about going upstate for school, even when we were still planning on staying together. But I was having fun just shooting the shit with her and so I tried to forget about anything that had to do with her relationship.

We exited the park at Sixtieth Street, walking past that monument of a dude on a horse. "What'd be your ideal job, then?" I asked Iris. "International business sounds worldly and stuff, but I don't actually know how the real world works and what kind of job you'd end up in."

"To be honest, I don't really know either. I'm kind of picturing a job that pays me to travel the world. I know it would be a lot more corporate than that, but I'll let future Iris worry about that part. For now I think I'm allowed to dream of a more idealized version of the job market."

"Dude, I'm pretty sure you're not allowed to say 'job market' until you're twenty-five."

Another throaty laugh from her. "Don't *you* have a job?"

"Two, technically. But that's totally different than *discussing* the job market. Hang on to your youthful innocence, new friend. The world will rip it away soon enough."

"You're a bit of a cynic, aren't you?"

"Depends on the subject. I totally believe in aliens, ghosts, and that the world is slightly more good than bad. But I've got serious side-eye toward the Illuminati, karma, and anyone who's not a fan of cilantro."

"You talked shit about being alone with your thoughts, but you've clearly spent some time mulling this over."

"Exactly! And look at the disastrous nonsense that comes from it."

She reached over and gave me a light smack on the arm. We went on like that for about an hour, making our way vaguely downtown. We snaked our way around Times Square, because no matter how much love one had for New York, it never quite extended to those few hellish blocks.

My mom did call about half a dozen times, but I managed to get permission to call this a free night out on the town. They happen rarely with Mom, who still has memories of New York in the crime-ridden eighties when she moved here. But I'd been feeding her a steady stream of statistics and some guilt-tripping tirades about how if she doesn't let me have some freedom I'll overcompensate as soon as I move out and she'll only ever see me during major holidays or familial crises.

When we hit Union Square I realized I'd forgotten to text Pete back, so I sent him a quick, apologetic message then put my phone away, leading Iris quickly past the Barnes and Noble. It was dark by then, and in the distance we could hear thunder rolling in, the occasional flash of lightning visible between buildings.

Iris didn't seem too worried about oncoming rain, and that kind of confidence about your possessions' impermeability is really contagious. There's a certain momentum to walking through Manhattan with someone.

"I'm hungry," Iris said, when we were deep into NYU territory. "You know anything good around here that's not insanely expensive?"

"Oh sure. Are you a souvlaki girl like myself, or are you more into hot dogs?"

"Definitely souvlaki, but I'm feeling something a little more special today." She stopped walking when we were in front of the Comedy Cellar, nearly colliding with a group of college-looking bros on their way to a nearby bar. I cringed, waiting for them to turn around and say something gross. Thankfully, they spared us. "What about this place?"

Coincidentally, she was pointing at Mamoun's. "Ah, it's fantastic. But I just ate there the other night."

"Don't like repeats?"

"I would eat at Mamoun's every day of my life. But I went half-insane on the hot sauce and I think my digestive system probably needs a break."

"Respect," Iris said. She looked around a little longer, then pulled out her phone. I would have done the same thing but I was relishing the fact that my mom hadn't texted or called in an hour and I decided to let Iris do the Googling.

"Comedy show, ladies!"

I looked behind us. The door guy at the Comedy Cellar was sitting on a bar stool, looking bored. He had his hands on his knees, a tight V-neck showing off his biceps, a diamond stud in his nostril. "Ten bucks, two hours of comedy," he said, already looking away from us, directing the pitch at anyone who happened to be nearby. Probably wasn't working off commission.

Iris looked at me and raised an eyebrow. "The internet says the food here is surprisingly good. Could be fun to have a comedy show with dinner."

"Oh sure, laughter is a fun thing. Easily top five on my all-time hobbies list. If I could laugh every day I would."

"You're such a weirdo."

"I just love to laugh, Iris, what can I say," I deadpanned.

We approached the doorman, who very quickly requested our IDs, since apparently you have to be over twenty-one to laugh when you're in the proximity of alcohol. I was about to turn away, thinking maybe Mamoun's again wouldn't be too bad. Then Iris touched my forearm and gave me a look, mouthing a few words that I didn't understand. She pulled out an ID and confidently handed it over to the buff doorman. I tried to act chill about this so as to not ruin our chances, though I had no idea how I was about to get in. Maybe Iris was so cool she didn't have just one fake ID, but a whole slew of them, for everyone she'd ever met.

That's an extraordinarily stupid idea, which proves that I was right to shut up. Iris managed to convince the door-man that I was visiting from out of the country and had not thought to bring my passport along for dinner. He eyed us suspiciously, but halfheartedly, as if he was only doing it in case someone else was watching. Then he said, "Ten bucks," again and waved us through after we handed him the money.

Between the cover charge and the food, I ended up spend-ing way more than I ever should have on dinner. But I real-ized during a bathroom break why I was so happy to keep the night going, why I could shrug off the financial irrespon-sibility: I hadn't thought about Leo in hours. You can't put a price on that kind of inner peace (and if you could, forty bucks seemed like an okay deal).

We watched a pretty great lineup of comedians, a couple of which were marginally famous, and one of them a little more famous than that. We got a few weird looks from the other customers and our server kept eyeing us as if we were plan-ning to run out on the bill, but the food was, as the internet had predicted, surprisingly good for a comedy club. When we left, I was a little sad that the night would be over, but thank-ful that I'd met up with Iris, and that I'd decided not to push the subject of her and Cal so I could have this night. A wave of panic started to build over the fact that I hadn't. Back on

MacDougal Street, we could hear a rowdy crowd at Mamoun's, one girl's voice carrying over the street noise.

"This was fun," I said. "I'm glad we met up."

Iris smiled, but then furrowed her brow. "I'm not ready to go home. Stay out with me."

I looked at my phone to check the time. I still had a couple hours until my curfew, and going back home might mean having to face thoughts of Leo and my still-unwritten article. "You make a very compelling argument. Where to next?"

11

SPEAK EASY

Iris and I were crammed into a phone booth at a gourmet hot dog restaurant.

"We might get lucky, since it's a weeknight," I said. I'd read about this spot on *Misnomer*'s nightlife section. At the time, I'd felt it was the most asinine idea for a speakeasy that I could think of, but now that I was standing in the phone booth waiting for some unseen voice to grant me permission inside, I couldn't help but feel like the gimmick was working on me.

The phone rang on my end a few times. Iris was so close to me I could smell her, something fruity and almost musky, covered up by a sheen of cigarette smoke from the comedy club. A hostess picked up the line from somewhere unseen.

We were told in a very snooty voice that it'd be a twenty-five minute wait at least, so we went out to the street and talked about some TV shows we'd binge-watched lately. Three minutes later a text message told us to go back to the phone booth and dial 1, after which the wall gave way to reveal an astoundingly attractive Asian girl in a high ponytail. She eyed us up and down, then grabbed two leather-bound menus and walked us over to the tiny bar. A food menu with secret hot dog options was hanging over the bottles of alcohol, the writing on which was hard to make out in the dark. A few candles in glasses flickered on the bar, casting a pale glow around the closet-sized room. Only a handful of other people were at the bar, their conversations carrying over the lounge techno music playing from the speakers.

"I'm confused as to why hip twentysomethings choose to hang out here," Iris said to me. The hostess looked at us over her shoulder. "Er, fellow twentysomethings," Iris added.

"It's all about wanting what you can't have. This place has room for about seven people, so they're always sold out and it's super hard to get in. Which makes everyone want to be here."

"That's so transparent though. How do people fall for it?"

"Dude, we're here. We fell for it."

"Well," Iris said, looking around. "I've never been to a speakeasy. I was picturing something a lot more…"

"Like a gangster from the '20s?"

"Exactly. I wanted to drink out of a bathtub."

Two napkins landed in front of us. "Lucky for you we serve our gin in tiny bathtubs." We looked up to see another astoundingly attractive employee, this one a Latino bartender. He looked like he was about to burst out singing a deeply romantic ballad and then star in a Mexican soap opera as a doctor with an evil twin and illegitimate quintuplets or something. "What'll you have, ladies?"

This was Daniel, who became the love of our lives. For the night anyway. Especially when he served us without asking for ID, then kept the drinks coming without ever letting his gorgeous smile falter.

"Seriously, how is he doing that? He's been smiling nonstop for an entire hour and it doesn't even look like he's faking it. He must have the strongest cheek muscles of all time."

"I think they just call them cheeks," Iris said, trying to get a hold of the curly straw in her tiki drink while not looking away from Daniel, so her tongue kept feeling around blindly for it. A couple times she went face-first into the glass.

"They can call them whatever they want, those bad boys are muscles." I looked into the bottom of my glass, scooping out a piece of fruit with my straw. "Leo has great cheeks," I mumbled. "I liked rubbing my face on them."

"Who's Leo?"

"Oh, right, you don't know him." I sucked down the last few drops from the bottom of my glass, feeling light-headed when I tilted my head back. "It's a pretty astonishing feat that I haven't brought him up until now. Pete would be proud."

"Girl, who is Pete?" Iris giggled, then motioned for two more drinks.

"I don't know if I should have more. It's late and I have to work like two and a half hours to pay for each of these."

"It's on me," she said. "Anyway, I'm not ready to leave Daniel yet. Now tell me about these boys." When Daniel had acknowledged her and started working on our drinks, she leaned her elbow onto the bar, turning her body so she could face me. The place had filled up as the night went on, every seat taken by überhip people in unseasonable leather jackets and plaid shirts.

I told her about Pete first, thinking I'd avoid mentioning the fact that I think of him as a wise, old uncle, but almost immediately saying that. "I don't even know how his advice is always on point, because the dude is technically younger than me and doesn't even seem to have a life outside of me and books. Which should make him smart, sure, but just book smart, right? You can't learn everything from those wonderful papery bastards." I took a breath to accept another drink, thinking it was a really bad idea but also kinda hoping my fingers would brush Daniel's. "There's just no one I feel more like myself around than Pete," I went on. "I'm funnier around him, completely unembarrassed."

"Are you into him?"

"You shut your goddamn mouth," I said. "No. Didn't you hear me say the word *uncle* to describe him a second ago, you freak? Plus, I don't think Pete is really attracted to anyone. We have this game we play at the theater called I Would Bone That Person, and… Well, the details don't really matter. No, Pete's a friend, and he's been my moral compass in this whole Leo thing."

"Still don't know who Leo is," Iris said. The woman sitting next to me shifted in her seat, accidentally bumping me with her elbow and making me take heed of the moment. A subdued pop song played on the speakers, competing with the din of conversation at the bar. At a glance, I could see how Iris and I could fit seamlessly into this crowd. Iris was stylish enough anyway. She was smiley, her eyes glazed over with booze and newfound friendship. For the first time since my breakup, I felt the possibilities of being out and about with strangers, the strangeness of where your life could go, and how easily.

"Leo's my ex. The one who dumped me for the same reason you kind of broke up with Cal."

"Right! You'd mentioned him." Iris pushed herself away from the bar, straightening out and then stretching a little to get her back to crack. "Tell me about him."

I looked down at my drink, rolling little snowballs out of the napkin Daniel had set beneath the glass. "He's a prick and I love him."

"Great, now with a little more nuance."

I bit my lip and kept rolling snowballs. "He's not really a prick. But I do love him." Bits of conversation from the lady who'd bumped into me kept floating over my shoulder, and it took a lot of effort not to chase after them. She'd used certain words that usually promised a rich eavesdropping session, especially when used within the same paragraph: *cheated, shotgun,* and, most notably (though I have to admit that I hadn't ever heard this particular string of colorful words used together), *that stripper from Alabama.* I turned over my shoulder to get a glance at the woman and whomever she was with, but there was nothing particularly interesting about them, and their conversation got too quiet to overhear.

My pause was excessive, I knew, but I did mean to go on and be open with Iris. But then I took a long gulp from my drink, and then another, and before I knew it the moment had become this awkward avoidance of a topic I was more than happy to talk about. Just, not then. I wanted to enjoy the night.

Thankfully, Iris was better at being a human person, and instead of dwelling on it, she changed the topic, asking me if I'd heard what the people behind me had just said. We finished our drinks right as it was about to turn midnight, which meant I'd have to pay for a cab to get home, even though there was zero chance I was going to beat my curfew. Like clockwork, Mom called just as we left the bar. I didn't want to answer because I was afraid of the background noise and my voice slurring from Daniel's magical elixirs of booze and sexuality, so I let it ring, then texted back.

Lu
sorry! at the subway but train's running late. :/
don't be mad.

Mom
I'm mad. Ur grounded until yur 21. 23
if I have trouble waking up in the mornng.

Lu
Har har. You can go to bed now. I'll be home soon,
promise. I'm okay, with a friend.

Mom
Can't sleep. Wht if I Wake up and ur dead?

Lu
Mom.

Mom
Good night, Lucinda.

I sighed with a semblance of relief, hoping she really would go to bed so she wouldn't smell the booze on me when I got home. There were a few other notifications on my screen, but reading them made my eyes hate the world, and the fact that it contained things other than me and Iris and this lovely night, so I tucked my phone away.

"Was that a sigh of relief I just heard?" Iris did a little shimmy where she stood, raising her eyebrows up and down repeatedly as if she was saying something suggestive. "Which means your mom's probably not going to wait up for you, which means you're in the clear to hang out a little longer."

I groaned. "How are you that smart? Such powers of deduction. I'm gonna call you House."

"What? Is that a weight joke?"

"No, like the TV show about the doctor. You never watched that?" Iris shook her head and shrugged, pulling out her own phone and typing out a message. "I binged three seasons and then had a bunch of dreams that I had cancer."

"Sounds like a blast," Iris said, still looking down at her screen. Then her phone vibrated and a smile spread across her ruby-red lips. "C'mon, I've got a cool spot we can go to." She started walking away before I could protest. Although I guess that's not quite true. I could have protested at her retreating back, or maybe protested louder than my initial instinct would dictate. But anyway, I decided to hold my protest and just follow her because inertia or psychology or some other science told me it was easier to do so.

I rushed to catch up to her, noticing that she was smiling as she was walking. Her hands were in her dress's pockets, and she had this absolutely serene look on her face, like she was exactly where she needed to be in the world. I don't know if I've ever felt that in my life, much less the same day I was weeping about the heartbreak of a relationship I knew would be over in August.

The way Iris Castillo walked through New York City made me envious. I'm not sure exactly of what. Just *her*, I guess. Or maybe not envious. I was in awe. Which is why I followed her back up Broadway toward Madison Square Park, avoiding puddles from a rainstorm we'd apparently missed while at the speakeasy. It almost looked like we were heading *to* the park, which made me wonder if I should tell her about how I'd met Cal on that bench. Then she made a turn and started knocking on the front door of the Flatiron Building. I'd lived in New York City my whole life and had admired the hell out of this particular landmark's aesthetics, but I had absolutely zero knowledge about what went on within its diagonal walls. For all I knew it was a factory where they pounded iron into flat sheets or something. All I knew then was that it probably wasn't a place two buzzed eighteen-year-olds belonged after-hours.

There were a couple of guys seated at the security station, their faces illuminated by the glow of what were probably— if television had faithfully portrayed security stations even slightly—a dozen different monitors. Iris knocked again, and the Latino one glanced up. At first he scowled, and then he squinted and stood up, approaching the door to get a closer look. His hand went to his nightstick, which is right around the time when I felt like it would be a good idea to retreat.

Then his body relaxed, and he took his hand away from the nightstick and grabbed his keys.

He unlocked the door and pushed it open, standing in the doorway, his bulky frame blocking most of the entrance. "Hey, cuz. You here to get me in trouble?"

"Yup," Iris said, dragging out the vowel for a couple of seconds and smiling.

He laughed and shook his head, turning to look at me and then at her. "You guys drunk or something? You know your moms would kill me if I let you up there and you fall to your death."

"Oh come on. My mom's a sweetheart. She's not capable of murder."

"Not literally," the security guard, whose name tag read Hernando, said. "But she'd beat me down with guilt. My life would be over. I'd have to carry that weight around until my actual death."

"We're good, man. I swear we'll stay away from the ledge. Except for when we're throwing stuff."

"Right, the usual rules." He chuckled and shook his head again, then stepped back to let us through. The other security guard, an older black man, looked up from the monitors and started to stand up. Behind us, Hernando locked the door again. "Roy, this is my little cousin, Iris. Gonna let them up to the roof for a bit. If anything happens I'll say I snuck them past while you were taking a leak."

"Fair enough," Roy said, offering a head nod.

We thanked them, then headed up the elevator to the highest floor, taking the stairs the rest of the way, probably too excitedly because when we pushed the door open we were both out of breath. Iris put her hands up behind her head, taking big heaving breaths. "Totally should not have run."

I was taking the hands-on-the-knees approach, trying to

appreciate the view while wheezing. "Yeah, that was stupid. Remind me not to ever do that again." When my head and insides begrudgingly returned to normal, Iris and I walked forward to the front of the building, where the diagonal walls converge and look out at Madison Square Park. "Damn."

"Yeah, right?"

Manhattan twinkled all around me. We took a lap around the roof. I looked around for The Strand and my movie theater, the bench where I was supposed to talk to Leo but ended up sitting next to Cal instead. The noise up there wasn't the usual cacophonous orchestra of competing sounds. All the sounds of the city had time to merge together into something more complete, and quieter. (Duh, Lu, it was past midnight.)

"Of course you'd have access to the freaking Flatiron's rooftop."

Iris laughed, leaning her elbows forward on the waist-high ledge. Her dark curls hung over her shoulder, nearly brushing the stones. "What do you mean?"

Below us, I could see some cops in the park, talking to a homeless guy sitting on the curb. An Indian man scrubbed his hot dog cart clean, headphones in his ears. There was that lovely post-rain smell in the air, instead of the usual smell of hot garbage. "You just have that kind of life, don't you? Charmed more than the average." Iris frowned, and I rushed to elaborate in a way that didn't make it sound like I was accusing her of something. "That didn't come out right. It's just...you're so cool. You're going to California because the ocean fills you with calm, you've got a fake ID and flawless style and seem so comfortable with yourself. You're my age and you have the maturity to not delude yourself into thinking long distance will work with your high school boyfriend, and then the absurd level of maturity to stay with him with a predetermined breakup date." The expression on her face was definitely not the reaction I was going for, like I was still complaining about her instead of the opposite. "I'm not saying all of this to bitch. I'm just saying...it feels like you deserve this kind of life. Like you're one of those people that has it a little more figured out than the rest of us."

A quiet moment followed, which made it feel like I'd messed up this awesome night and probably the rest of my friendship with Iris by being overly earnest. That thought almost made me want to cry, so I turned my head up to combat the threat of tears by having them fight against gravity. I was shocked to see a few stars visible overhead. There's such little sky visible in the city, it almost feels like a waste to look up in search of stars. There's a lot more interesting stuff going on down here.

"Well, I'm glad you think I'm this beacon of awesomeness," Iris finally said, breaking the silence. "It's not quite true, but it's nice to be seen that way, I guess."

I found myself mimicking her lean on the ledge, even though I felt like I hadn't looked away from the view in front at all. It was hard to pinpoint what made the sight so beautiful. It was just a different angle of the same buildings and lights I was well versed in. "Which part did I get wrong?"

A breeze blew and Iris tossed her hair over to her other shoulder so it wouldn't hit her in the face. "It's like you're seeing the duck above the surface, but not the feet paddling beneath. Things may look smooth, but there's more to it than that, you know. I'm not saying I have this crazy difficult life. But I'm definitely more than what you've picked up from our two times seeing each other in person."

An urge rose up within me, and I decided I'd try one more time. "So, let me see it. Let me see more of you and Cal, instead of this glossy, romanticized version that's formed in my head."

I thought maybe she'd just walk away, tired of my shit. Or that she'd groan and make a joke about how I didn't quit. Instead she just stood there, looking out at the city, not quite swaying from the booze but not motionless either. "Why do you like writing about love?"

"I just like exploring the topic," I said. No one had really asked me why I write about this stuff before. Maybe they just assumed because I'm a teenage girl that it makes sense, but I never felt like someone who obsessed over love. "This is when a lot of us experience love for the first time, and all we really know about it comes from books and movies and songs, which sometimes offer good advice, or a glimpse of what the experience is like, but it's not the same thing as really experiencing love. We're unprepared, all of us. We see a filtered version of love in art and media, but what do we really know about it? What have we seen, outside of our parents? And even then, how much is there? I don't know what your parents are like but mine are divorced, and I have no memories of what they were like together. They've both dated other people, but they aren't exactly open about that part of themselves. And the rest comes from our friends, but they aren't exactly experts either." Iris's phone buzzed a few times in her hand. She glanced at the screen then set it facedown on the ledge, giving me her attention. "I don't know. Maybe I think it'll make me better at it all."

Iris smiled, her eyes starting to droop with sleep. I was getting tired too, and had an early shift the next day. A yawn escaped me, and I thought of how Leo would make fun of the exaggerated scope of my yawns, how long they built up for. He would sometimes try to interrupt them by tickling me. It got annoying by the end of our relationship, but I remember how much I loved it when we were still just flirting. The rush of his touch, the intimacy of laughing together. I used to fake yawns just to get him to do it.

That was gone now. A joy in my life just flittered away. The thought caused me sadness, but not the kind of sadness I'd been feeling for weeks now. I didn't think I was healed from the heartbreak, but I started to realize in that moment, looking out at a relatively quiet Manhattan, that I would, with time. A few more nights like this, a few more nights to forget the things I liked about Leo, a few more run-ins where he acted like a jerk. I'd heal, in the end.

I just didn't know if I wanted to heal.

What We Talk about When We Talk about Talking about Love

BY LU CHARLES, NOVEMBER 10

Sometimes I wonder how people know that the feeling they're experiencing is the same thing others experience. Like, when I call something "love," am I talking about the same thing a certain boy with sexy stage presence is talking about when he talks about love?

The boyfriend and I exchanged L-words recently. I've written about this momentous stage in a relationship before, but I had no idea what the moment really felt like, could only imagine the layers of thoughts and hopes and fears that rush through a person's mind in the lead-up and afterglow.

I would think it'd be a full relief, something akin to how it felt to finally become uncrushed and enter into that elusive stage of actual dating and kissing. Don't get me wrong, there is joy. An unclenching deep within me. Since the beginning of our relationship, I had been wondering if it was one-sided, if I was deep in the pool while he was sitting at the edge watching me with only his ankles submerged.

Now that we've talked and agreed that we are both in the deep end, I wonder how deep we're talking about. I wonder about the quantifiable measurability of love, and how evenly it can match up. We talk about love, but do two people ever mean the exact same thing when they say they love each other?

It probably depends on your outlook. If you're a romantic, you say of course. If you're a cynic you say we're in actuality always alone and even relationships are an illusion. If you're at a party, you back slowly away from the cynic and come up with a signal with your friends to make sure you don't get stuck talking to him again.

Or. Maybe it's just me. My neuroses. Maybe it's just this relationship. Maybe it's still too new for me to feel complete reciprocity. To trust that it's there. I want that trust, but maybe that's one of those stupid grown-up things that comes with time. Although the most neurotic part of me says that no, that's not the case. Real love doesn't come with a minimum age requirement.

Tell me, readers, is it just me? Does this ring a bell for anyone else, or are these insecurities mine alone?

12
EXCUSES

The next day, as I was walking to work, Hafsah called me. I stared at my phone, wishing I hadn't been a huge tool and missed my deadline. Mornings are hard enough on a day-to-day basis, but I hadn't gotten much sleep the night before because I was out so late with Iris. I'd tried to improvise a last-minute article, but my head started lolling with booze and sleep and I had to succumb to bed. Mom had passive-aggressively grilled me during breakfast, which for sure helped with the whole sleep-deprivation thing.

Other than that, morning phone calls generally made me feel like some alien had zapped my brain and replaced it with one of those flimsy decades-old couch cushions my tita Marian refuses to throw away. So that's the state of mind I was in.

"Hey!" I said, really lingering on the *y* to make it seem like I was totally cool with this phone call and how it would undo my future.

"Where's your column, Lu?"

Small talk isn't the greatest thing in the world, but I would have really loved the opportunity to let my panicking mind ease into the conversation. I sighed, and then decided on a bold, albeit not superintelligent approach. "What was that, Haf? I couldn't hear you!" I even covered up my off-ear to the city sounds, as if it was onlookers in my vicinity that I had to convince.

All that did though was turn up the volume on Hafsah's end of the line. She was so quiet that I could hear the subdued sounds of the *Misnomer* offices gearing up for the day. Interns chatting in the coffee room, office doors opening and shutting, people saying their good mornings. Someone tapped softly on their keyboard, a fridge whirred. I swear I could hear those things. Hafsah was really freaking quiet.

"Can you hear me now?" I could tell she hadn't moved to a different spot in the office or closed her door or anything like that. Which meant she probably could sniff through my bullshit.

Abort, abort. "Yeah, that's better."

"I was expecting your column yesterday. What happened?"

I quickly ran through some possible excuses:

- A grandparent dying. (Too disrespectful to my dead grandparents, too awful to imagine for my still-living grandparents.)
- My dog ate it. (I don't have a dog, and I don't think dogs ever eat entire laptops or, for that matter, someone's ability to access the internet.)
- Someone elbowed past me so hard on the subway that it caused a weekend-long concussion and paralysis in my fingers. (Plausible, but Hafsah would probably ask for a doctor's note.)
- Heartbreak had rendered me wordless and now my future as a writer was over. (Not an excuse that would solve anything for me vis-à-vis losing the job.)

"I need more time," I said. "The couple I'm interviewing just had a busy weekend and they kept canceling our phone call appointments."

Another silence from Hafsah, during which I could physically sense my future falling apart. I was gonna work at the movie theater my whole life. I'd turn into Brad. Except Brad married his high school sweetheart, so I'd probably be a slightly sadder version of Brad, keeping an eternal stockade of notebooks which I would fill only with doodles because I'd never write another word again.

"You should have turned something in, Lu. A draft. A proposal. You're putting me in a bad position."

"It's gonna be really good, Haf. I promise. They're…" I reached around the empty recesses of my brain for a descriptor that would sell Hafsah, somehow landed on "…entrancing. It'll be worth it, but I do need more time. I'm sorry." Were they entrancing? Or was I just desperate?

I was still walking, and at that point I came within view of the movie theater. How this phone call ended could make the next eight hours excruciating or filled with sweet, sweet relief. I stood on the corner of Third Avenue and Eleventh Street, eyes glued to my feet and the sidewalk. I wish I could say I felt a moment of inner peace, knowing that the decision was out of my hands and worrying would achieve nothing. But that's not how my mind works. I focused on a piece of trash rolling along the street, carried by the draft of passing cars.

"Since I needed something by the end of the month, you get one more week. After that, I'm going to look to fill the love column with someone else."

"You are the best person alive. You won't be disappointed. It's gonna be great," I said, my shoulders shimmying with excitement of their own volition.

I hung up and hurried into work. In the back room, I found

Pete putting his things away in his locker. I stormed in and slammed my bag into the locker adjacent to his. "All is not lost!" I yelled.

"Oh good. I was worried when you bailed on me last night that you got stuck watching global warming docs. Clearly not the case." Pete grabbed his maroon work polo and slipped it over his head.

"My editor is giving me another week," I said, grabbing him by the shoulders and shaking him as violently as I could. "I get another chance!"

Pete shrugged his way out of my grip. "You're really excited for the extra rope to hang yourself with."

I clapped my hands together. "I'm gonna ignore the rudeness of that comment because I bailed on you yesterday and you're entitled to some snark. But this is good news! My future has not crumbled like the ice caps."

"Now I'm confused. Did you watch documentaries last night?" We walked over to the clipboard on the wall to see where our shifts would start. We were both on cleaning duty.

"No. Iris and I hung out all night. It was actually really cool. We went to the Comedy Cellar and a speakeasy, and even made it to the roof of the freaking Flatiron." Pete's eyebrows went up. "I know!"

We both grabbed a broom and a dustbin and walked out into the lobby.

"Please tell me you're not doing that thing."

"What thing?"

"That '90s rom-com thing where you strike up a friendship for ulterior motives, which eventually blossoms into a real relationship, and then it all falls apart in the third act when the other person discovers the aforementioned ulterior motives."

"Don't be ridiculous" I said. We started making the rounds of the theaters, sweeping up popcorn that last night's cleanup crew may have missed. "I was completely up-front with her about my motives for friendship. But I could use some help in determining a way to trick her into agreeing to an interview."

Pete was a few rows up from me in the otherwise empty theater, sweeping calmly. "Still?"

"Yeah. Get this: they *are* breaking up. But they're delaying their misery by staying together until the end of the summer."

Pete stopped sweeping and looked at me, furrowing his brow. I waited for him to say it was a ballsy move on their part, a bold acceptance of how all good things eventually end, they were living in the avant-garde of romance!

"Weird," Pete said, going back to sweeping. "So she changed her mind about letting you interview them, then?"

"Well, no. She gets sad if she thinks about the breakup, so she didn't want to dwell. But I think she might feel differently if I asked her this morning. We, like, bonded last night."

"Hmm," Pete went. I took that as a sign that his mental cogs and wheels or whatever a brain is made up of were starting to churn. We cleaned six more theaters without saying another word. Except every time Pete made a little noise I assumed he was about to drop some wisdom and I'd perk my ears up like a cat.

By the time we got switched over to concessions, I was getting tired of his reticence. "Alright, dude. You've been brainstorming for a while now. What do you have for me?"

Pete was trying to jam as many napkins as he could in the dispenser. Our record was 258, which I'd set last summer by cheating and taking out the spring-loaded bottom, then throwing that particular dispenser away. "Vis-à-vis...?"

The doors to the theater opened, the first customers of the day arriving: a group of stay-at-home parents coming in for a matinee that they would not be able to pay attention to because they'd be checking in on their baby and running out to calm the crying. "Have you seriously not been brainstorming this whole time?"

Pete tilted his head at me like a pretty Irish puppy. "In regards to the napkin thing?"

"No, you dolt. A strategy to get Iris to yield!"

"Ah." He nodded once, then muttered something about losing count and went off to attend to the mommy-and-me crowd. I scooped popcorn for him, a little pissed that he hadn't been on the same page as me. We're usually pretty in sync, and it felt weird not to have him on board with me for this. I had to wait fifteen minutes for a break in the first-showing crowd, the whole while berating Pete in my head and trying to keep a smile on my face while toddlers pointed at the candy they wanted and then wailed when their parents opted for anything else.

During the shuffle of actually doing our jobs, we ended up at opposite ends of the concession counter. But people that had been working with us for a while had picked up on the fact that I would do whatever I could to talk to Pete, whether that was talking loudly across the entire row of coworkers or making them switch cashier spots with me, and they usually chose the latter. Brad tried to talk to us about it last summer, but quickly came to the realization that we ended up doing a better job if we were allowed to hang out together during our shifts.

"Okay, you've had more time now," I said once I'd finagled my way down the registers toward him. "What's my approach?"

"Forget about convincing her." He shrugged. "Write about you and Leo."

"I am going to eye-roll you so hard it'll reverse the earth's rotation, sending us back in time to before you were born, so that I can slap your mom about the terrible choice she made bringing you into the world."

"That's rude, my mom's lovely. And you really don't have to go back in time to slap her." He squinted, and looked up and to the right, like he'd just had an idea and was riding the thought off in to the sunset. "Also, the logistics of rolling your eyes so hard that you turn back time is—"

"Pete."

He came back to Earth, leaning against a popcorn machine and then jumping back when it tilted under his weight. "'Sup?"

"Stop suggesting I write about me and Leo. I don't want to think about him. I want to write about Iris and Cal."

He rubbed his elbow, a red welt forming where it had rested against the popcorn machine. "I think you have to accept the reality that this isn't something she wants, and that if you continue to wish for her to just change her mind, you might end up right back where you were the other night, worrying about missing your deadline. My best advice is to find someone else."

"There isn't anyone else," I said, resisting the urge to say it in the whiniest voice possible. Have you ever just sunk into that bratty whiny voice? It's fun. Cathartic, even, like stretching a particularly tired muscle. "My words won't come with anyone else."

"Force them to." Pete shrugged. "You said Iris gets sad when she dwells on her relationship? Allow yourself to dwell too. Write about it." One of the moms ran out from her theater and took the whole stack of napkins that Pete had counted for the dispenser. She cringe-smiled at him then ran back, her sandals clapping against the floor until she hit the carpet portion of the hallway. Pete turned to look at me, his expression kind.

In defiance of what he'd said, I thought of Leo, as if to prove that I could do it without being touched by sadness. I thought of the speech I'd prepared for him, how I still hadn't had the chance to read it. I thought about whether I still wanted to be back with him, even though he'd practically wiped me from his life. The answer was an immediate and resounding yes. I missed getting pho with him, missed walking home from school with him, missed coming up with stupid songs with him. My stomach dropped at the thought.

"God, you really belong as the voice of reason in a third act somewhere." I fiddled with the computer screen on my register, hitting random buttons and then canceling the order, just for the pleasure of the little beeps. "Too bad this isn't a movie and those truth bombs don't do anyone any good. I tried writing about Rachel and Diane, nothing happened. I'm gonna write about Iris and Cal."

Pete bit his lip. Always so damn calm, even when I just dismiss everything he says. Sometimes I wish he'd blow up at me and call me a selfish jerk. But that's not who he is. "I don't know what else to say. Keep trying."

Mom wanted me to stay home after work, complaining that she "hadn't seen me in so long that she wouldn't recognize me walking down the street." I managed to convince her to let me go to the coffee shop down the street from us though, just for a couple of hours so I could work on my column.

"Hmm," she went. "What do you mean by 'a couple'? Is it two or three or just a stand-in for an indefinite number you'd rather not name?"

"Mom, when you sniff out my teenage evasiveness it really makes you unbearable."

"Answer the question."

"I don't know, Mother. Writing doesn't work like that. There's no formula to it. I could be done in fifteen minutes. Or I could be done in fifteen hours."

"You only tell me it's fifteen hours when you want to get away with something."

"Listen," I said. "What I do with my time is none of your business."

"It is entirely my business what you do with your time. That's my job as your mother, above all other business. It is literally the number one item on my business agenda."

I squinted my eyes at her, knowing that I had no ground to respond, but also to convey that I didn't want her to press any further.

"Before I let you out of the house, I'd like to press further. What are you writing about?"

I don't know if my mom reads my column. We don't really talk about it much, but she gets this funny look on her face every time the topic comes up, and then she kind of lets me do whatever I want.

I squinted a little harder, hoping to scare her off. Teenage squints are powerful like that. She clicked her tongue and shook her head, "You think that look scares me." I stopped squinting and instead I activated my second phase of deflection, the I'm-confused-you're-so-weird look. "Fine," my mom said. "I'll respect your privacy. But don't let me slip into the back burner of your mind, or I might burn until I'm nothing but an ashy nuisance crusted into your best pot."

"Goddamn, Mom. Harsh."

"Language," she said.

Little Bean is hipster chic, all wood paneling and hanging ferns, string lights draped across the coffee shop like it was the patio at someone's wedding. I bought myself a drip coffee and snagged the only available seat next to an electrical outlet. It's my favorite spot, not just because the outlet gives me freedom to hang out for long stretches of time, but because it's in the corner near the window, allowing me to look out the window at pedestrian traffic, but also at the hip baristas with their septum piercings and couldn't-care-less affectations, and the curious array of customers that came in: those plugged into laptops and headphones, those on dates or friendly meet-ups, those rushing in for a to-go order, a quick detour in their lives.

I opened my computer and brought up the saved blank document that should've been my article, as well as my notebook, flipping to the notes I'd taken about Diane and Rachel. I pulled up Hafsah's last email to me, hoping that seeing her name would intimidate me into inspiration. For the same reason, I pulled up a picture I'd taken of Pete a few weeks back at Books of Wonder. In it, he was holding a graphic novel and eyeing me like I was disturbing the very fabric of his world.

"There! Now I'm ready to work." I would have said it out loud, if I were even more unhinged than I really am. Instead I thought it, and cracked my knuckles for the symbolic effect. Then I did absolutely fuck-all for forty-five minutes. I texted Iris that I'd had a fun night. I texted Pete asking him if he'd had any breakthroughs thinking of ways to convince Iris.

Pete
Dude, I can't even convince you to do
anything but pursue these lovebirds, clearly
my powers of persuasion aren't that great.
Interview yourself. Or someone else, if you must.

I slouched as low in my seat as a nonslug being has ever slouched. All the excitement after my phone call with Hafsah that morning had been swallowed up by that unfortunate whirlpool of writer's block hanging over my head. Then I spotted them. At a table across the coffee shop sat a blonde girl and a black guy. They had two different college stickers on their laptops and they were touching each other the way you would if you hadn't seen the person you love in months.

Sure, I was making, at the very least, a dozen assumptions about these two people. They may not have even been a couple. They could have been having an affair, or displaying stickers for colleges their parents went to. They could have met after college. But I was in the state of mind that allowed me to push away from my seat, grab my mostly empty coffee cup, and walk over to them.

"Hi!" I said, cheery as one of those people in Times Square who tries to get you on the tour bus if you look even slightly like a Dutch family of four on vacation.

The couple looked at me exactly the way they should have. The blonde girl put a protective hand on her boyfriend's forearm. The guy retreated slightly, as if I was accusing him of something. "Sorry," I said, "that was aggressive. I write a love and relationship column for *Misnomer*, the online magazine." The couple exchanged confused looks. "Anyway, I noticed your college decals. Do you two happen to be in a long-distance relationship?"

"Um," they both said, because of course they did.

I was moments away from fleeing and begging Iris to change her mind, but then the couple said yes.

"How did you know?" the girl asked, half impressed, half still-wondering-how-deranged-I-was.

"Have you ever watched the show *House*?"

They both blinked, and I knew it was time to dial back Normal Lu and call up Journalism Lu. I took a breath, thought of the joys of a column coming together, thought of how good it felt to write again, how this couple might be the ones that broke the block for me. "Let me start over. My name is Lu Charles, I'm a writer for *Misnomer*," I said with a smile that hopefully hid my mental state. "I'm working on a column about dating the summer after senior year, and I'm hoping I could ask you a few questions?"

They looked at each other and smiled, and I knew then and there that I had them.

For twenty minutes I sat with them, interviewing them, pushing my pen furiously across my page, taking note of all the details that made this couple unique, all the specifics of their love lives. I listened to the very best of my abilities, asking questions that would really get to the heart of who they were and how they let love be stronger than the circumstances fighting against it.

Then I thanked them, returned to my computer, and failed to write a single word.

All I could think about was two-person paintball teams, and Iris crying at the fountain in Columbus Circle.

At home, I tried to make my mom happy by not disappearing into my room immediately. I answered questions about my day monosyllabically, faking enthusiasm while slurping through some puttanesca. I watched Jase miraculously switch from murdering people virtually to playing football and virtually causing concussions. I wondered briefly about whether he was interested in romance yet, if he was starting to develop crushes, think about love, dream about people. Probably. But I wasn't about to broach the subject.

After a while of being a decent family member, I opened up my computer. Instead of writing, I perused social media, clicking through pictures of Iris and Cal, which then led me to clicking through pictures of me and Leo.

A text came in from Pete.

Pete
How's the writing going?

                                              Lu
                                        Splendidly.

Pete
Mmm-hmm.

Having a friend with ESP is really annoying. I clicked away from my blank document as if Pete might be looking over my shoulder. I had six days to interview someone and write a column. It usually took me at least two days to draft something worthwhile, especially if I was working at the theater. I could probably get some work done on the train ride to Princeton on Friday when Jase and I went to visit Dad, but I definitely needed to have someone locked in to write about by then.

I looked over at my computer screen at a picture of me and Leo from that day we went to Coney Island in the winter. We'd had this notion that it would look beautiful after a blizzard, and it kind of did, but it was mostly miserable and depressing with everything shut down. We'd had fun for about six minutes, taken some selfies, and then gotten the hell out of there as soon as we could. I think we watched a movie at his place that day.

In the picture, the wind is blowing his hair across his face. He couldn't quite get it into the samurai-esque man bun yet. Sitting there on the couch, I tried to remember what Leo smelled like. For some reason I couldn't conjure it up; that particular aroma of his skin and clothes or whatever je ne sais quoi results in the symbiosis of a person's scent. It felt strange not being able to remember his smell.

Maybe that's what made me stand up from the couch, set my computer gently on the coffee table and stare at my phone as if it were buzzing in my hand. What I was really doing was scrolling to Leo's name in my phone. I hadn't done that since the last time he'd stood me up, the day I met Cal.

I tiptoed out of the living room and down the hall to my room, shutting the door quietly as the phone rang.

"Hey," Leo answered. He lingered on the *y* kind of like I had with Hafsah, but not like that at all.

"Hey." I tried to decide between sitting or pacing, then realized my room had about two steps' worth of pacing in any direction and plopped myself down on the corner of my bed. "How goes it?" I asked, which is not how I usually talk, because I'm a normal human person. I swear.

"It's, uh, good."

Someone strike this conversation from the annals of history.

"That's good. So good. Really happy for you," I said. I examined my fingernails and brought my thumbnail up to my mouth to chew on it, even though I had literally never done that before in my life. Through the parted blinds I could see the neighboring building, the column of bathroom windows, one of which was currently lit up. A blurry silhouette was showering, one royal blue bottle of shampoo or conditioner visible in the portion of the window that was pushed out into the night air, allowing mellow billows of steam to waft out.

"So, what's up?" Leo asked. I could hear something on in the background on his line, a reality show, maybe, or a Broadway cast recording.

My showering neighbor reached over for the visible bottle of shampoo, his hand recognizably male. Was I heeding Pete's advice to interview Leo, or was I going against his advice to forget about him? I suddenly wished I'd prepared questions before dialing. Pretty terrible journalistic move to arrive at an interview completely unprepared.

"Leo, I was wondering..."

A long pause from his end. "Yeah?"

I chewed off the corner of my thumbnail, cursing myself when it peeled away into my mouth. I spat it out quietly into my hand and tossed it into the nearby trash bin. My eyes were glued on the showering neighbor, but I'm pretty sure that if a human-sized wolf appeared in the window brushing its teeth and waving at me, I probably wouldn't have reacted at all. I was remembering Coney Island, the excitement of the subway ride there, the quiet disappointment on the ride back. Leo had played a game on his phone, taking the spurned plans pretty well. No matter how I felt, Leo could make the best of bad situations. He was not easily angered or annoyed.

"Can we talk?" I reached for something to fiddle with in my hands, landing on a receipt from the Comedy Cellar from the other night with Iris. I was slightly jealous of teenagers of old and their ability to play with tangled phone cords, tethered to a place but at least free to play endlessly. "About us?"

A quiet sigh from Leo. "I'm not sure that's a good idea."

"Why?"

Leo didn't say anything. You ever hear your past with someone in the pauses they take?

I thought about telling him the real reason I was calling, but couldn't decide if that was more or less weird than just playing the heartbroken-ex card. I crumpled the receipt and then smoothed it out on my thigh. "I just..." I trailed off. "I wish we could talk about it. Analyze things. Figure out what went wrong, what would have gone wrong regardless, what we did right. I wish we could talk about it like it was a harmless thing."

More pauses from Leo. "I'm not sure what to say to that." An awkward chuckle. Not even a chuckle. A throat spasm at best.

"We went through something, Leo. Good or bad, it was *something*. Good and bad, probably. And I was thinking that maybe..."

There was a loud crash on Leo's side of the phone, then some rustling about. "Sorry, I dropped my phone. What was that?"

The receipt was mostly smooth against my leg, so I crumpled it back up and tossed it over to my desk. Across the street, my showering neighbor shut off the water.

"We had love, Leo. Whether it's gone or not, that matters, doesn't it? It's an incredible facet of life and we should be able to dissect it. Share our experiences so that others can learn from them, or at least relate to them." My voice felt small in my room. I wondered if I should have been writing all of this down. I could hear Jase still chatting with his buddies on his headset, though making a concerted effort to be quiet. Through the crack under the door, I could tell the hallway light was off, which meant my mom was getting ready for bed. She'd be in soon to say good-night and ask me for the millionth time what my plans were for tomorrow.

"Um," Leo said, because I was a raving lunatic.

"What did you feel when—?" I asked, at the same exact moment that he said, "I'm pretty beat, I think I'm gonna go to—"

"Sorry," I said. "What was that?"

Leo cleared his throat. "I, uh… I should let you go."

My neighbor turned off his bathroom light. Down on the street, a car zoomed past, then squealed on its brakes. Jase button mashed on the couch, the little clicks and clacks impossible to make quieter, and I thought about going to grab my laptop. It was still on the coffee table, I knew, a yellow light blinking slowly to show it was on but asleep. I wished I could say the same about my writing. It was still alive, still within me somewhere. It just needed to be opened up again.

"Yeah," I said, "you should. Sorry for calling."

Yet another pause. I could picture Leo, if he were in another time, tangling himself up in a phone cord, trying to come up with something good to say. "It's…fine, Lu. It's okay. I hope you're okay." One last pause, this one the briefest of them all.

I thought maybe I could slip into that pause. Maybe I could wedge myself between the boy I loved and whatever hesitation had caused him to put us here. Then he said good-night and hung up.

13
STARGAZING

The rest of the week passed by in a series of self-assurances that I still had time. It's only Tuesday, I'd thought when hanging with Iris. Plenty of weekdays left, plus a few of those sweet, sweet weekenders thrown in as a bonus. I told Pete how the phone call with Leo had gone, then shoved down the memory of the conversation, even though Pete said I could still write about our relationship without interviewing him. I could unload myself on the page, he said.

I shoved my empty notebook in his face and told him obviously I couldn't.

Wednesday I had work and then Mom, Jase, and I went over to my tita Marian's in Queens for a family dinner. It was hard to brainstorm backup plans for my column in that situation, because my family is loud and talkative and we have a tendency to end up gathered around the piano singing show tunes. Which was always great, except it was the first time we'd done it since Leo and I broke up. Show tunes reminded me of Leo, the way he looked on stage, the way he'd close his eyes when belting a note. I used to sit in his room pretending to redo homework while he practiced his lines and songs. He'd catch me staring and blush, which was completely uncalled for, because every note he sang was perfect.

At some point with my family, my cousin Cindy—who was living this awesome postcollegiate life in Brooklyn—asked me about how things were going at *Misnomer*. I almost answered honestly, but then Tita started playing a song from *Aida* on the piano and we all lost our collective minds belting out the lyrics. I was reminded how much my family loved Leo because he could belt along with us. Especially because my stupid aunt kept asking where he was.

Thursday I tried to eavesdrop and find another Iris and Cal, but came away with only an exchange which was either a recruitment for a pyramid scheme or a pitch for a cult. My words were nowhere to be found. My deadline approached.

By the end of my work shift, I was starting to get the feeling that I was just going to screw this up again, and that the screwup was almost entirely inevitable now. Even if I wanted to write about Cal and Iris against Iris's wishes, nothing was coming. "You need to forget about these two lovebirds," Pete said. He was throwing on a denim button-down over his black T-shirt as we walked out of the theater. "That's the only thing that's keeping you from writing."

"Writer's block is a thing, Pete."

"So is needless obsession with a distraction." He brushed the hair from his eyes. "You need to go home or are we hanging out?" I cringed and avoided eye contact. "Social cues tell me I'm not going to like what you say next."

"Iris texted me. She wants to hang out. I'd totally invite you but I feel like this might solidify our friendship and I don't want to ruin it with, like, a premature group hang." A trio of people was strolling in front of us, unaware that they were blocking the sidewalk. I sped around them, balancing on the edge of the sidewalk. Pete and I hate getting stuck behind slow walkers, but I was also making a conscious decision to keep him from making direct eye contact with me.

"Glad to see you're taking my advice," he said quietly. We headed toward Union Square, each swiping into an adjacent turnstile without saying much. We were taking separate lines so had to split up soon. It was not yet rush hour, and the station wasn't overwhelmingly crowded. A cute guy walked past briskly, thumbs hooked into his jean pockets like a fashion model. Pete was quieter than usual, and though I could see something bugging him, I didn't ask about it because (a) I was pretty sure I was to blame, and (b) Pete would speak his mind when he needed to.

We stood there for a moment, avoiding eye contact. "Is this gonna be how it goes for the summer?" he asked finally.

"Don't be dramatic. I told you I'll offer a group hang next time. You'll like her."

Pete nodded twice, then looked down at his shoes. "I leave in August too, Lu. You know that." Then he mumbled a bye and headed down the corridor toward the 1 train.

"I said *don't* be dramatic!" I shouted after him, eliciting stares from the fellow commuters not wearing headphones. "The quick departure after a sentimentally loaded statement is definitely a dramatic move!"

Pete turned around as he walked on his heels, giving me a shrug before spinning again and continuing on his path. I watched him go, then found my train to go meet up with Iris.

Iris and I met up at Columbus Circle again, this time going into the Whole Foods to grab supplies for a picnic. "I don't mean to be boring and repetitive," she said, "I'm just gonna miss this park so much."

"I will grieve for you while you suffer in the terrible land-scapes of Southern California."

"Fair point."

I let her lead the way around the store, picking out our snacks. I probably shouldn't have been surprised after seeing where she lived and our adventures the other night, but she didn't seem to pay much attention to the cost of things. A liter of kombucha, a tray of sushi, three mangoes, two varieties of organic kettle chips, some artisanal cheeses, a pound of sugar-free granola, about three other items with hyphenations in their descriptions.

Part of why Leo had said he didn't want to do long distance was the cost. Neither one of us had a ton of expendable money, even though we worked, and long distance meant more of it would go to trains or buses to visit each other. I'd wanted to oppose this reasoning and remind Leo that love was heaps more important than money, but I'd kind of seen his point. I'd needed a scholarship for my parents to even be able to afford NYU, and I had no idea how I'd visit Leo enough to see him as much as I would have wanted to. If, you know, we were still dating.

Seeing Iris shop so indiscriminately made me think that she and Cal were maybe better suited to staying together if they had chosen the long-distance route.

"By the way, Cal's going to meet up with us."

We were by the self-service spice station, where large containers of cardamom, star anise, and turmeric awaited for customers who went for that sort of thing in bulk. I said, "Cool," and pretended to read some labels. A funny feeling coursed through my body, or more accurately, my stomach and chest. Writers are liars. Feelings don't ever make it all the way down to your toes. I couldn't put my finger on what exactly it was. Probably a mix of things, one of them definitely being guilt that I hadn't brought Pete along. But who likes feeling guilty? I shoved that feeling down, making room for the slight thrill I was experiencing that I'd get to see Cal and Iris together.

We paid for our snacks and went out to Columbus Circle to wait for Cal to arrive. I spotted him in the distance, wearing black pants, a maroon T-shirt, and carrying a black backpack. I realized that I hadn't seen him in person since the day of their fight. I'd forgotten how cute he was, how I'd wanted Leo to walk in on us sitting together and feel a pang of jealousy.

Then I remembered that Iris had no idea I'd met Cal already. I hadn't ever confessed the fact that I'd eavesdropped on them, and of course I hadn't ever mentioned our encounter on the bench. I had no reason to.

When he got closer Iris pointed him out and waved, and he smiled at us, then narrowed his eyes at me as he approached. I cringed, kind of hoping he wouldn't recognize me. "Oh my God!" he said immediately. "Bench Girl!"

I narrowed my eyes the same way he did, knowing I should probably just act natural. Problem is, my natural state is human, and human beings are weird. I pretended to search the files of my mind for recognition of his face. Finally, an Academy Award–deserving ten seconds later, I snapped my fingers and widened my eyes. "Holy shit!"

I turned to Iris, who had this confused smile on her face, then back to Cal. "This is so weird! Like, super weird. So incredibly weird I can't believe the improbability of this occurrence of events!"

"Um, what's happening?"

"Is this Lu?" Cal asked, pointing at me. "We sat on a bench together one day. I rambled about paintball teams."

Iris smiled and rolled her eyes. "Damn it, did you tell everyone about that analogy?"

"It's a great analogy," Cal rebutted. Then he looked at me

and shook his head. "Even if it turned out to be not entirely true." His grin got bigger for a moment, and then he looked over at Iris and down at the ground.

I wasn't sure where to look so I turned to the French baguette I'd bought as part of my picnic and crinkled its brown paper bag, "Small world, huh?"

Iris had a few follow-up questions about our conversation at the park, which made me briefly panic at the possibility that the two of them could uncover the fact that I'd eavesdropped, but she was quickly sated and Cal soon changed the subject, the matter apparently put to rest way more easily than I could have anticipated.

We dodged a few joggers, heading toward one of the large grassy fields in the park. We picked a spot shaded by a tree, and then Cal unfurled a plaid blanket from his backpack, kicked off his shoes and used them as anchors against the wind. Meanwhile, Iris set out the spread of food she'd bought at Whole Foods, neatly arranging everything on the blanket as if preparing it for a professional photo shoot. We did all snap a few compulsory pics for social media, although in the end none of us posted them. I wonder about those pictures sometimes, the stockade we each have backed up online or on laptops, thousands of pictures of the minutiae of life. Someday, will I see all those forgotten selfies of me and Leo? Will that serve a purpose beyond nostalgia? Or are they just taking up digital space on some unseen server, never to be reexamined, and definitely not reexamined in any meaningful way?

Iris ran off to collect a few wildflowers from the edge of the field, leaving me and Cal alone for the first time since the bench. We made brief eye contact when she left, and I realized that he had beautifully dark eyes. As someone who's been told my whole life by societal representations of beauty that light-colored eyes are the only ones that can be beautiful, I have a deep appreciation for brown eyes that raise a middle finger to those beauty standards and simply slay with their beauty. Leo had eyes like that, and Cal did too, framed by dark lashes that almost made it look like he had eyeliner on.

"She likes a certain aesthetic to her pics," Cal said with a shrug, looking away from me to watch his girlfriend. He smiled after saying it, a smile clearly caused by Iris.

"Weird, the aesthetic I usually go for is not-good-enough-at-taking-pictures-to-be-allowed-to-share-pictures."

He laughed that laugh again, the one from the bench, the one that was like rising bread. "That's right," he said, snapping his fingers, "you're funny. I'd forgotten that."

"Um," I said, because you can't simultaneously confess to a near stranger that you really want to be thought of as funny yet be stricken by the constant insecurities that you're not at all.

"By the way, I've been doing that thing more often. The one I said I wanted to," Cal said.

I blinked at him like he had suddenly switched to a different language, one based on entirely different phonetics than any I'd heard in my life.

"The French tourists," he elaborated. "I've been trying to help people in small ways like that ever since we talked. Nothing crazy. Gave a homeless guy a pair of shoes, carried a lady's bags for a couple blocks. That's it." He scrunched his face up, as if he were embarrassed by this confession. "Both times, I thought of you."

Of all the reactions I could have possibly had, I somehow smiled at this. "Really?" I looked down at my legs, then reached outside the breadth of the blanket and ripped a few blades of grass from the ground. "Why?"

Cal shook his head. He was sitting with his legs up and crossed, his arms wrapped around his knees. "I'm not sure. I guess because you were there when I thought of it?"

A few moments later, Iris returned with a handful of daisies, arranging them expertly around our spread. We took a few more pics, Iris on a fancy digital camera, then started to eat. The park was busy for a weekday, lots of picnickers and shirtless dudes playing Frisbee, a few women in bikinis taking advantage of the last few minutes of afternoon sun.

Iris said that she'd invited Cal along because she liked hanging out with me, and thought Cal would too. That she liked sharing joys with him.

"You guys are so direct," I said, popping a piece of sushi into my mouth with my fingers, since we'd forgotten to grab an extra pair of chopsticks. "Do you always just say what you mean? How do you function in society doing that?"

They both laughed, not taking offense to my comment. "I told you she was funny," Iris said, raising her eyebrows at Cal.

"You didn't lie." He reached over to rip off a chunk of baguette, pairing it with one of the soft cheeses Iris had brought and a little bit of rose petal jam. "I don't know. Being direct just feels good most of the time. A little uncomfortable sometimes, maybe, but even on the other side of that, there's relief."

"I can't be direct unless I'm making a joke," I said.

"Not true," Cal retorted immediately. "You just did it." He turned over his shoulder as a neon yellow Frisbee landed a few feet away. A tanned white guy with absurdly square pecs jogged up and grabbed it from the grass, flashing a smile at us. "Try it again."

I groaned, then tore a few more blades of grass, twisting them into one thick strand in my fingers. A tightness spread in my chest, which I interpreted as my body not being down for this direct ride stuff. They fell silent though, waiting for me to speak.

A few weeks after I started at *Misnomer*, before Leo and I started dating, I asked Hafsah for some tips on interviewing, since I was afraid every article would be just me ruminating repetitively on unrequited love.

"People are jacks-in-the-box, awaiting the chance to spring," she'd said. "You keep winding that crank."

"Ugh, is that really the plural of *jack-in-the-box*? It's gross," I'd responded.

I ripped my grassy braid into shreds, tossing them into the breeze, pretending I was still thinking. The sun had dipped beyond the horizon, causing the tanners to start to gather their things. Dozens of orange reflections glimmered in the windows of Midtown. "Cal, don't be like that. If she doesn't want to—"

"I'm jealous of the time you have together before breaking up," I said. A pause after, not just because I couldn't believe I'd brought myself to say it, but because I'm a goddamn pro and I know that letting the confession sink in might lead them to retaliate. Screw my deadline and my writer's block, screw Pete's advice, screw writing about Leo. This was the story I wanted. I shrugged at Iris, then looked at Cal, wondering how much Iris had told him about my article. "You guys have chosen momentary happiness, and I'm jealous of whatever it was that allowed you to do that. A lot of people would be."

Another Frisbee whizzed by us. This time a light-skinned black guy with sparse curls on his chest and a white bandanna tucked into his yellow shorts jogged past us, offering a smiling "sorry" before tossing the disk back across the field.

"See?" Cal said. "Feels good, right?"

Iris didn't say anything, her eyes following the black guy's light jog back toward his friends.

"A little bit," I said, watching Iris, waiting for her expression to change. She kept her gaze distant until Cal changed the subject, turning the conversation toward his plans to do as little as possible over the summer, before college and adulthood came around to drown him in responsibilities and the need to pretend to be busy. Iris snapped out of her daze and scooted a little closer to Cal, saying that she was going to walk as much of the city as she could manage before California beat her into its sedentary lifestyle.

"I'll photograph the whole city," she said, smiling at the thought. "I'll need something to look at when I'm missing it."

Other than that moment, they looked completely comfortable in each other's presence, even in front of me. They held hands and smiled at each other warmly without making it feel like they were about to start making out, which is honestly how almost every couple I've seen has ever acted.

I spent more time with Pete than anyone else, and sometimes I still felt awkward around him. Hell, I feel awkward when I'm alone in my room sometimes, like maybe my limbs are at strange angles or I'm doing something weird with my face and the whole world can see. I tried to remember if I was like this with Leo, but I couldn't recall. I remembered being happy with him, and in love, and turned on. But I'm pretty sure you can be all those things and still be awkward.

That two eighteen-year-olds could be in front of a third wheel and make each other laugh without making the third wheel uncomfortable astounded me, especially because I kept remembering the fight I'd witnessed, kept remembering that this was a couple that knew they were going to break up at summer's end. I'd never really looked at two people who were in love. I'd listened in, sure. But every couple I'd ever seen, I'd only glanced at for a few moments at a time. At the movies or at school or just walking down the street. I'd seen people and recognized them as a couple, but I'd never really studied the way two people acted when they were together. I wondered if this was what Leo and I had looked like, at least for a time.

"So, Lu, doing anything exciting this weekend?" Iris asked.

"Does New Jersey count?"

"Not normally, but I'm going to New Jersey this weekend too," Cal said. "Where in Jersey are you going?"

"Princeton, you?"

"No way! Me too."

"Whoa. Weird. Are you visiting my dad too?"

Cal laughed. "Yeah, he and I haven't had a night out on the town in a while, so we figured we'd go tear it up like the old days."

"Cal, be normal," Iris said.

"Do you take the train?" Cal asked.

"Friday afternoon," I replied, stealing some more rose petal jam for my baguette.

"Cool, I was gonna go on Saturday, but I'm sure my mom would love it if I showed up a day early, and a little company on the train is nice. If that's cool, I mean."

My mood was already the best it'd been in a while, and his awkward self-invite made it surge even further.

As the sky turned cotton candy colors and the air got a little less suffocating, Cal and Iris lay against each other on the blanket. He ran a hand through her hair. The noise of everyone else at the park came into focus—the joggers, the cyclists, the cheers from the baseball field nearby—and the three of us fell quiet, watching the clouds. I was starting to wonder how long this would go on for, but I was comfortable, and I wanted to see how quickly my statement would cause them to spring like a jack-in-the-box. I was so ready for them to start talking that I'd already started composing the article in my mind.

Cal and Iris were going to break up. Then they didn't.

The summer before college starts is riddled with the casualties of high school romances. Some couples survive the minefield of long-distance dating and opposing ambitions, some only think they can.

Other people on the field packed up their blankets and their books and Frisbees and went back to their lives. The joggers dwindled, the tourists disappeared. A breeze picked up.

"When does it start?" Iris asked.

"When does what start?" I asked, but too softly and Cal spoke over me.

"Technically, it already has. They say the best hours to view it are right before dawn."

"Cal! My parents will kill me."

"Don't worry, we can leave as soon as we see one."

"And how long's that going to take?"

"Well, we are in one of the brightest cities on Earth, it's a bit cloudy out, and there's a half-moon tonight, so chances are we're not gonna see a damn thing. But you've never seen one, and you've always wanted to. While I still hold the title of Guy Trying to Bring You Joy, I'm not going to let a meteor shower pass us by without you being around to witness it."

"I have questions," I said.

"Oh right." Iris sat up, reaching for a handful of kettle chips. "I forgot to mention, there's a meteor shower happening tonight. You wanna stick around for it?"

"Um," I said because I wanted to shout "Yes" for six full seconds but wanted to be cool about it, and also probably had to check the time and come up with some excuse for my mom as to why I wasn't coming home yet again.

"Come on," Cal said, propping himself up on his elbows. His hair was messy from lying down, sticking out in the back in two perfect cowlicks. Iris noticed too and tried to comb them down with her hand. "It'll be fun." When his hair refused to comply, Iris chose to instead muss it up some more, and he grabbed at her wrist with a chuckle, his fingers crawling to hers to clasp around them.

I know this is a weird thing to say, but it felt so good to be just near their love. It was complicated, sure. Doomed to end up like mine and Leo's, maybe. But it just felt good to be near them. To be in the presence of a love like that.

I smiled and pulled my phone out of my bag, to text my mom that I was crashing at my cousin Cindy's tonight. "I'm in."

14

LIKE THE MOVIES

I woke up early to Cindy and her roommates getting ready for the day. The smell of coffee was in the air, and I had a vague notion that I'd had a dream about Cal and Iris, though I couldn't recall any details from it.

I already had six missed calls and three poorly spelled texts from my mom telling me to call her as soon as I woke up and that I was an awful sister for leaving Jase alone. What my mom probably meant to say was that I was an awful daughter for having escaped the tight clutches of her umbilical cord.

After calling to assure my mom that I was alive and had no plans to abandon the family, I joined Cindy and her roommates Melissa and Sal in the kitchen. Melissa had been up last night to let me in, and now she asked what I was doing in Central Park until 2:00 a.m. I wanted to tell them, but I thought the details might be a little hard to explain to anyone other than Pete, so I just said I was working on a writing project and left it at that. They shrugged and went on with their morning routines, which was great, but left me with the urge to talk about the previous night.

Okay, so Cal and Iris hadn't quite unloaded on me the way I'd been hoping, but I'd gotten to see more of their relationship, enough to write about. I'd even written out something on my phone in the middle of the night: He turns and kisses Iris on her temple, which is the most appropriate word for a body part that Cal can imagine, since the place it occupies feels sacred. What a thrill it is to have someone to kiss every day, someone to watch the skies with, someone to treasure, someone whose happiness is at least as important as your own.

Not quite the makings of a relationship column, especially since I'd taken the liberty to go into Cal's perspective. Fiction, basically. And a little cheesy. Still. I woke up with the thrill of writing inside of me. I didn't care that it was Friday and I still didn't have my column written, or even a backup plan. The writer's block wasn't quite unblocked, but at least I'd written *something*. I didn't even need their permission, really, if I changed the names.

I poured myself a bowl of cereal, and texted an assurance to my mom that I'd see her at Penn Station before Jase and I headed off to Princeton. Then I chewed happily, a little exhausted but thrilled to be hanging out in the kitchen with Cindy and her roommates. They had already graduated from college but the whole morning had such a college-y vibe to it, or at least what I imagined college would be like, and it made me excited that I'd be going off to college in the fall.

Sal kept glancing at Cindy, and I wondered if anything was going on between them, even something unrequited. The whole world is mad with love, I realized. All the time, if they're not in the midst of it, everyone is seeking it out or hoping for it or recovering from it or looking for a better one.

I worked my morning shift, mostly bored out of my mind because Pete wasn't there. I tried texting him, but he wasn't the most efficient responder, and I couldn't always have my phone on me at work, so I had to keep myself entertained, which almost took the wind out of my I-wrote-something sails. Thankfully, my imagination kept going through my upcoming train ride with Cal, and I thought about how maybe just one more conversation would crack my writer's block. I still didn't have quite enough to comprise a good column without slipping into fiction, and if I fictionalized anything Hafsah would fire me quickly and ruthlessly, like a literal fire. So I needed just a little more.

After work I went straight to Penn Station to meet up with Jase and take the train to Jersey. A bunch of other divorcelings were huddled by the schedule board with their weekend packs. I'd noticed that more kids came into the city on weekends to spend time with their dads, but there was a good group of us that made the trek out to the suburbs every now and then. Mom was always more of a city girl, having grown up in Manila, and after the divorce, Dad had fled back to Jersey and the quiet he'd always been more comfortable in.

Mom had accompanied Jase to the station, bringing a bag full of clothes for me and several complaints about my life choices. After she kissed us goodbye at the platform, I pulled out my book and settled onto the floor near Jase, scanning the crowd every now and then looking for Cal.

Eventually I fell into my reading, thinking maybe Cal was a late-person who might show up right before the train pulled away. I felt some weirdo take a seat right next to me and ignored him as best as I could, but then the creep had the chutzpah to scoot closer, so that our legs were almost touching. Fuming, I had to keep rereading the same paragraph over and over again, until finally I decided to speak my mind. Granted, I suck at confrontation, but I give a solid stink-eye, and I figured that would be good enough.

When I put my book down though, I saw that it was Cal, and he was smiling like an idiot. "Wow, that took way longer than I thought."

I closed my book over my finger, responding with my own idiotic smile (to be honest, I don't have many other kinds). "Long time no see," I said, which is a stupid thing people say to each other when they've seen each other recently.

"How is this?" He gestured to my book.

"So far so good."

He leaned forward to take a look at Jase, who had a unique talent for concentrating on whatever was in front of him. I have no idea what he's going to be when he grows up, but, man, is he gonna be a good one. Unless it involves multitasking. Then he's gonna be only partly good.

The train pulled into the station just then, rumbling a few newbies to their feet. The rest of us knew an onslaught of people coming into the city for the weekend were going to take their sweet time and we stayed out of the way. Jase didn't even glance up.

Cal smiled and nodded, then put his knees up and wrapped his arms around them, looking out at the passengers. "How late did you guys stay last night?" I whispered, hoping Jase wouldn't hear me and deduce something he could blackmail me with at a future date.

"Sunrise," Cal said, smirking, but trying to hide it.

I caught myself staring at the side of his face. I wanted to ask him everything about the night but wasn't sure that was a conversation I was ready for. Then he pulled a book out of his bag and started reading, so I tried to do the same, though I kept thinking he was glancing over at me and couldn't focus on a word I was reading. After a few minutes the platform cleared and we boarded the train.

Cal walked behind me and Jase and helped us put our bags

in the overhead bins, since I'm tiny and, even though Jase seemed like he was huge to me, he was still only thirteen and couldn't lift his bags without struggling. I plopped down into a window seat, expecting Cal to say bye, but instead he hoisted his own bag over his head, his T-shirt coming up a little and giving me an unexpected glance at his stomach. It was just an inch of stomach or so, nothing of any note, but I caught sight of a faint trail of hair leading up to his belly button.

I turned to look out the window but saw only the tunnel wall and my reflection. Then I felt Cal's weight sink into the seat next to me. Jase was sitting across the aisle, looking for an outlet beneath the seats to plug his phone charger into.

The train started moving, and one of those train guys came by to check our tickets. He punched holes in them without ever looking at our faces. Cal stretched his legs out. We each opened our books, but I found myself rereading the same sentence again. I closed the book, and even though Pete and I have a golden rule never to disturb someone reading, I just couldn't help myself. "Do you and Iris do stuff like that all the time?"

Cal furrowed his brow. "Like what?"

"Picnics at Central Park, watching a meteor shower until dawn. Crazy romantic stuff that people in real life don't do."

He thought for a moment, setting his book down on his lap. "I don't know. I don't think we're all that different from other relationships."

I rolled my eyes. "I'm not the most romantically experienced person in the world, but I do write about relationships. Semiprofessionally. And I'm here to tell you, you are. No one does that. My ex and I once went out for a sit-down sushi dinner, and that was about the pinnacle of our romance." I paused as a couple walked down the aisle wearing huge traveler backpacks with straps flapping all around. I wondered if what I'd said was true. Surely, Leo and I had done something more romantic than that. Nothing came to mind, but I made a mental note to dig deeper into my memories. "Oh, and once we picked a rom-com on Netflix and held hands the whole way through, reaching for popcorn with our free hands."

Cal laughed and sat up straighter. "I think people want to be more romantic. They just keep themselves from being romantic because they don't know that it's actually pretty easy to do stuff like that. All you have to do is open the door."

"Open the door?"

"Yeah, it's this thing I think about often. It's from a story called 'Light of Lucy' by Jane McCafferty. There's this quote Iris and I love about how we all have just one life and every night is numbered and could be more like the movies if only we opened up our hearts, not all the way or all the time, but like you open the door for a cat, just enough to let it out into the open air."

I stared at him. "See? Who does that? Who quotes stories all the time? Both of you have done that already and I've barely even hung out with you guys."

"You don't love quotes?"

"Of course I do, but I can never work them into conversation that easily. Or remember a whole freakin' paragraph." I totally do and can, but it was fun to have a little outburst anyway. It felt justified.

The train came aboveground at that point, the darkness cut by the Manhattan skyline reflecting off the clouds and making the whole sky look orange. Jase was asleep in his seat, his phone dead in his lap. Someone a few rows away was listening to music loud enough for us to hear.

"I'm sorry I'm being weird," I said. "But now you see why I want to write about you, right? You guys do open that door, instead of all of us schmucks who just watch other people do it in movies."

"What do you mean write about us?" Cal asked.

I frowned. "Iris didn't tell you?"

The train screeched to a halt, sending Cal's book tumbling to the ground. He reached down for it, his arm brushing past my leg. A few of the divorcelings got off, their bags bumping into the backs of seats. Jase woke up and asked me if he could borrow my phone, and by the time I'd turned back Cal was looking out the window and it felt like too much time had passed to nudge him about it.

The car lurched forward again, and we stayed quiet all the way to the next station, which was a repeat of the last. A handful of people got off, most of them recognizable divorcelings.

Cal smacked his book into the palm of his other hand, the noise pulling me from my thoughts. "So, you should come to my friend's party tomorrow night," he said, as if the book-smack had obviously been a way to end the conversation.

"Uh, I don't know if my dad will let me." I'm not great at parties. I go to the corner and start writing in my head and I either get all quiet and judgy, or I come up with something good and have to write it into my phone, then everyone thinks I'm an antisocial jerk.

"Okay, I'll talk to him. I'm good with parents. What side of town does he live on?"

"Palmer Square. But, seriously, my dad usually likes us to spend the whole time together. He hands us itineraries when we walk in the door. There's no way he'll let me go to a party with someone he's never met."

"Don't worry. The party's super close to that area. I'll convince him." He pulled his phone out of his pocket and leaned into his seat, putting a foot up on the armrest in front of him.

"Iris says you should come," he said, showing me the conversation which had somehow been going on this whole time.

"Okay," I said, not really believing I'd go to the party.

The rest of the train ride, Cal read from his book, occasionally pausing to text Iris. I stared out the window, watching New Jersey towns go by. I usually couldn't stand being on the train without reading or listening to music, but I was strangely at peace, happy with my thoughts.

We got to Princeton and Cal helped us with our bags again, and then he took off to catch a bus. "I'll text you when I'm on the way tomorrow," he called back.

A few moments later our dad showed up wearing his typical khaki pants and royal blue blazer. He gave us one of his patented awkward hugs, Jase first and then me. It started as a side hug, then about a second into it he decided it was too impersonal and went for the full hug. But he assumed that as teenagers we'd be embarrassed by it, so he did it halfheartedly. I missed the hugs we used to get. The ones that felt like he'd spent the whole week missing us. Then he asked about the train ride, like he always does, despite the fact that we have never once answered in an interesting way.

"It was okay," Jase and I both said. Dad picked up my duffel bag but made Jase carry his own, and then we walked toward his car. I kept expecting him to purchase a midlife-crisis sports car, but it was still the sensible sedan he'd had for years. My dad was too broke and responsible for a midlife crisis, it seemed. It would have been sweet to have him unexpectedly fall into some college-tuition-level dough, but apparently Dad was "happy at his position," which is adult for "I have failed to buy into the American ideals of always wanting more money."

We went out for dinner at the one Filipino place in town—Dad's ongoing way to either poke fun at Mom's Italian food obsession, or his way to keep close to her, I'm not sure. These dinners usually consisted of Dad catching up on our lives at school, but because it was summer both of us had very little info to provide.

"How's the writing going, Lu? Is there any more paperwork I need to fill out for the scholarship?"

Ugh. I hadn't even thought of the scholarship in a while. For the past week, whenever my panicky thoughts came, they were still all about Hafsah and blank pages, and they'd been quickly repressed by good cheer and fantasizing about how incredible my eventual Iris and Cal column would be. "It's, uh, yeah. Going well. I pitched this idea for a series to my editor, and she was really into it."

"Taking initiative, way to go. When's it publishing?"

"Er." I stabbed at a comically large piece of chicken adobo and shoved it into my mouth with a little side of rice. "Shmomoni shmoon," I said.

"Dad, she's so weird," Jase said. "You think I'm kidding, but this is how it is, like, all the time."

"Right." My dad smiled politely. A lifelong academic, he was thrilled for me when my writing led to school opportunities, especially since his lack of tenure meant he had no sway and no money. He loved hearing the details of *Misnomer*, the process I went through with Hafsah, how many views each of my columns got. He especially loved hearing about my scholarship. The writing itself he never really asked about. It probably made him uncomfortable. And I don't really have any complaints. I think I've used the word *boner* two or three times throughout my career. "Well, I'm proud of you, hon. Do I say that enough?"

"Shmo shmuch," I said, still chewing.

"Good. Just want to hammer that point home. I couldn't be prouder of all you've done, and all you're going to do." He smiled, and I think I may have seen a tear glimmer in his eye.

Which meant that for the rest of the evening—as we finished our meal and headed home, sat in our usual spots in the living room, tried to remember whose turn it was to pick a movie to watch, went about watching that movie, talked about it when the credits rolled, talked about plans for the next day, said good-night, and finally went our separate ways—I was screaming internally, watching my life teeter on the brink of some nameless abyss, all of it about to fall apart.

15
ATMOSPHERIC PRESSURE

The next morning I woke up to an email from Leo. Well, I woke up to the desire to pee, but then when I got back to bed I checked my email and saw Leo's name in my inbox for the first time in weeks. And right next to it was the subject line: Do you know that I still... And then the character limit cut it off so I couldn't see how the sentence ended.

It's a terrifying thing, seeing an email from an ex. Especially when you were kind of managing not to obsess about them lately. Kind of. I stared at it for a long time, wondering if I really wanted to read the message. All day, really, I'd look at my phone and wonder how the thought ended.

Hey, Lu, do you know that I still inexplicably hate sea salt and vinegar chips?

Hey, Lu, do you know that I still really like Nic Cage movies? All of them. A lot. Anyway, have a good day.

Hey Lu, do you know that I still am the most comfortable person on the planet, even though you don't get to experience it, and probably never will again, since I ended things over four weeks ago and haven't changed my mind at all? Do you know that I still feel exactly the same way I did the day I dumped you? Just checking. Best, Leo.

But, out of bravery or fear, I'm not sure which, I left the email in the bold font of the unopened. Which was a pretty freaking impressive accomplishment, because for most of the day I had my laptop and my phone directly in front of me. I needed to write. I needed what I knew about Cal and Iris to come flowing into my fingertips and onto the page where I was at my best. I needed to forget about Leo.

Pete
How's the writing going?

I needed Pete to shut up.

In the afternoon, Dad said he had to go take care of some errands, so I had him drop me off at a coffee shop near the university. Watching people flow in and out of a coffee shop usually helped stir my creative juices. I brought earphones with me to help me resist the temptation to eavesdrop, and as soon as I had set myself up, I looked up as many writer's block cures as the internet could provide:

Inspirational quotes, advice from some of my favorite authors, ten minutes of freewriting (which resulted in mostly gibberish, but one really great paragraph about what kind of homeless person I'll be in my desolate future), taking a walk (twice around the block), stepping away from my writing to do anything else (probably hadn't earned that one yet). Nothing worked.

The only strategy that felt slightly good was bashing my fingers up and down on the keyboard as if I were killing a whole slew of spiders, and resting my forehead on the table and making slight whimpering noises. Which definitely made me look like the most with-it person at the coffee shop. But it wasn't quite as productive as I'd hoped. How the hell had I gotten to this point in my life? Why had I even accepted the terms of the scholarship? I should have, like, haggled or something.

I composed several texts to Iris, begging her to change her mind and let me interview her, but deleted all of them before sending.

Another ESP-level text from Pete came in.

Pete
I think you're going to have to write about yourself, Lu. Just send something in. It doesn't even have to include Leo's perspective, so you don't have to interview him. Didn't Hafsah tell you to write yourself into the pieces anyway? Start with yourself. The rest, whether it's the lovebirds or not, can come later.

Lu
Your texts are entirely too long

Pete
Trying to help. Not sure how else.

I groaned.

Lu
I know. Sorry. We'll talk later.

I got myself another coffee, used the bathroom, returned to my little self-made hell. It should have been a breeze to write about myself. Just tap into how it felt when I saw Leo's name in my inbox again.

I thought about the day after the breakup. I'd had to work

at the theater, which had felt like an unnecessarily cruel blessing. I didn't want to be in public and every moment of it hurt, but I was grateful for all those moments away from my own brain. From the fact that Leo had ended this thing that had been so good.

I remember scooping popcorn into a bucket for a customer that day, my mind lost in the soft swish of the kernels hitting the steel scooper. It sounded like Leo tossing in his sleep, a sound which I thought was going to increase in my life, not suddenly cease. For good reason too. He'd said the words to me.

"One day, we'll be able to do this freely," he had said. It was weeks before the split, an afternoon nap we used to take too many of, forcing ourselves into sleep in the yellow light of day, since our parents didn't allow sleepovers and we weren't going to abstain completely.

He'd said the words into the back of my neck as we spooned, the position in which all the best things get said. "You think we're happy now, just you wait."

"Oh yeah?" I'd rubbed my nose on his forearm to scratch an itch, then let my lips rest against his skin. "How so?"

"Well, for one, we'll be done with school."

"You love school."

"Yeah, but we'll finally have enough free time to record our R & B album," Leo had said. "And once it goes platinum, our parents will come to terms with the fact that our adult lives have arrived and they'll stop freaking out at the idea of us lying down together behind a closed door."

"So in this scenario, we are platinum-selling artists and still live in our parents' tiny Chinatown apartments, but they're now okay with us having sex."

"They've matured so much, haven't they? I'm proud of them."

"Are we still going to college?" At that point we hadn't talked about it yet, and I'd tried to toss the words out casually, broaching the subject because I was hoping that doing so wouldn't ruin the moment but only increase its joys.

"Don't be silly, we have an international tour to go on. We'll be spooning in five-star hotels."

After a couple of hours swimming in memories like that at the Princeton coffee shop, my dad picked me up and we headed back home. *Do you know I still want to go on an international R & B tour with you?*

As promised, Cal showed up at my dad's that night. He'd texted me to get the address, and told me to pretend not to know anything about the party. By the time he showed I was ready to get out of my head for a bit, to surround myself with the distractions a party had to offer, to stop actively resisting opening Leo's email.

Cal knocked politely. He was wearing his usual skinny jeans with a button-down plaid shirt over a plain gray T-shirt. His timing couldn't have been better, as Dad was busting out the Scrabble. Look, I have nothing against Scrabble. But there's something despairing about playing it with your family on a Saturday night.

Dad, bless his optimistic heart, thought I'd invited Cal over to play with us. His face lit up when I introduced them. "I always say this game is best with four people playing," Dad said, setting down the board on the dining room table. "Maybe you'll finally lose," he said to me, winking. Winking is the weirdest thing in the world, and no one should do it, especially not middle-aged men.

"Absolutely!" Cal said, before I could argue.

My dad looked thrilled. Jase looked like he did not care how many people were at the table playing as long as the game was over within three minutes or so and he was allowed to return to something with a screen. Cal took a seat, and I just stood there, figuring Cal was buttering up my dad a little, but still not wanting to stay at the house any longer.

I suppressed a sigh and took a seat, hoping I'd be strong enough to resist opening the email even longer. Meanwhile, Cal made small talk with my dad expertly. Jase played the first word: *but*. My dad wrote down the score. "At least we have one literate person in the family," he chided, though Jase didn't care enough to be insulted.

Cal laughed politely. He was pretty good at Scrabble but he was much better at putting on the good kid routine. My dad's not really the overprotective type. Truth be told, he was probably thinking that Cal and I were dating or something, and might have been secretly thrilled about it. I never talked about Leo with my dad, he might not have ever heard the name.

Halfway through the game I was up by a decent amount, which made everyone think harder about the words they were playing, which made the game go excruciatingly slowly. And that was when I finally caved and opened Leo's email.

It was a mistake to do that.

Hey Lu, do you know that I still love you? Thought maybe you should know.

I closed the email, reopened it, closed it again. I wanted to throw my phone across the room but also hug it to me.

For the rest of the game, I had to be reminded it was my turn and played only three-letter words. When we were finally done, I looked eagerly at Cal to make our break, and he seemed to catch on that I was not looking to stick around. He told my dad that we were meeting some friends of his for a movie night.

"I'll have her back before midnight," Cal promised.

We walked quietly in the warm night, our steps loud on the sidewalk until we turned a corner and hit a strip of college bars that drowned out the sound. "Everything okay?" Cal asked.

"So, what's this party we're going to?" I said, pretending I hadn't heard him. "Another Scrabble party, I hope."

"Funny," Cal said, nudging me with his shoulder. "Just a couple of guys I went to high school with. Should be pretty low-key."

Now, in reality, there was about ten minutes of mild-mannered walking and about twenty more after we walked into the crummy frat house before the party really got going. But in a movie they would have totally smash-cut to the scene I saw not all that much later: a group of dude-bros each carrying a case of beer and an iguana on their shoulders. That's four cases of beer and four iguanas. For one party. That's an unreasonable ratio of iguanas to beer, especially in the northeast.

The music got loud, and by extension so did everyone else at the party. The hot tub in the backyard was uncovered and promptly filled up with guys eager to take their shirts off, maybe in the hope that the handful of girls at the party would too. The other girls at the party seemed just as uninterested as I was in joining a six-person hot tub with twelve dudes in it.

Cal and I grabbed some beers, and while I had a strong desire to go off to the corner and watch the madness ensue from afar, Cal ushered me around the party saying hi to a couple people. He was staying with his friends Johnny and Raul, but had clearly made more friends since his arrival.

It was a distraction, exactly what I needed to keep myself from repeating Leo's email in my head all night, or even worse: responding. I did not trust myself to say anything coherent or sane, much less something that I would feel good about having said in the morning. My first instinct was to gush back, tell him everything that I'd been planning on telling him at the bench that day, and all those other times before. Then what though? He hadn't written anything about getting back together. Could I handle another instance of him not showing up, emotionally or otherwise?

Since I didn't have that skill some people seem to have for being able to hear things when the music is too loud, I mostly sipped from my beer and nodded while Cal chatted with his friends. I didn't really drink often, so I tried to pace myself, but when you're just being quiet and listening as best you can to a conversation that's being drowned out by a bassline, it's hard to keep track.

The frat house was run-down. I'm getting ahead of myself here. It was a *frat house*. Greek letters were plastered all over the place, numbering almost as many as the stains on the gray carpet. The only person I even slightly knew was Cal, who was still somewhat of a stranger, though one whose love life I felt completely immersed in lately. In the moment that didn't make any sense to me. There were drinking games to my left, dudes dancing like idiots to my right, and here I was obsessed with a relationship that wasn't even mine. I looked over Cal's shoulder as he talked casually with a group of girls, seemingly impervious to the music.

A half hour into the party I'd reread the email about seventeen times. Do you know that I still love you?

No, goddamn it, Leo. I did not know that.

Because he hadn't talked to me in weeks, and the last time he had, save for one stupid, heart-wrenching exchange when I was at work and he was my customer, was when he told me he didn't love me enough to stay with me, in so many words.

Why now?

I drank more from my beer and read the email and thought back to our 0.9% of a life together. I thought about how many times he'd said something as sweet and charming as he had in this weeks-too-late email that contradicted all of his actions.

It was hard to count, because it felt like a time in my life so far-removed from the present, but maybe also because of the beer. But as I stood there in a darkened frat house, surrounded by freakin' iguanas and conversation, I thought to myself that it hadn't been enough. And suddenly I was angry. I felt like Leo hadn't meant a word of his email, but had only missed me for a moment, had only felt the guilt of his actions and thought a stupid confession like that would help.

I felt like I was a receipt that had stayed in Leo's pocket too long; proof of something he once thought worthwhile but no longer needed. What I really needed to do was text Pete. He would get me through this.

Except when I tried to do that, I just ended up reading the email another eight million or so times and stewing.

I decided to put my phone away and see what else the party had to offer. Wandering away from Cal, I stepped through the door that led outside. Immediately one of the hot tub dudes beckoned me over to the steaming cauldron of germs and general grossness.

I thought about Cal and Iris at Central Park the other night, thought about how good those months with Leo had been when they were good, and how quickly it had all gone away. Could either of those relationships ever come from me allowing myself to be beckoned into a hot tube by some dude at a frat party? Maybe I'd throw caution to the wind. Just kiss the first cute boy I saw. Not in the hot tub, of course. But some other more presentable cute boy. I looked around the party but my eyes didn't really land on anyone. My beer was empty all of a sudden, so I put the can down and went hunting for another.

Oh, look. There was one. Not a beer. A cute boy. He was

leaning against the wooden pillar of the little hand-built-patio thing they'd put the hot tub on. White T-shirt and blue jeans, sneakers that had somehow managed to stay clean at the party. He had dark brown skin and a small afro, a silver bracelet on his left wrist. He looked bored, but in a content way. Like he understood boredom was transient and a part of life and he was just patiently waiting for someone to come along and pull him out of it. I could be that person. I'd wait for eye contact and then just strut my little self confidently over there and kiss him, forgetting about Leo entirely. I'd take him by the hand and say something, like... I don't know. Something really...mmph! It would come to me.

Oh no, he'd looked at me. Dead on, eyes-on-eyes, pupils, irises the whole thing. Had he smiled too? Holy shit, that was intimidating. I was definitely not going over there and kissing him. Who the hell did things like that?

I went back inside, running from my embarrassment, and found another beer in the fridge.

Scanning the room, I spotted Cal talking to yet another group of people. I felt my phone in my pocket, the email basically poking me in the thigh, like Jase used to do when he was smaller and wanted attention. Not to be outdone by an email, the fact that it was Saturday and I had another deadline on Monday exploded into my mind too, burning a hole in my thigh. Or the thigh part of my anxiety. Anxiety is human-shaped, therefore has thighs, right?

Maybe I'd had enough beer.

I checked my phone, reread the email.

Okay, one more beer and then I'll go, I thought to myself. *I'll stay up all night writing about myself, fueled by beer and the terrifying proximity of my deadline. Catharsis after catharsis will find me in the middle of the night, bathed in only the gentle glow of my computer screen, the way all brilliant writing happens.*

There was a cute Asian guy on the couch, but his face was zoned in on his phone. I pictured him reading an email from an ex too, feeling the same things I was feeling. Does love ever come up from two people just trying to stick it to someone that's left them behind? If not love, I'm sure there had been good make-out sessions founded on just that. Except I kept looking over in his direction and trying to catch his eye, but he was only interested in his phone.

I didn't know what I had expected from that party. A distraction from thinking about love and its absence in my life? Time spent with Cal? Normal teenage behavior? Then I felt that unique tingle of my cheeks going into blushing-drinking mode, looked around the party, and realized I was tipsy.

I'd only been at that stage a couple of times before, and I'd forgotten how downright pleasant it could be, at least physically. I looked over at the guy on the couch and he actually looked back. I wanted to smile at him but I guess I wasn't quite there yet. I drank a little more.

Now, I'm not one to condone teenage drinking or anything. But at that moment? I was ready to condone the hell out of it. If I drank a little more, maybe I'd even be able to smile at Couch Guy. I should have really texted Pete already. Pete was great. He'd talk me through this party. He'd convince me to delete Leo's email before I could respond to it, before it burrowed itself into the scars that had somewhat healed, ripping them apart anew.

I pulled my phone out and sent him a message, waiting for the ellipsis that said he was writing back. Meanwhile I took another sip from my beer and watched the party, this time not scanning for cute boys, or being too judgmental of bathtub bros, just watching the sight of a hundred or so people interacting. Five minutes later Pete hadn't even checked my message yet, but I was feeling all warm and chatty, so I found Cal and worked my way into the little circle he was standing in.

This took a little work. First, I stood by and waited for him to notice and open up the circle. When that didn't work, I tried to catch what they were talking about and chime in with my own comment. But they were talking about some people they knew, and so I just pretend-laughed whenever they laughed. Then I realized I wasn't sure what my real laugh sounded like, so I had to practice laugh a few times, which is what finally made Cal notice I was there.

"Are you drunk?" Cal asked.

"Probably," I conceded when I caught my breath from my practice laughter.

Cal and I stood quietly for a while, watching the party unfold. An uncomfortably grindy dance party had broken out, the music getting even louder than it was before. Several couples around the party were deep into make-out mode, the beer pong table was surrounded by people who seemed to have a moral imperative to high-five every eight seconds.

Cal leaned in so I could hear him over the music, his mouth close to my ear. "How do you feel at parties?"

I tilted my head at him, then leaned in to him, our shoulders touching as I shouted to be heard. "Awkward and buzzed. Why do you ask?"

"You don't feel this deep curiosity about everyone? Like, this amazement that humanity is a thing that exists in the world, and that you get to be surrounded by it?"

"Cal, there are literally six dudes peeing against the fence in the backyard, and another one passed out in the dirt."

Cal turned to look and laughed. "Still."

Somehow, this led to us deciding we'd go around the party talking to as many people as possible and introducing each other as someone else every time.

The first few attempts went horribly, since I was still in quite the giggly mood, and Cal tried to introduce me as his newly adopted sister, then as his newly adopted daughter, then as an extraterrestrial refugee that his family had taken in until the war ended on my planet. The last one didn't have much of a chance of fooling anyone, even without my giggling.

Cal pulled me aside as I recovered from my fit. "Come on, Lu," he said, a little giggly himself, but managing to put on a straight face. "You need to get it together. A lot is on the line here."

"Like what?"

Cal grabbed me by the shoulders and shook. "*Like what?* The joy of fooling someone!"

"That doesn't sound like a very honorable mission."

"It isn't!" Cal cried out, a smile breaking through. "But what of the memory of tonight? Remember, you have but one life, and this is one night in that one life." He pulled his hands away then gestured toward a couple that had just walked in. "Perfect. There are two people neither of us know, and who we won't ever see again. Now, what are we going to do?"

"Lie to them?"

"Exactly! We're going to bring fiction to life. Follow my lead."

He took off across the house and I followed behind, starting to get a little stumbly, but otherwise feeling great. The only thing on my mind now was not writing or Leo, but just this comparatively simple task of not giggling while lying to strangers.

Cal reached the couple and put his arm around the guy, who was tall and muscular, with one of those chiseled jaws that always make me think of action figures and cartoon superheroes. "Norton! So great to see you again."

"Uh, my name's not—"

"And, Matilda, darling! How are things?" Cal stepped away from the guy and gave two Italian air-kisses to the very confused girl. I stood by, focusing on not laughing the same way you try to resist a sneeze in class.

The couple got understandably wide-eyed. "You've got the wrong people, man. We're not—"

"Nonsense!" Cal said. He stepped over to me and put his arm around my shoulder. "Don't you remember us, old chap? We're the Kaminskys! The safari last year? Dar es Salaam?"

"We shared a tent," I said, not really knowing where the hell the improvisation was coming from. Maybe it was from Cal's arm on my shoulder, which gave me a little rush of warmth and joy. "The sound of hyenas kept us up at night, and we each confessed our secrets to each other, so that we wouldn't take them to the grave."

"What the hell?" the girl said, grabbing her boyfriend by the arm and trying to pull away from us.

Cal sidestepped and blocked their path. "You don't need to worry, Matilda. Your secret's been safe with us. No one will know about the homeless man you murdered."

"Or about your fear of chickens," I added, putting a reassuring hand on her shoulder, which she immediately shrugged off. "We haven't told a soul."

They made a few more evasive maneuvers around us, managing to sneak away, casting furtive glances back at us. "You gave us the best night of our lives!" I shouted.

When they disappeared into the crowd, Cal and I turned to each other and immediately burst into laughter. Then we decided that we probably didn't need to have any more beer, and that it was a good note to leave the party on. I stepped outside to get some fresh air while Cal went around saying bye to his friends. It was perfect out, unlike the mugginess of

Manhattan summer nights, a cool breeze blowing in through the trees lining the street.

The last time I'd had this much fun was with Iris, and I gave a quiet thanks to past me for being in the right place at the right time and meeting these two. They hadn't saved me from my writer's block, but they kept saving me from nights thinking about Leo. I hadn't even checked my phone in a while, and had no desire to now. A minute or so later Cal came out, stumbling a little bit and smiling widely.

"God, that was fun," he said.

"Yeah. It reminded me of being little." We walked down the driveway and turned in the direction of my dad's house. "Playing pretend. It's like childhood's one big game of improv that we lose the skill for when we hit puberty."

"At least the cringing sticks around," he quipped. "Kind of sad though. Why do you think that happens?"

I shrugged. "Hormones and society. I don't know." I laughed and looked up at the sky. There were way more stars out than there had been at the park that night, but I somehow felt like even if there was a meteor shower today too, we wouldn't be lucky enough to see any. Only Iris and Cal would. I glanced at Cal, a little surprised by how well we'd gotten along all night. "I like to think there's an unexpected explanation for it. Not something reasonable, like self-consciousness or social norms or anything like that. Something sillier."

"Like what?"

I thought for a while. "Piggyback rides."

Cal burst out into laughter, and I wanted him to keep on laughing the whole way back. "God, I love that idea. That if we just gave each other piggyback rides more often we'd find our inner children."

I didn't say anything. I was happy. Even if I knew part of it was the alcohol. Happiness is always chemically induced, whether the chemicals are naturally occurring in your head or ingested. I slowed down my pace, not just because I was swaying to the point that every now and then I'd bump into Cal, but because I wanted to prolong this walk back to my dad's. I didn't want the feeling to go away, didn't want to be alone at home, didn't want to think about Leo's admission that he still loved me.

"Give me a piggyback ride!" Cal shouted out suddenly into the night air.

I laughed. "Cal, my legs are so stubby they can barely support *my* weight. I don't think it's a good idea to load you on top. No offense."

"Okay," he said, undeterred, "then let me give you one. I'm sure giving a piggyback ride is as effective as getting one for the purposes of being a kid again. And if that doesn't make any sense, just pretend it does." He smiled, and his eyes were wide and gleeful. I like to think that, somewhere deep down, in whatever part of me was still sober, I knew it was a bad idea. I like to think that I hesitated, that I was at least initially responsible and intelligent, even if that wasn't the part of me that won out.

But the truth is that as soon as the words were out of his mouth, I was ready. I wasn't just ready. I was thrilled. The happiness I'd felt just a second before had in an instant multiplied, if happiness is a thing that *can* be multiplied. Whatever. There was more happiness than there was before. I was elated. I was thrilled. There was nothing in the world I wanted to do more than to jump on Cal's back and have him carry me down the street, laughing.

"That is such a good idea!" I cried out, even though—heavy-handed foreshadowing here—it wasn't.

We laughed into the night like a couple of cartoon villains, and then Cal turned his back to me, flexing his knees, ready to take my weight. I took a few steps back to get a running start, which made sense at that point. Like, I was short and I thought I needed that running start to jump high enough. I landed with my arms wrapped around his neck, his hands holding my legs on either side of him.

"Hold on," he said, and then he shifted a little, readjusting me on his back. My arms weren't all the way up on his neck anymore, but secured tightly against his chest. "That's better." He turned over his shoulder to look at me. "Ready?"

I nodded, holding on, feeling my heart pounding against his back.

"And away we go," he said, and he took off running.

The air rushed past me, like we were going way faster than we possibly could have. I pictured my hair flowing in the wind and closed my eyes for a second, basking in that breeze. When I opened my eyes again, trees were blurring on either side of us. We were either accomplishing impossible feats, or I was kind of drunk. A curb was coming up ahead, and I braced myself tighter against Cal. I became aware of my hands against his chest, the skin and rib cage that I could feel through his soft T-shirt.

Cal hopped off and landed without a problem, running on with another one of his doughy laughs. I let my chin drop to his shoulder. I could see a bead of sweat forming at his hairline, right behind his ear. I forgot about everything else and watched as it traced down his neck, around the curve of his collarbone, soaking into his shirt. Without a clue as to why the hell I was doing it, I leaned into him. Nothing obvious, but just enough so that our cheeks grazed against each other.

"Oh shit," he said, a breathless whisper. Then I felt us start to tumble forward, gravity tugging at us.

The next thing I felt was a shooting pain on the side of my face. I closed my eyes, dizzy, and when I opened them again

I saw Cal's head framed by trees and the New Jersey night. His face was drawn with concern.

"You're okay," he said, moving his hand to wipe hair from my face.

"How bad is it?"

"Not bad at all," he said. He took off the plaid button-down he was wearing over his T-shirt and bunched it up into a ball. Then he pressed it against my face, and the pain came to life again. I couldn't tell exactly where it was coming from.

"What happened?"

"I lost my balance. I'm so sorry."

I blinked a few times, and I could feel tears forming in my eyes. One of them scuttled down, focusing the stinging pain on my cheek.

"Come on. Let's get you home and cleaned up."

"Okay," I said. Then I let out a giggle. "You shouldn't piggyback under the influence."

He smiled, still dabbing his shirt at my face.

Then he helped me up and held my arm as we walked the ten blocks or so to my dad's house. I was dazed and in pain. I was worried about the fact that the pain was coming from my face, and how I would explain that to my dad. I was worried about permanent damage, scarring, a concussion. But Cal kept saying reassuring things to me, one arm around my shoulder, and it was helping. The tears were flowing, but it was more of a physical reaction than sadness or worry or panic. Somehow, a trace of the night's joys remained, and maybe that worried me too.

When we got to my place all the lights were off except for the one at the front entrance. Cal shut the door softly behind us. We went upstairs quietly to the bathroom connected to my room. I kept Cal's shirt against my face when I turned on the lights, not wanting to see the damage quite yet.

"Am I gonna freak out?" I asked him, lowering the shirt and motioning to the mirror without looking.

"Umm. I don't know if you're the freak-out type. I won't lie, it looks kind of bad. But I think maybe you should let me clean it up first. There's dirt and stuff that's making it look worse than it is."

I turned to the mirror, covering up the right side of my face again. That half of my reflection looked normal, aside from my eye being red from crying, which I guess shouldn't have been a surprise. I lowered my right hand and gasped inadvertently. There was a long scrape going from cheekbone all the way to my upper lip, bloody and flecked with dirt. The tip of my nose and my chin were bright red, and there was a deeper gash below my nose that was also bleeding.

Through the mirror, I saw Cal wince, whether at my pained reaction or at my face, it was hard to tell. "I thought you said it wasn't bad," I said, trying to keep my voice even.

"It's not. I really think it looks worse than it is."

I leaned in closer to the mirror, watching blood start to pool on my upper lip. There were little specks of gray in there too, like the force with which I'd hit the ground had guaranteed that I'd have a piece of that sidewalk with me forever.

The tears started flowing again, so I turned away from the mirror and sat on the lid of the toilet while Cal grabbed a washcloth and ran it under the tap. He kneeled down in front of me and tilted my head up by the chin.

"I'm never giving anyone a piggyback ride ever again," he said.

I managed to chuckle, tasting tears, but then he pressed the washcloth to my cheekbone and the pain shot through again. "Sorry if this hurts." He steadied my head with one hand as he kept cleaning off my cheek. His eyes were focused and concerned and a lovely shade of brown, tinged with yellow,

I now saw. Like autumn leaves. It did hurt, but I looked at Cal's eyes and it wasn't all that bad. It was hard to tell what I was more aware of: the sting of the scrapes or the light touch of his hand.

"Your elbow's bleeding," I said.

"I got off light." He dabbed the washcloth on my nose a few times then moved to my lip. "When I felt myself losing my footing I tried to turn so we'd land on our backs. I think I messed that up." He stood up and rinsed the washcloth off, then opened the medicine cabinet and rummaged through the bottles. "You have some really gross diseases, Lu."

"Shut up," I laughed, which made my face hurt more, which made me tear up again.

He took a seat on the edge of the bathtub this time, a tube of Neosporin in his hand. I watched him unscrew the cap, studied his fingers for the first time, followed them down to the sinewy length of his arms, faintly muscular despite his thinness. "Neosporin is the greatest thing on the planet," Cal said. "It'll make your face all better."

"Maybe we should put some on your face too, then."

He laughed and shook his head, then squeezed some of the ointment onto his finger. Then he paused and looked at me. "I'm sorry I slammed you into the ground." His eyebrows arched at that perfect apologetic angle, and I almost felt bad for how bad he felt.

"It was a stupid idea and you shouldn't have suggested it," I said. "But I agreed to it. Don't feel bad."

"Okay. I'm probably going to feel bad anyway, but I'm glad you don't hate me for it."

"No, I don't hate you. I actually had a really good time with you tonight. Before you assaulted my face."

He smiled, then brought his finger up to my cut lip and spread the Neosporin. Goose bumps tingled down my arms, and I tried not to shudder, though I wasn't sure if pain or relief was to blame. He had a light touch, caring. Was Iris constantly being touched like this? Constantly cared for, treated as precious, goose bumps tingling down her arms?

I braced myself for the familiar feeling of my cheeks reddening, but maybe they were already too red from the booze or the pain. Cal kept applying the ointment with a natural tenderness, and when he touched a spot that hurt, I reached out and put my hand on his leg, squeezing his knee. "Ow," I said, to distract him from what I was doing, or maybe to distract myself.

The atmospheric pressure in the bathroom increased.

Okay, I don't really know much about atmospheric pressure and how it works, or if it could shift based on the feelings of people in a room. But something increased. "So," I said, trying to get that something to return to normal. "I have a question. About you and Iris."

"Shoot," Cal said, still dabbing gently at my scrapes.

"Why break up? Why not let the relationship run its course? If it ends, it ends. But why force it?"

I take back my previous statement about atmospheric pressure not being affected by feelings. Because oh boy did that room get tense.

Cal didn't respond for a moment, his eyes clouding over with what could have been sadness or focus or just too many drinks. "I told her whatever I could so that we would stay together as long as possible."

Now it felt like there was a full-on storm brewing. Like, if for some reason my dad had a barometer in the bathroom, it would be going berserk right now. It's amazing the impact words can have on the feeling inside a room. For a moment it even felt like we should switch roles, like I should be tending to his wounds, instead of the other way around.

"I want to interview you," I blurted. Cal stopped for a moment, and we made eye contact. The house was so quiet otherwise, no city sounds like I was used to, the constant whir of life outside. Once the words were out it was all I wanted to talk about. "Iris seemed hesitant but maybe you could convince her that it's okay. I just think you guys have something special worth writing about. I could do it without your names, but I'd rather be allowed in."

Cal bit his lip while I talked, saying nothing, his eyes reddened by the beers and lack of sleep.

Maybe those same things were responsible for me continuing to talk. I told him about my writer's block, about eavesdropping being the only stand-in for writing since my breakup. Then I told him that I'd eavesdropped on their conversation outside The Strand. As soon as I said it, I braced myself for him to run out.

"That's why I found your wallet. I was there. But I swear that's just a coincidence. I am no creepier than what you've seen in person."

Thankfully, he laughed that comment off, which made me want to confess even more. So I told him about the scholarship too, and how I was probably going to lose it, since I didn't have a single thing written yet.

He paused, which confirmed my immediate fear that I'd unloaded too much and he was seconds away from sprinting, leaving a cartoonish human-shaped hole in the bathroom wall.

"I'll talk to Iris," he said, and I was shocked I'd ever felt fear that he would run.

We went to my dad's backyard with full glasses of water, sobering up, looking out at the leaves rustling lightly in the night breeze. Every now and then we turned to look at each other, maybe to check that we hadn't fallen asleep, maybe for other reasons, and we'd break out in laughter that we'd try to contain. Mostly, though, we were quiet. I tried not to think of the pain radiating from my face, tried not to think of anything at all. I just wanted to stare out at the dark with Cal, and watch the night cement itself into the past.

16
PROBABLY SWITCH GAMES

On the train back to the city, I took a window seat. My laptop was open, but any sentences I attempted sputtered halfway through, like cars breaking down and dying along the side of the road.

Cal was sitting next to me, his head lolling as the train rocked. Jase sat across the aisle, staring at his phone, every now and then casting strange looks my way. My face had healed surprisingly well, considering it hadn't even been a full day. Much better than I thought it would. All hail Neosporin.

Dad had wanted to rush me to the ER first thing in the morning, but I'd managed to calm him down, insisting that at the current rate, my face would look better than new in a matter of hours. My story had been that I had slipped on ice on the sidewalk. It was an awful excuse, because summer. But I spun a masterful tale about a careless restaurant and a very narrow cold front caused by an AC unit pointed in the wrong direction, and my dad had ended up calming down. Instead of going to the emergency room I had spent the rest of the day thinking about stuff other than my face.

Namely, Cal. His touch. The fact that he got my sense of humor perfectly. That damn doughy laugh. How I hadn't been able to stop watching his fingers or his eyes as he took care of me.

How much of last night had been shared, I wondered, and how much had I made up?

For the life of me, I tried to remember what I had been like with Leo, but it was as if the memories had been wiped out. Or not the memories themselves, since those were still popping up when I didn't want them to, the good and the bad alike, but who I was during those memories. What I'd actually felt. Had there been this much doubt, this much uncertainty? Had the joy always been tinged by something else, or was that just in the beginning?

Every now and then Cal's screen would light up with a notification, bringing to life the picture of him and Iris cheek-to-cheek that served as his background. I watched time tick away in the corner of my computer screen. I didn't need to read Leo's email again, its entire stupid contents were probably graffitied somewhere in the folds of my brain.

Do you know that I still love you?

What was I supposed to do with that? Return to a boy who'd fled?

On the train, back at home, at the coffee shop, at home again, I tried to write. Nothing. It was like some force field had been set up on my keyboard, or around my brain.

Pete
Dare I ask?

Lu
Please for the love of god don't. I'm broken.
Will you spare change when I'm homeless?

Pete
You're not going to be homeless, Lu.

Lu
I certainly won't be homefull.

Pete
That doesn't make sense.

Lu
SEE?!? I'm broken.

Pete
Want me to come over for a pep talk?

I sighed and told him that I probably shouldn't invite any more distractions, and that I'd talk to him after I'd sent in the column, or during the end-time, whichever came first. Moments later, another text came in.

Leo
Hey can we talk sometime

So much for avoiding distractions. Something in my chest fluttered, but I didn't feel the way I might have if the text had come a couple of days earlier. Before, I probably would have called Leo back right away, hoping to get my face on his face as soon as possible. But now my reaction was to let out a quasi-humanoid groan and put my head on my desk again. Which caused me to groan again, this time in physical pain, because of the whole piggyback accident.

A few seconds later there was a knock at my door. I looked up and saw Jase standing just inside my room. "Mom sent me to check on you. She's worried about the noises you're making and wants to know if you're hungry."

"Does she think I'm making those noises *because* I'm hungry?"

Jase shrugged, a video game controller still in his hand. "Should I say you're okay, then?"

"Sure, just make sure to mention that the fabric of my being is slowly unraveling and I will soon be a pile of mush, vaguely shaped like the human I once was."

Jase widened his eyes and stared for a second. "'Kay," he said, then started walking away. I called after him, sitting up. "Yeah?" he asked, reappearing in the doorway.

"Don't say those things."

"Yeah, I know. You were kidding."

"Oh. Sometimes it's hard to tell if you get me."

He shrugged again, the most thirteen-year-old expression there is. "Sometimes you're hard to get."

I nodded. "Fair enough." He turned to go again, but I called him back one last time. The controller in his hand was starting to shake. Withdrawals, probably. "I'm sorry, I just…" I trailed off, thinking that maybe he was far removed enough from my weird situation to be able to chime in with something helpful. Some bit of unexpected wisdom that would jar me into inspiration and productivity, saving me from myself.

"What's up?"

I turned to my computer screen. My Word document wasn't blank anymore, just littered with the corpses of false starts and random paragraphs that I didn't feel brave enough to delete. "What would you do if you were stuck and didn't know how to move forward?"

Jase looked down at his feet. "Like, physically? Is it glue? Or did I go into a small tunnel? Because if I was in a tiny tunnel I'd just die. That is the scariest thing I can imagine and screw you for putting that in my mind."

"Wow, you are more my sibling than I give you credit for." I shook my head, tried to put it in a way that Jase might understand. I ran a hand through my hair, fluffing it out the way Iris did. "Okay, so what if you were playing a video game and you were trying to get past this level. And you knew what you had to do, like, all the steps you had to take, the exact bad guys you had to shoot down. But you just couldn't beat it. And you've looked online and talked to all your expert buddies that have advice, but you still can't seem to get past it. No matter how hard you try."

My brother leaned against the door frame for a moment, looking lost in thought. He scratched his chin and made a face like he was hurting a little bit, which momentarily filled me with confidence that my unexpected-nugget-of-wisdom theory might actually play out, because he was looking solidly pensive. Then he shrugged and said, "I'd probably switch games."

I squinted at him, trying to find a metaphor in his response. He stared back, jiggling the video game controller more violently now. "That doesn't help me at all. I don't have another game to switch to. I could theoretically stop playing altogether, I guess, but quitting in this scenario has intense real-world ramifications."

"I don't know what we're talking about."

"Me neither!" I shouted, returning to my forehead-on-the-desk position a little too violently, sending shooting pains from my scrapes and bruises. And that's how I stayed for most of the evening. I gobbled down some lasagna Mom made, then went back to my room, slammed my face on the desk, stared at my computer screen, and stewed in my own uselessness.

Before going to bed, as my deadline approached single-digit-hours, I emailed Hafsah. It was the most concise thing I'd written in weeks. I'm sorry. I suck.—Lu.

When I woke up drenched in sweat and dread, I looked at my phone and saw that I had a missed call from the *Misnomer* offices. A creeping sense of shame oozed down my arms. Yes, oozed. I felt gross with regret. The thought of calling Hafsah back brought tears to my eyes. But I couldn't just leave her hanging. She'd been the first person who made me feel like I was a real writer. She'd given me a platform, given me readers, given me confirmation that I could really do it, not just for myself, in the privacy of my notebook.

I took a long sip of water, rubbing the sleep from my eyes. Then I sat up, trying to rouse myself into a semicoherent state by scrolling through various social media feeds. I had a handful of texts from last night I hadn't responded to, but I wasn't quite ready to dive into that can of worms. After some time, I clicked on Hafsah's name in my recently contacted list. Each time the phone rang it felt like the breath was getting sucked from my lungs. It rang four or five times, then finally there was that terrible click which told me I was going to have to speak.

"What happened, Lu?"

I was instantly choked up, which kept me from saying a single word. I bit my lip and looked out my window, trying to will away the tears. Unfortunately, my blinds were closed, and all I could see were little freckles of gray light, the hint of a cloudy sky. More time than I realized must have gone by, because eventually Hafsah broke my silence.

"Look, I'm sorry, but I'm gonna find someone else to take over your column. I wish I didn't have to, but I need someone who's reliable and—"

A sob escaped me, taking me by surprise. I hadn't known it would feel this way, hearing Hafsah say the words out loud. Like I was losing a part of myself. It felt like getting dumped.

It must have taken Hafsah by surprise too, because her speech trailed off, something which rarely happened. I looked around my immediate vicinity for a tissue, but couldn't find any. Somehow, Hafsah's silence only made me cry harder, and I lowered my head, hiding my face behind my hand.

It hadn't even been like this with Leo. We'd been in his

apartment, sitting on the fire escape like we sometimes did, watching the city while behind us his family argued over the sounds of the television. Leo'd been quiet and distant all day, something clearly off. It had taken him about fifteen minutes of beating around the bush, during which I had plenty of time to prepare for the actual words. When he said we should break up, I'd stood up so that I wouldn't be able to see him at all. After a couple of minutes, I shook my head, told Leo he was making a mistake, then stormed out, muttering a goodbye to his family, not a single tear shed to show my pain.

Now I couldn't stop the tears, and I knew that Hafsah wasn't making a mistake. I'd messed up, and this is what I deserved.

"Lu," Hafsah said, her voice all soft with concern.

"I'm sorry," I managed to eke out between my sobs. "You can hang up if you want. I know you're busy."

For a while I assumed she had. I slunk back into bed, not even thinking of my scholarship and my sudden inability to afford college. I was just thinking of my column, and how I'd miss the act of writing it every week. Going to the coffee shop, transferring my thoughts onto the page, tweaking them until they said exactly what I wanted them to say. The stupid, superficial, but absolutely wonderful moment when I'd check *Misnomer* to see my name up there. The "likes" and comment count rising, people tagging me on Twitter when they shared the column. More than all of that though, I was afraid. That it was gone: my ability to comprehend the world through my writing. That Leo had stolen *that* away from me too.

Then there was a loud intake of breath on the phone, and Hafsah spoke again. "One more week, okay, Lu? I love your writing and want you to stay with us, but I can't stretch it any more than that."

My breath caught. "Wait. What?"

"Just get me anything. It doesn't have to be what we talked about. But send me something. End of day Friday."

I blinked, the tears suddenly stopping. My blinds fluttered with a breeze, which sent a trickle of refreshing cool air through my room. "Really?"

"Last chance, Lu." She stayed on the line for a second, then hung up.

I dropped my phone in my lap and rubbed my eyes clean. Hafsah was too good for this world. I went to the bathroom and splashed water on my face, telling myself that I was going to take advantage of this second—er, third—chance.

I started by calling Pete and telling him the news. "I just wanted to let you know I'm not gonna waste this opportunity, and I want you to remind me I said that."

"Does that mean you're done obsessing over the lovebirds?"

"Probably not, but I'm not gonna try to write about them," I said. "I'm gonna take your advice and write about me and Leo." I hesitated, wanting to tell Pete about Leo's email, but not sure I was ready to talk about it. "There've been some developments. I can tell you at work though."

"Alright. And can we hang out after? I feel like I haven't seen you in several millennia."

"I don't think that's accurate," I said, the first smile of the morning creeping onto my face. I suddenly became excited about the day ahead. Working and shooting the shit with Pete, having him help me brainstorm, maybe even writing something out at work and getting his feedback. Still on the phone, I double-checked to make sure I had one of those pocket-size notebooks I could carry with me throughout the day, and plenty of pens in my bag.

"Pretty sure it is."

My phone buzzed in my hand. "Alright, dude, my phone's blowing up because I'm extremely popular and people clamor for my time. I'll see you at work." I figured it was a social media notification or something, or some follow-up pep talk from Hafsah, so after I hung up with Pete I went out to the living room and had breakfast with my mom and Jase. I only checked my phone again right before heading to work. It was a text from Cal.

Cal
You can write about us. You can interview us. Whatever you need, we're in.

At work, I found Pete in a projection room, changing over from one film to another. I walked up to him with my phone out, showing Cal's text message.

He stared at me, his eyes wide. "Whoa."

I thought he was reacting to the text message and so I nodded and smiled. "I know!"

"I'm talking about your face. Goddamn, Lu, that looks worse in person. How did it happen?"

"Oh that." I waved my hand. "Drunken piggyback ride, you know how it goes. It's healing quickly. But read this text."

"You're definitely gonna have to elaborate on 'drunken piggyback ride' in a sec." He turned his attention to my phone and read. Now, I wasn't exactly expecting an over-the-top reaction. I didn't need Pete to do somersaults and shoot confetti out of his butt or anything. But some overt expression of joy would have been nice. A smile or a high five or something. Instead he shuffled around the projection room, checking switches that we never had to look at before. "Interesting timing," he mumbled.

"Interesting my ass. This is perfect! I have their permission, right during my last chance. It's all going to be okay."

Pete brushed the hair out of his eyes and kept fiddling with the projector. "You said there were developments with Leo? He didn't do that, did he?" he asked, motioning at my face.

"What? No. It was Cal."

Pete nodded. "Right. I have no follow-up questions." He looked up at the official theater clock on the wall, then started the trailer reel and we headed out of the booth. "So, what happened with Leo?"

"I don't want to talk about Leo. I'm finally forgetting him and moving on from him, like you wanted. You should be excited for me."

"I am," he deadpanned. Oh, I got it. He was joking. We walked out into the theater lobby and saw Brad walking by, clipboard tucked under his arm. "Brad! We need responsibilities!" Pete called out.

"Hot dogs and popcorn," Brad called back, barely missing a beat before disappearing into the back office.

I belched a groan out as we shuffled our way to the concession stand. Throwing more hot dogs into a fake rotisserie thingy and reloading kernels and prepackaged popcorn into a machine wasn't the worst thing in the world, but we long ago decided it was the worst part of our jobs. Then I realized Pete wasn't joining me in the exaggerated parade of complaints we usually indulged in.

We fell into a silence, heavy only because of its timing. We'd never loaded the popcorn machine without making some sort of guess as to what they made the fake butter out of. "What do you think?" I asked. "Liposuction extractions, hippopotamus eye boogers, Saint Bernard drool?"

"Those are repeats," Pete muttered. He shut the glass door for the popcorn machine, then pulled out a package of hot dogs from the freezer. "What do you wanna do after work?"

"Er, did I not scroll down from that text message I showed you? Because there were more."

Pete pinched the bridge of his nose. "You're hanging out with the lovebirds again."

"You can come if you want!"

As Pete and I moved on to the second popcorn machine, we muttered a hello to our coworker Rahim, who was manning the one open concession register, a handful of people lined up waiting to be served. "I'm gonna be interviewing them for the article, so you'll totally be a fourth wheel, but it might help to have you there. I think you'll like them. Iris is doing a little photo shoot in Brooklyn, so at least it'll be a change of scenery."

Pete crossed his arms in front of his chest. He had his pouty face on. It wasn't a full pout, just a hint of sadness behind the eyes. I think it might be an Irish thing, pouting with your pupils.

"Don't get all broody on me. It's bad timing, but it's not like I'm spending every waking moment with them." Rahim turned over his shoulder at us, clearly hearing the conversation. I finished refilling the popcorn machine and lowered my voice. "You know how important this column is to me. Once the column is written, I promise we'll return to our regularly scheduled time-killing activities."

Pete nodded his head quickly, offering me a tight-lipped smile. "You're right. I'm happy for you. Not sure if I'll make the trek out to Brooklyn, but I'm glad you've got another chance." He sighed and uncrossed his arms, running a hand through his hair. "What game are we playing today?"

The Sound of Settling

BY LU CHARLES, NOVEMBER 21

What did couples do before movies and television were widely available from the comfort of your home, flashing from a computer screen set up in a bedroom while you pressed yourselves against each other?

I'm not being facetious here, I'm seriously asking. What did we do as a species to pass the time in the company of someone we loved? When the conversation dries up after months together—not entirely, obviously, not for good, but for now—and economic limitations prevent you from going out into the world, when the mental and physical onuses of senior year have taken their toll, and it's exhausting to do anything but lie around and be entertained by stories, what did couples do? Did they have to do anything? Do we?

I'm asking less out of a sincere interest in the dates of the past (no pun intended), but because, as my relationship has settled itself into comfort, I find myself wondering about options. I'm not knocking the Netflix-and-chill approach to modern romance. Few things sound more romantic to me. I've just been asking myself, is this all there is? Am I falling too deep into comfort and complacency?

When these thoughts float across my mind, it's hard for the questions to contain themselves to the literal. I start thinking that the questions are not just directed at the activities my boyfriend and I choose to partake in for our dates, but at the relationship itself.

I get a thrill when I see him for the first time in a few days after I've spent a weekend in New Jersey. I get a thrill when we fall asleep on one of these Netflix-and-chill dates and he wakes me up with a kiss on the temple. I get a thrill when I make a joke I'm sure is stupid enough to be grounds for a breakup and he responds with honest laughter, the sound rising up from his sexy belly, which juts out in a way that makes me think of teacup pigs.

But these thrills are few and far between now. Three months later, I don't keep myself awake all night texting him, thinking about him, writing him into my AP English essays just for the chance to talk about him. A natural part of the whole relationship thing, maybe. I've heard of this so-called honeymoon phase, and I think it's stupid to think feelings should lessen, even if I believe it's a real thing and a natural part of being a human.

Love that isn't thrilling is still love.

But thrills are nice too.

Maybe the only thing that happens to relationships as they go on, is that we forget that variety is the spice of life. We seek the same thrills from the start of the relationship, but those have been tired out, and don't provide the same jolt they used to. Or we've elevated those experiences in our minds, colored them gold with nostalgia, so that any new thrills that enter our lives feel lesser in comparison.

But there are new thrills to be found, right? We just trick ourselves into thinking that a relationship that has gone on for a while has tired them all out. We are blind to the possibilities because we're complacent.

What I'm saying is: I could find more thrills for me and my beau (ew, sorry, I won't repeat that term again) to partake in. From you, maybe. Thrills that you've tired of might hold some novelty for us.

Comment below with thrills you've experienced, so that someone (cough, cough) might try them out for herself.

17

OUT OF SHAPE

Cal and I stood leaning against a brick wall by the Dumbo waterfront while Iris walked around us, finding the best angle for the Brooklyn Bridge, with Manhattan coloring the background. It had been overcast all day, but a few rays of sunlight poked through the clouds now, as if the skies had parted just for Iris.

"Face looks good," Cal said. I started to blush, even though I knew what he meant.

"All hail Neosporin," I responded.

Iris waited for some tourists to step out of her shot. She was in another pinup-style dress, red with white polka dots. Again, I thought about how she seemed entirely at home in New York, but I could also picture her fitting into California perfectly. She moved through the world like she belonged in it.

I slipped my pen inside my notebook, where I'd been scribbling notes for the past hour or so. Not just my questions and their answers, but the way they looked at each other, how many times Iris reached out to put a hand on his forearm, anything they said that might have been an inside joke. I wanted to capture anything that could have been a key to answering why they survived and Leo and I had not.

"How'd you convince her?" I asked.

Cal squinted against the sun and shrugged. "I didn't try to convince her. I just told her that it would be a gift to have a little reminder of us. We might be splitting up come August, but what we had—what we *have*—is special. I don't want time erasing that, don't want myself thinking in the future that what I feel today was an exaggerated teenage feeling. That it wasn't actually love." He shifted his stance, resting one foot against the wall and turning to look at Iris, who was changing her camera lens. "Iris told me that it was silly, that we already have two years' worth of exchanged emails, texts, Tumblr messages, mementos like that receipt that was in my wallet you found. Plus, two years' worth of memories."

"But I want more than just memories. I wanted a love story. Our love story." If Pete were around, he might have burst out in laughter at the earnestness with which Cal said this. But there was something to how he said it that made my heart break on his behalf. "I just want an account. Something I can turn to months/years down the line and relive." He shrugged again, a very different gesture than when Jase shrugged at me while standing in my doorway. In the distance, Iris fluffed her hair and checked her camera's display, then turned to us and raised a finger to say she'd be a minute. "Maybe," Cal added quietly, almost like he didn't want me to hear the thought, "I could even use it as a way to figure out what went wrong, and how to fix it."

Then he turned and smiled at me, motioning at the notebook. "What's next?"

It took me a second to recover from his little speech. I couldn't even remember what I'd asked. I flipped my notebook open again, looked at the questions I'd scribbled throughout the day at work and on the subway ride over to Brooklyn. Nothing seemed pertinent or poignant enough. "Tell me about your first date," I said, right as Iris caught up to us.

"Ooh, I love telling this story."

Cal smiled. "Go ahead."

We started walking away from the waterfront, Iris switching up her lenses again as she started to tell the story.

We turned down a random street, me and Iris in front and Cal walking behind us. I turned over my shoulder to glance at him. He had his hands in his pockets, a little smudge on his glasses, which he didn't seem to mind or notice.

I kept quiet as Iris described reaching for Cal's hand for the first time outside of an Indian restaurant in Hell's Kitchen. I had to open up my notebook and start doodling while we walked in order to distract myself from the memory of holding hands with Leo. Not for the first time, but the last. How we'd lain in bed with our fingers limply intertwined, the air in the room so clearly heavy, though I had no idea why at the time. A few hours later we were out on the balcony ending things.

We'd been walking along Flushing Avenue, getting close to Williamsburg. Leo lived nearby, which was something I would have rather not thought about. Thankfully, Iris had been giving plenty of details about their date, her memory almost suspiciously good, providing me with plenty of fodder to occupy my mind. I checked my phone to make sure my mom wasn't getting pissed and threatening to hunt me down, but all I had was a text from Pete asking if I was still in Brooklyn. I texted back, Yes, hanging around Dumbo interviewing the lovebirds, and then added a string of random emojis because I couldn't think of what else to say as an apology for bailing on him again.

"I don't mean to bring down the mood after that lovely

reminiscence," I said, "but I just have to know, why are you guys breaking up?"

Iris slipped her hand away from Cal's, shoving her hands inside the pockets of her dress. "You wanna take this one?" she asked. I tried to detect bitterness in her voice, tried to detect pain in the air around them. But there wasn't anything so obvious as that. Cal fiddled with his rolled-up shirtsleeves, trying to even them out.

"We just know the path that we'll likely end up on if we stay together," Cal said. "We're not one of those couples that assumes first love is last love. Everyone knows it's irrational to think that, but they also believe they're one of the exceptions. It's better to end things on a good note."

I made eye contact with Cal, certain I'd see some of the hurt I'd seen the other night. I listened for his voice to waver.

"We know it sounds ridiculous," Iris added. "And we know it's not necessarily avoiding any pain. But we're avoiding the ugly parts, the sad unraveling. Everyone that doesn't marry their first love has it ruined by the breakup."

With just those few lines, I probably had enough material to put together into something Hafsah would accept. All I had to do was arrange it into something semicohesive. I couldn't tell if I was officially past my writer's block, but I felt close enough that a sigh of relief was appropriate.

Before I could, though, I felt a tap on my shoulder.

I turned around and when I saw who it was I let out an exasperated, "Of course!"

Leo furrowed his brow, then turned to look behind him, as if I might have been talking about someone else. "Hey," he said.

I searched the scene for further context as to why the hell he was standing in front of me right now. Then I saw his parents and sisters standing outside of a restaurant across the street.

Cheryl, his younger sister, looked over at me and waved. She went to our school too and seemed to think I was cool. The rest of his family didn't seem to give me much thought.

"What are you doing here?" I asked, although I'd picked up enough context to guess.

"You never answered me," he said, scratching at his neck. He looked over my shoulder at Iris and Cal, who'd picked up on the fact that something awkward was in the works and had taken a couple of steps backward. "I texted Pete, and he said you were around here."

"So you convinced your entire family to stalk me?"

I expected him to flatly reject this statement as me being ridiculous, but he combed a tress behind his ear and looked down at the ground. My stomach lurched. Why wasn't I throwing my arms around his neck, telling him that I still loved him too? Wasn't this exactly what I'd wanted? "I was just hoping to see you. I convinced them to go for Italian." He smiled. He had such a great smile, the prick. "It's been harder than…" He trailed off, looking again at Iris and Cal. "Wow, new friends already?" He forced a smile, then awkwardly waved.

Cal and Iris waved back, and then I saw Cal lean into Iris to say something, but their exchange was interrupted by Leo shouting his name at them, like a child with a weak grasp on social etiquette. Before Cal and Iris could respond with a slew of questions about his understanding of how the world works, Cheryl jogged across the street toward us.

"Our table's ready," she said to Leo. Then, turning to me, she smiled and waved. "Hi, Lu! How've you been? I haven't seen you in a while." My eyes flitted toward Leo, whose downturned eyes made it obvious that he hadn't told her we'd broken up. Maybe he hadn't told any of them.

"I'm okay," I said. "Just, you know. Hanging. Say hi to the

rest of the family for me," I added, making a point to say it to Leo.

Iris, Cal, and I walked away, wandering through Williamsburg as the sun dipped down. Iris stopped every few blocks to take pictures of buildings, a group of friends hanging out in stoops, two guys taking a smoke break from unloading a beer truck. They looked at the camera, one of them staring blankly, the other smiling, his hands resting on his hip. I could picture Iris printing this shot out, hanging it up in her California dorm, a shrine to all things New York.

"Was that the ex?" Cal asked.

I nodded, feeling physically exhausted from thinking about Leo. It was like I'd been in shape for a while, lifting that heavy load week in and week out. But since hanging out with Iris and Cal, I'd slowly lost my conditioning, and now the slightest exercise got me winded.

"I may not know what you're feeling now, but I can confidently say the dude made a mistake." Cal turned to look at me, pushing his glasses up the bridge of his nose, looking a lot more tenuous than the person who spoke about love and paintball teams to strangers on benches. He gave me a little smile. "You're great, Lu."

About an hour later, riding back on the J/M/Z toward Manhattan, the city lights starting to flicker on as twilight grew, Leo texted me again, telling me he missed me. If only I had the strength to delete it. Instead I stared at it for a long time, wishing it hadn't come, or that it had come from someone else.

18

THE SUBTEXT SNEAKS IN ANYWAY

What should have been a night of feverish writing and transcribing all I'd learned about Iris and Cal, unleashing all that pent-up desire to tell their story, unpacking everything I'd been wanting to say about relationships through the specific lens they existed in was instead spent curled up in bed trying to empty my brain of thoughts. My laptop was set up on my laundry hamper playing cartoons on Netflix, my notebook forgotten beneath a cup of water and some discarded tissues. I'd purposely left my phone charging in the bathroom.

The next morning, all I wanted to do was see Iris and Cal. Even in passing, from afar, for a single moment. It was strange how specific that desire was, almost like a craving for a favorite dish at a restaurant.

At work too I was thinking about Cal, reliving our night in New Jersey. Or I was thinking about Iris, and our adventures in Manhattan. Or I was thinking about them stargazing, kissing on the sidewalk, cardamom and the heat of vindaloo on their lips. This is what inspiration felt like, and if it hadn't been for Leo, these thoughts would have already turned into writing. I just needed to give it a little more time.

Thoughts of them slipped in between my breaths, in the space between my words when I was talking to customers, in the accidental brushing of fingertips when I handed people their change or their popcorn. It was hard to focus on anything else, and I wondered how the hell the world was in such relatively good shape, if everyone who was in love was constantly distracted like this.

Not me. Them. Everyone out there, constantly in the throes.

Or maybe those people weren't in love either. Maybe that's why teenage love got its reputation for being more intense and all-consuming, and "adult" love was tapered and comfortable, focused on compromises and commitment. Teenage love was the real version, but the world wouldn't be able to function that way. People gave up on it after the first time or two, because they couldn't get anything else done. They opted for something that left room for other activities. Like breathing, and conversing with people who are present, and purchasing movie tickets. They loved in a way that made the heartbreak less severe, in a way that made the love less suffocating.

I spent my shift not in the least bit present, constantly being nudged back to attention by Pete and other coworkers. Pete acted normal for the most part, although the fact that we were avoiding each other felt as obvious as if we were both dressed in lucha libre outfits. Or I guess I wasn't aware enough of my surroundings to really say that for sure. Pete could have been talking at me all shift. Come to think of it, when I snapped out of it, he was standing right next to me, looking expectantly, as if maybe he'd said something that, in a typical social interaction, might have elicited a response.

"Sorry, what?"

"Your plans today?" He leaned back and shoved his hands

in his pockets, staring at a crowd of people letting out of a theater, a trail of spilled popcorn at their feet. His eyes followed along with someone, and I turned to see who it might be. An attractive group of girls, an attractive group of guys, some dude in a tracksuit to add to our running tally (544). Hard to tell, it had been a full theater, and everyone had exited at the same time. "Starla said she got some advanced copies of winter releases and that we can go sort through them."

"Coolio," I said.

Pete eyed me sternly, then sighed. "Don't invoke the holy one's name when you're clearly not Coolio. You haven't listened to a word I've said all day."

"Whaaat? I'm a great listener."

"Name three words in succession that I've said today."

I bit my lip. "That's so many words though." I looked around the theater for ideas. "Oh! I know. 'That'll be eight dollars.'" I smiled smugly, sure that he at some point said that, since it's what most of our concession items cost.

Pete looked around for a moment, as if looking around for someone, then stuck his hand in the nearest popcorn machine and tossed a fistful at me. "Hopefully that'll snap you back to our reality."

"One of us is gonna have to clean that up, you jerk."

"No, one of our coworkers will. We're off in fifteen. Seriously, where've you been all day?"

I had a miniflashback to the daydreams I'd had throughout our shift: me, Iris, and Cal riding bicycles through a meadow, happy pop music playing in the background. The three of us in a car with the windows down and our feet sticking out, sunlight dancing on our toes, wind getting whipped around everywhere as we headed somewhere vague yet adventurous, happy pop music playing in the background. There was even one fantasy I had—brief, and quickly dismissed by the rational part of my mind, even though it was fun to be in its illogical clutches for a while—where the three of us were living in the same Brooklyn apartment, exposed brick on the walls, sparsely but tastefully decorated, so comfortable with each other that all of us walked around in our underwear without batting an eye. Happy pop music, of course, played in the background.

Pete waved a hand in front of my face. "I mean, what happened, Lu. Did you get hypnotized?"

"What? Sorry. I've been…um…brainstorming. You know I've got this column due. I'm just an utmost professional and it's been hard to think about anything else."

Pete cocked an eyebrow at me, then rolled his eyes. "Right. So, should I tell Starla we're swinging by?" He raised his phone up to show me the texting screen he was on. I knew I'd been a less-than-ideal friend lately, and I'd been spending plenty of time with Iris and Cal and should probably let them have a day off from me. But I wanted to have my damn cake and eat it too.

"Sure," I said because I'm considerate but also a coward. Plus, I hadn't talked to Iris and Cal all day, so assuming that they'd be down to hang out would be a little presumptuous, even if it felt like we'd been hanging out all day in a golden montage of carefree, adolescent good times.

When we clocked out, I called my mom to let her know I wasn't going to be coming straight home.

"Is that you, Lucinda? It's been so long, I can hardly remember what your voice sounds like," she said because she's a goddamn comedian.

"Very funny, Mom."

"I'm not being funny."

"Well, then, you're being dramatic. I'll be home for dinner," I said. Then added a quiet, "Probably."

"Now you're being funny. I know it's been a while since

you saw me, but I haven't aged enough that you can sneak in that 'probably' and expect me to miss it. What are you doing that's so important you're abandoning the woman who cares most about you in this world?"

How to begin? "Well," I said, choosing to go with the easy answer first, "you know how Pete's leaving for school in August? I want to make sure I'm being a good friend and spending time with him."

There was a pause on the phone, and I thought maybe she would complain about the fact that I was making time for Pete and not her. "I hate to admit it, but I did a good job with you."

"Why would you hate to admit that?!?"

"Anyway, since I've been granted the generous gift of your voice, at least over the phone, tell me, how are you?"

"I'm good, Mom."

Another pause, which meant either Mom was getting distracted or she was gearing up for some sort of lecture. Since I was hoping for some leniency during the afternoon, I motioned to Pete to give me a second. He mouthed, "Tell her I say hi and also…" And then he quietly continued mouthing a speech about—I think—US foreign policy.

"Lu, are you depressed?"

"Um," I said, because Mom had just taken the conversation from about a three to a nine.

"Because I know that boy broke your heart, and if you have to get out of the house a little more to help with it, that's okay. But I want you to know that you can stay home and talk to me about it too. Or stay home and not talk to me about it. Whatever you need."

I felt that pressure behind my eyes that could only mean that my emotions had also gone from a three to a nine. I turned away from Pete, who was still mouthing words, so that he couldn't see me tear up. Instead of staying at a nine along with my mom, though, my stupid brain somehow decided that what it really wanted to do was deflect. "So I can go to that all-night warehouse rave with all the drugs? Thanks, Mom, you're the best!"

My mom sighed. "Very funny. That'd be a great way to get disowned."

"Love you too, Mom," I said.

After I hung up, Pete and I went to The Strand and loitered at the information desk with Starla. Pete sorted through advanced copies while Starla leaned her chair back against the wall. I stood by, trying to remember if there was something specific I was supposed to be doing other than aching to hang out with a couple I'd met recently.

"What's with the notebook and the idle pen, girly?" Starla asked.

"Right, that's what I'm supposed to be doing."

I opened it up randomly, landing not on the pages of scrawled notes from the other day, but on the one lame attempt at a poem about Leo I'd written post-breakup. *Eyes the color of desert cliffs.* Ugh. I'd never even seen desert cliffs. I threw the notebook down on the help desk.

"You gonna tell me what happened with Leo?" Pete asked, halfheartedly reading the back cover of a fantasy novel. "You can't throw around the word *developments* and then not fill me in for a whole day. It's too loaded."

"Are we still talking about fart boy?"

Pete widened his eyes and nodded dramatically.

"Such a lingerer," Starla said, wrinkling her nose.

"To be fair, I think last time we talked we'd decided that I was the fart. Or my pain was. I don't know, I'm foggy on the details." I uncapped my pen and started fiddling with it, just to give myself something to do. I didn't want to talk about Leo, he had delayed my writing long enough. And if I brought up Iris and Cal, Pete would probably disown me, if that was a thing that friends could do to each other. "Friendship breakup" doesn't seem like an adequate description.

"Also, I don't want to be rude," Starla said, looking at my face in a way that made it easy to guess what she was about to say next. "But what happened to your face?"

I propped my elbows on the desk, then rested my chin in my hands, cupping slightly so that my cheeks pressed together and muddled my words when I answered. "Drunken piggyback ride."

"Oof. Kids these days, so irresponsible. When I was your age we—"

"Had the highest ever rate of drunk-driving accidents?" Pete chimed in.

"Probably. Stop being clever around older people, we don't like it." Starla smirked. She stopped as a customer approached the desk, putting on her professional smile. But the customer had a change of heart and awkwardly walked past us, pretending to check her phone as if she'd just gotten a text that instructed her not to talk to us. "Lu, you were saying?"

I mumbled some more into my hands, not wanting to reduce the memory of that night to a funny, somewhat embarrassing story.

Starla furrowed her brow, clearly not understanding my mumbling. She turned to Pete and asked him if he wanted to translate. He shrugged. "I don't know this story yet. We haven't had the chance to catch up."

They both turned to me expectantly, and since it would at least allow me to talk about Cal and Iris (or at least Cal) without judgment (er, mostly), I told them about the party and the regrettable transportation choice we'd made on the way back to my dad's place. There were moments from that night that I didn't share, of course. The way Cal had cared for me. Sitting out there on my dad's back porch with him, my face sore but tingly with Neosporin, the hum of summertime bugs in the New Jersey night, the deliciousness of a cool glass of water nursing me back into sobriety. I wasn't embarrassed by these moments or anything, I just didn't know how to include them without causing some intense eyebrow raising.

"Wait, do I know who this Cal person is?" Starla asked, her bracelets jingling as she gestured.

"I don't even know this dude. One of her eavesdropping victims. It's this whole thing."

My phone dinged with a text message at that point, which was cartoonishly good timing because it was the exact moment that I was struck by a brilliant idea. "Pete, you are so right!" I said, as cheerfully as I could manage.

"Um," Pete said, backing away a step because I'm not a normal person. "What's that thing your voice is doing?"

"You *should* get to know Cal. That's a great idea." I grabbed my phone and unlocked it. "What a crazy coincidence, Cal *just this moment* texted me to see what I'm doing." This wasn't true. It was my mom sending a string of emojis that equated to: Every moment you're away from me breaks my heart. "Why don't you and I go hang out and you can get to know him! Yay friends coming together!"

Pete looked legitimately scared. He turned to Starla. "I think she's been body-snatched."

"Ooh, you know *Body Snatchers*? Good flick. You just got old people points." She held out her fist, and Pete tapped it.

While they did that, I texted Iris and Cal in a group message.

Lu
Sorry to be clingy, but I'm thinking I need
just a little more for my column.
Are you guys free?

Iris
Hmm. When/where were you thinking?

Lu
Now-ish? Wherever you guys can.
I'm the worst, sorry.

Cal
Sure! We were about to learn real-world
skills making spaghetti Bolognese at Iris's.

Lu
No way. My mom cooks that like
twice a week. You could basically call
me Spaghetti BoLugnese.

Lu
Please don't call me that.
Please delete that text.

Iris
Ooops we just screenshotted it and
tweeted it and now that's your
official nickname. See you soon!

Lu
Okay if I bring a friend?

Cal
👍

When I looked up from my phone, Starla was typing something into her computer, helping a young Asian woman find
a book. Pete was flipping through more of the advanced copies, avoiding eye contact with me.

"Pete."

"My head's in a book, Lu. You're breaking our rule."

"Your eyes aren't even moving across the page." I could
see him suppress a smile. "Now they're moving way too fast.

You're gonna give yourself a seizure." I reached out and lowered the book from his grip. "I promise that this is the last time I'll do this. After today, I have to write the column or I'm for sure fired and my life is over. Then I'll move on. And I'm really sorry I bailed on you before. That's why I want you to come with me now."

Pete chewed on his lip for a while, eyes up, flitting around the store. "Please tell me they're not excessively PDA. They sound like they make out more than they breathe." He brushed his hair out of his eyes and glanced over at Starla, who'd stood up and was going to walk the customer over to find a book, which was our cue to back away from the help desk.

"They kiss so rarely, they're practically mouth virgins."

Pete winced. "Don't say mouth virgins." He sighed, and we started heading toward the exit. "I'm going to come with you," he said. "But I want you to know that if it sucks as much as I think it's going to suck, I reserve the right to complain about it for the rest of our friendship."

"Pete, darling—" I hooked my arm into his, leaning my head on his shoulder as we walked out onto Broadway "—I will listen to you complain about anything you want."

When Pete and I exited the subway uptown, the late afternoon light was golden and dazzling, shaping the people around us into nothing more than silhouettes, the cars and buildings nothing more than glares, everything a canvas for the sun. The air was magically fresh, a slight, natural breeze that carried no humidity and none of the city's sour summer smells. I noticed leaves swaying gently, people laughing with friends, an old man in a suit whistling as he strolled by, his fingertips trailing the sides of buildings as if reminding himself of the pleasures of touch.

We got to Iris's building and I rang the apartment number, expecting the world to literally become rose tinted at any moment. An unfamiliar voice answered, only slightly pulling me out of my daze. I told the intercom that I was Iris's friend, then struggled to open the door when they tried to buzz me in, because intercoms are hard.

When Iris opened the door, she revealed a much different scene than when I'd first come over to return Cal's wallet. The TV was tuned to a baseball game, and a set of twin black-mop-haired boys were at the dining table wielding crayons like swords and speaking to each other at an inhuman volume. Iris's mom was at the table on a computer, looking like she was somehow managing to get something accomplished despite the ungodly noise of two seven-year-olds interacting. Her dad was on the couch, and he glanced over and waved.

"Hey!" Iris said. She gave me a quick hug then looked to Pete, extending a hand and introducing herself. Then she introduced us to her family as "some friends," said something in Spanish, and we went into the kitchen. Cal was seated at the island, looking intently at his phone. When he looked up and saw me, he smiled. I'd forgotten how it felt to be smiled at just for my presence.

"Your face!" Cal said, still smiling. "It's healing so well. It's like magic."

He just called my face magic, I thought, triggering my stupid, blushing blood vessels. I turned away so he wouldn't notice, gesturing toward Pete. "Cal, Pete. Pete, Cal."

I let them shake hands and walked around the island to the counters, where tomatoes, garlic, and onions were resting on a wooden cutting board. A pot with water sat on the back burner, the flame set to high.

"I should have told you not to trust his piggyback rides," Iris said, joining me at the counter. "I've seen him drop glasses of water he was holding with both hands. He should not be trusted to carry a human being, ever. If he ever gets married, we'll have to warn the girl not to go for any of that carrying the bride nonsense."

Cal laughed, and I heard the rattling of Pete pulling out the stool to take a seat next to Cal. "So, what are you guys up to?" Pete asked. He was making a concerted effort to be normal, I could tell. If this were me, or random people he didn't care about, he would have cracked a joke, or settled deep into himself without attempting to interact.

"Researching spaghetti Bolognese recipes," Cal said, taking up his phone again.

"Lu, we should call your mom and tell her to join us." Pete turned to Iris and Cal. "She makes the best spaghetti."

"Do it," Cal said, still looking at his phone. "I want mom-quality spaghetti, not whatever spaghetti-like food we're about to come up with." He sighed as he scrolled, his glasses reflecting his phone screen, his pretty eyes narrowed behind the lenses. "Reading some of these recipes is like doing AP Physics homework. Blanch the tomatoes? Mince the garlic? Reduce the sauce? What are these words? What kind of magic spells do chefs use?"

"You guys want me to help? I've picked up some stuff from my mom over the years."

"Actually," Iris said, "I'd rather you didn't help. I want to learn, and I do better if left to my own devices." She stood up and grabbed one of the saucepans hanging over the stove, then started filling it with water. "I mean, if you see us doing something incredibly stupid, stop us." She chuckled warmly, and I found myself thinking: *like bread baking.* That's what her laugh sounded like to me, tasty and nourishing. Which made me think, somewhat sadly, of Cal's doughy laugh, and how perfectly suited they were to each other.

Cue the fun cooking montage.

Except, instead of a fun montage of us getting flour on each other's noses and making an eggy mess while laughing, it was me and Pete sitting at the kitchen island, watching Iris and Cal work through a fairly simple online recipe. Cal dropped half an onion on the floor, and some of the sauce bubbled over onto the counter, but there were no shenanigans. I kept my notebook within reach, since my reason for being there was ostensibly to take more notes for my column. Instead, I watched them cook. Cal would look over at Iris's chopping/mincing garlic technique and imitate it for the onion he was attempting to dice. She watched his oniony tears and then dropped her knife, walked over to him, and moved him away from the cutting board by placing her hands on his hips and gently repositioning him farther down the counter. They blended blanched tomatoes with basil and then Cal stuck a spoon in the not-quite-sauce, tilting it to taste-feed Iris. She looked into his eyes as she tasted, thought for a second, then announced she had no idea if it was any good. Both of them burst into laughter which did not include me or Pete.

God, how does anyone leave a relationship when they have that? Even if love itself is gone, how do you step away from that? How does happiness dissipate from something that looks so effortless? Was that what Leo and I'd looked like?

The four of us ate in the kitchen, since Iris's dad was still watching baseball on TV and the twins were still screeching their way through some indecipherable game which involved the dining table. Somehow, Iris's mom managed to eat, continue to work on her computer, and keep the twins from wreaking complete havoc. Iris and I sat on the bar stools, while Pete and Cal stood next to each other and across from us, leaning over their plates as they ate.

"So, Pete," Iris said, adding some more parmesan cheese and a tablespoon of red pepper flakes to her pasta. "What's your story? Are you a writer like Lu?"

"Nope, I'm just a cinema employee. We met when we started working at the theater, and I haven't been able to rid myself of her yet."

"Rude," I interjected. I knew he was kidding, of course, but there was something to the comment that felt a little passive-aggressive. Aggressive-aggressive, maybe. Or whatever it is you call a comment that isn't meant to be cruel but just sort of strikes at your insecurities.

But I didn't say anything else, not wanting the conversation to turn toward me and Pete. I wanted to sink into Iris and Cal, in all of their Iris-and-Cal-ness. We all fell quiet, slurping at our pasta in our different ways.

Iris's parents brought the twins by the kitchen to say goodnight to Iris and Cal, then told us we could use the living room if we wanted.

Cal stood first, clearing our plates and rinsing them off. "You guys up for a movie?"

"You don't have to do those," Iris said. "Just leave them in the sink."

"It's okay, it'll make your mom happy," Cal said. I checked the time on my phone, and even though my mom had been in I-miss-our—umbilical-connection mode, I thought to myself that I had plenty of time to get back home and see her. Plus, Pete's departure was only a few weeks away, and I hadn't yet cashed in on those pity points.

"I'm up for a movie!" I said. I looked at Pete, giving him a look that I'm sure conveyed that I wanted him to stay too.

"I dunno," he said, looking away from me. "I have to open tomorrow."

"Dude, our shift starts at ten, and it's only 7:30 p.m. That's practically the afternoon."

"Seven o'clock is definitely not the afternoon," Pete said. "It's evening."

"Maybe in this prudish country. I have it on good authority that most countries don't consider night to have fallen until at least 8:00 p.m. Or, you know," I said, gesturing to the open blinds in the living room, where the floor-to-ceiling windows showed a beautiful pretwilight skyline, "until it's dark out."

We looked at each other for a moment, trying to communicate through eye contact the way most best friends have attempted. This took place through a series of eye widenings, squinting, and eyebrow movements. And we clearly had zero clue what the other was trying to say, because we both ended with our heads tilted and our foreheads creased with furious confusion.

"Well, I'm up for a movie if you guys are," Iris said, pushing away from the island. "My mom's a huge movie buff, so we've got a crazy collection. Some of them are even hard to find on the internet."

So, Pete and I may have failed at the silent eye-convo thing a second earlier, but we did get the same thought at the same exact time. *"Troll 2!"* we shouted, then realized there were two seven-year-olds probably trying to sleep and we shouldn't be assholes, so we cringed.

"Sorry," I said. "But please tell me you have *Troll 2*."

"What's *Troll 2*?" Cal asked from the sink, setting plates into the drying rack.

"Legend has it, it's one of the worst movies ever made," Pete answered.

"It's so hard to find online unless you pirate it, and we've been holding out hope that we could watch it legitimately. And this night has been lovely and all, but literally all of my nights that don't end in watching *Troll 2* are a complete failure and add to the general meaninglessness of my life."

"Wow, that's a little heavy," Iris said. "Fortunately…"

Four hours later, we'd watched *Troll 2* twice back-to-back, and my whole torso was sore with laughter. Iris hadn't quite made it through the second viewing, and was currently curled up on the three-seater, her feet just barely resting on Cal's thighs.

Pete was yawning too, looking at his cell phone in a super obvious way that made it clear he wanted us to leave. I'd barely even bothered checking my phone since the break between viewings, and then it was just to tell my mom that I'd be home late (and a few follow-up texts to convince her not to disown me and that I still loved her).

"I don't think I understood any more of it the second time around," Cal said. His hand was resting on Iris's exposed calf, fingers lightly rubbing up and down. I wondered if Iris could feel that in her sleep.

An idea crept into my mind. "There's only one possible thing we can do, then."

Pete lolled his head in my direction. "Please no."

Cal, though, was nodding vehemently. "Yes."

"Too much *Troll 2*," Pete moaned.

"No such thing," Cal and I said at the same time.

The end credits rolled again. Pete was snoring now, and Iris was so deep into her REM cycle that she hadn't even flinched when Cal and I burst out laughing yet again at the scene where the kid stands up on his chair in the middle of dinner and pees directly onto everyone's food.

Cal and I shared a look, as if we'd just gone through something life-changing together. Which, honestly, jury was still out on, because maybe we had. Watching that movie with anyone is a life-changing experience.

That was probably around the time I should have woken up Pete, called a car service or whatever back to Chinatown. Except Pete looked so peaceful snoring with his eyes slightly open and that adorable stream of drool in the corner of his mouth, and I didn't want to disrupt him. I stood up and stretched, then caught the door that led to the balcony with the corner of my eye.

"I think I spoke too early. There is such a thing as too much *Troll 2*." I tiptoed over to the balcony door, looking out at the buildings across the street, the city lights. I couldn't see a huge stretch of the city like Iris and I had seen at the Flatiron, but it still felt magical. I looked back at Cal, who was drinking from a glass of water. "You think it's okay if we go out there for a little bit?" I asked, turning my voice into a whisper. "I think I need some fresh air to recover from that marathon of madness."

There were two patio chairs on the narrow balcony, arranged at angles so that they could fit, pointed half at the railing and half at each other. We plopped down after shutting the door gently behind us to keep out the sounds of the city.

"I wasn't too pushy, was I?" I asked, stretching my feet out and resting them on the railing.

"About what?"

"Forcing everyone to watch *Troll 2* all those times. I sometimes get carried away and don't want things to end, so I force everyone to hang out longer than they want to."

Cal chuckled. "I know what that's like."

Most of the lights were off in the building across the street. I hadn't looked at my phone in a while, and I could only guess what time it was and how much trouble I was in with my mom. She might actually ground me. Which wouldn't be the worst thing in the world, seeing as how I had two and a half days to send in my column and after that my life would be over anyway. My chest tightened with the realization that it was technically Wednesday already, but I managed to quell the panic by turning to look at Cal.

"Are you talking about paintball teams again?"

He snorted. "I wasn't going for subtext on that one."

"And yet it snuck in there anyway."

Cal put his hands on his thighs, rubbing them up and down as he let out a long breath. "Funny how that happens more and more as the days go by. It's like everything is suddenly steeped in symbolism. I saw a poster for a missing dog the other day. It said, 'Missing: The Best Thing That Ever Happened To Us.'" He made a sweeping motion with his hands to show that that was the headline. "Then under that it had a picture of a cute dog, whose name is, get this..."

"Oh my God, are you about to tell me that the dog's name was Iris? That'd be some heavy-handed symbolism right there. Like, come on, universe, have you heard of subtlety?"

"Well, no. The dog's name was Sir Barks a Lot."

I stared at Cal, maybe extending my reaction a bit because he was really nice to look at. "Human beings are the worst."

"Yeah, I know. But below the name it said, 'Without her, love has left our lives.'"

"Wait, *Sir* Barks a Lot is female?"

"I guess. But my point is—"

"I mean, I respect the refusal to adhere to society's oppressive gender rules, but that's really a mouthful of a name. Do they like, call out the whole thing when they're out looking for her? Ugh, they probably have a really gross, cutesy name that they use more regularly. Something like Barksy. Or Lottie." I noticed that Cal was staring at me with his eyebrows up. "Sorry, not the point. Yeah, that's harsh."

Cal sighed. "You're telling me." He yawned, stretched his arms out, and rested them behind his head. Then he leaned back in his chair and put his feet up on the railing, his left shoe resting against my ankle.

God, how much comfort could come from a touch like that. I remembered all those instances of first contact with Leo. How they lost their meaningfulness after a couple of months of dating, but never their comfort. Never the joy of being touched by someone whose presence you wanted near you all the time. How sometimes Leo and I would be lying down together in his bed, touching almost our entire bodies together, and yet we'd want to get closer and closer. We'd press ourselves tighter, feeling all our skin. Even through clothes, touch was something to marvel at.

I wondered briefly when the next time I would do that with someone would be. Then I thought, in a quick flash, about all the things Leo had said in the last few days. His email, his texts, running into him. What had felt like finality a few weeks ago had suddenly opened up, like a knot coming undone. There were all these loose strings flapping around now, and I couldn't even see how far they extended, what they might lead to.

"I can't believe she's leaving this city," Cal said, softly. "She's gonna miss it so much."

"Hey, Cal?" I said, making my voice go soft.

"What's up, Lu?"

"Do you think that, maybe, in the statement you just made, 'the city' might be a stand-in for something else? An easier way for you to say a difficult thing? I'm not claiming I have any proof." I raised my hands up in mock-defensiveness. "I'm just, you know, reading into things."

"I don't know what you mean," he said, then tapped his shoe against my ankle, giving me a smile. It was like we were back in New Jersey, except my face hurt a little less.

Then the balcony door opened behind us, making me jump in my seat. "Jesus, Pete. Don't sneak up on a girl after she's watched *Troll 2* three times in an evening. You're liable to get peed on."

His hair was ruffled, his eyes droopy with sleep. "I'm gonna take off, you want to come with?"

I looked beyond Pete into the living room. The TV was still on, and I could see Iris now fully stretched out on the couch. From the sounds of the city, and the number of neighboring apartments with their lights off, I could tell it was much later than I'd thought.

I realized that I'd slipped my legs from the guardrail, which meant Cal's shoe was no longer resting against my ankle. I didn't want to leave, but I couldn't find a normal-human reason for staying.

"Yeah, sure," I said, standing up. Cal remained seated, looking up at me and Pete.

"It was really nice meeting you," Pete said.

"Back at you. Sorry it was in such a weird setting. We don't always just hang at home trying to improve our cooking skills. I swear Iris and I are normal."

"No they're not," I said.

"Yeah, sorry, man." Pete ran a hand through his hair, trying to get it back in its usual sweep across his forehead. "I've heard too many stories about you to believe that."

Cal shrugged. "Fair enough." Then he held up a hand to wave goodbye, which I mistook for a call for high fives, then tried to play it off like goodbye high fives were a thing I regularly did by high-fiving Pete too, even though we were obviously not saying goodbye to each other.

"Well," I said, when the air around us had grown sufficiently awkward. "I guess all good things come to an end."

"Jerk," Cal laughed.

19

THE MOMENT THEY FIRST KNEW

Pete and I entered the nearly abandoned subway station. Two white guys wearing untucked button-down shirts sat on a bench, both looking at their phones. At such a late hour you can reasonably expect at least one drunk person to be stumbling about, or if not that, then at least someone doing something shady. I guess the Upper West Side got less of that though.

We'd been quiet since leaving Iris's building, which I'd assumed was a normal 2:00 a.m. silence. But then Pete, apropos of nothing, looked at me with those piercing, soulful eyes of his as if we'd just been in the midst of a meaningful silence. I knew that look well. He was about to say something honest and tactless.

"You're getting a crush on this guy."

I scoffed and combed my hair back behind my ears. "I got scared there for a second. You went into your nugget-of-wisdom voice. It sounds exactly like your having-an-aneurysm voice, which is clearly what's happening right now."

"You're denying it?" His hands dropped to his sides.

"I don't find the need to deny preposterous statements. If you called me a fish, I wouldn't really worry about correcting you." I turned my body away from him, scanning the tunnel for any oncoming trains, even though the signs overhead clearly said the next one would be arriving in thirteen minutes.

"Fine, deny it. But I've got an official prediction for this—it doesn't end well for you."

"What's the 'it' in that sentence?"

"Your emotional well-being."

"And the west will always be at war with the east. Bold pick, Nostradamus."

"Don't get defensive, Lu. I'm not saying anything bad about Cal or you or Iris or any of it. I'm just worried that you're setting yourself up for more heartache."

One of the dudes in the button-downs looked away from his phone and toward us, staring for a moment and then glancing too-quickly away to show he hadn't meant to hear anything. I could spot the maneuver with ease because I employed it often when I was eavesdropping.

"I don't have a crush on anyone, Pete. I'm writing about a couple. And, yes, becoming friendly with them. But that doesn't mean I suddenly wanna bone him. Or her, for that matter. Or them." I was going for a laugh, but Pete didn't provide one. He kept his Irish brooding up at full capacity. "They're interesting, cool people. I think they might be my friends. That's what's happening here."

Pete clicked his tongue. It looked like he wanted to say something else, but then he just leaned back against the wall and crossed his arms, looking everywhere around the station except at me. I mimicked his pouty stance, hoping again to defuse whatever this was with a laugh.

The minutes ticked away. The train arrived with a rumble and a sweep of stale, warm air. We climbed into a different car than the buttoned-down white guys, into one with only three other people in it. Pete and I still had about fifteen stops or so to go though, so when we took our seats I thought I'd try to convince him that he was reading too much into things.

"I know it looks like I fell into a weird friendship with them really quickly. I get that it's weird I've been spending so much time with them. But remember what happens if I lose my job? I don't qualify for the scholarship? My whole world falls apart? I spend the rest of my life at the theater, mumbling about the life I could have had. Like a high school athlete reminiscing about the glory days."

Pete had a Gaga-level poker face going. I sighed and leaned my head back against the train window. I closed my eyes, a wave of tiredness spread over me like a blanket.

I don't know how long it was before Pete spoke up again. I wasn't even sure he had spoken at first, since the rumble of the train was so loud. I opened my eyes and looked over at him to find him glancing down at me. "Maybe that's how it started, Lu. You were interested in them. And I'll grant you the fact that they're cool people. I liked spending time with them tonight. But you're pursuing this so diligently because of him, probably as a stand-in for Leo, and I think it's gonna cause you pain. Or at least sadness."

I put my hand over his. "Pete, hon. You're wrong. You're imagining things."

He looked at me for a long time before turning away. "Good," he said.

Over the next two days, I kept meeting up with Iris and Cal. First together, then individually. Despite pages of notes, I still didn't have a column written that I could send to Hafsah. When I tried at the end of the day to sit down and get something cohesive written, my thoughts refused to focus. I'd start thinking about Leo's eyes. I'd start thinking about sex. About when I'd have it again. I'd start thinking about college breakups, and even about the very idea of love and what that meant. God knows you can't write something concise with that kind of shit on your mind.

All this felt increasingly terrifying, especially when I received an email from the foundation that was giving me my scholarship. They needed some paperwork from me. I'm not sure exactly what paperwork, since I panicked when it all started feeling too real and closed out of the email.

Iris and I met up first. She was still spending her days photographing as much of the city as she could, and making her way around Brooklyn on Wednesday. We met in Bushwick, at a hip Caribbean restaurant with a sweet rooftop patio, which made me look forward to the days when I had enough money to spend at rooftop patios in Brooklyn. Well, I did do that, but I couldn't afford any of the food. Not after our last foray out on the town.

It was, if I'm being honest, the most journalistic I'd been around her. I came with a specific list of questions prepared, everything that I thought could flesh out that goddamn column which should have been written weeks ago. I was focused, and had even arrived at the restaurant with the idea that it was a professional meeting and not a friendly one.

I tried not to be too enamored with her cool composure, the way the pain of her oncoming breakup seemed to roll right off her, not in a callous way, but because she seemed to understand pain was a natural and often transient part of life. I tried not to imitate that hair-fluffing thing she did, or appreciate how well she continuously pulled off her pinup model look. Instead, I tried to pry as much as I could. I wanted to get stories from their relationship, not just facts.

"When did you first know?" I asked her when we were done with our food, our plates pushed to the side in defeat.

Iris stirred her virgin daiquiri, beads of condensation dripping off the glass and forming a ring on the wooden picnic table. "Know what?"

"That you loved Cal."

She paused, did that hair-fluffing thing, then told me that it had been such a tiny thing that made her realize that she had almost missed it. It was just like joy in that way: if you didn't pay attention you might not know it was ever there, or believe that it had been there at all.

Cal had borrowed his mom's car for a date, and they'd driven out to Long Beach for the day after a recent snowfall. The idea had been to build Calvin and Hobbes—esque snowmen near the shore. They'd purchased thermoses of crappy gas station coffee near Montauk, then wrapped themselves up in their best snow-proof gear and trekked out to the beach.

"Look!" Cal had called out. "White sand beaches!"

They'd done their best to re-create the grotesque snowmen from the books they'd both loved as kids, mostly failing.

The cold reddened their noses and stiffened their joints, and whenever they would stop to kiss, the warmth of each other's mouths kept them close for long periods, almost causing them to forget the snowmen entirely.

They went back to the car and turned down the music, rolled up the windows, and got the heat started. A quiet moment passed, their breathing normalizing from the mayhem and the laughter, fogging up the glass. Iris looked at Cal's face and felt something within her shift. He was smiling, leaning back against the headrest. Then he pulled his glove off, warmed his hand against the vent, and then moved it to Iris's knee. He sighed pleasurably, as if he were punctuating their day.

"That's when I knew. At the sound of his sigh, with his hand on my leg. It was a feeling before I knew what to call it. As distinct as hunger, originating somewhere similar, but entirely different. Only a moment later the words came to identify what it was, and as soon as they were there, I moved my hand over his, and leaned back into the seat, knowing what it was I'd found."

"And you're letting it go," I said. Not a question, but a crowbar, meant to slip into the crack and unleash all she might be hiding. Tears would be good, or maybe even a confession that the feelings she felt weren't actually as strong as how she described them. That a part of Iris and Cal was the version of themselves they portrayed to the outside world. A fabrication on par with books and movies. That the love they had did not really exist. And if it did, it wasn't ending for the same reasons that my and Leo's comparatively muted love had ended.

In that moment, when I had that thought, I tried to dismiss it. I tried to tell myself that the love I'd experienced wasn't muted just because someone else's sounded more romantic. But then I had this little flashback, if that's what you'd call it. It wasn't a specific memory, just the recollection that, every now and then during our relationship, I'd look at Leo—while he was joking around with his friends, while he was staring at his phone, while he was kissing my stomach—and wonder what it was about him that I was drawn to. It was as if every now and then, I'd simply forget that I loved him.

Iris didn't cry or confess after my question. She simply shrugged. "We are."

When I met up with Cal the next day after his shift at the coffee shop where he worked near Washington Square Park, I wasted no time in asking him the same question.

"Jeez. Firing on all cylinders. So much journalism. I'm impressed."

"Answer the question," I said, sliding my phone closer to him. I'd taken to recording our conversations because (a) it made me feel cooler, and (b) not sure you've noticed, but my mind tends to wander and that leads to poor note-taking.

Cal leaned forward on the table, his elbows almost halfway across the wooden surface toward me. He cracked his neck and looked over to the register, as if wanting someone to call him back over to work. Then his eyes met mine, and goose bumps shot down my arms.

Just because I knew he was about to tell me another incredible story. Not for any other reason.

Cal let out a breath and clasped his hands together into a double fist, which he brought down gently onto the table. "She came over to my house for dinner, and to do homework together. At that point I hadn't known what exactly we were, but I knew I loved *that*. Sitting at the kitchen island with Iris, each of us focused quietly on our own thing, music playing from Iris's computer. Knees touching, cheesy as that is." He chuckled, as if no one had ever acknowledged that touching knees is a cliché of love that we all nevertheless indulge ourselves in.

"The thought came quickly. Just like that. I can't even tell you what spawned it, at what time, how long into our night. Just that I knew. Without a doubt, all at once. What I'd previously thought was true is wrong. Soul mates are not about finding the one person meant for you. 'The one' does not mean *the only one*. It's just that...there are others, but they are lesser. They have their qualities, but if you add them up they don't equal the qualities of this person you've found, this one person who has so many things you crave, so many joys to provide. Not all the things you crave, but more than anyone else does." He took a sip from the coffee he'd ordered when he arrived.

"*I did not know love would be this calm.* That was my thought."

I stared, because, duh. How was I the first to write about these people? How had Cal not already been featured in numerous *Misnomer* articles and Jane Austen novels? I set my pen down. "I think I have all I need."

Cal raised his eyebrows, smiling. "Yeah? Article's all done?"

"Probably. Just needs typing," I said. I even tucked my notebook away inside my bag and set it at my feet. I looked at my phone. "I still have time to hang, if you do."

Cal shrugged. "Sure." He took a sip from his iced-coffee-frappe-concoction thing, which he'd loaded up with extra flavors and caramel drizzles because he got them for free. "So, now that you've gotten what you need from us, you're gonna stop hanging out, huh?"

"Oh, one hundred percent. You guys are lame."

"I guess it makes me feel special in a way. That I've been screwed over by a writer, my trust betrayed."

"There's a support group that meets Tuesdays at Jefferson Market Library."

"Damn it, I'm busy Tuesdays."

"Ha! I screwed you again."

Phrasing, Lu.

The door to the coffee shop opened behind us, letting in the noise of Washington Square Park, along with two girls that walked in talking about whatever meal they'd just had. For some reason I was blushing again when the door shut and Cal looked back at me.

"So," he said, his voice trailing off. His eyes caught the light coming in through the windows, a pretty glint of auburn in his irises. I remembered the bathroom again, and found myself reaching up to the scrape on my cheek. The scab had subsided to the point where I felt the urge to pick it away, bit by bit. What is it about scabs that make us want to peel them off and leave scars behind? What evolutionary purpose could there possibly be for that? "What should we do now?"

20

DOING NICE THINGS WITH CAL

There's something about walking aimlessly with a person that passes the time like nothing else. That could be another instance where movies have worked their influence on me. Watching characters talk as they wander, smooth cuts that make it seem like they've been transported to a whole other place in a city. *Before Sunrise*, which is basically ninety minutes of walking and talking, is one of my favorite movies because that's the basis for how everyone falls in love, the basis for humanity. I think 90 percent of our existence is spent walking and talking.

We left the coffee shop, talking for the first time without my having to worry about writing everything down or even remembering it. Then we were passing through Canal Street's jam-packed sidewalks, stores overflowing with knock-off sneakers, loaded up with electronics and racks with cheesy T-shirts aimed for a very specific kind of tourist. Before I knew it, we had ended up at the South Ferry piers, sweaty from walking in the heat. "Why is lower-back sweat the worst feeling in the world?"

"Ugh, I know," Cal said. "We should start a summer fashion trend where T-shirts have that part cut out. Get a nice draft going back there."

Without thinking about it, I reached for the back of his T-shirt and gave it a tug, pretending I was trying to rip it.

"Oh my God, yes. You just gave me a little draft. That felt so good." He stopped walking and spread his arms out, his eyes closed.

I held on to his shirt, fanning it gently. We were at Pier Eleven by the water, near a pretty stretch of colorful flowers that had been landscaped into the structure. A breeze hit us, and Cal smiled, his eyes still closed. The breeze blew a little stronger, and Cal almost seemed to lean into the draft. My knuckles, gripping the inside of his shirt, brushed against his lower back, which did not feel sticky with sweat, but warm and thrilling. I gave myself the liberty to keep them there for just a second, just long enough to let the sensation sink in and take hold of me. Then I pulled away, letting his shirt drop. Pete didn't know what he was talking about.

"A-plus draft making, Lu." He opened one eye and smiled at me, and we kept walking to the edge of the pier. There we leaned against the guardrails and looked out at the sun shimmering on the Hudson, and the boats zipping their way across the river, streaks of white in their trail. New Jersey in the distance, an uninteresting skyline of drab buildings. Even Jersey was looking pretty good.

"Do you think human beings are overly obsessed with love?" I asked.

"Overly?" Cal shrugged. "It's better than a lot of other options, I guess. We're obsessed with plenty of other things."

"Like porn?"

"Yeah, I was thinking of porn specifically. So many types." He chuckled. "What makes you ask?"

"It's just been on my mind lately. I have a weekly column where I get paid to share stories about love, or just my thoughts on the subject. And people read it. I'm far from the only one too. It's all over the world, almost every story you hear, love's at the core."

"What else would be worthy?"

I turned my back to the water, wanting to make eye contact without craning my neck to see him. "Piggyback rides?"

"Definitely."

"Doing nice things for others. Helping bring joy into others' lives. That's a pretty worthy obsession. Have you been keeping up with it?"

He grimaced. "Not as much as I'd like."

On the pier, a handful of people milled about, same as everywhere. Tourists, mostly. "What about one of these fine folks?" I gestured to the crowd.

Cal smiled, then turned to face the same direction as me, leaning his elbows back against the railing, scanning the pier.

"What do you look for when you're trying to find someone to be nice to?" I asked.

"People with signs that say Help Me are ideal. French tourists looking at maps." I smiled at the memory. "It's kind of hard to find obvious ways that people need help. I gave my shoes to a homeless guy, which is an easier one to figure out, but I only have so many pairs of shoes." He pushed off from the railing and we started walking again down the pier, toward the street.

"Have you tried just asking people if they need help with something?"

"No, Lu, I've got social skills."

"Well, then, it's probably not a surprise that you haven't done as much of the being nice to strangers thing as you wanted to."

"But just approaching and talking to people is terrifying. They'll think I'm selling them something."

"Yeah, but you get used to it. I do it all the time for my pieces." We walked off the pier, strolling along the path near the water. There were plenty of joggers out, and a few people sunning themselves on the grass. "When Iris still wasn't on board for the column, I was getting close to my deadline and panicking about not having a topic, so I was at a coffee shop kind of harassing everyone who looked remotely like a couple."

"Judging from the fact that you haven't had an article in a while, I'm guessing that didn't go well."

I stopped walking. "How do you know that?"

"Oh, it's this thing called the internet. It allows you to find out stuff about people's lives. Crazy, right? You should check it out."

"You've read my stuff?"

He squinted as if I'd just suggested something immensely stupid. "Yeah, dude. I showed it to Iris and it helped convince her. You're a great writer." He took up the stroll again, hands in his pockets, turning his head back and forth as he gazed.

I had to jog to catch up to him. "Thanks."

He may not have heard me though, because as soon as I said it, Cal approached an elderly Asian couple that was walking hand in hand toward us, shuffling their feet, adorably wearing matching long-sleeve shirts and floppy hats. "Excuse me," he said. "Is there anything I can help you with?"

They looked at each other and then at him. "What?"

"My friend and I are just wondering if there's anything we could do for you." He gestured to me, probably trying to show he wasn't a murderer, like his introduction suggested. "See?" his gesture meant to convey, "here is a person I know whom I have not murdered. Now please answer my normal question."

The man furrowed his brow. "Like what?"

"Oh, could be anything," Cal said, putting his hands on his hips. "Give you directions somewhere, write a particularly difficult email that you've been having trouble writing, clean your house."

"You want to clean our house?" the man asked in a monotone voice.

"If it would make your life easier, sure!" Cal smiled warmly, and I tried to match his smile, though it was hard not to cringe instead.

Not surprisingly, the couple shuffled away without another word. Cal turned to look at me, eyebrow raised. "That went well."

"Eh, at least they stopped and heard you out. Most people will do anything they can to avoid talking to a stranger on the street. It's surprising they didn't just keep walking."

"I don't know if I can handle that."

"I'll take the lead on the next few," I said.

A group of women pushing strollers, a guy standing on a street corner flipping a sign that advertised a good deal on cell phone plans or something stupid like that, a cook taking a smoke break in an alleyway. Every single one of them looked at us like we were exactly as socially challenged as we seemed.

We kept tweaking our approach, trying to be as unintimidating and normal as possible.

My legs were sore and sweaty, even with the sundress I was wearing. I thought about suggesting we go get ice cream, but I didn't want to break our momentum. My mom had already called and given me a hard deadline of 7:00 p.m. for dinner, which was too quickly approaching. Heading away from the Hudson, we started meandering through the streets again, passing near Wall Street and its onslaught of suited bros hitting up the bars after work.

"I don't know how I feel about helping out finance dudes," Cal said.

"I mean, me neither. But helping someone is helping someone, right? Someone here might be really struggling with something heavy. Like, that guy," I said, pointing to a semi-attractive white guy in a blue suit, the top shirt of his button undone, his tie just a little loose, like he'd given it one good yank as soon as he left the office. "Maybe he's second-guessing his career, and really hates the environment he's put himself in. Maybe he's begging for someone to tell him it's okay to leave. Or maybe his parents are sick, maybe he's lonely and…"

"Okay, I think I get the picture. Wall Street bros are human too."

"Don't put words in my mouth." I walked up to the guy, who was looking at his phone outside of a generic Irish pub. I tapped him on the wrist. "Hi. Sorry to interrupt, and this is going to sound weird, but please don't let the weirdness undermine the sincerity of the question. Is there anything nice I can do for you today?"

He blinked, like so many others had. "Something nice?"

"Yeah. Maybe something you can't do for yourself. It doesn't have to be big, just something that could help make your life a little better. Even if it's just for today."

He looked at Cal. "Is she serious?"

"Super serious. Me too."

Wall Street Dude considered us for a second, then reached into the breast pocket of his jacket and pulled out one of those unabashedly douchey vaporized cigarettes. He inhaled slowly and thoughtfully, then exhaled a huge puff. To his credit, he turned his head so that he wouldn't blow it directly into our faces. "Actually, yeah. There is something." He craned his neck back toward the bar, which was not quite full but getting busier. He could have been there alone, or a part of any of the groups hanging out in booths and those high-top tables that don't have seats, but are only meant to rest your drinks on. "There's a bartender in there. Charles. Tall, fit, cute as a button." He took another pull from his e-cig. "I've been in love with him for months. But I don't want to make him uncomfortable by hitting on him at work, and I'm not sure if he even knows I'm gay. I'm only ever here with coworkers, and it's not like it comes up."

Of course it would be love related. Cal's eyes were practically gleaming with joy. "Yeah, we'll help. What can we do?"

"You tell me, kid."

Cal bit his lip and looked sideways at me. "What do you say, love columnist? Have any ideas?"

For a second, I thought they were messing with me. The solution felt so simple that I couldn't help but roll my eyes. Then Cal and Wall Street Dude shared a look, and I realized that they really didn't know what to do. People can be so stupid about love. I sighed, and walked into the bar.

"Where's she going?" I heard Wall Street Dude say to Cal, a hint of worry in his voice.

The bar was as equally loud with music as it was with chattering. There were two male bartenders working, and it became clear quickly which one was Cute As a Button. He, however, was busy punching something into the electronic tablet that served as his register, so the other one noticed me first.

"No!" I said when he locked eyes with me. "The other one."

The bartender continued his approach. "What?"

"I said the other one!" I pointed at Cute As a Button, or whatever his name was. "Bring him to me."

The guy looked like he wanted to ask me for my ID. Then someone else approached the bar and so he shrugged, tapped the other bartender on the shoulder, and tended to the new customer. Meanwhile, my phone started ringing. I checked to see who it was. Leo.

"ID," Cute As a Button told me, as soon as he saw me.

I hit Ignore on my phone. "That's not important right now," I said, waving him away. "Do you see that guy outside?" I pointed toward the door, where Cal was standing with his hands on his hips, looking so happy that just the sight of him made me break out into a grin. Wall Street Dude had been staring a moment ago, but as soon as Button looked over, he pretended to look at something very important on his phone.

"Who? Scott?"

"Sure," I said. "He has a crush on you but is iffy about hitting on you at work. Are you interested in him?"

He didn't even have to answer. His smile said it all. "Great," I said, matching his grin. A little flutter shot through my chest. "You want to write down your number or something? He seems like he's so nervous he might run away waving his arms in the air at any moment."

I left the bar and handed Scott the napkin I had with Button's phone number on it. "Wow, the classic digits-on-a-napkin," Cal said. "I feel like no one's done that since the early 2000s."

Scott grabbed the napkin, staring at it with mild disbelief, holding it gently, as if it were a butterfly that could flitter away at any second. "He says to call anytime," I said.

"That's all it took?" Scott said softly.

"'People are vines, awaiting the chance to cling.'" Both he and Cal looked at me with eyebrows raised. "It's a quote. From *Look at Me* by Jennifer Egan." Scott returned his gaze to the napkin, but Cal kept his eyes on me, a slight smirk on his face. My chest flutter grew. "What? You and Iris are allowed to quote stuff all the time. I can be deep too."

Cal laughed, putting his hands up to say he wasn't judging. Scott thanked us, a big smile on his face and a new glow to his skin, even though his hand was shaking when he took his next puff. Cal and I waved goodbye and started heading back to Chinatown toward my place.

"You feel that?" Cal said, when we were a few blocks past the hectic streets of downtown.

I did. I wasn't sure if it was exactly the same thing Cal was feeling, if he meant just the fact that we'd helped Scott out, or if he meant something else. "Yep," I answered, leaving it at that.

"That was surprisingly simple. If we ignore the six thousand failed attempts before this one."

"We got lucky that it was love related."

"Why's that?"

"Because love's pretty simple to figure out."

Cal laughed. "Is that right?"

"Not always. But when you're outside of the situation, hell yeah. It's easy to see the solutions to someone else's problems. Especially an early stage. This was just the approach. Things may get messy later, but the approach is easy. You have feelings for a person, you try to see if they reciprocate. Then you get closer to each other."

"That's all it takes, huh?" Cal said, scratching his chin.

"In a nutshell."

Again, that stomach flutter returned. I checked my phone to see how I was doing on time, if I could stretch the day out any more, but I had about fifteen minutes before my mom threatened to disown me again, and we were ten minutes away from my place. Also, there was a voice mail on my phone. Probably from Leo. Which made sense, because who even left voice mails anymore, other than ex-boyfriends intent on making your life more confusing than it had to be.

For the rest of our walk, Cal and I were quiet. I was wondering how much of what I'd said was true, that love is easy when you look at it from the outside. Like Iris and Cal. For me, it was easy. They should stay together. They should extend the rare thing they have until it can't be sustained, not give up on it because there were obstacles in the distance. Was there some easy solution for me that I was failing to see? If there's an easy solution for love, is there an easy solution for heartbreak too?

"Well, this is me," I said because that's the thing everyone says when you're walking and you arrive at your house. It's practically a law that those are the words that leave your mouth.

Cal looked up at my building because that's what his role dictated he had to do. Then he smiled at me. "Well, Lu, thanks for hanging out and doing nice things with me today. It's always great hanging out with you."

"You too," I said, averting my eyes in hopes of quelling my overactive blushing mechanism. Pete's accusation flashed through my mind, not for the first time that day.

Then Cal took a step toward me. "Are you a hugger?"

I shrugged. "I could be." I stepped forward into his arms.

Goddamn, was it a good hug. I could feel it on me long after it was gone, long after we'd said goodbye and I went upstairs and had dinner with Jase and my mom. It clung to me like a scent, like a feeling, refusing to let go.

In my room, later that night, I listened to the message Leo had left on my voice mail. His voice was cracked with hurt and regret, which was enough to convince me that the words he was saying were honest. "I fucked up, and I'm sorry, and I think I want you back. I don't think, I know. I want you back." A beat on the phone, no static because the quality of the call was good, but I could imagine it hanging in the silence, just like I could still feel Cal's touch on me. "I can't believe I'm leaving soon and that I might not see you again." He sighed into the phone. "I hope it's not the last time. I'm sorry."

Then, a click.

21
WHY NOW?

How had I arrived back on deadline day without having written a word?

Well, Lu, as soon as you find yourself in an emotionally healthy state, ready to tackle the task set before you, your idiot ex-boyfriend says or does something that throws you back into a confused place where thoughts are the last thing you want to face.

Also, your words have probably left you for good, revealing to the world that all you are is a love-obsessed teen. You don't pay enough attention to your family, or your closest friend. You allow a job, and therefore a scholarship, and therefore your ability to attend an institution of higher learning, to slip through your fingers. Because of something as superficial and, frankly, nonexistent as writer's block. Writer's block is nothing but cowardice. The fear of facing what you should really be writing about, or the fear that what you will write won't be good enough to meet some lofty and vague standards that only you yourself have set. Either way, you put yourself here, so don't blame stupid Leo and his change of heart.

Blame, maybe, the memory that lingers of that incredibly silly, stupid, and wonderful thing he used to do when you found yourselves in a room all alone. He'd rush over to your backside, place his butt against yours, then do a little side-to-side shimmy.

Blame, even, the fact that every story about heartbreak you've ever read has made you expect his smell to cling to your bed. Except he only lay on it a handful of times, and never slept in your room overnight, so no matter how much you burrow your nose into the pillow, you cannot reclaim those moments spent lying next to him.

Blame your stupid desire to address yourself in third person.

It was Friday. The morning light slipped in through my blinds, weak and gray. I woke up right before my alarm went off. It felt like I was waking up from a bad dream, but the truth was that I was waking up *into* a bad dream. This was it. I was going to lose my job and my scholarship. My whole life from that day forward was going to look very different from what I had imagined, and it was all because Leo suddenly agreed with me that he was an idiot and that we shouldn't have broken up.

I hadn't responded to him yet, but as soon as I'd had a sip of water and had a moment to adjust to being human in the morning, I grabbed my phone.

Lu
Why now?

Someone started knocking on my door.

"Lucinda, are you awake?" my mom shouted, clocking way too many decibels for the morning. "You have work, right?"

"Yeah, Mom, I'm awake and capable of meeting my responsibilities, thank you!"

"Except for making yourself available for an adequate

amount of family time!" Mom yelled. "Come have breakfast before your brother eats it all."

I kicked the sheets off and stumbled to the shower, putting on a podcast so that I wouldn't have to listen exclusively to my thoughts. That didn't work out great though, as I just ended up peeking my head out of the shower every thirty seconds when I imagined I heard my phone buzz. I wondered if Leo would respond at all, or if in the course of the night he'd changed his mind again.

My mom knocked on the bathroom door this time. "Lucinda Philomena Charles, stop wasting water and come out to have your breakfast!"

"Mother, you named me, and you know that's not my middle name."

"I'm trying to annoy you so that you come join us." She knocked again. "Love you!"

I toweled off and went back to my room to get dressed, pausing the podcast and rewinding it to the beginning so that I could actually listen to it some other time.

Mom had made strawberry-basil French toast. If you need something to further illustrate the state I was in, I only managed to eat two pieces. Jase ate the other fifty-one.

I kept doing math in my head, trying to figure out how much time I'd have to write my column (not counting the previous three weeks or so). My shift would be over at three, and Hafsah had given me until the end of the workday, which ostensibly meant 5:00 p.m. I could maybe stretch it to six, but it probably wouldn't behoove me to stretch anything at all with this last chance I'd been granted. I could also add thirty minutes for my lunch break, plus a few stolen trips to the bathroom which could be productive, especially if I came in announcing I'd eaten a bad kebab and was feeling queasy and could sneak away to the bathroom more than usual.

Oh right. Faking an illness. That was a thing people did.

"Mom," I said, "I'm not feeling great. I think I might call in to work."

"You better be sick, to only eat two slices." She stopped doing the dishes and walked over to me, placing the back of her hand on my forehead. She frowned, then touched my cheek. "You don't have a fever."

"I think it was something I ate."

My mom gave me a look that I was breaking her heart.

"Not the French toast. Or last night's dinner. I think something before that."

She put her hand over her heart and started looking seriously wounded. "You ate something before dinner? Do you not like my food?"

I said it wasn't that, and then stammered to think of some other thing I might have eaten between leaving the house and coming back for dinner, but my brain was still not in tip-top shape and I failed. Then my mom took a seat next to me, her eyebrows angling with so much worry I was afraid that if I kept thinking up excuses, she might never recover from the heartbreak. "So you are depressed, then. Should I call Leo and yell at him? You want Momma to do that?"

Oh good, I wasn't going to have to fake throwing up. The thought of my mom confronting Leo made me queasy but also strangely emotional. There were too many feelings happening for the time of day. I didn't have time to deal with feeling things.

I groaned. "Never mind. I'll go to work."

"You sure?"

"Yes, your food is wonderful, I'm okay."

"Okay," she said, still pouting. She put her hand back on my forehead. "Should I be worried about you?"

I thought about the shitstorm that would come when I lost

my scholarship, how I could possibly explain the reason why
I had failed to deliver one stupid measly column. "No, I'm
fine. I think I'm just gassy."

"Gross," Jase mumbled as he chowed down on three slices of
French toast at the same time, syrup dribbling down his chin.

"Yes, I agree, chemical reactions are gross when they occur
inside my body." I pushed my chair out. "I guess I'll see you
guys later when my life is over."

"Sounds great, honey. Drink a mineral water when you get
to work, it'll help." Mom smiled at me then went back to the
sink, slipping on a pair of blue latex gloves. Jase was already
deep into a game on his phone. I gave one last wave to my
former life, then grabbed my bag, slipped my computer in,
just in case I found time to type up the column, and headed
out the door.

It was a slow walk to work, since I had my notebook open,
trying to write as I weaved around other pedestrians (or, if
I'm being honest, as I let them weave around my annoying,
slow-moving self). I did manage to write a paragraph on the
fifteen-minute walk though:

This is an introductory paragraph about a very interesting couple who I thought were breaking up but aren't
really. This is their story. Did you read that in a *Law and
Order: SVU* kind of way? Because I wasn't going for that
at all. Tonally, it's just not what I write. I write about love
and stuff. You probably used to read my stuff, but then
I stopped writing because love messes you up like that.

Good, right?

I pushed the door to the theater open, that familiar blast
of AC hitting me, yet offering no relief. A second later, Pete
came in behind me, a backpack slung over one shoulder. He

brushed the hair away from his eyes. "What's with you? Did you not hear me calling your name for the last block?"

I blinked at him, then showed him the notebook. "I was working."

He read silently. For like six seconds because I hadn't accomplished all that much. "Jesus, Lu, this is all you have? You can't send that in to Hafsah."

"Oh really? I thought I might pitch a new relationship column written by a toddler."

He shook his head. "I dunno about that. Hell of a vocabulary for a toddler." We crossed the lobby toward the employee room. "I don't mean to pour salt on a clearly gaping wound, but what the hell have you been doing for the past week? I thought you had more than enough material."

"It got complicated."

"What, you're in love with Cal?"

I smacked him on the chest, harder than I would normally. "Shut your face, man. I'm not in love with anyone."

"Right." Pete slipped his work shirt over his head and threw his backpack into a locker. "So where's the complication? Write a few paragraphs about how they're hanging on to love while they can and that you and Leo couldn't and then move on."

"Wow, that's really reductive. It's harder than that to write something compelling. You just threw together a sentence about the main idea. Not even the right one. *A* main idea."

Pete rolled his eyes. "I apologize. So why haven't you written more than one borderline toddleresque paragraph?"

"Leo's still in love with me."

Silence filled the employee room. I looked at Pete, begging him to just say the right thing again, like he always used to. Just tell me what to do, what to say, what to think, how to live.

"Oh no," he said. "Have we gone back in time? Are we still at the start of the summer? Has your obsession switched back?"

"This isn't wishful thinking or delusion. He told me."

"Your ex-boyfriend, Leo Juco, said those words."

"Yes."

"I'm gonna need you to run those exact words by me."

We walked over to the computer system where we clocked in for the day. "Beginning quote from Leo Juco, in an email sent last Friday at eight thirty in the morning: 'Do you know that I still, dot, dot, dot—'"

"He said 'dot dot dot'? Just wrote out the words like that?"

"No, it was in the subject of the email, so the ellipsis naturally popped up."

"Ah, got it. 'Do you know that I still, dot, dot, dot.'" He motioned for me to continue with his hand, and his eyebrows, and basically his entire body.

"'That I still love you.'"

Pete raised his eyebrows the farthest they could go. "Those were the words he wrote?"

"In their entirety. Oh wait, he also added, 'I thought maybe you should know.'"

He relaxed his facial muscles, and we walked over to the whiteboard to look at our shift assignments. "Who's the 'I' in that email?"

"Pete, focus."

"This happened last week? These were the developments you mentioned? How the hell did you keep this all from me for a freaking week, Lu?" I waved the notebook in front of his face. "Right, the lovebirds." Pete rolled his eyes, then used his wiry index finger to trace his name along the clipboard that listed our duties. "Yay, box office."

I checked to make sure I was there too. "Oh thank God. I'll be able to work on the column during the lulls."

"I take it this means we won't be hanging out after work."

"We'll get back to our routine soon enough," I said, opening the door to the box office for him.

"I've heard that one a few times this summer," he muttered, plopping down into the farthest chair. The shutters were still down on the box office window, so I flicked on the lights, then powered on the register computer. "What'll be the next obsession that keeps me from hanging out with my best friend before I move five hours away?"

"Come on, that's not fair."

"I agree. I tried to help you get over Leo, I tried to help you find topics to write about. Instead you jumped into this unhealthy obsession with the lovebirds and I've spent the summer twiddling my thumbs waiting for you to be available." Pete was raising his voice a little, which he never did. He was also resolutely looking away from me, even though he'd already logged in and there was nothing to see on his computer. I was about to respond when Brad came in, jiggling his keys.

"Hey, gang," he said.

"Gang?" Pete and I responded in unison. We shared a look then fell back into silence, a tension building that I wasn't expecting.

"Yeah, that felt weird to me too." Brad whistled a little bit, searching through his comically large key ring, until he found the one needed to automatically raise the metal shutters. They were painfully slow, creaking with every inch they moved.

"Why are these even automatic?" I said, tossing a pen at them. I was hoping Pete would laugh or smile or something, but he seemed to be stewing in his annoyance at me. By the time Brad finally left, Pete was exemplifying textbook restless leg syndrome and brushing the hair out of his eyes so regularly it was as if his movements were guided by a metronome.

Obviously, he was upset, but I wasn't really in the mood

for a Pete diatribe. Tactless honesty would have to wait until after my column had been sent in. "Wouldn't it be great if Brad started talking in really outdated slang? Which decade do you think he'd pick? I'm picturing him speaking like someone who was a little cool in the '50s. Calling people 'cats' and saying 'neat-o' and stuff. That'd make this place a little more lively, huh?"

No response from Pete. He even pulled out his phone, which is not something he usually did at work, or at least not to the same extent as most of our coworkers. I could see him scrolling through Twitter, then closing out of it, and immediately opening it back up.

I scooted my chair closer to him, using the pen I'd tossed at the shutters to poke him in the ribs. He swatted at me. "Read the room, Lu."

"I did, and the mood didn't appeal to me, so I'm trying to move it in another direction." Pete sighed and set his phone facedown beside the computer mouse. "Come on, give me a decade of slang for Brad. Maybe '60s grooviness? Early '80s hip-hop?"

Pete chewed his lip, which gave me hope that I'd successfully turned the room in my favor. But he just kept staring out the window at the intersection of Third Avenue and Eleventh Street. The stoplights went through a couple of cycles. A homeless man with a mess of dreads and dangerously low-riding pants shuffled by. No one approached our window.

I leaned over and poked Pete again in the ribs. "Will you help me with my column?"

Suddenly, Pete pushed away, smacking the pen out of my hand. "For fuck's sake, Lu! Take a hint."

I froze, feeling my jaw succumb to cliché and gravity. The hurt kicked in a moment later. "Fine," I said. "Whatever." I faced forward like he was, grabbing another pen from the holder in front of me. I twirled it in my fingers, tapped it on the edge of my notebook, remembered that I had a deadline that afternoon and I was going to need every second that I could get to formulate something deliverable that wouldn't cause my life to unravel.

I looked around for any approaching customers, then opened my notebook to a fresh page and pressed the ballpoint tip to the first line. But now I had that goddamn restless leg thing going on, and the only thoughts in my mind were definitely not deliverable to Hafsah. I put the pen down and turned back to Pete. "I get that you're upset, but that was messed up, Pete. All I'm doing is—"

Pete swiveled his chair to face me. "Is what, Lu? Please, I'd love to know exactly what it is you've been doing all summer."

I scoffed, tears unexpectedly rushing to the brink. I had to look away to keep them from coming. Some guy carrying a closed umbrella was standing on the corner, looking up at our showtime display boards while texting. "Writing! At least trying to. It's how I process the world, Pete. And it's what I want my future to be, a fact that becomes infinitely less likely if I don't get this column done. So I'm sorry if I haven't been lavishing you with attention while I work on that."

"Oh bullshit. You're not processing a thing. You're using this column as an excuse to do the exact opposite." Pete glanced outside, probably thinking like I was that the umbrella-toting guy better hold off on his desire to purchase a ticket until we were done. "You've spent all summer clinging to the notion that because Iris and Cal survived their precollege breakup, then so can you. You've been in denial about Leo, and instead of writing and processing your heartache, you've plunged yourself into this weird fantasy where they are the golden standard of love, and you're hoping that their love will somehow rub off on you." Pete took a long breath, then exhaled through his nose. I couldn't help but wonder how long he'd been holding this in.

"That's not what I'm doing." My voice came out as a whisper. Umbrella Guy chose that moment to walk up to my window. I went through the motions of getting him his ticket, and dropped his change onto the floor when I tried to slip it into that little slot beneath the window.

"You haven't written anything, Lu. You're not processing the world around you. You're trying to distract yourself from your pain. And I get that. Of course I get it." Rather than brushing the bangs out of his eyes, Pete ran his hand through all of his hair, mussing it rather spectacularly. "I've been here just wanting to help you in whatever way I could. Instead, I get left sitting at home waiting for texts from you, while you feed an unhealthy crush on Cal."

"I don't have a crush—"

Pete waved his hand in the air. "That's not the point." He swiveled his chair from side to side, our eyes not meeting. His leg had stopped shaking. Outside, the clouds parted and a beam of light hit the building across the street. "You know I put in my two weeks here, right? And that a week after that I leave the city? You know that all I wanted for this summer was to hang out with you as much as I could, to enjoy your company while I had it? And you've acted like that doesn't mean a thing to you. You could have listened to me. You could have written about anything else, like the heartbreak that's causing all of this. But you've chosen not to. You brought this on yourself."

I couldn't look at Pete anymore. My stomach started churning, like maybe I really had gotten food poisoning at some point. I stared out our window, begging everyone who entered my periphery not to approach. I waited for my retort to come, but all I could feel was the stinging threat of oncoming tears, and a queasiness in my gut.

So I grabbed my notebook, rushed out to the lobby to find Brad, told him I was sick, and then fled the theater.

Indie Folk Album
BY LU CHARLES APRIL 17

You ever have one of those days where you feel like you're stuck in a particularly sad indie folk song? More like one of those weeks, maybe.

I've discovered loneliness is still something you can feel in a relationship. I think we're all taught to believe that love inoculates you from certain unpleasant feelings, but that's either a lie or I'm still bad at this whole love thing.

I guess that's to be expected. I'm doing it for the first time, and it's no longer just in my head, where everything can go swimmingly all the time. There's someone else involved, and that always complicates things. As a writer I understand this discrepancy between what's in your mind and what shows up in real life. It's just a little more difficult to deal with when it's, you know, not just writing.

Like in writing, it's hard to know whether the problems are real or just in my head. I'm critical of myself when I write, and so I guess the same could be true of my relationship. I don't know if the silence I've felt this week has a reason behind it, or if its significance is imaginary.

It's not like anything tangible has changed between us. Our

touches don't feel lesser in any way, our silences aren't heavier, none of the usual indie-movie indicators that something is astray are present. We're still saying I love you and spending time together, and I couldn't point at anything in our relationship that I would change. But I feel a weight somewhere, just off on the horizon, like a storm brewing, and I have no idea what it is.

I'd ask him if he feels the same way, but calling attention to it might just reveal my insecurities. So I'm putting them here, where I can have strangers tell me whether I'm being silly. And if he's reading, he can bring it up (Hi, babe).

I've gone back and read my previous columns, searching for clues as to how to help myself. I've also gone through the vast resources of relationship advice columns, self-help blogs, that wonderful archive of human emotion that is Tumblr.

Nothing's helped. Maybe because this is a wave of emotion that will pass. It has no specific cause, and therefore no specific solution. Or maybe the problem is specific but I can't put a name to it, and so, like an undiagnosed disease, it's impossible to know what solution will work.

Maybe it's too much for us to expect an instruction manual for love. It's a complicated thing, and even those who have loved before and loved well cannot promise us a step-by-step guide.

I'm only a chronicler, in the end. Take in what I see, process it through my particular lens of experiences and insecurities, spit it back out at you to do with what you will. Just because the experiences are a little closer to home now doesn't mean I'm suddenly an expert. This is my one relationship, and it looks like no others, can be treated like no others. The human heart is layered and complex, and it'd be foolish for even a love columnist to pretend she knows exactly what goes on within its thin walls. (Are heart walls thin? Probably not. All the cardiologists reading this feel free to go nuts in the comments.)

All I can claim to do is see what happens to us teenagers in love and share it with the world. I'm content with that, at least.

22
A FLIGHT TO NAIROBI

I found myself at Madison Square Park, eavesdropping on a woman's phone conversation with what sounded like her grown son. She was wearing traditional Orthodox Jewish garb and picking at a blueberry muffin that she'd laid out on her lap, the crumbs attracting pigeons which she would intermittently shoo away with a lethargic wave of her hand.

"Did you call your landlord about it?" she asked, brushing crumbs from her skirt.

I wrote down her words out of habit, out of a desire to shut my brain up.

"Mmm-hmm," the woman continued. "Right. Yeah, no, I know. But what about asking him again? You have to bug him a little or he'll never do anything about it."

Really compelling stuff, I know. I kept writing, filling almost two pages with lines from her conversation and the meaningless details of the park surrounding us. The scruffy brown pigeon that looked a little diseased and was unperturbed by the woman's halfhearted attempts to make it go away. A dumpling food truck was parked behind us, and every now and then the girl working inside called out a name and an order.

I tried to remember if I was on the same bench where I'd met Cal, but I hadn't quite taken note of it at the time. I'd taken note of his attractiveness, and the way he talked, and of Leo's absence.

My pen stopped moving. I moved my notebook beside me on the bench, rested my elbows on my knees, rubbed my face a few times, tried sighing to get it all out. Then I buried my head in my hands and begged the tears not to come.

Thankfully, at that moment, my phone buzzed. God bless these little computers we carry around with us, and their ability to pull us far away from our thoughts and pains and public meltdowns.

Iris
Hey! Doing anything tonight?

My mind flashed forward to me on my bed weeping while Netflix played a cartoon for no one.

Lu
No set plans. Why, what's up?

Iris
Cal and I are going to a party, wondered if you wanted to come.

Iris
It's in Washington Heights. 7 pm.

I looked at my phone. It was barely ten in the morning.

Lu
Sure! I'm in. You guys wanna get dinner or something first? Lunch? Coffee? Piggyback rides?

Lu's Conscience
Hey. Aren't you forgetting something?

Lu
Shut up, I'm not talking to you.

Iris
Haha. Sure, let's keep in touch. Either way,
I'll send you the address and let
you know when we're on our way?

Lu's Conscience
Dodged a bullet there. You need
to gety our column done.

Lu
WTF. How are you sending out typos?

Lu's Conscience
It's been a weird day. Just write your
column, will you?

Lu
Sounds good! Thanks for the invite!

The good news was that I'd now weaseled myself out of work, and could focus the next few hours on keeping my entire life from falling apart. So, naturally, I went to Cal's coffee shop. Look, it was nearby, and sometimes when you can't decide where to go for a writing session you end up wandering around being nitpicky and wasting entirely too much time, so it was a very responsible decision on my part.

I walked there listening to that same podcast from the morning, still not listening to a word of what was happening, but happy to have some other noise blasting directly into my brain. Also, it made me look super casual when I walked in, as if I didn't know where I'd stumbled into. A cute black girl with a septum piercing was at the register, not the cute bespectacled white boy I was hoping for. I ordered a regular coffee which came with refills, set up my computer in a spot that hit all of my checklist items (outlet, view), and only then looked around the coffee shop for Cal. And I swear to the god of reliable narrators that he walked in at the exact moment I turned to the door.

Which, of course, meant I started staring intently at my computer, setting my fingers on the keyboard and chewing my lip like I was reaching desperately for a word, or mired in the internal suffering of a true artist. My Word document wasn't even open yet, and I'd paused the podcast, so there was nothing distracting me from the fact that I could see Cal walk toward the register, pause, do a double take, then head my way.

It was hard to not burst into a smile when he arrived at my table, but I managed to keep the charade going. Then he reached out and tapped my shoulder. I jolted out of my fake focus—my fauxcus—taking a moment to process who'd dared to interrupt my intense work session. He was wearing a gray button-down shirt with his sleeves rolled up, the strap of a laptop bag slung diagonally across his chest. He smiled at me and waved, and I made a show of raising my eyebrows in surprise and taking my silent earphones out.

"Hey! What are you doing here?"

"Hey! I wasn't sure if you'd be here today or not," I said. Then I pointed at my computer. "It's deadline day, so I pretended to be sick at work and came here to put the finishing touches on the column."

"Oh man, that's exciting. I can't wait to read what you really think about us." He leaned over to sneak a glance at the screen, which made me almost panic and throw the laptop to the ground. Thankfully he didn't seem to really process the blank Word document I had open.

"It's a scathing indictment of your relationship."

"I'd expect nothing less." He chuckled. "I'll let you get some work done, then. Iris says you're coming to the party later?"

"Yup!"

"Awesome. No piggyback rides though."

"Aww, come on. It's my turn to give you one."

"Fair enough. By the way, your face?"

"Magic, I know."

We smiled at each other, and then Cal went back into the kitchen and reemerged behind the counter wearing an apron. I put my earphones back in and stared at my computer screen, feeling so much better than I had all morning.

For the next two hours or so, I proceeded to accomplish absolutely nothing, even with my phone buried deep in my bag to avoid distractions. I typed a bunch, but it was mostly gibberish or freewriting so that if Cal glanced in my direction I would seem like I was really getting work done. My leg didn't stop nervously shaking. I flipped through the notes I'd taken over the last couple of weeks, rereading them at least two or three times. Every now and then, I allowed myself glances at Cal steaming milk and grinding coffee beans, chatting amiably with customers and coworkers.

I checked my email obsessively, half hoping that Hafsah would message and say that she was actually super busy and could I hold off on sending the column until next week/next month/whenever I was ready? I also looked up flight options that combined the cheapest possible ticket with the farthest possible location. I even worked out a formula in a spreadsheet where I'd plug in all the numbers so I could rank the flights in order of cost per mile. I drank so much coffee that my stomach hurt and I got heart palpitations.

When I looked down at the right-hand corner of my computer screen and noticed what time it was, a fresh wave of panic washed over me. Why the hell had Pete chosen today to pick his little fight with me? Why had Leo left his stupid voice mail last night? I could have been at work focusing on writing. Instead, my brain was mush and the only thing that helped me feel semicoherent was looking up at Cal. I closed out of all my internet windows, put on my favorite playlist to write to, closed the spreadsheet, angled my body a little bit so that I couldn't look over at the coffee counter without craning my neck.

I cracked my knuckles because that's a thing that helps according to writing montages in movies. "Okay," I told myself, "no distractions, get this thing done." Then I got up to use the bathroom because I'd had approximately twelve cups of coffee and my bladder was not happy with me.

To get the key to the bathroom, I had to go ask someone working. So of course I found myself talking to Cal. "How's it going over there? You look like you're in the zone."

"I'm in a zone alright."

"Almost done?"

"Is a piece of writing ever really done?"

Cal used a dishrag to wipe down part of the super fancy espresso machine beside him. "Yes?" he asked, cracking a smile. "I think yes."

"I was asking philosophically, you philistine. You know—" I made air quotes "—'Art is never finished, only abandoned.'" I fidgeted with the silver ladle that they had attached to the key to keep people from forgetting it inside the bathroom.

"So is that the stage you're at now? Editing and perfecting?"

My mind flashed to the image of my computer screen, the word count on my document. "Ish."

Cal smiled, and then his coworker with the septum ring came over and said something to him, pulling him away so that he could complete some task or the other. I used the bathroom and then returned to my computer. It was only about noon, so I still had five hours to figure out how to do the thing that had eluded me all summer. No big deal.

Plus, anytime I let my guard down for a moment, my treacherous thoughts returned to what Pete had said. To what Leo had said. To how he still hadn't answered my text message. To all the angles and cracks of my stupid heartbreak.

I looked over at Cal, trying to examine what it was I felt for him. Yeah, he was cute. He was great to hang out with. But a crush? I chewed on my thumbnail and shook my head to rid myself of those thoughts. Of all thoughts. Instead, I looked back down at my notebook and flipped through my notes. Maybe what I could do was start the column with something Iris and Cal had said during that first eavesdropped conversation.

We have love. What else matters?

Or, no. What if I started the column with an introduction to them?

I would have called bullshit on the whole thing from the beginning if I didn't see both Iris and Cal get the same look in their eyes. Constantly. When Iris hums to herself as they walk hand in hand, when Cal insists on doing the dishes at her parents' house, when she underlines whole paragraphs in novels then simply has to voice her appreciation for what she's just read, and how he'll stop whatever he's doing to listen, even if he clearly has no idea what she's talking about.

One eighteen-year-old gets that look, you start feeling sorry for them. Two of them give that look to each other and no matter what kind of cynic you are, you start thinking only teenagers really understand love. How insane it's supposed to be.

Ooh. That wasn't bad. Except Hafsah wouldn't let me get away with using *bullshit*. I deleted the word and brainstormed possible replacements for it. Which led me to click over to the internet for a few seconds to find a thesaurus, decide that I could just use *bull* instead of the full version, but then continuing to click around the internet instead of going back to my Word document. Before I knew it I was plugging more flight options into my spreadsheet.

There was a crazy cheap flight to Nairobi out of Newark leaving the following month, which I'm not entirely sure how I found. I had enough money saved up to get myself on the flight and then maybe pay for a place to stay for a couple of weeks, and pay for meals, according to a quick search on the currency exchange rate and cost of living in Kenya. It was satisfyingly far away, and I had a fantasy of getting a job as a tour guide, wowing Americans with all the Kenyan knowledge I'd accrued over the course of a few short months, how seamlessly I'd slipped into the culture, my nuanced understanding of how things were different and how they were the same. My familiarity with the best restaurants and food stands in the city would become legendary, and my tour group would become highly sought after as an exploration of Nairobi's culinary highlights. On one of these tours, I'd meet a boy. A Spanish boy. Sparks would fly. We'd spend a night walking around the city talking, ending up on...quick Google search for the best views in Nairobi...the roof of the Best Western Premier hotel, watching the sunrise as we made out. He'd cancel his flight back to Madrid to stay with me a little longer. We'd become more and more intimate, eventually coming so close to one another that we could really *see* who the other was. Until one day he finally brought himself to ask me about what brought me here, what did I run from in America. I'd go really quiet and stare off into the distance. He'd put his hand over mine.

"Hey, it's okay. You can talk to me." A single tear would drip down my cheek, and he'd rub it away with his knuckle, softly palming my cheek and moving my head so I could look into his beautiful brown eyes. "It's in the past. Whatever happened, it's okay. It's over. You have me now."

Then I snapped out of my fantasy, wondering what I would do for the next month until that flight. How would I hang around the house without telling my mom that my scholarship was gone? I checked for a flight leaving tomorrow. The price went up three thousand dollars. Damn it.

I clicked back to my Word document, reread my introductory paragraph, feeling okay about what I had until I saw the time. One o'clock. Four hours to go.

I slammed my forehead down on the table.

At four forty-five, I shut my computer.

I had just emailed Hafsah, and did not want to think about the contents of that email, or the lack thereof. Another apology, another failure to save myself. I finally pulled my phone out of my bag to distract myself. Within the slew of notifications I saw Leo's name, and I clicked to that first.

Leo
Idk. I'm sorry. Can I see you sometime?

I typed out a dozen different responses, deleting them all as soon as I read them back to myself. The longest-lasting one was, Do you really still love me?, which I stared at for almost a full minute, my thumb hovering over the send button before I decided that I was in no condition to be thinking about this stuff. I threw my phone back in my bag and walked up to the register, where Cal was counting out tips from the two different jars (one of those cutesy do-you-prefer-this-or-that ploys which I always fall for).

"Finally taking off," I said.

He looked up from the pile of singles and quarters. "Yeah? The column's done?"

"Oh, I'm done alright."

"I can't wait to read it," he said. "Wait, what time is it?" He pulled his phone out of his pocket. "Oh sweet, I'm almost off. You doing anything between now and the party?"

I shook my head.

"You mind waiting? I'll be done in like ten. Iris was trying to think of what to do before the party. Maybe we could grab something to eat to help soak up the booze."

"You're such a responsible drinker."

He laughed, rubbing the side of his face with his hand and then taking off his glasses to clean them on the hem of his shirt. I don't know why, but I had the sudden urge to help him. I wanted the familiarity of being able to reach over to him, gently pull them off his face, and clean them for him.

"Okay," I said. My voice came out soft and shaky, like I'd just been woken from a dream. "I'll wait for you outside."

Cal and I rode the subway all the way up to the 103rd Street station. Our knees didn't touch, not really, but we were sitting side by side, and other parts of us were in nearly constant contact. Not that I was hoping for that, or whatever. But I did notice. I'll grant Pete that. I noticed Cal's laugh too, and how I felt like myself around him.

We met up with Iris at Xi'an Famous Foods on Broadway, not too far from the party. When we saw her, Cal's eyes lit up with joy, but a little bit of sadness too. Which made sense. She looked fantastic, but he'd soon be me.

He leaned in and gave her a kiss on the cheek, and we headed inside for some insanely delicious hand-pulled noodles. We sat at the counter looking out at the street. Somehow

I got the middle seat, which meant I didn't feel like a third wheel at all. I felt like I was the center of their attention. It felt natural, and comfortable, like by writing about them (or at least meaning to) I'd somehow carved out a little place for myself in their relationship.

It was exactly what I needed, eating spicy noodle soup with Iris and Cal. They didn't pry about the column, they didn't bring up Leo, they didn't even touch on the not-so-distant future in which they'd be broken up and I'd be dropping out of college before I could even begin. August 4 was three weeks away, but rather than delve on that future heartache, they knew how to appreciate the happiness they had in front of them. They joked, talked about each other's days, laid hands on one another in small but deeply affectionate ways. There was no subtext to the conversation, just two people who loved each other. I was in awe and thankful of their presence. It would get a little more complicated than that by the time the night was over, but at that point, I didn't want to be anywhere else but by Cal and Iris's side.

23
THE TRUE MEANING OF PARTYING

The party was at a swanky apartment with its own roof-top terrace. It wasn't huge, but there were about thirty or forty people around, split up evenly between the living room and kitchen inside, and the terrace outside.

A blue-haired girl with a pixie cut let us in without much fanfare, and then Cal and Iris led us straight to the kitchen where the bottles of booze and soda were lined up.

"Mmm, alcohol," Iris said, wiggling her eyebrows at me. "'Drink up, young man, it'll make the whole seduction part less repugnant.'"

"Solid reference," I said.

"Wow, first time someone's caught that," Cal said, reaching for a bottle of whiskey and the stack of red plastic cups.

I eyed the bottles for what I should drink. Again, I swear I don't go straight to the bar at every party, and I'd definitely been given reason to think twice about doing it now. I didn't even believe that drinking could drown your sorrows or worries. Those jerk feelings are good swimmers and will just be there to greet you in the morning. But if there was any night in my life that I needed an artificial way to push them down, it was that night. "So, who do you know at this party?" I asked, pouring myself some tequila and grapefruit soda, which is a concoction Cindy discovered while doing a semester abroad in Mexico.

"Not a soul. Pretty smooth party crashers, right?"

Iris smacked Cal on the shoulder. "Don't listen to him. It's our friend Monica's party." She pointed across the room to an Asian girl wearing jean shorts and a plaid shirt sitting on the couch's armrest. Just then, Monica looked over at us.

She stood up and waved. "Clarice! You made it. Come play twenty-one with us!"

We finished pouring our drinks and went over to her, where hugs and excited hellos were thrown around briefly and then I was introduced to Monica and a handful of others around. "Why Clarice?" I asked.

"Eh, I'm into couple names. Cal and Iris don't really mesh well with each other, so I had to really stretch for one. It stuck, though."

"That's not true," Iris said, "no one else calls us that."

"I didn't say it stuck universally, did I? Just with me. Which counts." Monica smirked, and then she led the group over to the dining room table. "Okay, everyone who's going to play twenty-one, come now!" She called out over the music, which was playing loudly but not ridiculously so.

About ten people gathered around the table, six of us sitting down, the rest standing or squatting wherever they could. Cal had been sitting next to me and Iris, but gave up his seat for a guy with crutches, and ended up standing on the other side of the table, where I could slyly stare at him every time I drank or made a joke or just kind of wanted to.

I tried to follow the rules of the game, which involved counting to twenty-one one by one as a group, but every time we succeeded, the last person had to come up with a new rule for a number. For example, Cal came up with the rule that instead of saying "four" you had to name a city that started with the letter *F*. And for "twelve," Monica came up with the rule that we all had to stare silently at each other for five seconds without laughing. Any time someone messed up a rule or the wrong person counted, we all drank and had to start over.

Needless to say, my goal of forcing my sorrows to swim in a deepening pool of alcohol went pretty well. Now, we all know people that put "I love to laugh" on their social media profiles and senior yearbook pages and online dating profiles, and hell has a special eye roll reserved for those people. But holy crap did laughing on that particular Friday feel like a godsend.

The game was nonstop hilarity. I can't recall accurately whether it was merely drunken hilarity or an honest-to-goodness great time, but who really cares about the difference when you're in the moment.

Eventually the game lost its steam, as we'd all become sufficiently sloshed, at least for that time of the night. We were now ready to party.

And by *party* I mean stand near Iris and Cal all night and joke about whatever came up and look out at city lights twinkling in the Manhattan night while a few people around us talked and shot the shit with their preferred subgroup and some of them danced a little bit.

"How would you guys define *party*?" I asked. I was on my nth cup of tequila and grapefruit soda.

"A festive gathering of people, usually to celebrate a specific occasion," Cal said.

"Okay, Merriam-Webster. Now using your own words. Also, I meant the verb. Like, someone saying, 'we're going to party tonight!'" I added a wooh for effect.

"Hmm." Cal thought for a little bit.

Iris peeled the label off a beer bottle. "It means dancing." She'd asked Cal if he wanted to dance several times throughout the night, but he said he wasn't feeling it. Since then she'd been eyeing the improvised six-person dance floor inside the apartment with a palpable sense of longing.

"Not a universal definition, but respect for working in that subtle dig." He rubbed Iris's back. "I'll dance with you later. Right now I'm feeling more of a buzzed stupid conversation kind of partying."

Iris rolled her eyes, then put her beer down on a nearby charcoal grill, which was already a graveyard of abandoned bottles and red plastic cups. She kissed Cal on the cheek. "Well, I'm not. Lu, care to join?"

"Sorry, I'm with Cal on this one. To party is to banter while buzzed."

"Lame."

We watched her go back inside and join the modest dance floor with three other girls and two guys who were way more skilled at moving their bodies than I would ever be. I looked around the terrace, trying to come up with more definitions. Another summer thunderstorm was brewing in the distance, lightning flashing in the clouds on the horizon. "Thanks for inviting me to this. I needed it."

"Oh yeah?" Cal said, taking a pull from his whiskey ginger. "To celebrate finishing your column?"

I drank to buy myself time to come up with a good answer. "I don't know. I just like spending time with you guys. It's been an easy part of my life at a time when life isn't so easy."

Cal frowned. "Sorry if this sounds flippant or naive or presumptuous, but what in your life isn't easy?"

I stared into his eyes for a moment, then took a sip. "No, it's nothing. Nothing that I'll have to move to Kenya to escape from anyway."

Cal laughed. "Okay, good. And I'm sure this goes without saying, but just because you're done writing about us doesn't mean we have to stop hanging out. You know that, right? We like hanging out with you too. I'm gonna need a friend to help me take my mind off the heartache of my oncoming breakup."

His words brought to mind my conversation with Pete. I took another gulp. Drown, stupid sorrows, drown. I winced, then turned to Cal. "I feel like we haven't put this *party*-definition thing to rest yet."

"You're right. I think we should take a piggyback lap around the party, I hear it's a great brainstorming activity."

"Come on now, we've done a piggyback joke today already. Don't get lazy on me, Cal," I said, giving him a little hip bump, trying real hard not to leave my hip on his. Then I had to add some more liquid to my sorrow pool. "Broaden the definition. Regardless of *how* someone chooses to party, what's a definition that's all encompassing, whether it's dancing or buzzed banter or yelling 'woooh' repeatedly."

Flashes of lightning made us pause for a second. A few people at the party oohed, but most didn't seem to notice. Monica was on a lounge chair making out with the girl with the blue hair, and there were a few other hookups happening. Most everyone was just kind of standing, talking, laughing, drinking, sitting, not drinking.

"I guess I'd say that to party is to live in the moment," Cal said.

"Hold my drink, I have to throw up on you."

"Yeah, I'd like that stricken from the record. Permission to rephrase?"

"Granted, but do it quick, my stomach is lurching."

Cal laughed his rising-bread laugh, then took a seat on the ground, resting his back against the wall and stretching his legs out in front of him. He patted the floor next to him, and

I was more than happy to oblige. We were at the far end of the terrace, with the railing at our left, the inside of the apartment at our right, and the whole party in front of us.

"I think the true meaning of partying is..." He gestured vaguely with his hand, then dropped it into his lap. "I was going to say 'living in the moment' again. It sounds so lame, but I think it's kind of true. Parties aren't necessarily about celebrating life or anything like that. I mean, some of them are. Birthdays and New Year's are quite obviously a celebration of still being alive. But, parties in general, their biggest goal is to provide enjoyment, right? To be aware of the joys of the moment." He brought his drink up to his lips. "Whether it's in the form of a chemical buzz, or..." he pointed at Monica "...the chance of meeting new people you can create a bond with, or..." he motioned toward the mini dance party "...letting loose with your body..."

"That's a weird way to say 'dancing.'"

"Those are all acts of enjoying the moment. Forgetting the not-easy parts of life in the company of others, just for a night, just for a few hours." He crossed his legs at the ankles and leaned his head back against the wall, his eyes glimmering with joy and alcohol, and I want to say "moonlight," but it was overcast to the point where the city lights were reflecting off the clouds and the shimmer in his eyes probably came from a nearby lightbulb.

That's when I felt it. Or, I should say, that's when I recognized the feeling for what it was. The warmth in my stomach, the inability to look away from his face, the desire to keep the conversation going all night, the slight appreciation for the fact that Iris had stepped away to dance and had left us alone. Pete was right.

"Somehow I don't feel like throwing up anymore," I said quietly.

What a realization, to know that you are in love with someone. Even if it was just a crush, even if it was ill-advised, even if it was confusing. It was still some degree of being in love. Cal was appreciative, attentive, shared my sense of humor. He was warm, thoughtful, *good.*

He wasn't a distraction from my heartbreak over Leo. He was the cure. Hell, these were things I missed about Leo that now felt like qualities Cal had in excess. And he didn't like me only after making the mistake of leaving me behind. He liked spending time with me, he'd just said so.

I put my drink down on the ground suddenly feeling like I didn't need it anymore. I could see Iris in the apartment, moving to the music, her hands in her thick, curly hair as she danced. She looked so happy. Like these were the only moments that mattered, not whatever was to come. I wondered if I would have been happy if I'd known the breakup with Leo had been coming. I wondered what would happen on August 4, after Iris had left, after Leo had left, after Pete had left, when it would only be me and Cal together in the city.

But then I pushed the thought down. I stole another glance at Cal, then watched the partygoers standing around, drinking, flirting. "Do you think you can identify the people at this party who are in love?" I asked.

Cal made a little humming noise somewhere between a laugh and the noise people make when they want to indicate that they're thinking. "I dunno. Probably not. Do you think you can?"

"Yeah," I said, nodding. "It's pretty easy. All of us here. Everyone, all the time. Just walking around being in love. It's what people do. We can't get away from it, no matter how much we try."

The song playing on the speakers inside changed to something slow, and the dance party broke away. Iris moved to

the kitchen and grabbed herself a fresh beer, apparently forgetting the one she'd set down on the grill. Monica and the
blue-haired girl had stopped kissing and were now just holding each other on the lounge chair. Another flash of lightning overhead, this time followed closely by a loud rumble
of thunder. Cal turned toward me and our eyes met, the song
getting louder in the background. A few seconds later the first
few drops of a light rain started to come down.

"No complaints from me," Cal said.

24
NORMAL HEART THINGS

I hadn't looked at my phone all night, so I wasn't sure at what time I got home. I fumbled with the key for a little bit, finally creaking the door open as quietly as possible. My mom was asleep on the couch with the TV playing quietly, her phone resting on her chest. I turned off the TV and the floor lamp that was still on, got myself the largest glass of water I could find, and went into my room quietly.

I took my laptop out of my bag and set it on my desk, opening it up but not moving past the log-in screen. For a long time, I sat on the edge of my bed, staring at the screen. I still hadn't changed the background picture away from one I'd taken of Leo in front of our school. It was hard to reconcile the image I saw with who I was now. High school already felt like so long ago, and so did Leo. Even the breakup felt long ago.

While I considered whether or not to log in and attempt one last-ditch effort at the article, or at the very least change the background image, my door creaked open. Under normal circumstances I might have jumped in fear or surprise, but I guess my reflexes were mellowed by the night of drinking. I turned to see my mom in the doorway.

She looked at me for a moment and yawned. "You have fun?" she asked in a whisper.

"I did," I responded.

"Good. That's the last fun you get to have until you can afford to pay rent somewhere in Manhattan."

"Yeah, I figured as much."

"I'm not sure if you've heard, but Manhattan is expensive. You'll probably be here until you've graduated from college, and had at least two to three jobs. I fully intend to ground you that whole time."

I gave her a smile. "Fair enough. At least I'll eat well."

She scoffed and walked over to me, planting a sweet kiss on my forehead. "Suck-up." On her way out, she paused in the doorway. "Are you okay?"

"Yeah, I think so." I bit my lip and looked over at the picture of Leo. She stood there for a while, waiting for me to continue, or maybe trying to figure out just how drunk I was, and whether her bit about grounding me until college graduation was hyperbolic or not. "Mom, how highly would you rank love on your list of priorities?"

She chuckled and walked back over to me, putting her hand on my shoulder. "You're not just asking to get out of your punishment?" I shook my head, and she sighed in response. "In theory, I'd say it's the most important thing. But that downplays the complications that surround it. I'm sorry I don't have a clearer answer for you."

"Yeah, I could have used a clear-cut 'number one.'"

"Sorry, love." She kissed my forehead again. "If you need to talk in the morning, please do. I don't hear enough about your life. You know I want more than just to feed you and complain that you're not home, right?"

Then she left my room, leaving me in the glow of my computer again. I stood up from my bed and closed my laptop with a cathartic click. It felt like letting go of a rope I'd been clinging to for way too long, and the relief in my metaphorical knuckles made me want to sing.

Or maybe that was the booze still in my system. I stumbled to the bathroom, brushed my teeth, washed my face, and came back to my room. I pulled my phone out of my bag and plugged it into the charger, finally looking to the screen to check for notifications, but it had died at some point during the day, so I laid it facedown on the nightstand and slipped into the cold comfort of my sheets. The room was threatening to spin, but I let out a slow exhale, took a long sip of water, and managed to keep it at bay. As soon as my head hit the pillow, I closed my eyes, and allowed myself to dream of Cal.

In the cruel, cruel morning, my serenity had evaporated and left in its place a headache, nausea, and a drained pool where all of my sorrows were now walking around and making it known that the alcohol had not drowned them even a little bit.

I reached for my water, but found that I'd drank the entire glass at some point in the night. "Blurgh," I said into my pillow, which only made my terrible breath waft back toward me, sending my nausea into high gear. "I hate life," I said out loud, hoping that voicing my opinion to the universe would cause it to make some adjustments.

Somehow, I managed to stumble out my bedroom to the bathroom across the hall, grabbing my phone from my nightstand before I left. Opening the door led to a barrage of noises: Jase's video games and the accompanying button mashing and smack talking into the headset, my mom cooking something and the accompanying pans clanking around and blenders going. I swear there was more than one blender going.

"Ahhh," I said, trying to keep this complaint under my breath at least until I made it into the safety of the bathroom.

As soon as I shut the door though, it felt like the noises all got louder. Maybe I was imagining it, but I'm pretty sure Jase was yelling, "I swear my mom wants me to do this! I don't know why! I know I'm screaming! Shut up, Jerry!"

Immediately afterward, there was the hellish sound of someone pounding on the door with the full force of their open palm. "Morning, honey!" my mom shouted at the top of her lungs. "How are you feeling now?"

"Not great, Mother!" I shouted back, very quickly regretting expending the energy it took to do so. I groaned and turned on the faucet, drinking hungrily from the cold Manhattan water. Mom kept pounding on the door. "Why?" I moaned.

"This is your punishment," she shouted, somehow hearing me through the cacophony she was creating.

I shut off the faucet, then crawled to the floor and curled up into a ball, pressing my cheek to the cool tile, staring through one eye at my phone and yesterday's barrage of missed notifications. "Why don't you just ground me?"

"Because of your speech last night."

"What speech?" I felt like crying and puking at the same time.

"Okay, not a speech. You asked me about how highly I'd rank love on my list of priorities. My guess is you didn't just pull that question out of nowhere but were asking for a reason." She blissfully stopped pounding on the door for a second. "As much as I believe you should stay indoors for the rest of your young adult life so that I can keep my eye on you, I'm your mother and want the best for you, and I have a sneaking suspicion you being relegated to this apartment all summer might cause more harm than good."

"Wow. That's actually really cool of you. What's with the noises though?"

"I want this hangover to be so traumatic that you think about it next time you drink." She resumed the pounding while I scrolled past more Leo texts that I didn't want to think about. "Now take a shower to wash your shame away and come out to have breakfast. I finally made Filipino food like you asked. Dinuguan."

"Blood stew? Are you fucking kidding me?"

"Hey! Language. And it's not part of the punishment, it's actually a great hangover remedy. I'm having fun with your misery, but I'm not a monster."

"Where does one even find blood to cook with…?" My voice trailed off. I'd found an email from Hafsah from exactly five o'clock yesterday. *I'm disappointed in you.*

"A butcher, dummy." She pounded one last time on the door, then her footsteps sounded down the short hallway.

My shower was long and painful and provided almost none of the comfort I wanted from it. I kept wanting to lie on the floor of the shower and just fall back asleep under its wet blanket of warmth, but managed to resist.

I'd screwed up so bad. I'd lost my column. I was going to lose my scholarship. I'd wasted my summer away being heartbroken. I'd sullied my remaining time with my best friend in pursuit of a stupid idea that only resulted in… Well. It *had* given me Cal. And it was a weird situation, but the only thing that felt okay during that shower were thoughts of Cal. The fact that he was staying. Everyone would be gone, except for him.

I turned my face into the water, closing my eyes, trying to find a way to make everything okay again. Instead of solutions though, all I got was a montage of the time I'd spent with Cal over the past few weeks. The bench, the subway, the party in New Jersey, the pier, last night.

What if I didn't have to make *everything* right?

What if I just held on to one good thing the summer had provided for me? This boy who was part of a ridiculously romantic, albeit doomed relationship. What if the reason I'd met him wasn't to write about him and Iris?

I opened my eyes again, my heartbeat starting to quicken, a smile managing to break through my hangover's defenses. A closed window means an open door, right? People say something like that? What if a bunch of facets of my life were coming to an end, but something else was set to begin? A cliché, maybe, but who cares about lacking originality if a cliché leads to joy?

After I toweled off and ate my bloody breakfast (way too rich for my queasy stomach, but surprisingly tasty), I sat on the couch while Jase played his video games at full volume, trying to think of what my next course of action would be. I wanted to reach out to Pete, but he hadn't texted me at all yesterday after I left the theater, and I had the sneaking suspicion he wouldn't be on board with my plan to salvage my summer/disposition/love life/life.

I brainstormed to the best of my ability under my current conditions. It actually wasn't all that bad, because at long last I didn't have the pressure of trying to write. That part was over now. It hadn't exactly been a quick pull of the Band-Aid, but I no longer had to worry about it. I could let my writing come to me whenever it was ready. The way love did. Or something.

In the end, I decided that I didn't need a big plan. I just needed to see Cal, maybe talk to him openly, see if he felt the same way I did. He had to. The way he'd cleaned up after me after slamming my face into the ground. How well we got along. He called my stupid face magical. That meant something, didn't it?

Under normal circumstances I would have stepped far away from someone in a relationship. Especially someone as clearly in love as Cal and Iris were. But these weren't normal circumstances. They themselves had decided that the love was secondary to timing. In the space they carved out for that sensibility, I could see how feelings for me could sneak in. Even if he didn't know it yet, there had to be something there, right?

Lu
Good times last night. Thanks
again for the invite.

Cal
To party would not have been
the same without you.

Lu
☺
Are you as hungover as I am?

Cal
I was, but then I went for a run.
It works every time.

Lu
A run. While hungover.
You either have incredible mental fortitude
or are a way bigger idiot than you make
yourself out to be.

Cal
Say what you will, but I am now hangover-free.
What's your go-to remedy?

Lu
Er. I had blood soup today.

Cal
Ugh. Sounds offal.

Lu
Clever. Wasn't bad, actually. Wouldn't
recommend while hungover, but I'd try it again.
What are you up to today?

Cal
Relishing my non-hangoverness by
walking around the city.

Lu
Coolio. Iris too?

Cal
She holds similar views to you about
running after a party, so she's still in bed.

Lu
Want some company?

Cal
Sure!

The High Line was unsurprisingly busy. After yesterday's late-night thunderstorm, the sky was a brilliant blue and the heat had been momentarily washed away, leaving a cool breeze in its wake. I was in my favorite gray dress, carrying nothing with me but my phone, keys, and a few five-dollar bills. No notebook, no laptop, not even the earphones I usually jam in as soon as I leave the house. Physically, I was still feeling less than perfect, but mentally and emotionally I was feeling… Okay, still less than perfect. I was still in deep, deep shit, and suddenly on a life path that I had not planned on.

But I was going to see Cal. And I would get to keep seeing Cal. I took a seat on a long bench that looked out at the water and was near a stretch of food kiosks and coffee stands.

To my right, a couple speaking in Spanish were toying around with a selfie stick, laughing tirelessly at their poses and private, whispered jokes. I wished I understood enough Spanish to pick up on some of the details of their conversation, but could only catch the occasional word.

The foot traffic was constant, tons of people holding iced coffees and popsicles and each other's hands. I looked around, hoping to see a couple on a date to eavesdrop on, or even a couple breaking up, since last time it hadn't gone so bad, in the end. I didn't spot anything like that, but I was content to look out at the parade of humanity passing by in front of me.

Every now and then my thoughts turned to Cal, and what I should say. Should I have a speech prepared? Should I wait until August 4? Would it be a completely selfish and inconsiderate thing to want him the way I did, to burden him with these feelings I'd developed? Or would I be doing what I'd been told to do by nearly two decades' worth of art: following my heart, putting love above all else? Would I be doing what Iris could not do for him?

I didn't want to think about Iris. She was letting him go. I liked her and admired her and wanted to keep her as my friend. Maybe she would understand. It was love. I turned my attention back to people watching, emptying my thoughts, still feeling a little physically miserable but nevertheless enjoying the sun on my skin and the breeze in my hair and my ass going numb from sitting on the wooden bench too long.

Cal took a seat even before I had noticed him approaching. Which was awesome because it totally saved me from spotting him and then trying to figure out if I should pretend I hadn't or if I should hold his gaze the whole time.

"You look very content for a hungover person," he said, squinting into the sun. He had an iced coffee in his hand and looked freshly showered, his hair too damp to take on its normally tousled look.

"I *am* content," I said, by way of a greeting. I felt like reaching out to grab his coffee and take a sip, but withheld the intimacy for the time being. "It's a beautiful day out. I got drunk without someone pile-driving me into the concrete, so—"

"I think it was more of a suplex last time."

"I'm hanging out with you. My worries, however big or small, will be dealt with some other time, by a future version of myself that is more ready to deal with worries because she's already had this little moment of joy."

Cal smiled at me and took a sip of his coffee. "I can tell you're a writer." Then he lifted his cup at me like he was offering a sip. I tried to maintain my short-lived reputation for being chill by not knocking it out of his hands as I rushed to grab it.

"How's your day going?" I asked when I handed back his drink.

"It's good. Again, the run helped. It's a cool feeling to defeat a hangover. Like a superpower." He swirled the ice cubes in his coffee, then looked around the park. "I've actually been thinking a lot about the…" He trailed off, making a halfhearted motion in the air with his hand. "You know, the breakup."

I know people describe all sorts of nonsense things that they think their hearts have done. Backflips, somersaults, lurches, skipped beats. That's ridiculous. Hearts just beat until they don't. Contract and expand. Pump blood in and out. Maybe an arrhythmic beat here or there due to a medical condition. But when he said that, I almost understood what they meant. I twirled my hair as nonchalantly as I could manage. "Oh yeah?"

Cal bit his lip, scooted back on the bench so that he could lean all the way against the backrest. I had noticed he was not the most relaxed sitter, often falling into poor posture. Now he looked at ease. He crossed one leg over the other and set his drink on the bench between us. I could see little indents of teeth marks on the straw, and I thought to myself: *He's a straw biter. That's a thing you know about him now.*

"Yeah," he said. "And I feel strangely at peace about it."

My heart upped its non-heart-like activities. "Really?"

"Not, like, thrilled or anything."

"Of course not. No one expects that."

"Yeah, but not... I don't know. Not devastated. Zen, almost. Like, I know it's going to hurt more than this at some point. Probably a lot more. But I had a lot of joy over the last two years with her. And this isn't the last I see of joy in my life." He turned to look at me as he said this, holding eye contact with me for far too long for it to not mean something. I smiled at him.

"No, it's probably not."

"Yeah," Cal said. He picked up his drink and looked away from me, toward the water. "And it's weird to come to terms with that. That I'll have joy again, it just won't be coming from her. It'll be from someone else." For good measure, another glance in my direction. I hadn't bothered even pretending to look away, so our eyes met again. Now it was my entire body doing un-body-like things. Chills, waves of goose bumps, floating. All the possible hyperbolic descriptions people use. "It's weird, you know? Thinking like that. But I know it's true. Here comes another quote for you. 'Love was not a quantifiable substance. There was always more of it somewhere, and even after one love had been lost, it was by no means impossible to find another.' That's from—"

At that moment, all my questions flittered away. All my doubts about what I should do, what things could mean, whether he felt the same way. It was clear to me that he did. That we would be each other's unquantifiable new love. I cut the distance between us, parting my mouth and waiting for the beautiful, inevitable moment when he would part his too and kiss me.

But it never came.

Cal pulled away. He stood up. His brow furrowed. He looked like a skittish animal about to bolt across a meadow. "What was that?" he asked.

My heart went back to doing normal heart things.

"Lu, what was that?"

"I thought…" I started. But nothing else came. I couldn't look at him. I pulled my knees up to my chest and stared at my shoes. The Spanish-speaking couple next to us said something in their beautiful quick tongues, then stood up. A family of four squeezed into the space they'd occupied.

It felt like several groups of people took a seat, enjoyed themselves, then made way for someone else. The earth rotated several times. Cal and I didn't say a word. He stood there, clearly not knowing what to do with himself. "Lu," he said, tenderness in his voice. But not the tenderness I was expecting. Or hoping for.

"I'm sorry," he said. I dared to look up at him. He had one hand on the back of his head and was looking up and down the pathway, like he was worried someone had seen, like he didn't know how to proceed.

Then his eyes met mine. I didn't know what to do with that gaze. Whether I should plead or apologize or avert my eyes so that he wouldn't have to. I didn't have to second-guess much longer. He walked away, leaving me alone on the bench.

25

DARK DAYS

Dark days were ahead.

Well, not literally. They were bright, summer days that stretched way too late into the evening and started well before I was ready for sunshine.

I went to work and came back home, leaving my phone buried in a drawer so that I could stay far away from all the people in my life. Pete and I severed our attached-at-the-hip workplace relationship, and Brad or one of the other managers must have noticed the tension because they stopped scheduling us for the same shifts and the same duties. When we did see each other at work, we didn't say much. Pete's jaw was perpetually tensed, like he was trying hard to hold back all the wise, honest, tactless things he wanted to unleash on me. One shift we sat together in the box office, each of us staring resolutely out the window, or down at the books we'd brought with us and kept hidden on our laps.

At home, I helped Mom cook. I sat with Jase on the couch and asked if I could play a game with him. I did all I could to keep my mind off the topics of love or writing or human relationships or the future or escaping to Kenya.

It didn't really work.

As soon as I let my guard down, my mind attacked itself, entering loops of the same stupid thoughts repeated over and over until I had to go to the bathroom and pretend I was taking cold showers to combat the heat. I barely ate, claiming I'd been tasting so much while cooking with my mom that I'd filled up on spoonfuls of marinara sauce and bites of meatballs.

For some reason, Mom didn't call me on this obviously terrible excuse. She smiled and said, "Okay, honey. Thanks for helping." Every now and then she'd ask me if I was okay, if I wanted to talk, but I didn't. I wanted to never talk again, since I obviously couldn't be trusted to understand other people in the slightest. I especially didn't want to talk to anyone about love, since I was in no way qualified to do that. Honestly, Hafsah should have fired me a long time ago.

Every now and then in bed I found myself tearing up suddenly, feeling like the world was too much to handle. Or I'd start to tear up because I was just another stupid teen going through another stupid heartbreak. But knowing that didn't help ease the pain at all. I wasn't even sure anymore who I was feeling heartbroken about, Cal or Leo or Iris or myself or my writing. Most of the time though, I tried to go numb. That's all I really wanted. I listened to songs like "What Happens When the Heart Just Stops" by the Swell Season and "To Wish Impossible Things" by The Cure for the comfort of their mopiness, but couldn't even handle listening to the lyrics, so I tuned them out as best as I could.

There was also that small matter of figuring out how the hell to tell my parents that I was about to lose my scholarship. A few times I came close to confessing to my mom, when she was looking at me super sympathetically like she'd already guessed everything I'd gone through. But then I'd have to talk about it all. That felt like something Future Lu was better equipped to handle. I decided to wait on that particular disaster when it naturally arrived in the form of a notice email or repo men showing up to take back that NYU sweatshirt I'd bought when I'd gotten accepted, or however it would happen.

I got one text from Cal, which I never responded to.

Cal
I'm sorry I bolted like that. But that really
took me by surprise.
Things between us aren't like that, Lu.
I care about you, but not romantically. I'm not
mad or anything. Love is weird and hard. I know.
And Iris isn't mad either. Maybe the three of us
should meet up and talk this out?

I had a few texts from Leo too, most of them classic ex-boyfriend texts like:

Leo
You up?

Leo
Hey, hows it going

Leo
I've been thinking about you.

Leo
Please answer me Lu. I miss you. I'm sorry.

Leo
I'm trying here, but you're not making it easy.

About a week and a half after my disastrous decision to unravel my own life and scatter the pieces like an oversize game of Jenga, I was at work taking tickets. It was a Wednesday night, and since I was tearing tickets I had few ways to get my mind off of the tiny, not-at-all-overwhelming mistakes that I had made.

Pete was working that day, but thankfully he was at concessions behind me. I was trying to keep myself entertained playing one of our people-watching games, I Would Bone That Person. Unfortunately it being a Wednesday night meant there weren't all that many people coming in, and every time I tried to play out a fantasy with an attractive person who came by, my daydream would turn to me fleeing the country well before it progressed to anywhere sexual.

So I made up a new game for myself called I Would Be a Completely Normal Human Being around That Person and Not Act like a Total Weirdo. There was one inherent flaw in the game, which was that I didn't come up with any rules and wasn't playing with anyone, and so I just thought the name of the game every time a person came to hand me their ticket, and that's where the game ended. I put my elbows on my little podium and leaned forward, making it tilt as I sighed. Maybe I could count how many popcorn kernels were on the floor. Or how many times the ugly pattern on the bright red carpet repeated itself within my periphery. Or how many scholarship dollars I'd lost.

Then a wave of panic would creep in, reminding me that I was alone and jobless (well, kinda) and when I'd made a friend who I felt like myself around, I'd proceeded to embarrass myself by projecting my feelings of affection onto him.

"Girl, you look like you're a million miles away."

I looked up. Starla was standing in front of me.

"Hey, Starla." I took her ticket and handed her back the stub. I wanted to follow her into the theater, sit in darkness for two hours while a story took over my mental functions. "No work today?"

"What's going on with you?" She tossed the ticket stub into her open purse and then waved her hand around like she was tracing the outline of my body. "You do not look as sprightly as usual."

The mere fact that she asked me the question threatened to send me into a tailspin of tears. I wanted to leap into her arms and weep into her tattooed bosom while she shushed me and told me everything would be okay.

I blinked back my neuroses and tried my best to fake a smile. "I'll admit I'm not feeling peppy. What are you watching, by the way? I didn't actually look at your ticket. Don't tell my boss."

"You are not just sidestepping that conversation that easily, girl." She moved aside to let a group of high school boys come through. When guys my age come through, I usually do a little scan for attractiveness, or at least try to recognize attraction for me in their eyes. This time I just took their tickets and waved them through, not bothering to count how many tickets they'd handed me. "What's got you upset? Who do I have to beat up? Is it Fart Boy?"

This time tears did fight through to the surface, and I had to take a deep breath to not let them loose. Starla reached out and put her hand on top of mine, her bracelets cold against my skin. She didn't break eye contact, her look kind but unrelenting. I looked over my shoulder toward the concessions and caught Pete watching the exchange, an eyebrow raised until he realized I'd caught him and he pretended to be doing something else.

When I looked back at Starla, I realized how little I knew about her life. We talked about books and bounced one-liners off each other, but I knew nothing about this cool woman I'd been seeing consistently for two years. Other than what she looked like, her place of employment, and her reading tastes,

I didn't know her story at all. I knew she wasn't married, but I didn't know what kind of love she had in her life, if at all. I didn't know the shape of her life outside the bookstore at all, and at the realization that I hadn't ever bothered to ask, a couple of tears fought through my weakened defenses and trickled down the bridge of my nose. I wiped them away with the back of my hand, then saw Brad walking in my direction, looking down at his clipboard as he crossed the lobby. Starla noticed me eyeing him and she gave a little nod with her head, motioning me away from my duties.

I called out to Brad and begged off for a fifteen-minute break, which he acquiesced to quickly.

Starla and I sat on a bench by the bathrooms. "I feel bad. It's like Pete and I have just been mooching advanced reader copies from you for years and unloading our teenage drama on you without asking you about you."

Starla gave a little chuckle. "Are you kidding? I love having you guys around and not having to talk about myself. You're more interesting than I am. Plus, I go to therapy once a week, not to mention the therapy sessions forced upon me every six to eight hours when my mom calls to check in on me."

"I don't know, Starla. You have tattoos and have lived like four times as long as we have. You *must* be interesting."

She pointed her index finger at me and mock-scowled. "Check your math, girl. But fine, I'll say stuff about me first, if that's what you want. Ask away. But then I need you to open up the way the Red Sea parted for Moses or the way my legs parted for anyone with a pixie cut when I was nineteen."

"Wow, okay, that's already quite a bit of info." I looked around the theater for a bit, wondering what exactly I wanted to know, wondering if I was just trying to delay talking about myself. I shrugged. "I don't know, I guess I just want to know your story."

* * *

As it turned out, Starla was much more interesting than she'd let on. I don't know how she'd ever managed to keep this from me and Pete, but she had been married for five years not long after college. Then her husband got sick and his health deteriorated even quicker than the doctors had expected. By thirty she was a widow. She'd had an office job before that, but after her husband died, Starla's main comfort came in books, so she decided to surround herself with them. Hence, The Strand.

"Wow."

"I see that look on your face," Starla said. "Save your comments about not being able to complain about your life now that you've heard about mine. A terrible thing happening to me doesn't mean your pain isn't valid."

I stammered for an excuse a little, then, like with every other situation in my life, opted for a stupid joke. "No, I was just wondering if your husband had a pixie cut."

Starla laughed, then smacked my leg lightly. "Your turn."

I told her everything. How the summer started with Leo dumping me, then my writer's block, eavesdropping on Iris and Cal, the whole of the past few weeks recounted so easily it was hard to believe that it had all happened to me. Once it was all out, I didn't know whether I felt any relief, or if I was closer to tears than I had been at the start. "I know this probably sounds stupid and juvenile," I said, looking down at my lap. "But... I just don't know how I got here. I don't know if anything I've been through is worth this feeling."

At that point Starla put her hand on my knee and raised her voice. "Hon. Wishing you weren't suffering is a whole other beast than wishing you hadn't experienced anything good. Just because I will never stop grieving my husband doesn't mean

I'm going to erase our life together. The bad cannot possibly erase the good."

She looked around, waiting for the people coming out of theater seven to clear out. "That couple? They have the right idea. A weird way of doing it, but they've accepted the bad will come, and that it won't cancel out what they have. My only surprise is that they didn't agree to you writing the column earlier."

"Why's that?"

Starla sighed. "A few years after Larry died, I moved. The memories that I was clinging to at our old apartment had turned more painful than comfortable, so I got out. Along the way I lost a photo album we'd been keeping since we started dating. Mostly of our travels, little paragraph descriptions on the back of each picture. The whole trip summarized into a few lines."

"Oof. I can't imagine."

"You can." Starla gave a tight-lipped smile, then patted my leg. She stood up. "Maybe to a lesser degree, but you understand the feeling, I'm sure. If there's one possession I'd love to have back from all my life, it's that photo album. Just because it's gone doesn't mean the memories are gone. But having a tangible reminder of something that's no longer around means being able to return to bygone comforts. It's proof that what was once gone did exist, however briefly. A reminder that you *were* granted that time, and that can never be lost. If I were that couple, I'd beg you to write the column." She gave me another smile, then checked her wristwatch again. "Perfect. Just in time to catch my movie."

I stood up too, not wanting to go back to actually working. I wanted to sit there and soak in the conversation with Starla. I was afraid if I moved away from the area, I wouldn't absorb some of it, whatever *it* was. The lesson in all she'd said. The wisdom she'd passed on that I was still too hurt and ashamed to fully feel. I wished I'd brought my notebook with me or recorded the conversation. I had the notion that what she'd said deserved its own column too, though I no longer trusted myself with the ability to capture anything of importance.

"Take care of yourself, kiddo. Don't let the heartbreaks silence the love." She reached out and ruffled my hair, then disappeared down the hallway toward the theaters, her bracelets jingling as she walked.

26

JUST HOW LOVE KIND OF WORKS

I spent the rest of my shift deep in my thoughts rather than trying to escape them. When it was over I stood outside the theater and waited for Pete to come out. He had his earphones in and almost walked past me, but then we made eye contact and he stopped in his tracks, pulling out his earphones and wrapping the cord around his phone. "Hey," he said.

For a moment, I tried to read whether he was angry. I'd never known Pete to hang on to a grudge for a long time, but I'd never seen him as frustrated as he had been the other day. I'd missed his presence in my life. Our banter, his advice, the mere fact of his company. The past few days had been the most emotionally draining of my life, and I knew that part of that was because he wasn't around.

"You were right," I said, afraid he might walk away before I got the courage to unburden myself. "You were trying to help, and I'm sorry that I was stubbornly resistant to that. I was..." I chewed on my lip for a second, looked across the street at the sushi restaurant, reached for a word. I couldn't land on one though, and when I looked back Pete was nodding gently.

He pocketed his phone and brushed the hair out of his eyes. "Have there been developments? Your face looks like there've been developments."

"Yeah, but I want to do this first. You mean a lot to me, and I've always trusted your judgment. I don't know why I didn't this time." I shrugged, less of a gesture expressing my quandary and more to show Pete and the universe that I was really at a loss. A moment passed, during which I was afraid Pete would be thoroughly unimpressed by my apology and decide he was done with me. Traffic rolled by, people entered and exited the theater, a bike messenger sped past behind me, blasting music on speakers rigged hidden within his backpack. "Did you know I think of you as my wise, old uncle?"

Pete smirked. "That makes a little more sense than it should."

"I should have listened to you, and I didn't. I went further down the rabbit hole with Iris and Cal, and ended up in a sort of nightmare situation that could have easily been avoided if I'd just paid attention to you. If I'd admitted what was going on. If I'd spent the amount of time I normally spend with you so that your wise, old, avuncular qualities would rub off on me and I would stop being such an idiot."

Pete smiled, then motioned with his head. "I need to get home soon. Walk with me? Or was that it? Because I'm ready to forgive."

Tears rushed to the corners of my eyes again, persistent little fuckers. "I don't know if I deserve to be forgiven yet."

"It's okay. I was hurt and wanted all your attention. I could have done better too. I could have been more supportive."

We started walking down Third Avenue, our gaits slow. Night had fallen already, and the restaurants and bars we passed were filling up. Our shadows stretched behind us as we walked, then receded when we approached the next streetlight, then shifted ahead. "I wasn't the easiest person to be supportive of," I said. "I was obsessed, like you said."

I filled him in on what had happened since our fight, my realization that he was right about my feelings for Cal, how I'd missed my deadline again. That goddamn attempt at a kiss, and the look on Cal's face afterward. Leo.

"I just kind of lost it, you know."

"Oh, I know." He nudged me with his shoulder.

We'd walked past at least two subway stations that Pete could have taken to get home, so now it felt like we were committing to the whole walk to his place on the Lower East Side. "At least you don't have to worry about writer's block anymore, right?" Pete said. "I kept thinking throughout this whole ordeal that you could easily write, if only you weren't so tied down to one idea. It sucks about the job, and the scholarship, and—"

"And the rest of my life falling apart as a result."

"Yeah, that. But at least you don't have to carry this burden of writer's block around with you anymore, you know. You can just write when you feel compelled to do so, about whatever topic is in your heart."

"Yeah," I sighed. We passed by a busy strip of bars, where of course there seemed to be a disproportionate number of couples, people flirting, making out, smearing love and dating and sex all over each other. That was a weird way to put it. "Rub it in, assholes!" I yelled.

Pete laughed. "Been holding that in for a bit?"

"Is it that obvious?"

He laughed, and we slowed our gait even more, looking in at bar after bar of people laughing and pawing at each other. "You never talk to me about your love life," I said. "I don't wanna just unload all my stress on you and make this a one-way friendship. You can lay it on me too, you know. I don't even know what kind of people you're attracted to. I can't believe I've never asked."

Pete shoved his hands in his pockets and shrugged in the same motion, which I filed away as a really poignant gesture which I wanted to use in some future conversation. "I haven't really found anyone that inspires that in me," he said. "Male, female. I don't know if I really have that same drive you and your readers and the rest of the freaking world have."

"Now I get why you suck so much at I Would Bone That Person."

Pete laughed. "Yeah, I figured you might have picked up on it by now."

"I'm sorry, that was shitty to say. Don't let me make you feel bad about that. I'm gonna try to be a better friend. Starting, like...now."

Another laugh, which made feel like I hadn't immediately screwed things up again. "It's okay, I don't always feel like I want to talk about this. It's just not something that's on my mind all the time. I like people, and intimacy. But I don't find myself wanting anything more than what we have, you know? I don't need romantic love, or sex."

"I wanna say you're lucky, but I don't know if that's a stupid thing to say too."

He reached out and gave me a little side hug. "We can go back to our normal dynamic and not talk about me. I kinda like dishing out advice on what to do. Being the wise, old uncle."

"Okay," I said. "But if you ever want to. I'm here, you know. I may suck at it because I'm self-indulgent and self-centered and terrible. But I'm here."

He gave me a little shoulder bump. "Thanks, Lu."

We walked in silence for a few blocks, or at least the relative silence Manhattan can provide. We weaved through a crowd standing in front of a kebab truck, a group of smokers standing outside a bar, a man walking four dogs on a leash. "So, what are you gonna do next?" Pete asked.

"Beats me. Any ideas?"

"You could try to find another writing gig. I bet Hafsah would still write you a decent recommendation. Maybe you still have time to save your scholarship."

"Yeah, I don't know if she will. She might have a soft spot for me, but she won't abide what I put her through."

"Just send in writing samples to other publications, then. Everything that you've been through doesn't erase the fact that you're still a damn good writer."

"Thanks. I'm gonna miss *Misnomer* though. It's so...hip. I don't know if I'll ever be that hip again."

"True. But you don't need to be hip."

I laughed. "Yeah, I guess if I'm being honest it just felt good to fake it. I'll always write for myself. And I'm okay with that because I have no choice but to be okay with that. But the validation feels good. It makes me feel like it's okay that this is how I process my feelings and the world around me."

"Dude, just start a blog, then. Outside validation doesn't have to come with a paycheck. Hell, I'll be your outside validation. You have Twitter followers. You have the internet, and you have talent. Forget about everything you can't control, and just do this thing that comes naturally to you. Everything else will fall into place. Maybe not the exact place you had in mind at the start of the summer, or even a week ago. But there's no use in worrying about all that. Just, you know, keep writing."

I smiled at him. "There's the Uncle Pete I know and love."

We said goodbye with a long hug, and then I made my way

back home and ate Mom's food, and sat with Jase and gave him shit. Mom even joined us on the couch and jumped in on berating him about not contributing to the household. Before she went to bed, she gave me a long forehead kiss and asked me if I was doing okay. I didn't think I could answer with a flat-out yes, but I nodded my head and told her that I was doing better. "Good," she said. Then she told me and Jase she loved us and to keep it down, then disappeared into her room.

We still didn't talk about love deeply, but we'd established a sort of trail, some stepping stones that might someday lead to conversations about it.

Jase turned down the volume on the TV, and I sat there for a while longer, feeling the simplicity of that joy. What a marvelous thing it is, to feel like you've marooned yourself on an island, surrounded only by worries and regret, most of your own making, then suddenly find that the island is an illusion. That you have people there with you, and that they're constantly offering lifeboats.

It still hurt me to think of how wrong I'd gotten things with Cal. I still felt like I wanted to repeatedly hit the undo button on my decisions with the column, just go back on each missed deadline and have a chance to redeem myself. I still felt heartbroken that Leo had left me, and confused about what he wanted us to be, what I should do with his change of heart. But I no longer felt like I was on an island.

A little while later, I said good-night to Jase, went into my room, and opened up my computer.

Iris and Cal

BY LU CHARLES, JULY 20

I would have called bullshit on the whole thing from the beginning if I didn't see both Iris and Cal get the same look in their eyes. Constantly. When Iris hums to herself as they walk hand in hand, when Cal insists on doing the dishes at her parents' house, when she underlines whole paragraphs in novels then simply has to voice her appreciation for what she's just read, and how he'll stop whatever he's doing to listen, even if he clearly has no idea what she's talking about.

One eighteen-year-old gets that look, you start feeling sorry for them. Two of them give that look to each other and no matter what kind of cynic you are, you start thinking only teenagers really understand love. How insane it's supposed to be.

This started out as a plan to profile a series of couples dealing with the question of what happens to a relationship the summer before college starts. When I first pitched it to my editor, it was very timely, since it was the start of summer. Also, I'd just been dumped.

The weeks have gone by though, and my goal of helping out those couples who might have needed some outside perspective is now mostly moot, as I'm sure most of you have also been dumped. If not, good for you. Or maybe bad for you, I don't really know.

Then I met Iris and Cal. Rather, I should say that I eavesdropped on what sounded at the time like their breakup. They were happy, but worried about the challenges of being long-distance, and how that could mar this wonderful thing they had between them. Iris worried that they were too young to survive it, that four years apart was too much. Cal responded with almost the same thing I responded when I'd been dumped by my ex: "We have love. Isn't that enough?"

They went their separate ways. I assumed they'd fallen victim to the precollegiate breakup like so many eighteen-year-olds do. I thought about my ex. I thought, no, it's probably not enough. Not when you're eighteen. Then, through a twist of fate in the form of a dropped wallet, I saw Cal and Iris again.

They were still together.

With a caveat: they were going to break up at the end of summer.

Like any good journalist, I became single-mindedly obsessed over this decision, and convinced myself I had to write about them. Mired in writer's block since my breakup, I convinced myself that they were the only thing I could write about. I had to explore all the nuances of their decision, of their unique relationship, the love that they wanted to hold on to but were okay eventually letting go of. Under the guise of this column, I started spending time with them, eventually forming a friendship based on the mere fact that being in the proximity of their love made me feel better about love itself.

I kept expecting to see dramatic flare-ups caused by their

unique arrangement. I kept expecting their self-imposed expiration date to strain the way they were with each other. But somehow they resisted the dramatic. I saw them both struggle with the thought of losing the other, but throughout the past few weeks, I've also seen them dive into their love so deeply that they achieved what we all hope to achieve—everything but the love faded to the periphery.

Iris has impeccable vintage style, and the confidence to pull off her pinup-model aesthetic. She's funny and insightful, and knows exactly what she wants to do when she goes to school— she's already declared as an international business major at Pepperdine, a school she knew she wanted to attend as soon as she saw the campus.

Cal is charming and considerate, less sure of what he wants from life, but certain that he loves New York too much to leave it. He's got a hipster aesthetic and a few cheesy tastes, but is to his core a good soul that wants the best for others. He'll attend Columbia in the fall.

Together, they make storybook love feel possible. They actually go out of their way to remind me that it is. "It's all about keeping the door open to the possibility," Cal says, quoting a short story, a habit they both share, though it's unsure whether they're drawing on the same material or each have come into this admirable quirk separately. They go on dates to Central Park in order to watch meteor showers, even on overcast days, because Cal doesn't want Iris to go through life never having seen one. Their first date would be the envy of even the swooniest contemporary YA novels. They learn how to cook pasta together, even when they know it's a skill they won't get to share together for long.

In my mind, if I managed to capture the magic of their relationship in one of these columns, then I would be better off. I would have learned something valuable about love, understood relationships better, gotten marginally better at this thing we're all walking around obsessing over all the time. Maybe I could help some of you avoid the same fate I'd met by teaching you to hang on to whatever love is in your lives.

What I managed to do was miss my deadline a bunch of times, lose this job, lose my scholarship, neglect my friendships, neglect my family, fall in love with Cal, and not know what to do when my ex succumbed to my silent wishes and changed his mind, begging to see me again.

This is the point in the column where I tell you how I learned to let go of my broken heart and move on from my ex, how Cal and Iris taught me that love that ends is, even with that bitter end, still love. Or I tell you Cal and Iris's secret for maneuvering the minefield of the summer before college. I tell you how they succeeded where I—and maybe many of you—failed.

Except love isn't that tidy. You've all seen that, if not firsthand then at least in this column. Spending time with a couple doesn't mean I know how they've cracked the secret to love. Hell, the fact that they're happy and facing a difficult decision with level-headed maturity doesn't mean they've cracked the secret to love at all. It doesn't mean they've learned how to avoid heartbreak.

Did I learn a lesson through all this? Kind of. It didn't come from Iris and Cal, but from a bookseller named Starla that I've become friends with. Love that ends was still love.

Have I absorbed that lesson deep in my heart so that it can

fight off all the hurt swirling around inside? No, not really. I think that's just how love kind of works.

I finished the column, finally. It wouldn't run, but I guess I needed someone to read it, and that someone may as well have been Hafsah. It wouldn't fix anything, but at least I'd know that I had turned something in, in the end. I shut my computer and creaked open my window, then slipped into bed. Somewhere nearby, I could hear neighbors arguing, their voices carrying through enough that if I truly listened, I could have made out what they were talking about. Instead, I closed my eyes, and let the conversation fade into white noise.

27
YEAH WHATEVER

The weekend passed by uneventfully, a definite weight off my chest now that I'd managed to write again. Not that my chest was particularly weightless.

I went to work, happy that I could do so next to Pete again. Afterward, we jumped around from bookstore to bookstore. We hung out with Starla for a bit. Then I went back home and had dinner with Mom and Jase. It was supposed to be another New Jersey weekend for us, but Dad had to take a last-minute trip to a conference in Denver, which was fine by me because I don't know if I was ready to face New Jersey again, or his questions about my scholarship.

I resisted texting Cal or Iris, the shame creeping down my spine every time I even looked at their names in my phone. It was weird to miss not just Cal, but Iris too. And on top of that, I couldn't ignore the fact that Leo was still in love with me. I couldn't help but imagine being by his side again, doing it better this time. Going on Cal and Iris–esque dates in Central Park, keeping the door creaked open for life like the movies to sneak in.

On Monday morning, as I was walking to the theater for a shift, I got an email from Hafsah. I didn't want to get my hopes up, but hopes are rebellious little buggers that do what they want. I clicked on the email immediately.

> **Hey Lu,**
> **I'd guessed there was a reason for the missed deadlines. Wish you would have channeled some of those frustrations and heartache into writing, but I understand that's not always how it works. I talked to the team and we decided we will run this column next week. I've attached my notes.**
> **Unfortunately, it will be your last column, as I've already filled the position. If you have any pitches for one-offs in the future, please do reach out.**
> **Take care,**
> **H**

That felt like something. I didn't know what, exactly. But it was something.

Later that night, I found myself with Pete traversing the particular circle of hell that is Times Square. "I can't believe Leo is holding his going-away party at Dave and Buster's," Pete said, avoiding contact with one of those dudes that dressed up like the methed-up nightmare version of your favorite superhero.

"I think he's doing it tongue in cheek."

"But you're not sure."

I sighed, avoiding accidentally photobombing about six different selfies happening at the same time. "No, I'm not sure."

We pushed open the doors and entered the adolescent casino. Baseball and soccer games were on every one of the approximately three hundred television screens around the bar/restaurant/arcade. Dudes were running around holding their twenty-ounce beers and jumping from machine to machine

317

like they never wanted to grow up. I couldn't blame them much. I scanned the crowd, looking for a place Leo and his group of dweebish friends might be hanging out, and spotted them at a long table littered with half-drunk sodas, half-eaten nachos, and fully-eaten chicken wings. Leo himself was not far off from the table, at one of those basketball games where you have to shoot a tiny ball into a tiny hoop to get a tiny amount of tickets.

"We could leave," Pete said, looking around the room, clearly uncomfortable at the abundance of noise and absence of books.

"As much as I want to, I should probably have this interaction. Closure, and all that."

"Alright. Want me to come with? Or should I go pretend I know how to play Skee-Ball, kind of keep my eye on you and watch for some sort of signal that it's all going terribly so I can come intercede?"

"Yeah, the second one." I watched Leo shoot small hoops for a while. He was wearing the outfit I thought he looked best in, his black jeans, a light green T-shirt, and his gray hoodie, which he brought everywhere with him even in summer because he hated intense air-conditioning. I remembered wearing the hoodie a few times, its oversize sleeves feeling like Leo himself was wrapped around me. I remembered the first night we'd ever kissed, how he was wearing a similar outfit, but with a couple of added layers because of the weather. His skin had been warm, his cheeks flushed from the fleece and body contact. The night we'd broken up he was also wearing those pants, only with a tank top instead of a T-shirt. And he'd pulled away as soon as I'd tried to touch him, so there wasn't a clear memory of how his skin had felt.

Pete clapped a hand on my shoulder. "I don't mean to be

an unsupportive friend right now, but can I borrow five dollars for tokens?"

I sighed and gave him the money, then crossed the mayhem of the arcade to approach the stupid, beautiful jerk of an ex-boyfriend who'd landed me in this predicament in the first place. He was next to his friend Miguel, who saw me approaching and thankfully peaced out.

"Lu," Leo said, combing his hair back behind his ear. I wondered if he knew what my name in his mouth did to me. "You came."

I crossed my arms in front of my chest, now wondering if this was a good idea. I tried to look anywhere but into his beautiful brown eyes. There's much to be said about the attraction of new people, but so much more to be said about someone whose eyes hold history for you. "Yeah, I thought it'd be best to say goodbye in person."

Leo rubbed the back of his neck. "Oh. Yeah. Right. I'm glad you're here." Then he broke into a wide smile, his eyes shimmering with what could well have been tears. "Can we go somewhere a little more quiet?"

I looked around. "We're at a Dave and Buster's, I don't know if that exists here."

He chuckled, then walked over to a Jurassic Park shooting game where you could sit down in your own little private booth thingy that was maybe meant to represent a car. He pulled the curtain aside and peeked in. "This is open."

I bit my lip, thinking of sitting in an enclosed, private place with Leo again. I turned over my shoulder and saw Pete playing Skee-Ball, but then spilling a handful of tokens out of his shirt pocket as he tossed a ball. He leaned over to pick them all up, not looking in my direction. "Sure," I said to Leo, stepping inside the booth.

"So, you're leaving."

"Next week. This was just the only day that worked for everyone." He put his hands on his knees, fidgeting. I'd never known him to be a fidgeter. I was the restless one between us, the one who didn't know where hands were supposed to go, didn't know if at any point I looked like a weirdo who thought too much about where to put her hands. A couple of kids ran past the game, causing the curtains to flutter a little. Outside the booth, there was incessant dinging and shouting and simulated explosions. But inside the noise seemed to fall away. "I'm sorry about all the messages. It's just that—"

"It's okay," I said, cutting him off. "I'm sorry I didn't respond. It's been a crazy few weeks."

"Anything to do with those new friends?"

"Partially," I said. Then I took a breath, readying for what I'd come here to say. Pete had helped me figure out exactly what I needed to get off my chest, and I thought the words were on the tip of my tongue, but I suddenly didn't know anymore if I should even bother. He was leaving, my life would continue without him. I looked at the screen, which was in demo mode, outdated but still pretty decent graphics of velociraptors getting shot. I should leave, I thought, let Leo have his fun day with his friends.

Then Leo scooted closer to me, reaching for my hand. I was surprised, but managed to look him in the eyes instead of running out terrified. "Let's try again," he said. "I'll do better. I don't want to lose you." Then he moved his hand to my cheek, and leaned in to kiss me.

God, it was so hard not to accept the kiss. His voice sounded so sincere and tender, and I had no doubts that the regret I could hear was authentic. I'd have his company, even if it was only a couple of times a semester, or in text form. Someone who'd ask after my day, make me feel attractive, funny, loved.

I'd have love back in my life. My words were back. Now all I needed was this.

But somehow, I managed to shut up that part of my brain. I pulled back and put my hand on Leo's chest. And as great as his chest felt, the thrill of touching someone, the memories of slipping my hand beneath his shirt and feeling his skin for the first time, all the times I'd laid my head on his chest while we watched TV, I pulled my hand away.

"I came here to say bye, Leo. That's it." I saw his lip quiver for a moment, and then he turned his head away. "You hurt me when you broke up with me. I wanted us to have a chance. I thought we did. But the truth is that it was probably the best decision. We had what we had. It's over now. We're obviously both struggling with that, but that doesn't mean we should try to erase our hurt. We just have to move past it."

Leo turned his head even farther away, and that annoying part of my brain was momentarily moved and flattered that he could be crying. "Yeah, whatever," he said, his voice almost breaking.

On the screen, the demo started again, all the same dinosaurs getting shot in the same spots. A stegosaurus swung its tail, and the computer simulation failed to shoot at it, so Leo's side of the screen flashed red and he lost a life.

"Yeah," I agreed. "Whatever." I reached over and gave his hand a last squeeze. Despite his tears and terse dismissal, his fingers quickly weaved themselves into mine. He wasn't just regretting the breakup out of loneliness, I knew. He loved me. Still, this felt good. Our love had run its course. We weren't Iris and Cal, weren't a storybook love. What we had was real, but it was also over.

"Take care, Leo," I said. Then I slipped my hand loose, and left the booth.

28
AIRED LAUNDRY

It was mid–August. The heat had only gotten worse as the summer stretched on, but on this particular day another morning rainstorm had cooled the air down, so I decided to go to Madison Square Park and do some people watching and maybe a little bit of eavesdropping. I had to go to work at the theater in an hour, so I wanted to enjoy the nice day as much as I could.

I got myself an iced coffee from a street cart and found a spot on a bench with a good view of foot traffic. I kept my notebook within reach, but still tucked away in my bag. It was one of those days where I felt okay with losing my *Misnomer* gig. Some days weren't as easy going, especially as I was still getting emails from NYU trying to prepare me for the fall semester, which I wouldn't be attending.

My parents had not been thrilled to hear that I'd lost my scholarship, but after a few days of tension, anger, and apparently brainstorming, my mom had come up with the simple solution to defer for a semester or two until I found another job that would allow me to keep the scholarship. If that didn't happen, I'd look for other grants or take out a loan. "You are young, with your whole life ahead of you," my mom had said. "Starting college six months or a year after other people will not change anything. And it'll keep you at home longer, which I'm perfectly happy with." My dad was a little slower to come around, but he still deferred to my mom's judgment on almost everything, and if he was still pissed, he hadn't shown it on my last visit to New Jersey.

I looked around the park, trying to scope out any potentially interesting interactions. Most people were on their own or talking quietly to each other though, and I was kind of happy just watching instead of actively listening. There was a cute boy on the bench across from me too, and he was laughing every now and then at whatever he was listening to through his earphones. He had a great smile, and really clean shoes, which I know is a weird thing to look at but I somehow always notice it first. I wasn't about to go talk to him or do anything outrageous like that, but I was okay sticking around and just watching him laugh and eat his way through a bag of chips until he got up and left or I had to go to work.

My phone buzzed in my pocket, and I pulled it out to see that Pete was trying to video chat me. I answered, holding the phone up to my face but switching the camera function so that it was showing Pete the cute boy instead of me.

"Lu?"

"I'm here. Just showing you this cute guy sitting across from me at the park. Look at how much he's laughing. He's so pure."

"Are you at Madison Square Park scoping out cute boys on benches again? I thought you were morally opposed to reboots. This feels like one."

"I'm not scoping anything out, I was just sitting here having a coffee." I switched the camera again so Pete could see me. He was on his dorm bed, his pillow propped up against the wall. I could see the corner of a *1984* poster above his head. "How's your institution of higher learning treating you? Is your roommate still sleeping twenty-six hours a day?"

"He got up and had a meal the other day, so he's officially not hibernating," Pete said. Then he filled me in on how his orientation and first week of classes had gone. He complained about the paltry number of bookstores in his college town in Rhode Island, and then we bickered for ten minutes because I said him leaving meant I could now legitimately call dibs on Alice.

Right as I was about to hang up, I looked over the edge of my phone to get another glance at the cute boy on the bench, when I saw something else entirely. "Oh my God," I said.

"What? Is someone doing something surprising even by New York standards? I miss the unexpected sights of the city. Nothing here is surprising. Lu? What's happening? Your jaw is doing that clichéd dropping thing that we agreed never happens in real life."

I glanced down at the screen to give Pete a look, then returned my gaze to the couple entering the park. I hadn't been sure at first, but now they were close enough that I had no doubts. It was Iris and Cal, holding hands.

"Pete, I think I'm gonna have to call you back."

Right as I said that, Iris looked up and made eye contact with me. She paused and tugged at Cal's arm, and then they started walking toward me. That was a good enough sign. They weren't fleeing from me or storming at me with rage in their eyes.

"Yup, definitely hanging up now. I'll tell you more later," I said, and put my phone away, wondering if I could also fit my entire body into my purse. Cute boy laughed again, and I silently begged him to rescue me from the interaction I was about to have. My prayers worked well enough that he looked up at me and smiled, but not enough to get him off the bench.

"Hey," Iris said.

Cal squinted through his glasses, avoiding eye contact. I couldn't help but stare at their clasped hands. If they noticed they didn't say anything. "Hey," I said finally. "You're still here."

"Yeah, I changed my flight," Iris said. "We haven't heard from you in a while." I looked at Cal, wondering if he had somehow kept it a secret what I'd done, forgetting for a moment that he'd texted after my stupid kiss attempt and said there were no hard feelings.

"Sorry," I said lamely. "I just…" I let the statement peter out. I looked down at my lap, but their shadows were cast in my direction, so it was hard to pretend that they weren't there anymore.

"It's okay. It'd be awkward, I get it. I almost didn't come over here, but I wanted to say that I read your article," Iris said. I could feel myself blushing right away. My heart was thumping in my chest, my hands sweaty right away. "It was really good. It felt weird to read about ourselves like that. I felt a little naked, equal parts proud and embarrassed."

I finally looked away from my lap, and through the space between the two of them I could see the cute boy laughing again, shaking his head a little. I kept my eyes on him. "Thanks," I said. "I'm sorry if I stuck my nose in your business too much." Like, all the way in Cal's face. "I got carried away."

"You don't have to apologize, Lu," Cal said, speaking up for the first time. I didn't have the guts to look up at his eyes.

Over the past couple weeks, I'd thought of what would happen if I ran into them again. What I would say to them. Shame still crawled down my spine anytime I thought about them, but I still couldn't help but fantasize about a redemption. I'd even fantasized about thanking them. If they hadn't come along I might still be moping around about Leo, mired in writer's block and swearing off love entirely.

"I probably should," I said. "I was inappropriate. And clingy. Then I aired out all your laundry for the world to see."

"At least it wasn't the dirty laundry," Iris said with a laugh. "You were pretty complimentary. Made us look more interesting than we really are."

I examined my fingernails, looked back at cute guy. He was looking at his phone, no longer laughing, his brow furrowed in concentration. "Anyway," I said. "I'm sorry."

We didn't say anything for a few moments. It was hard to tell how much time had gone by. It could have been ten seconds or ten minutes. I was suddenly sweaty, like I had been all damn summer. So much for a refreshing day. I noticed Cal rub his thumb against Iris's hand, tried not to dive into memories of his touch. "So, when's the new breakup date?"

Again, the thumb rub against the soft flesh Iris's hand. I'd been avoiding thinking of Cal romantically at all, but it was hard not to want that. I forced myself to look up, see their faces when they answered. The sun was shining behind them turning them into more silhouettes than human faces. Seemed fitting, and I was glad to not see Cal's eyes.

"We've postponed it," Cal said. It sounded like he was trying to restrain a smile. Behind him a cotton-candy cloud moved in the way of the sun, and then I could see his eyes clearly again. "Indefinitely."

"Really?"

"After reading your article, how could I let go of what we have?" Iris said. She was definitely smiling. "If it goes sour, if we can't survive the minefield of long distance, so be it. But we're gonna try. We have you to thank for that."

Behind us, a woman shouted out something that could

have been my name but was probably one of a million words that end with the same "oo" sound. I looked back, trying to hide the fact that tears were coming to my eyes again. I took a breath, gaining control of myself. When I faced them again, I noticed cute boy looking in our direction. I tried smiling at him, but his eyes flitted away, guilty at being caught.

"I don't know why that makes me feel good," I said. "But it does. I'm happy for you guys. You really are…" I bit my lip. "I want to find a better word than *special*."

"Cheesy? Hopeless? Treacle? Naive?" Cal said.

"Hey!" Iris said, letting go of his hand to smack him across the arm. "We'll take *special*."

We shared a laugh, and I felt something within me relax. "I should be the ones thanking you anyway. You broke me out of my writer's block funk." I noticed my iced coffee sitting beside me, forgotten, sweating beads of condensation onto the bench. I picked it up and took a sip. "This is going to sound cheesy and treacle and naive, but seeing what you guys have let me hold on to romantic ideals. Maybe a little too much. But I think it's better than the alternative. I want to believe that love can be special at this age. And you guys showed me that it can be. So, thanks."

Both of them were smiling now, and I could sense my cheeks blazing up to a fiery red. Iris fluffed her hair out, and Cal pushed his glasses up the bridge of his nose. "Well, we were gonna go meet up with friends for coffee," Iris said. "You want to come with?"

I considered it for a moment, before the smart part of my brain nudged the rest of me and suggested that maybe it wasn't a great idea to dive back into obsessing over them. "I have to go to work," I said, nodding with my head in a direction, even though I wasn't entirely sure that it was the right direction for the theater.

"Cool," Iris said. "It was nice seeing you again."

"Definitely."

"Don't be a stranger," Cal said. "We can still be friends."

I chewed on my straw a moment. The cloud that had moved over the sun blew away, and the two of them turned into silhouettes again. "Yeah," I said. "Maybe someday."

They nodded, and then we gave each other awkward hugs that still felt emotionally fulfilling, even if the physical aspect was a little more complicated than that. I didn't stand up all the way, and tried to keep my body away from Cal's, even though it felt good to be in his touch. I counted to three on both hugs, wondering if I was squeezing too hard or not enough. When the hugs were over it felt like they'd been entirely too long, and not nearly long enough. Then they took their leave, and I watched them cross the park, hands clasped back together.

My phone buzzed in my pocket, Pete asking what the hell was going on. I waited to respond until I couldn't see Iris and Cal anymore, and even then I kept looking in the direction they'd walked off, trying to catch sight of them. Before I could respond to Pete, I felt a shadow pass over me. I looked up, and Cute Bench Boy was standing over me.

"This is gonna sound weird," he said. "I couldn't help but overhear your conversation. Do you mind if I join you?"

★ ★ ★ ★ ★

ACKNOWLEDGMENTS

Since I've started writing, this book has been the one that has taken the longest to fully form. It couldn't reach this final stage without the help of a ton of people. First of all, my agent, Pete Knapp, for guiding me to the heart of the story. To TS and the team at Inkyard Press, for giving Lu a home, and for continuing to give my writing a home. I'm lucky I get to keep doing this, and that's thanks to the hard work of the editorial team, the publicity team, marketing, sales, design and many more. Thanks to all those who help make my books a reality.

Thanks to the hundred people who filled out my survey on what teenage love feels like. Your answers helped remind me, as well as tap into experiences I did not have.

Thanks to Laura for constant inspiration and for helping me leave behind a lot of the crappy things about love and break-ups that I wrote about here.

To Drea Walter, Leah Kreitz and Marianne Reyes for help with representation matters.

To my family for their love and support and absurd group chat messages.

And of course, to you. I get to do what I love to do because you have this book in your hands, and I'm very grateful for that.